CW00969371

DEADLINE

James

With best wishes

Geoff M

GEOFF MAJOR

**Grosvenor House
Publishing Limited**

This book is published by
Grosvenor House Publishing Ltd
Link House
140 The Broadway, Tolworth, Surrey, KT6 7HT.
www.grosvenorhousepublishing.co.uk

This book is a work of fiction. Any resemblance to people
or events, past or present, is purely coincidental.

A CIP record for this book
is available from the British Library

ISBN 978-1-83975-253-7

To Lucia, for supporting my dream.

To Becky and Lauren; all this started on our morning walks to Woody Primary.

ALSO:

With heartfelt thanks to Iain, Jon and Jenni. Your help, advice and feedback (and hours of painstaking proof-reading) helped create this. I could not have done it without you.

To Gary, for your endless positivity and support.

To Jo (@agoodwriteup) – I owe you a Curly Wurly.

To Catherine Knibbs Ph.D, MSc, PGDip, BSc Hons – because there's no right answer to what he is, or isn't

PART 1 – CAUSE AND EFFECT

Chapter 1: 11th December, 1971

Pain coursed through Kathy Mason's body; her nerve ends screaming. She lay on her back, in the middle of the road, unable to move her torso. Her eyes danced, erratically, in raw panic.

"*Robert? Robert?*", she cried out. "*Robert, where are you?*"

Her right arm reached out and her hand groped the wet tarmac, hoping to feel her husband's re-assuring hand grasp hers in response. She couldn't see it, but just inches behind her, lay Robert's left hand. It was lifeless, like the rest of his body.

"*Madam, I need you to please lie still*", pleaded one of the medics at the scene, who had arrived to support the ambulance crew. He was trying to inject some pain relief into Kathy Mason's arm. "*We're going to take you to Scarborough General Hospital. You appear to have a broken collarbone and your left leg has multiple fractures. We need to stabilise it before we move you. It will help ease the pain, so please lie still*", he continued. Kathy Mason simply stared into the distance, wide-eyed and unable to concentrate on anything being said to her.

Another movement regained her focus, as she saw a figure carrying her baby to a nearby ambulance. The baby appeared motionless.

"NOOOOOOOOOOOO! Edward!" she howled. "Where are they taking my baby? EDWAAAAARD!"

As she desperately tried to reach out to him, she shrieked in a physical pain that matched that of her emotion. Her collarbone was completely shattered, and the pain consumed her.

"It's alright, your son is alive, but he needs some emergency treatment", assured the doctor. For a moment, Kathy Mason became calm and closed her eyes. She murmured a brief prayer of thanks. The doctor took this opportunity of calmness to inject morphine into her right arm, and he exhaled in relief at having been successful. He then looked across at the ambulance driver carrying the child, who motioned his hand to indicate that the child's chances of survival were only probably fifty-fifty.

Just twenty minutes ago, Robert and Kathy Mason had left the comfort of their beautiful home, that was perched on the top of the limestone cliffs above the south bay. Their six-week old son, Edward, had been suffering with a fever. A short walk to a local late-night health clinic had followed, and ended when one of two cars, which seemed to be racing each other, had struck a kerb and spun through the air, striking right into the young family. All Kathy could remember was holding Edward tight, just before the car slammed into her left shoulder. The force of the blow threw her into the air and, as she struck the ground, she lost consciousness immediately.

To the far left of the scene right now was the wreckage of that car. It had crashed down onto the road with sparks flying, as the cold steel roof skidded across the tarmac, before finally coming to a stop. The car was now leaning precariously against a steep stone wall. A fire crew worked to remove the side of the car so that medical help could reach its driver, Anthony Cleaver. Blood dripped from a gash to the side of his head, and he too was motionless, but apparently alive. He was soon eased out of the wreckage and transferred to an ambulance for immediate attention.

When Anthony came around sometime later, his head and right arm were covered in bandages. He wore a temporary splint and harness around both legs and his pelvis. A drip had been inserted into his left arm, and an oxygen mask over his face gently provided some pain relief. The ambulance's right rear door was open, and the view was like a framed nightmare. Blue lights were still flashing all around, and what looked like a white blanket lay on the road. The persistent drizzle quickly turned the blanket's crimson blood stains a pale scarlet as the colour spread. Anthony's stare was broken as a doctor stepped up into the ambulance and closed the door behind him. He picked up a clipboard, looked down at the notes, and scribbled on the paper. He then looked up at the drip and followed the tube to where it disappeared into Cleaver's forearm.

"*What happened?*" asked Cleaver. The doctor said nothing and reached into a black bag, taking out a syringe, a stethoscope and a small bottle of liquid.

"*Please tell me who that is, out there – on the road?*" pleaded Cleaver. The doctor started drawing liquid from the bottle into the syringe and sighed.

"*You seem to have killed some people tonight*", replied the doctor, concentrating on the syringe and still not looking up from his work. "*The father is dead, and the mother and baby are very close to the same fate. I don't think they'll be able to save them*", he added, solemnly.

The doctor now gave a hard stare at his patient, but Cleaver was too deep in reflection to notice. The doctor injected the cloudy liquid from the syringe into the drip and continued his prognosis; "*Just like I don't think anyone will be able to save YOU now, either*".

Cleaver snapped out of his daze and looked up to see the doctor placing the bottle and syringe back into his bag. The doctor turned to face his patient and Cleaver suddenly recognised him. His gaze switched from the doctor to the drip.

"*You deserved to die tonight, Anthony*", said the doctor. "*It's just a shame we didn't catch up with you before you attracted so much … attention*". And with that, the man removed his clinical white coat and exited the ambulance, disappearing into the darkness.

Anthony Cleaver started to sob. He felt the warmth of the injected solution sweeping through his body, knowing that the concoction meant his death was both inevitable and imminent. As his vision started to blur and his head started to swim, he found some solace knowing that at least the location of the file his enemies sought would continue to remain a secret. For now.

Chapter 2: 29th September, 2012

Albert Scargill was living out his final days in his 1950's red-brick semi-detached home in Leeds. He lived alone as a widower. Aged 82, he had a band of wispy white hair that ran from his temples all the way around his head, framing the top of his shiny hairless scalp. Despite his age, his weathered chiselled face, and a tall and slim - if slightly stooped - frame, it didn't stop the neighbours admiring how active Albert was for a gent in his 80s. He was proud, independent, and often quick to refuse well-meaning offers of help.

"Hello, Mr Scargill. Can we offer you a lift?" someone from the street might ask when they saw him carrying bags back from the not-so-local supermarket in the rain.

"Oh no, thank you", Albert would say, smiling back. *"I really find this weather quite invigorating. But thank you"*, and he would raise a hand, in thanks, as the driver of the car in question raised their window and slowly drove away.

On other occasions, Albert might be in the garden trying to keep the weeds at bay, when a neighbour might lean over the fence and comment, *"Back-breaking stuff, Albert. Fancy a hand?"*

"*That's very kind, but you have more than enough to do with work, your family and keeping your garden so lovely*", he would reply. He was nothing if not polite, especially when the 'lovely' garden in question was no more than a patch of land comprising four or five potted plants.

"*Well, maybe a refreshing cuppa then? We've got Custard Creams!*" the same neighbour would wink, conspiratorially.

"*Oh, thank you. That would be lovely!*" And with that acceptance, the neighbour would puff out his chest with pride in response to the one and only Albert Scargill having said yes to five minutes of chit-chat and a bit of help, just from him.

Albert used to love to play golf, twice a week, with an old set of hickory-shafted clubs he'd been presented with many years ago. The clubs were rarely used these days, of course, so he simply kept them in their golf bag, standing proudly in the corner of his lounge.

Although still physically able, Albert Scargill's mind easily wandered nowadays. He knows that tomorrow is the day the binmen come to his street, because the pin board in his little kitchen reminds his fading memory of the tasks he needs to complete each day and each night. He also keeps a message on a notepad by the side of his bed, which reminds him to look at the kitchen pin board, just in case he forgets.

Of course, most things about Albert Scargill were now a far cry from the physical and mental prowess of his younger days. In his prime, he would fell-run to national standards, and his IQ would have qualified him for MENSA, but rather than share this information, anonymity had remained Albert's ally, especially given that, despite the indications from his modest home and lifestyle, his considerable wealth had rarely dipped over the last 30 years. Indeed, Albert was a wealthy man, though you'd never know it.

Albert had purchased the house with the specific aim of maintaining a low profile; a desire his late wife, Alice, knew nothing about. In fact, she had died never knowing a thing of her husband's wealth. It wasn't that Albert didn't love her completely, or mistrust her with the real savings he had amassed, but any significant change in lifestyle would have been noticed by those who wished to find him, and that would put Alice in danger. That was the last thing Albert wanted.

There had been a point, around ten years ago, when Albert considered telling Alice a story that they had won the Premium Bonds jackpot. No sooner had this idea come to him, than the couple discovered that Alice had terminal cancer. With a diagnosis of only 3 months to live, Albert dedicated a significant proportion of his savings to fund private medical treatments. He would have done anything for his beloved wife, and this was the least he felt he could offer. None of the treatments worked, though, and in 2003, Alice Scargill was finally free of the pain that the cancer had wrought upon her.

Albert put a cardigan around his shoulders and walked into the kitchen. He unlocked the back door, stepped outside, and gently pulled it closed behind him. Grabbing a handle on one of the wheelie bins, he slowly and steadily manoeuvred the bin from its resting place onto the narrow concrete path that ran around the back and side of the house. As he moved, Albert glanced at the now overgrown vegetable garden Alice used to tend so lovingly. Covering nearly a quarter of the garden and requiring many hours of tending, it was now barely recognisable. Whilst the furrows were still faintly visible, the whole ground was now covered in weeds and wildflowers. A tear gently trickled down Albert Scargill's wrinkled cheek at the thought; a happy memory and yet, like all the others, tinged with such enduring sadness.

It took Albert a couple of minutes to wheel the bin around the side of the house and out onto the front of the short driveway. The outside lights he'd installed provided sufficient visibility without illuminating his or anybody else's garden with the sheer white floodlighting that so many of his neighbours seemed to favour nowadays.

After placing the bin at the end of the driveway, Albert stood and looked out at the street, pulling the cardigan a little closer as the crisp night air nipped gently at his body. It had been a fairly mild day, but the chill had arrived as soon as the sun had left the sky, and he found himself smiling at the memory of his wife who, in previous years, would have had a warm cup of Horlicks ready for him when he returned to the lounge.

A sudden stiff breeze whipped around him and broke Albert's thoughts. He shivered and made his way back to the rear of the house, where the breeze had blown the kitchen door slightly ajar. He made a mental note, should he remember it, that he really must make sure he closes it properly next week, so as not to let the warmth out of the kitchen.

Albert re-entered the kitchen, locked and bolted the door, and then checked that he had already put out his cereal bowl and spoon for the morning. He was a true creature of discipline and routine. After checking his to-do list that hung on the wall to the right of the rear door, he pushed open the door to the lounge and walked through into the hall. As always, he paused to pick up and kiss goodnight a photo of his wife, before replacing it on the radiator cover and enjoying a quiet moment of reflection. He then turned towards the chairlift on the stairs.

The swish of a hickory-shafted golf club broke the silence, as the metal clubhead sank into the back of Albert Scargill's skull. A natural and uncontrolled reflex forced a soft yelp from his mouth, before his body crumpled and his blood spattered across the wall. His flailing arm knocked the photo of his wife to the floor as he fell.

The killer bent down and retrieved the photo of Albert and Alice Scargill, taking care to lay it gently on Albert's lifeless body. He then reached into his own jacket pocket and took a small slip of paper out of a thin plastic wallet. He lay the note on Albert Scargill's chest. It had five words printed on it:

You reap what you sow.

Chapter 3: 16th October 2012

He walked into the room and everyone stood. This wasn't the military, and he wasn't a Judge, but formality and respect needed to be demonstrated, because when he called a meeting, people knew something serious would be troubling him.

Before he sat down at the head of the table, he casually tossed a thick brown folder into the middle of it. All five attendees glanced at the folder as it thudded onto the dark oak.

"*We seem to have a problem*", he said, uneasily, as he sank into his chair. Everyone knew his opening words served simply to set the tone and context, and that he has by no means finished talking. They had all felt his wrath at one time or another if they had dared to interject during the silence, so they remained quiet, and sat down.

"*Intel from our friends across The Pond suggests that a problem we thought was resolved, isn't. It's just been hibernating*". His eyes didn't make contact with anyone in the room, but his simmering temper was evident as he gazed up at the ceiling. "*Hargreaves, you'll take the lead for the team*", he added, as he casually leant forwards and pushed the brown folder towards one of the men on his right. "*Inside this folder, you'll find archives from the basement, and a couple of profiles. I suggest you read them, and then discuss your next steps*".

Hargreaves calmly took the folder and untied the Treasury Tag that sealed the paperwork inside. He scanned the contents, nodding with an assured self-confidence. "*Classification?*" he asked, closing the folder.

"*It's a Grade 3. Sir Trevor is interested in this one. Identify, verify... and then remove the risk*", came the order from their leader. He then glanced around the table before asking, "*Anyone have any questions?*" It almost sounded like a challenge so, unsurprisingly, nobody put themselves forward. "*Update on my desk by the close of play every Tuesday, please – starting today*".

He stood, slowly, so that everyone had time to quickly but quietly push their chairs back and stand in respect. They all remained motionless until he had left the room and the heavy door clunked shut behind him. Once he had gone, they transformed into a highly active team once more, keen to find out what Hargreaves had been allocated and how they were to play their part in completing this latest assignment.

Hargreaves re-opened the file and laid the contents out on the meeting room table. He allocated the archive files to his team but kept the profiles to read for himself. He browsed them with interest and intrigue as his colleagues buzzed around him, planning their next steps. Somehow, he'd need to get close to one of the names staring back at him -and quickly, so the more he could find out about them, the easier that would be. He'd done it scores of times in the past for his job; different people, different reasons and different circumstances. For some, his role was to infiltrate, befriend and extract information from them. For others, he would skilfully apprehend them and hand them over for colleagues to deal with in any way they saw fit for the task at hand. Occasionally, there might be someone who just needed to die, and he would be the man for the job.

"*Whatever it takes, for the sake of national security*", he would say to himself, as if to justify some of the unsavoury methods and the subsequent human collateral that had been necessary on his previous assignments.

Hargreaves formed an initial plan. "*Meet back here in two hours. I want a briefing from you all*", he said to his colleagues, before settling down at the desk, in readiness to review his information.

An hour later, he had finished his second full read – an approach he took with all case files, to ensure his concentration had not lapsed and that he had not missed anything material. He sat back to reflect on his conclusions. Whilst the mission appeared clear, his assessment of it felt unusually cloudy. There was something about this assignment that struck a nerve. There were things buried within his own history that resonated with what he was reading right now. Rather than feel indifference or abhorrence towards the person identified as his target, he felt a new and very different sensation in his role. Empathy.

Hargreaves knew his brief was to identify, verify and remove the current risk. His current *question*, though, was now more about what - or *who* - the true risk was.

"*I know where you are*", he mumbled to himself, "*I just don't know which side you're on.*"

Hargreaves slipped the paperwork back into the folder and began to think very carefully about how he might befriend his target. Little did he know that an ideal opportunity would present itself in the very near future.

PART 2 – DEATH RETURNS

FEBRUARY to MARCH, 2013

Chapter 4

It was difficult to tell whether the relentless hammering sound was someone knocking at the door, or simply the blood forcefully pumping through Adam Ferranti's head. A litre bottle of Jack Daniels stood half empty on a small table next to where he was lying.

After a few more seconds, the hammering stopped, so Ferranti ruled it out as one of headaches. He was begrudgingly awake now, and his eyes slowly opened and became accustomed to the usual view at this time of day - the artexed ceiling of his compact little lounge. The curtains were almost completely closed, but a bright shaft of sunlight cut across the ceiling of the cottage, and the animated yet polished voices of two ever-smiling TV presenters emanated from the screen in the corner, which meant it was already mid-morning.

The hammering started up again, and Ferranti looked over to see a silhouette through the frosted glazing of the front door. He knew it was probably Aarav Khatri, the taxi driver who had been hired to carry out the tough task of getting Ferranti into work before 11am every day of every week. This instruction hadn't come from a self-aware Ferranti, but from Ferranti's boss, Barry Clements, who hired Khatri for the seemingly mammoth task, and ensured that Ferranti's monthly salary was suitably docked to cover the bill.

Ferranti tentatively rolled over to ease himself off the battered old brown leather sofa he had fallen asleep on, so that he could get onto his hands and knees on the floor and prepare to stand up. He misjudged the manoeuvre, though, and flopped off the sofa; falling straight onto the empty pizza boxes that were strewn across the lounge floor from the night before. In shock and confusion, Ferranti tried to stand, but only succeeded in bumping into the coffee table, sending an empty glass and the whiskey bottle tumbling across the room. He closed his eyes and swore under his breath as he attempted yet again to rise. His body ached and complained at the effort required, but this was nothing new.

For a man fast approaching his 51st birthday, Ferranti was in reasonable shape and could still out-muscle and out-run many men 10 years his younger - a benefit of his training regime decades ago. Recently though, he had started to feel that age was catching up with him. Standing at just under 6' 2" and weighing a modest 78kg, he looked like an ageing jock who had kept up something of a fitness routine, but it appeared as if late nights and the lasting effects of excessive alcohol were slowly winning the battle against him.

As Ferranti stretched, arching his back and yawning, the letterbox flap opened and a pair of large dark eyes peered through.

"I thought I heard you. What was that noise? Are you alright?", came a voice with a soft Indian lilt. It was indeed Khatri. He was tall and slim, with a mop of hair that was quaffed and held in place by a copious amount of hairspray.

Aged just 24, Aarav Khatri had decided that the medical degree he had come to study in England wasn't now how he believed he would make his fortune, although he had yet to tell his parents he had dropped out of his expensive education. Khatri's alternative plan to become a millionaire was to develop a fleet of hybrid-fuel executive cars; promoting a reputation for multi-lingual drivers in command of sleek eco-friendly vehicles. So far, he had one 2012 Nissan Leaf, which he shared with his cousin, Jayesh. Despite this rather underwhelming standing, Khatri always dressed smartly and with some style, as he felt his professional image would overcome any sense of disappointment when clients climbed into the back seats of the Leaf.

Ferranti walked over to the door, unlocked it and pulled it open, but didn't go so far as to greet his visitor in any way. Khatri knew the peculiarities of his regular customer, however, so he knew what Ferranti did was not a sign of disrespect; just resigned disinterest.

Khatri walked into the lounge, which accessed directly from the street once the front door was opened. The scene inside was nothing new to him and, from what he could see in the semi-darkness, it was far from the worst he had ever found at this address.

"*Give me a minute*", mumbled Ferranti as he opened the door to the kitchen and went looking for some tablets and whatever there was in the fridge that could give him some kind of relief from the pounding in his head.

"*I'll, err, just pick up a few things, shall I?*" asked Khatri, rhetorically. This scenario played out more often than he could remember, and Ferranti would always hold up a hand, signalling 'sure, go ahead', without a word of thanks.

Once Ferranti had walked out of the kitchen and stumbled upstairs, cursing as he stubbed his toe, Khatri opened the curtains to let the light in, and began to tidy the room. The lounge was compact and just big enough for the furniture it held; a sofa and matching brown leather armchair, with a small television sat on a black lacquered glass unit in the alcove next to the window. The pale walls and white ceiling contrasted well with the black iron coal-effect fireplace and its cherry-wood surround. The small table, now lying on its side, and a bookcase in another fireside alcove, were made from a similar looking wood, completing the room's decor.

A small window looked out onto what was the old village square in Barwick-In-Elmet, with its First World War memorial stone cross and 86-foot candy-striped wooden Maypole. The estate agent who had originally showcased the property to Ferranti was an enthusiastic man in his very early twenties, wearing a bright blue suit that looked straight off the discount store rail. He thought the history of the village would be a huge selling point to any potential buyer:

"And, as well as the tranquillity of the countryside and convenience of having the booming city centre only 30 minutes away by car, you'd be living in one of the most attractive villages in West Yorkshire. Rich in history, this place was the capital of the Kingdom of Elmet and ...", but before he could continue, Ferranti pretended to receive an urgent message on his phone. It was a ploy he had used before, of triggering a fake text to his mobile, which was activated by a device he carried from time to time. Ferranti didn't care about any of the history of the place. His interest in the stone terraced cottage was purely because it was immediately available, clean, and required very little in the way of work or upkeep. Additionally, it was virtually next door to two of the three pubs in the village. Ferranti smiled, thinking about how well the gizmo had worked to cut off the conversation.

"Thank you, Justin", he murmured to himself, as he recalled who had given him this handy device.

The estate agent looked crestfallen at his client's distraction, but his demeanour quickly changed when Ferranti said, *"I'll take it. I'll put an offer in writing to you tomorrow"*. Clearly the agent's sales technique was better than he realised.

Ferranti had lived in this three-bedroomed cottage since he moved up from London just over a year ago. Although a few of the regulars in The Black Swan pub might strike up a conversation with him, he didn't have any real friends in the village to speak of. In fact, he didn't really have any friends in the UK at all beyond his army buddy, Justin. They had met in Afghanistan, where Ferranti had served as a war correspondent. After promotion through to Fort Monmouth, Justin left the army and moved to London to make his fortune in specialist and covert communications for the private sector. He and Ferranti had stayed in touch since Afghanistan, and Justin invited Ferranti to come stay - and indeed work with him – after hearing about Ferranti's mother's death. Within six months though, it was clear that whilst Ferranti was capable of some excellent work, the business relationship between the two men wasn't working. Ferranti's moods had become a risk to the company, so the pair agreed to part, with Justin putting Ferranti in touch with a newspaper owner in the north of England. In the past, Ferranti had quite a reputation with the main New York and Washington newspapers, but his drinking and the rapid decline in his mothers' health had started to take an effect. A sharp mind and an even sharper pen were both blunted, although they were not so useless that he couldn't now fill a column with an insightful commentary once a week, whilst providing general news and support for the Yorkshire Post, where he now worked.

Ferranti changed into his usual blue jeans, white shirt, dark brown cargo jacket and tan brogues, before picking up his courier bag and heading downstairs. It was deadline day for his weekly column and he still wasn't sure what he was going to write about. There were several emerging stories across the region - and the country - but no 'doozer' - the name he gave to a story that got his pulse racing and his brain buzzing. On his day, Ferranti was the best journalist at the Yorkshire

Post - perhaps even in the country - and everyone knew it, which made it even more puzzling that he seemed to drown his talent in whiskey most nights. It certainly smelt like that most mornings.

Once he reached the bottom of the stairs, Ferranti collected a coffee from Khatri who, as usual, was stood in the kitchen doorway with flask ready and waiting. Ferranti took it without breaking stride and gave Khatri a nod of both appreciation and guilt. The pizza boxes, glass and bottle had been cleared from the lounge, and the furniture had been straightened, just as it always had been since Khatri had come into his life. The gesture was not lost on Ferranti, and the first time this young man had made him a coffee was the first time Ferranti viewed him as more than simply a flunkie who drove a battery-operated toy.

Over the subsequent months, the two men began to talk. Initially, this was mainly about local and international news, but slowly, the focus would also zone in on Khatri's ambitions. Ferranti never discussed his own life, and enjoyed pouring humorous scorn on his new friend's optimistic views of global politics and local events, but he could sense that Khatri had a sharp and engaging mind, which brought the occasional smile to Ferranti's face - not that he ever showed that to Khatri.

Both men left the cottage and pulled their jackets a little tighter in the chilly February air as they walked across the square to the Nissan that was parked outside the local Post Office. As usual, Khatri opened the rear door for Ferranti and, still somewhat amused at this gesture of service, Ferranti supressed a smile as he mumbled, *"Thanks"*, before climbing in.

Ferranti sank into the back seat of the car and stared out of the window, watching as the retired villagers went about their daily business of collecting their pensions, paying their bills at the Post Office, and stopping and talking about the minutiae of their lives, including – most likely - the latest death amongst their friends and acquaintances.

It was 10:15am, and at that time of day, the journey from Barwick to the offices of the Yorkshire Post took around 30 minutes. Khatri did a u-turn in front of the Maypole and headed up Main Street in the Nissan, past the eclectic collection of old terraced houses and the more recent – and modestly opulent – abodes. He soon made his way onto the A64, which ran slightly downhill for almost 4 miles into Leeds city centre. After ten minutes of driving, Khatri heard the tell-tale sigh from Ferranti that signalled he was awake and sober enough to engage in a conversation.

"So, what do you think of the Pistorius charges?" asked Khatri, trying to hide his enthusiasm at the thought of out-thinking Ferranti with this one. He had stayed up late last night to do some thorough research. He was sure he was ready for a comprehensive debate on the subject.

"Why is that this morning's subject, rather than the pressing monetary crisis in Cyprus – you know they're

going to have to be offered a bail-out, right?" responded Ferranti, in a typical tactic that both allowed him more time to sip his coffee, and signalled to Khatri that he knew the young man would have put all his efforts into preparing for that one single debate. Khatri quietly exhaled, as he realised Ferranti had once again side-stepped the challenge. At least Khatri had been fortunate to grab some time to listen to some of the early morning debate about Cyprus on the radio before he collected Ferranti, so he wasn't completely underprepared.

Their talks usually lasted for the majority of the journey into the city centre, and this one was no different. As the building playing home to the Yorkshire Post offices came into view, Ferranti wondered whether the Cyprus situation should be the focus of his column, but as quickly as the idea popped into his head, he dismissed it.

It was no doozer.

Chapter 5

The Yorkshire Post office was like hundreds of other administrative office set-ups across the city. Occupying three floors of a modern office block, and housing a sea of characterless desks, the premises were a far cry from the paper's previous iconic abode and printing site on Wellington Street.

"Now that was an impressive newspaper site. The energy and noise within that newsroom were constant, rising to almost a frenzy level as the printing deadline loomed closer", mused Barry Clements on Ferranti's first day with the paper. Clements was Ferranti's editor, and both men remembered that first day very well; not least because it was the first - and last - time either of them could recall Ferranti turning up to work without the feint smell of stale alcohol on his clothing. Sadly, the Wellington Street site closed the previous year to help cut costs. Now, with 24-hour news services and a website to feed, deadlines were frequent and seemingly minor on most days.

On this morning, Ferranti entered the fairly innocuous lobby - shared with two other businesses – and nodded to Charlie, the security officer. Charlie gave Ferranti a broad smile and welcomed him with a genuinely warm, *"Morning, Mr Ferranti"*. Most of the workers in the building always seemed engrossed in their mobile phones, so Charlie loved to have someone to talk to on his shift. He was a warm and gentle burly man in his early sixties, whose shift covered the middle portion of the day, while the other security officers were on a break or a shift changeover. He and Ferranti had struck up somewhat of a rapport immediately, swapping small talk each time Ferranti arrived or left the building. Thanks to Ferranti, Charlie usually had an extra £20-£30 in his pocket every week, from the hot racing tips he'd happily shared with him.

As Ferranti moved through the lobby and entered the stairwell, he called back, *"I'm not your teacher or your boss, Charlie"*, but he couldn't help but smile as he spoke. He climbed the stairs to the 2nd floor and entered the newsroom, walking towards his cubicle on the far corner of the floor, nodding dutifully at colleagues who appeared to acknowledge him. He took off his jacket and turned on his laptop. Sipping his coffee, he browsed the new emails that had arrived in his inbox and, as usual, scanned the electronic bulletin board that Clements had proudly showcased in the new offices; to alert allocation of tasks and 'must-read' notices.

The desk phone rang.

"Ferranti - Newsroom", he muttered absently, focussing instead on the information on his laptop screen and scribbling down the extension number of a colleague looking to sell a bicycle. He needed to do something to start to recover his fitness, and this seemed like a good place to start.

"*Hello, Adam*", said a calm, measured voice.

"*Who's this?*" queried Ferranti, still distracted by the details of the bicycle for sale.

"*Stop reading the bulletin board and listen to me*", asserted the caller.

Ferranti paused, confused. He glanced at the receiver and then at the digital display on the console. The number was withheld. He looked up again and glanced around the office to see if it was a colleague playing a joke on him, but those on the phone seemed to be involved in animated conversations that took their focus elsewhere. Nobody was looking over.

"*Albert Scargill was the first, but certainly not the last. Tell the officer in charge of the Scargill investigation that I told you to heed the note: You reap what you sow. You should also tell them that there's another body – an early diner next to the O2 Arena. I don't think he appreciated the after-dinner wine though, if I'm honest*". With that, the caller gave a short cackle at his own joke. "*Hurry, Adam. You have a week to stop me, otherwise your next headline will be about another murder*".

The phone clicked, and the line went dead.

Chapter 6

The doors to the Charge Area burst open. Three burly policemen staggered through the entrance, man-handling a suspect as they strode forward towards the main desk. Custody Sergeant Bill Osbourne was in charge of making the decisions on this evening's over-night detention. He stood, staring, with clenched fists resting on the counter. He leaned forward and sighed.

"Welcome to another Friday at West Yorkshire Police HQ, Millgarth", he muttered to himself.

The suspect was over six-feet tall, thick-set and tanned, with muscular arms flexing against his captors and the handcuffs placed upon him. Although his head was bowed in a restraining hold, it was clear to see that his face and bald head were largely covered with intricate tattoos. He wore oily dark blue jeans, a t-shirt that probably used to be white but was now a grimy ashen grey, and a denim jacket with the sleeves cut off; no doubt to frame the rippling muscles in his arms and shoulders. Blood from a recent injury to his nose and lips still dripped, unchecked, onto his t-shirt. His sneering face and spittled mouth contorted in anger, as he let out an almost growl.

"I'll kill that bitch once I'm outta here!"

Following them into the Police Station was the arresting officer, Detective Sergeant Stephanie Walker – the very same 'bitch' the tattooed man was growling about. Everyone at Millgarth HQ knew DS Walker was a hard-nosed copper; unafraid to tackle the most brutal and determined of criminals. She stood a little over 5'8 tall, with her long dark hair in a ponytail and just enough make-up to accent her elfin face. She cast a steely stare of disdain at the suspect as she strode over to the custody desk, turning her attention to Sergeant Osbourne in readiness to brief him about their guest. Sergeant Osbourne transferred his focus from the burly suspect onto the split lip and black eye that DS Walker was this evening sporting; it's bruising already mature and prominent.

"*Ouch ... who caught you unawares?*" he queried.

Walker smirked and winced at the same time.

"*Not him*", she replied. "*My own stupid fault for stepping through some loose flooring as I chased him*". She then turned to look at the suspect. "*I whacked my face on the way down*".

"*I'll whack your face for you. I got rights, you know! You're only supposed to use 'reasonable force', but I've been victimised and tortured! My solicitor is going to fuck you right off, bitch!*", spat the suspect, as he lashed out at a nearby table with his foot, sending the magazines scattering across the floor and the table slamming into the nearby wall. Walker had seen the table coming and moved deftly to the left, both sighing and gently shaking her head as the table skidded past her.

"Looks pretty sore", said Sergeant Osbourne, peering at the bruising almost quizzically.

"Guess I must just have soft peachy skin", DS Walker joked, as she turned her attention back to the Custody Sergeant. She was hoping to deflect any further discussion about the damage to her face, as this wasn't the time or the place to try to build a believable lie that she might need to remember for the upcoming arrest report and charge sheet.

"Why's he under arrest?" enquired Sergeant Osbourne.

"Suspected of possession, dealing and ..." DS Walker began before theatrically touching her lip, *"resisting arrest. The Exhibits Officers are at the scene. They've already bagged up £30,000 in cash and several small containers of what appears to be cocaine, which they've now handed over to the temporary property store. Here are the evidence reference numbers"*, she stated, as she handed across the information.

Walker paused to give Sergeant Osbourne the chance to record the information on his chart before continuing with her report. *"I'd like him detained for questioning over the next twenty-four hours please, Sergeant. He's considered a flight risk"*.

The suspect was still straining against his captors, but he remained focused full of vitriol.

"When I'm out of here, I'll find you, and show you what pain is really fucking about", he sneered, as he looked Walker up and down, imagining her pinned to the floor and screaming for his mercy.

"Please process this ... gentleman, Sergeant. I'm going to fill in the paperwork, after I've thoroughly washed my hands", said Walker, unfazed by what this man - and so many others before him - had just threatened. DS Walker turned on her heels and made her way through the security doors that led from the Charge Area into the Administration Area of the station. She entered the nearby washroom and checked the cubicles to see if any of them were in use. To her relief, they were empty. She turned and looked at her battered face in the mirror, as tears began to well in her eyes. The make-up had covered some of the bruising and masked a bit of the swelling, but it was all still clearly visible and still very tender. As she looked at her reflection, she recalled how dramatically things had changed so recently in her seemingly perfect marriage.

Stephanie Walker had been promoted to Detective Sergeant just under a year ago, having passed the strenuous tests and training at the Bishopgarth Police Academy. On graduation day, she had gone out to celebrate her achievement with some of the other successful candidates from the course. A few hours and several cocktails later, she returned home to celebrate with her husband, Alex, only to find him drunk and far from being in a celebratory mood.

Alex Walker was 6'2 and a powerhouse of a man, having spent much of his twenties and thirties at the gym, enhancing his impressive physique with a regular regime of weights and cardio circuits. Stephanie had met him five years ago, when they were both competing in a 10km charity run. They found themselves accidently bumping into each other throughout the race as they jostled to get past pockets of slower fun-runners. As they approached the finishing line, Alex had accidentally knocked Stephanie to the floor.

"Hey!" she yelled, irate and frustrated. Getting onto her hands and knees in the mud, she looked up and was about to curse the clumsy co-runner, when she saw him slow down, stop and then turn around and jog back towards her.

Alex held out his hand to help her back to her feet. *"Sorry about that"*, he said, and a soft twinkle appeared in his eyes, as his handsome face melted into an apologetic expression. *"Here, give me your hand"*, and he pulled her to her feet. *"Please, after you"*, he added, as he gestured that she should run ahead of him to cross the finish line before he did. Thirty seconds later, they had both crossed the finishing line and completed the race. Alex jogged up to Stephanie and bumped into her again, on purpose. Stephanie smiled at his cheekiness.

"So, as well as buying the victor a drink, that unwarranted assault is also going to cost you dinner", Stephanie joked, raising an eyebrow and smiling. She had been immediately taken with this charming, gorgeous hunk of an athlete, and the feeling was clearly mutual.

"Deal, provided I can pick you up. Don't want you losing your way and having to follow me to find your way to the end ... again", Alex had teased. Stephanie feigned to punch him, and they both laughed.

Over the following weeks, the pair started to meet regularly for drinks or maybe something to eat. It became apparent that Alex had a wonderfully wicked sense of humour which, along with his good looks and athletic physique, explained why he had numerous advertising and sponsorship modelling deals. His clients already loved him, and now he had a stunning and intelligent woman in his life, Alex Walker was a promotional agent's dream. Meals turned into days out, which very quickly turned to nights in. Alex proposed to Stephanie just a year later whilst the couple were on holiday in the Caribbean. She had never cried such tears of joy and, as a result, she had struggled to get the word 'yes' out of her mouth to accept the proposal.

As soon as the newly-engaged couple returned to England, they moved in together, setting up home in Alex's expensive and expansive penthouse apartment, which overlooked the city centre of Leeds. Life as a couple was bliss, and Alex showered Stephanie daily with gifts as well as with continued affection and adoration. They were married two years later, at a small private ceremony on a cliff-top in Santorini, with just close family and a couple of friends watching over them.

With her growing reputation at work as a 'good copper', Stephanie Walker seemed to have it all, but just before their first anniversary, things began to change.

Alex lost a couple of promotional contracts and, with this, came a slow but noticeable loss in self-confidence. He never wanted to discuss why the companies terminated the contracts, and whenever Stephanie offered to help with some legal advice, he flew into a rage and told her not to treat him like a hopeless child. Increasingly, Alex suffered from mood swings, which weren't helped when he started using steroids to supplement his waning training regime. Over time, his commercial contacts declined to even take his calls, and work for him was becoming scarce. But, he insisted he and Stephanie still enjoy themselves. Exotic holidays, fast cars and lavish meals in fancy restaurants remained part of the Walkers' marital life until, whilst looking for some stationery in their home office, Stephanie found some credit card Final Demands tucked in the back of a drawer. In maintaining the luxury lifestyle façade, Alex had racked up debts of almost £400k, and it seemed he could barely afford the minimum monthly re-payments.

Stephanie felt sick in response to the discovery, the debts, and the lies, as well as the precarious position this would put her in at work. She was duty-bound to tell her superiors about the debts, but hopefully an upcoming promotion to Detective Sergeant would give the pair a chance to stabilise their finances, as her husband hopefully re-built his career. Stephanie knew though that whilst this was a great idea in theory, Alex made no secret of the fact that his ego felt increasingly threatened by his wife earning more money and having a higher status than him.

The night of her promotion celebration, Stephanie had entered their apartment, slightly tipsy, with a bottle of champagne she had bought on her way home. At first, she didn't see him, but as she moved through the apartment, calling out Alex's name in a cheerful sing-song tone, her husband appeared from the bathroom with a look of utter contempt etched on his face. Stephanie started to slur, *"Hello gorgeous. I brought some champagne, to celebr...."* but the newly promoted DS Walker didn't get anywhere close to finishing her sentence before Alex had grabbed her forearms and pulled her close to him; the bottle falling from her hand and smashing on the stone flooring at their feet.

"Been out with your new mates, have you? Laughing at how pathetic they think your husband is, are they? Off shagging some Senior Detective after a few drinks, maybe? A cheap bottle of bubbly isn't going to make that better, Stephanie!" he sneered, with the smell of stale whiskey on his hot breath and the spit from his vitriol now smattering across his terrified wife's face.

"Alex, you're hurting me", Stephanie trembled, as she attempted to break free from Alex's vice-like grip. *"Please, let me go ..."*

Alex didn't seem to hear or care about his wife's plea and, pushing her to almost arms' length, he released her left arm and swung his open right hand hard against the side of her face. She would have fallen to the floor, but Alex grabbed at both of her arms again and pulled Stephanie close; trying to kiss her face and neck, before he dragged her into the bedroom.

Stephanie Walker was still gazing into the mirror in the Millgarth washroom, reflecting on that first night of violence, and looking at the marks on her face from this morning's episode, when the door swung open and two female PCs entered the room, laughing and chatting amongst themselves. Stephanie quickly smiled at the two officers in the reflection of the mirror, before calmly looping a couple of loose strands of hair behind her ears and walking out and towards the CID. She reminded herself that no-one must ever perceive a weakness in Detective Sergeant Stephanie Walker.

Chapter 7

Ferranti sat with the phone still in his hand, even though the caller had cut-off the call a good thirty seconds earlier. He was taken aback not only by the content of the call, but by the calm tone of the caller. Yes, he'd had crank calls back in New York - pretty much every day, in fact - but this was a new experience entirely. The fact the caller seemed to know exactly what Ferranti was doing had got him worried. He turned around and looked out through the window, half expecting to see someone staring back at him, but his view was of a grassed area to the right and a derelict building with bricked-up windows to the left. Nothing else, and nobody there.

Ferranti slowly replaced the receiver, turned back to his computer, and searched the internet for 'Albert Scargill, murder, death, killed'. Within seconds, the search brought back a single result. A short memorial in the Yorkshire Evening Post - the sister newspaper to The Yorkshire Post. It read:

"Albert Scargill. Born 5th February 1930 - died 29th September 2012. Was never forgotten".

Ferranti tilted his head to the side, with a slightly confused expression on his face, as he read and re-read the entry. The wording seemed unusual. He returned to the search bar and tried similar or additional words to expand the search variables, but always got the same single result. Ferranti sat back for a moment and closed his eyes, blocking out the sights around him and slowly the sounds as well, so as to allow his mind to wander around the subject. Colleagues were used to seeing Ferranti do this, although with the smell of stale alcohol in the air and dark lines under his eyes from keeping late-night hours, most of his peers assumed he was simply sleeping off a hangover. It was, however, a tried and trusted method that Ferranti had used many times with great success throughout his career at the Washington Post.

As his mind cleared, Ferranti began to ask and answer a series of questions in his head. Why was an apparent murder not reported? Leeds was hardly the murder capital of England, with only 32 murders registered by the Police in the past 12 months, so why wasn't there at least some press coverage? Maybe it wasn't a murder but an accident? That would make the call a hoax and the voice on the phone that of an attention seeker, but given the tone of the mystery caller, and the fact he spoke of 'another body' being imminent, meant that Ferranti had to push that idea aside. For now, at least. The flip-side of that would be a murder disguised as an accident, and the time between the death and the call meant the murderer needed time for the trail to go cold... but then why would the caller talk about another victim that would be found tomorrow? What else would stop a murder appearing in the paper?

Ferranti played around with the idea that perhaps other, larger, more newsworthy events had taken up all the media focus that day. Another internet search showed that the Jimmy Saville scandal was a significant event at the time, but a hit-and-run death and a murder had also both been reported on the BBC News website. He also found the articles in the online archives of the Yorkshire Post. Perhaps the murder was discovered several days - or maybe even weeks – later? Ferranti focused the search for news on the following 10 days into October 2012, but again, only the one entry appeared. He looked into November, in case there was anything there; perhaps after a post-mortem found that the accident wasn't an accident after all. Still nothing, though. A final question that popped into Ferranti's head was why someone would want to stop this murder from appearing in the news?

During Ferranti's time at the Washington Post, the various security agencies in place in the US had frequently used their powers to influence the media. Whether it was a bombing they dictated be reported as a gas explosion, or something they wanted to ensure had no coverage at all. So-called gagging orders were commonplace and often justified under the banner of 'for reasons of national security'.

Ferranti was trained not to dismiss any idea, but this wasn't about a mass murder or a suicide bomber whose vest had exploded as it was being prepared. No, this was presumably a frail old man who had died, and no-one thought it was worth reporting. The phrase at the end of the obituary still nagged at the back of his mind, though, as did the words the caller used… "You reap what you sow". Both could imply something historical, although the phrase from the caller could also be a statement about a future event coming to fruition. Rather than continue to think through the various scenarios, Ferranti decided he needed to talk to the Police about the caller's instruction;

"Tell the officer in charge of the Scargill investigation to heed the note".

Ferranti re-opened his eyes and logged-off his laptop, before standing and snatching his jacket from the back of his chair. He was about to stride across the office and down the stairs, when he heard his name called across the room. It was Barry Clements, waving to him and indicating he wanted Ferranti to come over. Ferranti sighed, turned, and walked slowly towards Clements' office. This was a weekly event, where Clements looked for confirmation that his journalist i was on-track to deliver his weekly column, even if it was at the eleventh hour as usual.

Clements was perched on the corner of his desk. He was a rather short, plump, affable man of 56, who was used to managing people through gentle coercion, carefully worded challenges, and honest encouragement when a job was well done. He was a far cry from Seth Athenberg, who had been Ferranti's gritty cigar-smoking editor back in the States. Seth had been a tough-talking hard-nosed operator, who would happily berate you at full volume, with the office door wide open, so the feeling of fear could permeate the entire floor of your peers. But he would also defend you in the face of any external pressure or criticism, to the extent of placing himself in the firing line instead. Clements had done the same for Ferranti several times too, although much of the criticism was usually from *within* the company, given the reputation Ferranti had as a man who drank harder and for longer than he actually worked. Clements was also the kind of boss more likely to use an arm around the shoulder approach and inspire a sense of mutual achievement, to push people to hit a deadline - a kind of 'one fails, we all fail' ethos. Fortunately, for both men, Ferranti's articles were always of the highest quality; hard-hitting and objective. Few could argue against the content with anything other than emotion or personal bias.

Regardless of his leadership style, Clements was a damn good editor. Years ago, he could probably have had a job in Fleet Street had he wanted to move to London and work 17 hours a day. He didn't want that, though. Career ambition for Barry Clements included being safely tucked up at home most evenings with his wife, having dinner at the table and watching something light-hearted on television, before climbing into bed with a good book and then a good eight hours' sleep.

"How's it going?" asked Clements. *"Anything bubbling; a 'doozy', perhaps?"*

"A 'doozer', Barry", corrected Ferranti, suppressing a smirk. *"We'll see"*.

Clements raised his eyebrows, intrigued. He motioned for further insight from Ferranti, but the journalist laughed softly and said, *"Not yet, Barry, not yet"*.

Clements knew not to push, but his editorial instinct told him Ferranti had something exciting unfolding.

"Well let me know, and … Adam … let's not leave it until 9pm tonight, ok?" said Clements with a playful glare. It wouldn't have been the first time the office had stayed open late to accommodate the journalist's tardiness. Ferranti nodded to Clements, and that was all the editor seemingly needed to put his mind at rest. He hopped off the end of the desk and watched as Ferranti walked out of his office and purposefully strode towards the exit. Clements returned to the chair behind his desk, opened his flask of homemade soup and went back to reviewing a handful of draft online articles that needed his approval before going live on the website. He sighed as he started to read the first one, about a drunk woman who was saved by an alert petrol station manager, just seconds before going through a car wash with her convertible's roof down.

Clements looked up as the exit door on the 2nd floor swung closed, and wished for just a little bit of the excitement he imagined Ferranti must be feeling right now.

Chapter 8

Aarav Khatri had just sat down to enjoy a steaming hot cappuccino when his phone rang. It was Ferranti, asking him if he could pick him up outside the Yorkshire Post offices.

"*Err sure*", said Khatri, looking down at his delicious beverage. It would be his first coffee of the day, after five hours of driving of clients to and from locations across the city.

"*You busy?*" enquired Ferranti, sensing some hesitation in Khatri's voice. "*If you are, I can grab a black cab at the station...*"

"*No!*" exclaimed Khatri, a little loudly, causing the waitress and the female barista at the café to glance over. He saw them looking and smiled weakly, before responding to Ferranti.

"*I'll set off straight away and be there in 10 minutes*" he said dejectedly, as he took in the glorious aroma of the freshly brewed coffee.

"*Good. Make it five, will you, as I'm kinda in a hurry*", added Ferranti.

"*Ok, five minutes*", replied Khatri, trying to sound enthusiastic. He thought about adding, "*I'll just quickly finish my coffee*", in the hope that he'd be encouraged to take a little extra time to enjoy it, but Ferranti had already ended the call without even so much as a thanks. Khatri sighed, signalled to the barista that he needed a takeaway cup, and put his jacket on. As he walked out of the café, he broke into a lolling jog to make up for the lost time spent contemplating his cappuccino. He started the car engine and eased into traffic, reaching Ferranti within the allotted time with ease. He waited for his client to climb in.

"*Where to?*" he enquired.

"*Millgarth Police Station*", said Ferranti, sinking back into the seat and immediately losing himself in his thoughts. Khatri frowned. He had never taken Ferranti anywhere other than work or home, but he could tell from the distracted look on Ferranti's face that now wasn't the time to ask if everything was alright.

It only took 10 minutes to loop round to Millgarth Police HQ. Stopping at the taxi rank outside, Khatri turned to ask if his passenger would be long, but the door was already slamming shut as Ferranti strode across the road.

Ferranti entered the public enquiry reception and walked up to the front counter. Sat behind it was a civilian employee, rather than a Police Constable. With resources stretched due to public spending cuts, the use of civilian employees for non-specialist tasks, such as front desk admin, was an increasing trend across the country; not just here in Leeds. Ferranti paused momentarily to gather his thoughts and put on what he called his best 'people-friendly smile', before approaching the front desk.

"Morning, sir. How may I help you?" enquired the jaded Enquiry Officer, Henry. His tone was slightly sarcastic, as his eight-hour shift had thus far consisted almost entirely of foul-mouthed relatives of detainees who personally blamed him for not ensuring their loved ones' immediate release, or smug city office workers hoping to smarm their way out of a well-deserved fine for damaging public property whilst being drunk and disorderly over the weekend.

"Hi", said Ferranti, casually. *"I'd like to talk to the officer in charge of the investigation into the death of Albert Scargill, please."*

"Are you a relative, sir?" enquired Henry. Ferranti was aware there might not be an active investigation, or maybe that one had closed down by now, but he didn't want to assume anything. He put a conspiratorial 'just between me and you' look on his face, lowered his tone and leaned forwards slightly, to imply to Henry that privacy was of the utmost importance.

"No, but I've been told I had to come down here to speak to the officer. I have some information that might help".

Henry, aware that he only had five minutes left before shift changeover at noon, reached for a pad and a pen.

Lowering his tone slightly to reflect Ferranti's apparent request for privacy, he said;

"Let me take your details, sir, and I'll see if the officer is available. Please take a seat".

After passing on the basic information of name, contact number and nature of the enquiry, Ferranti took a few steps back and sat on one of the grubby blue plastic waiting room seats that was fastened to a steel frame along with three other seats. All but one of them had cigarette stub marks on the edges and clumps of old chewing gum stuck to the sides.

Henry picked up a handset and looked to his right at what Ferranti assumed was a list of extension numbers. He slowly dialled, mouthing the numbers silently, as his eyes flitted from the list to the phone and back. He held the phone to his ear and began to gaze at the ceiling, waiting to see if anyone answered his call. Often, nobody did, given their workload. A pile of messages was usually the end result of an eight-hour shift on the front desk; messages the CID team would read as they brewed yet another cup of coffee or tea in an attempt to stay awake and alert on their long shifts. Just as he was about to hang-up and add one more written message to the current pile, someone in the CID office answered the phone. Henry relayed Ferranti's message, and DC Hulme, who was sitting in CID filling out an arrest report on the system, told him that DS Walker had stepped out of the room, but that a message would be passed on to her. Henry sat, nodding, before putting the phone down. Ferranti sprang to his feet and walked over to the desk, optimistically.

"*I'm sorry, but the investigating officer on that case is currently unavailable. I'll be sure to pass your message on and they will be in touch*", Henry said, with a satisfied smile. End of shift, no issues. Unfortunately, Ferranti wasn't in the mood to walk away and wait for a call who-knows-when. He didn't know if the investigating officer was genuinely unavailable or just stalling, but the message from upstairs at least confirmed that there was indeed a case running in the Incident Room.

"*Hi. Sorry*", said Ferranti, attempting to both sound apologetic and sympathetic at the same time, "*but could you just call up one more time? My source seemed keen for your colleagues to know about the information I have, so if you could just pass on the following message straight way, please? Tell them, 'The note said you reap what you sow', and I'm sure that will help them understand*".

Henry responded firmly but politely. "*I'll add that to the message now, sir, and CID will collect these sometime this evening*". He picked up his pen and turned to retrieve the message from the CID clipboard.

"*Sorry, but they said it was urgent*", Ferranti quickly added, shrugging his shoulders and with his arms outstretched a little so that Henry could see the desperation when he turned back to look at him. Henry exhaled. This could turn into one of 'those' situations, where a member of the public just won't let it go. He looked down at his own feet, closed his eyes and exhaled; resigned to what he had to do next. He lifted his head and put on a weak smile, before picking up the handset again. Ferranti lifted his palm to feign gratitude, mouthing 'thank you' before stepping back and lowering himself back down onto the seats. The phone rang in CID as DS Walker walked back in from the kitchen area with a couple of steaming hot brews in her hands. She popped them down next to her colleague, DC Hulme, and reached into her pocket for a few Rich Tea biscuits she had also quickly grabbed from the kitchen.

"I'll get it, you grab your coffee", said Walker. Hulme nodded in gratitude, as his colleague picked up her mug of herbal tea and leant over to grab the phone with her free hand.

"DS Walker, CID", she said, as she manoeuvred around the corner of the desk and took her seat.

"Hello, it's the front desk", said Henry. *"I have someone here who wants me to pass on some additional case information, immediately. Can you let DC Hulme know, please?"*

"Err sure. He's right here … hang on", said Walker, as she put her hand over the mouthpiece and mouthed *"It's Henry on the front desk, for you … something about adding information to a message?"*

Hulme took the handset from Walker and, with the remnants of a hurriedly chewed Rich Tea biscuit still in his mouth, listened to Henry on the front desk. When

Henry had finished talking, Hulme replied, "*Oh right, well she's here now, so I'll let her know. Thanks, and have a good one*". And, with that, he put the phone down, as DS Walker looked up, eyebrows raised.

"*What was that?*" she enquired, curiously.

Reaching for another biscuit and already looking back at his paperwork, Hulme remarked, "*Oh a front-desk walk-in asked to speak to the officer in charge of the Albert Scargill death. Henry initially took a message, but the guy said there was some additional information that needed passing on straight away. Something about a note and reaping what you sow?*"

It only took a few seconds for the words to sink in.

DS Walker leapt to her feet and sprinted to the lifts.

Chapter 9

He sat in front of the mirror, removing the wig and the last pieces of the prosthetic nose. He was far from being a professional at disguises, but he knew the basics.

The room he was sitting in was small, with a chair, a tambour desktop and a pinboard sitting neatly in the corner. Behind the desk hung a small wall mirror. He felt cocooned from the outside world when he was in here. Such was his concern for security and privacy, though, he had a black-out blind fitted to the window and had set up a live video feed from CCTV cameras dotted around the room. The feed was accessible at any time from his mobile phone.

Spread out on the desk was a variety of equipment, all very neatly and carefully positioned - just how he liked it. He couldn't bear untidiness and disorganisation, but he had learnt to control his angst as he grew older. He certainly didn't see himself like some of the OCD people he knew or had read about, who would freak out if a picture frame on the wall was three degrees off-centre.

As he so often did in this secure space, he began talking to his reflection.

"So, *they know about your murder, Scargill, and they should have found you too by now, Yedlin*", he said, with a depraved grin on his face. "*I wonder if they will believe Ferranti's story? It should be an interesting ride, Adam. I do hope it doesn't bring back any nightmares.*"

His face turned into a mock sad frown as he thought pitifully about Ferranti and the Police, who had no clues and no chance of ever finding who they were looking for.

"*Hmm, is it time to tease the inept Met with a hint or a clue?*" he wondered. The mischievous side of his alter-ego thought about it for a few seconds, but he then gave his reflection a hard, angry glare. "*NO!*" he retorted. "*Don't get over-confident. Remember the plan! You have dreamed of this for years, so don't do anything stupid!*" He almost spat the final word out in disgust; furious at the momentary lapse in his thus-far meticulous approach.

He paused, closing his eyes and taking a few deep breaths, to give his heart rate time to return to normal after such an explosive outburst. After several minutes, he re-opened his eyes and looked up at himself in the mirror again. He stared at the familiar face that looked back at him, devoid of disguise. Who was he, really?

Deep down he knew, from the years of therapy he'd needed to endure, that he was no longer just one identity. The trauma throughout his early years had been sporadic, but extremely intense nonetheless, leading to the split personality he now both loved **and** loathed. His traumas had been compounded in his twenties and thirties, but the die was already cast long by then. He remembered the first psychiatrist he saw, after he first tried cutting his own skin; a typical trait of someone who feels they need to be punished for simply surviving.

"The diagnosis is simple. After such a series of traumas throughout your life, the typical response is either to self-harm or to harm others. Dissociative Personality Disorder - textbook stuff", the psychiatrist had said to him. He recalled the self-congratulatory smug smile on the doctor's face and how it made him want to pick up the pyramid-shaped glass paperweight on the desk in front of him and bury it into the psychiatrist's forehead. He imagined smirking as he watched the dying doctor's nervous system respond to the shock and the pain, before convulsing and then suddenly slumping back, with a vacant deathly stare.

"How text-book was that?" he would have goaded the dead man.

That was the moment he knew that self-harm really wasn't satisfactory. He felt a surge at the thought of ending this stupid man's life; an emotion so powerful he wanted to live out the fantasy, but he already knew he didn't want to waste his 'murdering virginity' on this imbecile.

The memory brought a malevolent grin to his face as he stared into the mirror in his tiny room.

The second psychiatrist he had been to see, five years later, was a woman. Kindly, mid-to-late thirties and not unattractive. He had not wanted to kill her, though. Instead, he wanted to feign tears. He was good - really good - at feigning sorrow, so the woman had stepped over the line when she gently put her arms around his shoulders in a sign of support. When she did that, he would close his eyes and pretend – just for a moment – they were the comforting arms of his mother, as if she was still alive. 'Mummy' had shown him nothing but love and understanding and treated him with respect; not as an equal, but as a child and then an adult she was proud of, and who deserved to have things explained:

"*It's okay, sweetheart, I'm here. Everything will be alright now*", he would imagine hearing his mother say, as the psychiatrist held him. He knew the feeling of salvation that the imaginary scene brought him would quickly desert him, though, and when it did, he found he despised himself for being so weak and needy.

He brought his thoughts back to the present. Shaking the loving imagery from his mind, he suddenly felt hollow. He needed to re-focus on something, to take his mind off the gaping hole he had in his life. He needed to fill the hole with hatred, again. As he continued to reflect on what he had been put through - what 'they' had done to his family - he shook his head in anguish and anger. They would pay.

They were already starting to pay.

"*You reap what you sow*", he said to his reflection, with a calm, slow diction and a steady gaze that reflected his calculating and vengeful attitude. The murders of

Scargill and Yedlin had gone smoothly, although he really did question his use of the term 'murder'; "*More like justice, if you ask me*", he said out loud but to himself, with a feeling of self-vindication.

He always knew he would eventually give this side of himself a name. He would probably start using that name soon when contacting the Police, whether directly, or indirectly through Ferranti. He looked at his reflection full in the face once more, changing his mood yet again, and smiling politely, as if looking at a stranger he was pleased to have met for the first time.

"*Well, hello. How lovely to be able to finally put a name to the face*". He snorted with derision at his own joke and then settled back into removing the final untidy remnants of his disguise. Yes, he knew what name he would give to the Police and to Ferranti soon enough, but not just yet. He let out a satisfied sigh and then looked down towards his desk. It was time to start thinking about 'what next'.

"*And now, Ricardo Goas, I believe it's time for you to die?*" he asked, rhetorically; deliberating his options. He stood up, stooped over the top of a small bookshelf that rested on the desk unit, and started to look for his map of York city centre; the last known place of residence for his next victim. The map was, of course, exactly where it should be in his filing system, causing him to smile at his own efficiency. He laid it out on the pull-out extendable desk and began to recite the short chilling poem he had made up several years ago, to help him remain focused on his dream:

"Scargill first, then Yedlin near water,
Goas to follow, then on with the slaughter.
Plenty of reasons to kill so many more,
Before Adam will die; the son of a whore.

The short, sweet memory of his mother's hug was now gone, and a cold, steely stare returned to the face of his alternative persona. He looked at the map and then briefly turned to the mirror one more time.

"And they will all find out and fear my name soon enough. Oh, Adam..." he said, grinning into the mirror, *"How I wish I could see your face when they first tell you my name".*

Chapter 10

DS Walker repeatedly jabbed the lift-call button on the 12th floor. "*Come on, come on!*" she cursed, impatiently, hoping the walk-in hadn't left and disappeared into the Thursday market crowds by the time she got down to the Enquiry Desk.

The lift light pinged and the doors opened, with Walker jumping into the lift and jabbing the ground floor button immediately. She stood right in front of the doors, primed to jump out as soon as the lift stopped on the ground floor and the doors started to open; her mind continually replaying the phrase, 'You reap what you sow; you reap what you sow'. Who was the person downstairs? Surely it wasn't the murderer, but who else knew about the message, and how? The lift stopped on the 9th floor.

"*Oh shit... what the fuck?*" exclaimed Walker, only then realising there were already two other people in the lift, who were now trying to pass her and get out onto their floor. She moved aside, temporarily adjusting her demeanour; "*Sorry*", she offered, "*Just in a rush to ...*" but her travel companions had already hurried out of the lift, mumbling to each other and throwing quick glances back towards Walker.

Several frantic button jabs and fifteen seconds later, the lift slowed to a stop and the doors opened on the ground floor. DS Walker ran out and punched in the security code to get to the Enquiry Desk. She rushed through the door, whilst trying to gather herself, so as not to spook anyone who might be waiting. As she looked out from behind the counter, she could see four people sitting on the chairs in the waiting area. The Enquiry Officer who had called upstairs would have already left for the day by now, so how would she know if one of the four people was the person she needed to talk to?

"*Good afternoon, DS Walker*", came a voice from her left-hand side. It was Dennis, one of the Enquiry Desk team, who had taken over the shift from Henry. Dennis was a gently-spoken man; some would say slightly effeminate, and everyone would definitely say a little camp, but he was also lovingly cheeky and able to defuse the tension of even the latest-night Enquiry Desk altercation.

"*Oh, good afternoon, Dennis*", Walker replied, only briefly turning her head towards him, before she returned to scanning the room for any clue as to whether the walk-in she was looking for was still on the premises.

"*This message was left for you, and you're looking for the gentleman on the far left, in the cargo jacket and …*" Dennis quietened his voice momentarily whilst leaning slightly towards her, and adding "*… the off-white shirt with the coffee stain on it*". He pursed his lips and gave DS Walker a faux-appalled 'fashion failure' look with his eyes.

Walker took the slip of paper and looked quizzically back at Dennis, who explained, *"DC Hulme called to say you were heading down ... rather quickly ... so could I ask the visitor to stay"*. Walker's face broke into a gentle grin; grateful for Dennis's actions and those of her colleague, DC Hulme upstairs. She also knew Dennis would be smiling to himself, content at appearing to have everything under control with the minimum of effort, but just a touch of drama. She opened the slip of paper and read the briefest of contents. Looking up, she saw Adam Ferranti leaning against the wall, smiling casually back over at her, as if he knew she was going to be looking for him. Walker felt instantly riled by it all. She smiled back and asked, rhetorically;

"Mr Ferranti?"

Adam Ferranti pushed himself away from the wall and raised a hand in casual acknowledgement as he started to stroll towards the counter. Walker didn't know what it was, but this irritated her, too. He was far too casual; almost smug. She maintained a fixed smile as Ferranti approached the counter.

"If you could come to the door on your left, Mr Ferranti, perhaps we could talk in private".

DS Walker directed Ferranti to the Interview Rooms, whilst Dennis called up to DC Hulme to request his attendance on the ground floor.

"Thank you, Dennis. You're a star", smiled Walker.

Dennis paused for effect and then whispered, "*I know*".

"*Step this way, please*", Walker said to Ferranti, ushering him into Interview Room 1. She held the door and, as Ferranti passed her, she caught the slightest aroma of stale alcohol. Walker rolled her eyes as Ferranti strode into the room. She waited for him to sit down before offering him a drink.

"*Coffee would be great. Black, four sugars, please*", Ferranti requested politely, whilst rocking onto the back two legs of the chair. He rested the palms of his hands behind his head and looked around the compact room.

When Walker returned from the kitchen with the drink, DC Hulme was already standing outside the interview room. He whispered, "*So what we got, Guv?*"

"*Not sure, other than an extremely cocksure man, late forties, maybe early fifties, smelling of last night's alcohol. Appears to know more than he should about a specific detail of the Scargill death*", Walker replied, matter-of-factly. Hulme, who had plenty of his own work to do, knew nothing about the note the killer had left at the scene of the Scargill crime. He looked at Walker, as if waiting for her to share her thinking.

"*It's ok*", she said, seeing the look of expectation on his face. "*Let's just see what he has to say. I'll let you lead and I'll chip-in if I think there's something that we need to dig a little deeper into*".

DC Hulme nodded in agreement and opened the door to the interview room.

"*Mr Ferranti, this is my colleague, DC Hulme*", explained DS Walker. Ferranti rolled forwards onto all four chair legs and partially stood, to shake Hulme's hand.

"*Hi*", said Ferranti, gripping Hulme's hand firmly and shaking it vigorously.

"*Wow, good firm handshake, Mr Ferranti*", said Hulme, apparently impressed. It was a well-rehearsed opening line to try and build some apparently submissive rapport, thus easing some interviewees in with an appropriate sense of informality. "*You work out?*"

Ferranti slumped back into the chair and shrugged his shoulders. "*Not as much as I should*", he lamented, framing his midsection with his hands, as a pregnant woman might do to imply the extra weight she was carrying. The two men chuckled, but not enough as to appear genuinely amused. All three sat down and Walker moved her hand towards a recording machine.

"*We'll be recording this conversation, Mr Ferranti, to allow us to listen to you rather than miss anything important if we're trying to write up notes*".

Ferranti nodded. "*Sure, no problem*", he said.

Walker pressed the record button and commenced the interview. "*Thursday, 28th February 2013, 12:05pm*

- interview with Mr Adam Ferranti. In the room are DS Walker and DC Hulme."

Walker leant back and glanced at Ferranti. She was just about to ask her opening question when Ferranti launched into the conversation with, "*So, what can you tell me about the Scargill murder?*". Both Walker and Hulme were taken aback; confused by the approach Ferranti was taking.

"*I'm sorry?*" said DS Walker, busy assimilating what had just happened. How had Ferranti become the interviewer and they the interviewees - and so quickly?

"*Well, that's why you're interested in the information I have, right, DS Walker?*" stated Ferranti. "*And I'm interested to know if the local media are aware of the murder. Is there a killer at large? Are people at risk? Is there any safety advice from the Police for members of the public at this time?*"

"*What's the local media coverage got to do with this, Mr Ferranti?*" asked DC Hulme.

"*Well, people do have a right to know if a murder has taken place, don't they? And I assume it was a murder, as neither of you have reacted to tell me I'm wrong. You've just questioned why I think I have the right to know about it*". He paused and looked from Hulme to Walker and back again; waiting for - hoping for - a reaction.

Walker responded quickest and with a degree of unexpected calm from Ferranti's point of view. "*Firstly,*

Mr Ferranti, this is an active investigation, and I am not at liberty to comment or indicate whether there was a murder or not. Secondly, I need you to tell me who you are and tell me why you came down here today". She leaned forwards, resting her arms on the table in a subtle but defiant and commanding gesture; to reaffirm her role as the inquisitor rather than of the accused.

"Wow, she's cool under pressure", thought Ferranti; immediately impressed by DS Walker. Many others would have fumbled their way through his question and stumbled straight into a far deeper hole. He gave Walker an admiring glance and congratulatory nod of his head. Walker was, in turn, appalled by such an arrogant condescending gesture, but gritted her teeth and allowed Ferranti the time to answer her questions.

"My name is Adam Ferranti. I work as a feature journalist at the Yorkshire Post. I came down here today because I had a phone call this morning; either from a killer or a whack-job". Ferranti confidently pulled out his reporters' pad, peering at his written notes through weary and slightly hungover eyes, and continued;

"... Albert Scargill; the first, not the last. Tell officer in charge I said heed the note: 'reap what you sow'. Another body near the O2 Arena. Something about him not being keen on the wine, or something".

Ferranti looked up at Hulme and Walker again. *"He also said I have a week to stop him, or there will be a third murder. So, now you know why I'm here".* He flipped the notebook closed rather theatrically as if to punctuate his statement. DS Walker gritted her teeth, as the small hairs on the back of her neck bristled at the arrogance of the man in front of her.

"*What else can you tell us about the phone call?*" asked DC Hulme, calmly, seeing that Walker was possibly about to explode, and therefore re-taking the lead in the interview from her. "*Where were you? When was it? Was there any caller ID? Did you recognise the voice?*"

Ferranti glanced at Hulme with what appeared to be both a smirk and a touch of disdain, as if surprised that the 'helper' dare ask questions. Ferranti restrained himself though as he could see DS Walker was clearly agitated and seemed to have taken a dislike to Ferranti and his mannerisms, so he replied quite coolly;

"*I was sitting at my desk at work. It was around 10:55 this morning when the call arrived. I checked the display on the phone and the number was withheld. And no, I didn't recognise the voice ... although, to be fair, I was a little distracted, trying to multi-task. It was only when he started to talk about there being another body that the caller really got my attention.*"

Walker looked up. "*So, it was a man? You didn't mention that before. And if you only started to concentrate on what he was saying part way through the call, how can you be so sure about what he said at the start?*" Her analytical mind was working hard as she scanned Ferranti's face for a reaction. Perhaps her points might actually make him stop, think and feel a little humbled.

"I guess I just have great subconscious recall", said Ferranti, shrugging his shoulders and sitting back. He slouched in the chair with enough self-satisfaction that made Walker's irritation levels peak. She paused, taking a moment to calm down. Then, thinking things through, she asked;

"What else did he say? Did he introduce himself in any other way than using a name?"

"No, no introduction really", replied Ferranti. *"Just straight into the message"*. But then Ferranti's expression changed and he looked upward, as people often do when replaying a visual or auditory memory. His mind was searching for something that he couldn't quite recall. Then, he tilted his head to one side, apparently having recalled a memory. The flash-back clearly perplexed him.

"It was weird, though, now I think about it", he added to his tale as he re-played the memory. *"He told me to stop what I was doing. He knew exactly what I was looking at on my computer"*.

Ferranti suddenly lost his smug disposition. He was trying to recall some more of the conversation, when he suddenly leant forward and abruptly slapped the edge of the table with the palm of his hand. *"Damn it …. He knew my name"*.

And, with that, he stared up at DS Walker and DC Hulme with a look of shock and realisation.

"He called me Adam".

Chapter 11

It was a cold morning, made colder by an easterly breeze coming down the River Thames. Police Constable Yvonne Nash wrapped a fresh, dry blanket around a woman who was sitting on a wooden crate; shivering and weeping. The woman's clothes and hi-vis tunic were dripping with water, and she was thoroughly soaked to the skin. PC Nash assured her that she was safe and that they were all there to support her. Was there anyone they could ring? The woman mumbled a phone number and the name 'Des', but added that he would be at work and might not be able to take any calls. PC Nash asked where Des worked and, in a flat distant tone, the woman muttered the name and location of a local haulage company. PC Nash assured the woman that they would contact Des, and tore the page of details from her notebook to pass it to one of her colleagues, just as the woman bent over and began to cry once again.

Detective Sergeant Steve Denton was in charge of the scene. He waved to Nash, signalling for her to come and talk to him. Nash put her arm on the woman's shoulder and explained that her colleagues would be stepping in to stay with her, as she had to talk to the Detective Sergeant. The woman grabbed Nash's hand as if to stop her leaving, but PC Nash explained that two other constables would be with her. They knelt down and started to talk to the woman, assuring her she was not being left alone. PC Nash gently eased the grip the woman had on her hand, stood up slowly, and backed away a few steps, before turning and walking over to DS Denton.

"*Is she saying much, yet?*" enquired Denton.

"*Not really, sir. I think she's still too shaken*", Nash responded, as she flicked open her notebook and read the notes she'd managed to take from the stuttering words the woman had uttered in-between the waves of frightened tears.

"*Her ID badge says her name is Julie Pritchard, and she's an O2 Arena Safety Officer. She was inspecting the waterline levels near the InterContinental Hotel when she noticed someone sitting in a chair at the water's edge. She walked over to ask if they were alright and to tell them it wasn't safe to be so close to the edge. As she got closer, she saw the man's face – and the corkscrews. She said that's when she screamed, stumbled sideways, and fell into the water. One of waiters at the hotel heard her scream and ran down to help her. He got her out of the water, shouted for one of the guests to throw down some blankets and towels, and then called 999. His English is pretty poor but PC Kyriakou speaks some Turkish. He's on his way down now, to take a more complete statement*", reported PC Nash.

Denton pursed his lips and nodded slightly, impressed with the reaction of the waiter, and grateful for the multi-cultural demographic of The Met. PC Nash closed her notebook and, after a short pause in case there were any other questions from DS Denton, she asked, *"Any news on the victim, sir?"*

Denton slowly shook his head. *"Not yet. No ID on the body and SOCO tell me there's no chance of fingerprints as they appear to have been mutilated. The body was held upright with six corkscrews twisted through the vent holes in the chair and up into the ribs and spine of the victim. There's trauma from the two corkscrews in his eye sockets... We'll let the coroner do their job; see what other identifying features they can find, if any. He can only have been there since late last night, otherwise the evening safety checks would have spotted him".*

Nash opened her eyes wide in shock. *"Whoever did this must have had some help, or must be some sort of muscle-man... or woman, I guess. It would take massive upper-body strength to get a dead body into a position where it can be manipulated to stay in an upright position, wouldn't it, Sarge?".*

Denton nodded. Both he and Nash looked over to the edge of the pier, where police hazard tape blocked the path and beyond. A dozen members of the London Metropolitan Police Force were still going about their business; some in uniform, some in wetsuits, and a couple of Scene of Crime Officers were starting to erect their investigations tent and equipment.

"Who goes to the trouble of killing someone and then making a big deal of theatrically presenting the corpse, leaving it so easy to find?" mumbled Nash to herself.

"Someone who wants to send a message", replied Denton, now looking up towards the hotel. A few onlookers up at the Intercontinental Hotel were now trying to view the morbid scene, but thankfully their view – and that of their smartphones – was almost entirely blocked.

"Sick bastards", muttered Denton, before turning away from the scene and beginning to reflect on everything he knew, or rather everything he *didn't* know. Who was the victim and why was he screwed to a chair on the banks of The Thames? If it was a message, who was it aimed at? The Police, maybe? How was the body transported here and where was he killed? SOCO had said there was no evidence at the current scene to suggest the murder had taken place here. This clearly wasn't a random killing and yet it didn't have the hallmarks of a gangland one, either.

Denton casually looked over to where some uniformed officers were standing, by way of blocking vehicle and pedestrian access to the quay. As he mulled over the current absence of facts, a black car with three occupants pulled up at the temporary barrier. One occupant stayed in the car, whilst the other two got out and walked over to the uniformed officers, flashing some credentials. The uniformed officer in charge of the temporary barrier looked between the ID and the faces of his visitors and then stood aside, gesturing for them to proceed.

*"What the hell are **they** doing here?"* muttered Denton. He excused himself from PC Nash and strode over

toward the two unexpected visitors. As they all got closer to each other, they stopped and held their ground, about two feet apart. For a couple of seconds nobody moved or said anything, then the lead passenger from the car held out his hand, ready to shake Denton's. His name was Simon McBride, and Denton was already familiar with his work at MI5.

"*Steve*", said McBride, with a small but perceivable nod of his head in acknowledgement to Denton, who extended his hand in return. They shook hands. "*Simon*", replied Denton, with an equally lukewarm but not unfriendly greeting.

"*What brings you down here, Simon?*" Denton asked.

"*Company business*", McBride responded, coolly. He then partially turned his head in the direction of his colleague, who was standing behind him to his right, adding, "*This is also Steve, he's working with me on our … research*".

Denton raised his chin in a gesture of hello, but the other Steve just stared back with indifference.

"*Two people called Steve? Might get confusing*", said Denton, dryly.

"*Not really*", added McBride, smirking back at Denton, as the apparent chilled indifference between them melted a little more. "*He rarely talks*".

McBride looked over Denton's shoulder and gazed at the Police hazard tape stretching out over the entrance to the crime scene. *"Messy stuff, murder"*, he said, subtly enquiring into the situation at the water's edge.

Denton glanced over his shoulder briefly and then looked back at McBride, replying calmly with, *"Who said anything about a murder?"*

McBride smiled, wryly. *"Just a guess. Anyway, I'm sure you'll cooperate with our enquiries? I've already spoken to your lovely DCI"*.

"Can I see you in my office, Mr McBride?" whispered Denton, leaning slightly forwards, which both men knew as code for 'dump the help and tell me what you can'.

McBride turned to 'other' Steve and instructed him to wait by the car, which he did without query. Denton and McBride then turned and walked across the concrete paving together, away from prying ears and eyes.

"So, what can you tell me and what can't you tell me, Simon?", asked Denton, canvassing for any clues into this unusual turn of events.

"Not much, Steve, other than the fact that MI5 have an interest in this particular case as part of a wider and longer-term investigation", proffered McBride.

"How wide and how longer-term are we talking?" questioned Denton. McBride just tapped the side of his nose, to indicate he really couldn't – or wouldn't - share any more information.

They walked a little further, before McBride turned to face Denton and quietly began to confide in him.

"All I'll say is you need to keep me in the loop on this. You cannot discuss what we've just spoken about to anyone, including your DCI. This is Chief Super and above only."

Denton nodded and resigned himself to having got as far as he could with the conversation. The two men had a long and friendly history that overarched their choices to join separate departments in the public service, so they both respected the boundaries.

As they stood in silence, the pair saw PC Nash striding over towards them. McBride took this as his cue to leave the Police to their enquiries. He clicked his fingers to attract 'Steve', motioning him to come back over, which he did without question.

"Sorry to interrupt, DS Denton, but could I have a word, please?" PC Nash asked, quite hurriedly.

Denton nodded and then, grinning cheekily towards 'Steve', added, *"Great talking to you, Steve"*. As McBride and his silent companion walked away, Denton and PC Nash moved slowly back towards the crime scene.

"Call from HQ, sir. A Detective Sergeant from West Yorkshire called into Control, asking if we'd found a body this morning near the O2".

Denton shot Nash a shocked look.

"*Got a number for that DS?*" he quizzed. Nash handed him a slip of paper. Denton took out his mobile phone and punched in the number.

Chapter 12

Khatri had waited outside Millgarth for nearly twenty minutes, in the hope that Ferranti was going to be quick. A traffic warden had knocked on his window and politely asked him to move on, as there was a time limit for waiting outside the building - taxi license or not. Khatri started up the Leaf and drove around to the other side of the building, where he found a car parking spot on the road. From there, it was a short walk to the central shopping area of the city, and to his new favourite place for relaxing - Mrs Atha's Coffee & Tea Shop.

This family-run independent cafe appealed to Khatri, who couldn't abide multi-national coffee chains. He would often spend time here, taking in the atmosphere and talking to whoever had the time and inclination to chat with him. This time, though, he hoped he could at least enjoy his hot drink in peace and quiet, without Ferranti calling to ask where he was. Instead, the interruption came from elsewhere. His mobile phone burbled from inside his jacket and, taking it out, Khatri's shoulders drooped as he saw the caller ID. It was his father, calling from India.

"*Hello, father*", sighed Khatri, trying his best to sound mildly enthusiastic.

"Hello, Aarav. Where are you?" asked his father, brightly but a little accusatorily, too.

"I'm at University, of course ....", lied Khatri. *"I'm on a study break"*.

He had yet to tell his parents he had in fact abandoned his studies, and he intended to keep it that way, for now. The line went quiet for a couple of seconds, which Khatri knew meant his father was reflecting on what his son had just told him.

"Your mother called the shared house, to talk to you on the landline. Someone called Celia said you were probably out with clients all day – 'as usual'. Your mother wants to know what Celia meant by that. Care to tell us?" his father asked in an assertive tone.

Khatri had winced at hearing of Celia's recount. Knowing this moment could - and would – arise at some point, he was at least partially prepared.

"Yes, yes. Err, I have taken on some work, to supplement my income, father. I am on a break, studying, until I meet my next client ... a first-year student who is struggling with the workload... he has asked me for some extra tuition".

He paused, holding his breath, to see if his story was perceived as plausible. He could hear voices talking rapidly in Hindi, presumably as his father was relaying the message to his mother away from the receiver, whilst his elder sister would be 'contributing' to the conversation in some way, for sure. He could always rely on her to throw petrol on even the smallest of fires and make it rage. Khatri knew, however, what sacrifices they had all made and were continuing to make for him, so he calmed his attitude a little.

The Khatri family lived in Kolkata. As the principal educational and commercial centre of East India, they were able to grow up with comparative wealth and easy access to good local schools. Aarav Khatri nearly followed his father into banking, but he persuaded his parents that he could excel with an English university education; giving back to the community one day as a wealthy doctor, who could afford to help the rich and the poor alike. Such was his enthusiasm and ability to paint the picture for his parents, they agreed to finance his studies – all at the expense of home comforts and early retirement for themselves.

Khatri's father's voice returned to the phone. "*Well, that is wonderful news and we are happy to hear other students are already looking up to you, Dr Khatri!*"

Aarav could almost hear the smile on his father's proud face, which just served to layer more guilt on his conscience. "*But don't take on too much, Aarav. You don't want to jeopardise your own success*".

Aarav Khatri suddenly felt very remorseful in deceiving his family. "*Oh, of course not, but please don't call me 'Dr Khatri' yet, father. There are so very many things that could go wrong over the next two and a half years, that could mean I...",* but his response was cut-off mid-sentence by his father.

"Nonsense! I will hear none of it, Aarav! You are a talented student and you make us all very proud... doesn't he!" asked his father, rhetorically, presumably turning to Aarav's mother and sister for confirmation.

The call soon concluded with love, best wishes and promises from both sides to call again soon.

Aarav Khatri let out a long sigh of relief and flopped back into his chair.

"Tough call?" asked Danny, the manager at Mrs Atha's, smiling as he replaced Aarav's now cold cup of Darjeeling. Khatri looked up, in surprise. *"Sorry, wasn't eavesdropping, but the look on your face suggested a top-up would be useful"*, Danny explained, hoping to reassure his customer.

"Oh, yes. Thank you, but I think I might need more than some tea after that call", Khatri chuckled, nervously, reaching into his pocket to pay for the fresh cup of tea.

"No need", said Danny, seeing what Khatri was trying to do. *"We all have days when a cup of hot tea can help make a whole lot of difference. And you're a regular, so this one is on us"*.

Khatri smiled. Oh, how he loved to spend time at this place! As he sat back, he lifted the cup towards to his nose and took in the aroma. The day was just starting to feel bearable again, when his phone rang. This time it was Ferranti. Khatri looked over at Danny, who smiled and just shrugged his shoulders.

"*You can leave a message*", thought Khatri, aloud, and he put his phone back in his pocket without answering it. The tea he had been waiting to drink for almost 20 minutes had never tasted sweeter. "*Some things are worth waiting for*", said Khatri, and he grinned, mischievously.

Chapter 13

Ferranti walked out of Millgarth Police Station, with the request from DS Walker to let them know if he received any more contact from the mystery caller. The detective had also made a less than subtle request for him not to leave the city in the next 72 hours, in case they needed to call him back in. As his eyes adjusted to the light, he looked around for Khatri, but wasn't surprised to see he had left. Ferranti called Khatri's mobile and left a message, but then started to walk back to work in the crisp February air and soft, warming sunshine.

As he walked, Ferranti reflected on the Scargill murder - and yes, he still intended to call it a 'murder', despite the pathetic protestations from an uptight detective and her less than useless sidekick. He also started to analyse how he had become involved in the case. He didn't understand why the caller had chosen him. Was it random? How did the caller know his name? And how in the hell did he know exactly what Ferranti was doing at the time of the call? He decided the best thing to do was ask an expert.

"Justin Grant", came the voice on the end of the phone.

"Hey Justin, it's me", said Ferranti.

"Hey man! How the hell are you? I've not heard from you in months!" There was a slight pause and Justin let out a light-hearted chuckle before asking, *"So, what do you want from me today?"*

"Go easy. Maybe I'm just calling you to say hi. You know, just checking in on a friend?" replied Ferranti, laying on an overly-dramatic wounded tone, in jest.

"Sure. Poor, poor Adam", said Justin, in playful response. *"So, what's up?"*

"I need to pick your brains on a couple of things".

"Shoot".

"Okay", ventured Ferranti. *"Firstly, if someone wanted to call an unpublished number, and withhold their own number in the process, how easy would that be? And, secondly, how easy is an office CCTV system to hack?"*

"Come on, Adam, we did both of those things - and more - when you were here in the business. Did you forget everything I showed you last year?" asked Justin, wondering whether Ferranti was acting dumb, or had started hitting the alcohol again.

"Well, I think they're pretty easy to do, but I just wondered what had happened in the world of tech in the last twelve months. Maybe things got more secure?" As soon as the words left Ferranti's mouth, he knew how ridiculous they sounded.

"Adam, you know as well as I do that the gap in tech security isn't going to get wider, only narrower", replied Justin, softly.

Ferranti knew this to be true. Some of the things his friend had shown him, whilst both of them were in Afghanistan and then in London, blew Ferranti's mind. When they'd first met, Ferranti immediately liked Justin's no-nonsense gallows humour, as well as his keen and inquisitive mind. Their time together was cut short when Ferranti had to return to New York. Sadly, his mother's health was declining rapidly, after years of struggling with the consequences of being brutally beaten to near-death by Ferranti's violent stepfather. Ferranti had arrived back home just days she died. That was when he began to drink again, heavily. Justin heard the news that the stepfather had disappeared, and knew the escape would feel like someone twisting a knife into his friend's gut, so he invited Ferranti over to London, hoping it would be a new start for him. To his delight, Ferranti agreed, and Justin spent several weeks bringing Ferranti up to speed on some of the latest technological breakthroughs in the area of expertise for his company; the legal yet dubious world of corporate espionage.

As their time together went on, Justin was pleased to see how alert Ferranti's mind still was, and took joy in the enthusiasm he showed whilst learning, although it was clear that alcohol apparently still played a significant part in Ferranti's after-hours activities. The work Ferranti did was excellent, but his mood swings, fuelled by his drinking, finally led to a couple of clashes with high-profile accounts. Things weren't working out, and ultimately, Justin had to think about his business.

"Look, Adam, both the clients are delighted with the work, and I'm delighted with it, too... but you've just got to be more... well, professional, when meeting the clients", pleaded Justin.

"I know. It was just that one time. When the work was finished, I went out to let my hair down. I... well... maybe I had one or two too many. I'm pretty sure that blonde spiked some of them, though Justin. I mean ...", started Ferranti, but Justin and he both knew this was not the first time this had happened. Justin held his hand up, to indicate that his friend needed to stop talking.

"No, Adam", Justin said, assertively. He exhaled and, in what was clearly a discussion-ending tone, continued; *"Ashcroft says if I send you in again, he'll walk. I think Delaney's have already started talking to CommPack. That's over $1m wiped-off the sales forecast, if they leave, too"*. Justin wanted to ease the conversation onto how Ferranti could become a back-office technician instead, rather than a client-facing operative. The problem was, they both knew that Ferranti would rather sweep streets than be locked in a secure window-less office, setting up tech for some other glory-boy - or girl - to later steal his thunder. Ferranti held up his hand, partially in guilt and partially to signal he'd heard enough. Looking down at the floor, too embarrassed to look his buddy in the eye just yet, Ferranti said;

"Look, Justin, I truly appreciate the opportunity you've given me, and getting out of the States was a big step

forwards... but...", Ferranti paused and then looked up at Justin, "*...but maybe it's time I lived or died by my own actions, rather than putting your reputation at risk*". Both men looked at each other in silent submission. This was the truth, and it was fair, and they both knew it.

"*I'm not going to cut you adrift, Adam. You've generated some great revenue for my company and I owe you your share of the bonus.*" Justin paused, then added softly, "*And buddies don't cut each other out of their lives, either; especially given what we went through together in Helmand*".

Both men stood in momentary reflective moods; silent and reliving the memories of war, death and the senseless waste of human life. Justin turned and walked to his desk, opened his top drawer and pulled out a business card. He closed the drawer, walked back around the desk, and held out the card to Ferranti.

"*I might know where you could go next, if the thought of returning to journalism doesn't make your blood run cold?*" offered Justin. The pair briefly chuckled at the joke, but it was also in relief that they had amicably agreed that things needed to change. Ferranti took the card, looked at it and waved it gently, as if weighing up the option and saying thank you, once again, to his friend.

"*I know it's time for me to stand on my own two feet again or die in a ditch of spilled whiskey and my own drunken vomit*", said Ferranti. "*Either way, I can't allow either of us to feel like I'm a problem anymore*".

No more words were necessary. They pair went to shake hands but ended instead with a 'guy hug'; the sort you see on a sports field, between two competitors who have the ultimate respect for each other. That past memory of the friendship the two men had forged made Ferranti smile, as he now continued on his way back to work, in the bright but chilly February sunshine. He had just started to mentally replay the call from the mystery man, when a breathless voice at the side of him made him jump.

"*Hello*". It was Aarav Khatri. He appeared exhausted, resting his hands on his knees, and bent over as if a little winded from running.

"*How did you know where I was?*" asked a startled Ferranti.

"*Easy*", said Khatri, still sucking in air. "*Your message said you'd walk back to the office, so I took a guess that this was the easiest and most straight-forward route. It avoids the crowds in the city centre that you hate so much*".

Ferranti thought for a moment and then smiled at Khatri. "*Good guess. Maybe you ought to be a detective*", he said, smiling, and they turned and walked together.

"*Were you just talking to yourself?*" Khatri asked after a few seconds. "*Something happen at the Police station?*

Are you in trouble? Sometimes it can help to share a burden, you know?"

Ferranti chuckled. *"No, I'm not in any trouble. It's just that..."*, and then he paused. *"You know what, I'm not sure I'm actually allowed to talk to you about it, unfortunately".*

Khatri shrugged his shoulders and half-nodded, forlornly. *"I understand. Police business and witness statements, huh? Well, I've probably got enough on my mind anyway".*

Without breaking stride, Ferranti turned to Khatri with a look and gesture that suggested that Khatri might be the one to want to share.

Khatri took his chance. *"It's my parents. They think I'm still studying medicine"*, he offered, slightly ashamed.

"And you're not, right?" enquired Ferranti.

"Right", replied Khatri, guiltily, *"But they've just called me and... I've now lied to them directly, rather than by email. They think I'm currently helping a first-year student out with their studies, just to earn some money. They don't know I'm actually spending my days - and their life savings - driving a small and seen-better-days taxi".*

Khatri hung his head, glancing over to Ferranti, sheepishly awaiting the lecture about family values and honouring your parents, but it didn't happen. Instead,

Ferranti walked for a few minutes and then, to Khatri's surprise and relief, stopped. He turned to look at Khatri, and said;

"It's your life, not theirs. Sometimes you have to do what you think is the right thing, not what everyone else thinks is the right thing for you. I'm sure you'll be a success and you'll pay the money back – believe in yourself and in what you're doing."

Both men paused, with Khatri unsure what to say. He had only ever heard the sarcastic or dismissive and disinterested side of Ferranti's character before, so this was a surprising but also gratefully received comment. He suddenly felt as if a huge burden had been lifted from his shoulders. He slowly started to nod his head and couldn't help but smile, with his eyes beaming brightly in relief. The nod became more pronounced and rapid, and then Khatri reached out with both hands and took Ferranti's right hand, shaking it vigorously.

"Thank you", he gushed, and then threw his arms round Ferranti in a spontaneous and unbridled outpouring of gratitude. Ferranti just stood there, arms by his side, unsure what to do.

After a few seconds, Ferranti said, *"Ok, I get it... you're grateful"*, and raising his arms, gently pushed against Khatri's shoulders, to recover his personal space. For an unemotional character like Ferranti, that sort of public display of gratitude was more than a little uncomfortable.

Khatri stepped back, nodding in understanding and wiping his moist nose with his sleeve. *"Sorry, but I think that was just what I needed to hear"*.

The two men shuffled awkwardly on the spot and Ferranti looked around, hoping nobody was looking. Thankfully for him, nobody was, so he cleared his throat and said, *"Right, I'll be heading back to the office"*.

Khatri blurted out, eagerly, *"But you must be hungry! I bet you haven't had lunch? My treat?"*, and then he looked a little sheepish again, before adding, *"No hugs expected or given"*.

Khatri was surprised yet again, when Ferranti's expression broke into a genuine smile and he said, *"Sure kid, why not"*. They turned and walked to the nearest restaurant together.

As it turned out, the lunch extended into most of the afternoon, as Khatri talked about his life, his family's ambitions for him to become a doctor, and his new life plan. Ferranti hardly said a word, but his keen mind took in every detail.

Chapter 14

DS Stephanie Walker had completed a marathon shift and was both thankful yet anxious about leaving work and returning home. She had not seen her husband, Alex, for 25 hours, although that wasn't unusual. These days, there were times when he would be gone for days and she'd have no idea where he was. In the past, Alex was usually very remorseful after an assault on his wife, but recently, her apparent lack of interest in his apologies had backfired. Today, Stephanie was exceptionally weary and just hoped to get home and go to sleep.

As she unlocked and opened the door to the apartment, Stephanie paused and listened for any tell-tale sounds. She had become quite adept at pre-judging Alex's mood by what she did or didn't hear when entering their home. Silence. That either meant he was out or he was asleep in a drunken stupor. She entered the hallway, hung her coat and bag in the cupboard, and listened again. Still silence. Closing her eyes and crossing her fingers, she softly called out, "*Alex?*" and found herself tensing in fear, should there be a response. No reply. On entering the open-plan kitchen and dining area, she saw flowers on the worktop and an envelope with her name on it. The relief she felt wasn't at this pathetic apologetic gesture, but that it indicated that Alex was out of the flat. She wandered over and picked up the envelope, raising a contemptuous eyebrow as she opened the back, and took out the note. It read;

'Hi. I know I did a terrible thing again last night, baby. It was the alcohol, not you, that made my frustration about money and work boil over. Again.

I'm out for the day, so rest, because I'm sure you're tired and don't need me around. I won't be back until late. Just popping out for a bite to eat with Jaggs. He says he wants to talk to me, so fingers crossed, eh? We might pop into town later, but I'll stick to soft drinks.

Love you, and sorry again. I know I need help and I'm going to get it and get us out of this mess. Just need Jaggs to come good on a deal and we'll be home-free.

Love you loads, Alex xx'

Stephanie snorted in derision. "*Sure, just soft drinks*", she said to herself. That was a new line from Alex, but she knew he wouldn't be able to contain himself. It would be a soft drink, which would lead to maybe a weak half-a-pint of shandy, and then escalate from there. She predicted the conversation ahead:

"*And then the time just went 'whoosh', babe. Don't know where a couple of hours went but, suddenly, I found the guys had popped a whiskey into my beer and, before I knew it, I realised I was smashed. I tried a coffee to help me out, but the bastard behind the bar made me a liqueur coffee – bloody double Tia Maria splashed in*", and then Alex would laugh in mock surprise. But the laughter would quickly stop, as he would see either the look of fear or disappointment in his wife's eyes. It would always turn to fear, eventually…

"Fucking hell, I couldn't help it, could I?" he would suddenly snap in those scenarios. *"It's not like you've never been pissed and done something stupid, is it?"* he would say, pointing an accusing finger at his wife. She knew that's when things could quickly escalate and, even stood in the empty kitchen right now, the thought of it filled her with dread. Cold sweat began to bead on her forehead, and she held onto the counter-top edge to steady herself. Her breathing became laboured, as she fought with the physical reaction to the déjà vu of the psychological scenario.

Her grip tightened as she gritted her teeth. *"FUCK!"* she screamed and kicked out at the cupboard door. She knew that expressing *her* anger would help when she was alone, but the cuts and bruises she had endured over the last year had taught her never to express it in front of – or towards - Alex. *"Like petrol and a fucking match"*, she said to herself, describing the combustible, explosive nature of one particular fight last month. Alex had struck her so hard that she needed to take a couple of days off work in order for the bruising to sufficiently fade and therefore not raise any questions. That was the only night she had ever struck him back; an instinctive and immediately regretted reaction. Yes, she had the satisfaction of watching him crumple in a heap, clutching his crotch, but once he had recovered, he had almost punched his way through the locked bedroom door to get to her.

Stephanie brought herself back to the present and hung her head as she leaned against the counter-top, releasing her grip on the hard surface. Her knuckles were white and the muscles in her fingers ached, such was the tension coursing through her body. She took a couple of deep, slow breaths and allowed herself to feel back in the present; in an empty apartment with a large L-shaped sofa she could sprawl out on. No matter how comfortable the bed was, it no longer felt like a restful sanctuary. It was a place of occasional nightmares and abuse. It felt dirty and always filled her with insecurity and a sense of impending sadness. Even when Alex was sober, she rarely slept when they shared the bed. She remembered one night a few weeks ago, though, when Alex was sober and she needed to feel close to him. She had slid under the duvet and put her arms around his waist, snuggling up to spoon him. For a few minutes, everything felt normal and she had fallen asleep hugging her husband – a feeling and an experience so heart-warming to her that, the next morning, when Alex had gone into the shower, she had sobbed with joy that she might have her husband back. But, it was short-lived, and Stephanie Walker promised never to make that mistake again.

Kicking her shoes off and unbuttoning her top two buttons, Stephanie felt too tired to eat or drink anything, although a shot of whiskey appealed. "*How ironic*", she muttered. She dropped onto the sofa and quickly faded into a deep, much-needed sleep.

She had no idea what time it was, but the buzzing of her mobile phone woke her with a start. She struggled momentarily to realise where she was and what the sound was. Bleary-eyed, slightly confused, and temporarily drained of energy, Stephanie roughly fumbled to find her skirt pocket before pulling out her mobile phone. She squinted, looking at the time. It was 3pm, so she'd only been asleep for around four hours. She answered the call, thankful that Alex's name hadn't flashed up on the screen.

"*Hello?*" she mumbled, sitting up and trying to gather her thoughts, yet still struggling to fully wake up.

"*DS Walker?*" came the question. "*This is DS Denton of the London Metropolitan Police*".

"*Oh, yes*", said Walker, desperately trying to sound natural whilst organising her thoughts.

"*Our Control Centre said you enquired about a possible dead body, to be found near the O2 Arena?*" Denton asked.

Walker recalled the enquiry. She was now wide awake and focused. "*We found one*", her caller continued. Denton didn't feel the need to add anything else. He waited for the news to sink in and for Walker to respond, but she just sat in stony silence. The interview with Ferranti swam back into her mind, but, returning her focus to the call, Walker enquired, expectantly;

"*My source made reference to the victim 'not appreciating fine wine'. Does that have any relevance to the body you found?*"

DS Denton replied without emotion. *"The body was screwed to a plastic chair, and both eyeballs were ruptured by corkscrews, too. I've also just taken a call from the coroner"*. He paused involuntarily, which only added to the tension. *"He told me a wine cork was rammed into the victim's oesophagus"*.

DS Walker closed her eyes, pinched the bridge of her nose, and whispered, *"Fuck"*.

Chapter 15

Andrew Jagger, known to most people simply as 'Jaggs', was in his mid-thirties and worked in the PR and sponsorship industry. Well-connected, he had a growing reputation for partying with the local media stars and being on the speed-dial list of several of the more prominent ad agencies. He was a polished professional, with a clean reputation, the smartest Armani suits, and an extreme loyalty to those who had helped him get rich. Loyalty was the only reason he had agreed to meet Alex Walker today, after Alex had called him and begged for work. Jaggs assumed either Alex didn't realise it, or had simply decided to pretend that his recent behaviour had not caused Jaggs both significant reputational damage as well as huge financial loss.

It started several months ago when Alex arrived at a promotional meeting with a high-end French fashion magazine. He seemed surprisingly pre-occupied and on edge, so Jaggs had taken him aside before they stepped into the boardroom:

"*You alright, mate? You seem a bit on edge?*" Jaggs queried.

Alex didn't make direct eye contact, but his response was an attempt to placate Jaggs.

"*Yeah, yeah, fine. Let's get this done*", he replied, clearly uncomfortable.

Jaggs placed the palms of his hands upon Alex's upper arms, patting them in a comforting act of assurance. That was when Jaggs noticed the feint aroma of alcohol on Alex's breath.

"*Had a quick swig of encouragement, have we?*" smiled Jaggs, uneasily. Such a scenario was unusual for Alex, who was normally the epitome of health and restraint. Alex looked down at Jaggs, who stood four inches shorter than him:

"*What?*" he sneered, instinctively defensive, as his eyes suddenly focused on Jaggs for the first time that after-noon. Jaggs unconsciously rocked back, before smiling warmly up at Alex. It seemed as if Alex was about to say something else in anger, but instead, he changed his expression and smiled.

"*Oh, you know, just the one*", he explained, trying to sound jocular at being found-out. "*I surprised Steph at lunchtime. I wanted to take her out for a bite to eat, so we popped into a place on Briggate. She had a small glass of wine, so I thought I'd join her*". Alex continued to force a smile, but he knew his story sounded flawed as soon as he mentioned Steph drinking in work hours. A newly promoted Detective Sergeant having alcohol at lunchtime? Utterly ridiculous.

For a split second, Alex thought about revising or adding to the story, but decided that would only make things worse. Jaggs knew the lunchtime drinking story was unlikely to be true, but Alex was one of his best earners and now wasn't the time to find out if there were unexpected issues they needed to talk through. They'd get through this meeting and then deal with whatever it was another time.

Jaggs smiled. *"Know what you mean, mate. Now come on, let's go in there and seal this deal!"*

As Alex and Jaggs entered the room, their hosts rose to their feet. Their lead was Alain Bernard, the MD of the UK division of Le Echelons magazine; a high-end quarterly fashion publication. With Bernard was their lawyer, Albert Dubois, and their UK Marketing Director, Tavia Stewart. It was a small, glazed office on the fourth floor, with just enough room for the five of them, and a small glass unit which had water and coffee laid out on the top. As the meeting progressed, Jaggs noticed Alex glaring at Dubois and Stewart. They appeared to be amused by something in Alex's portfolio and, to add to Alex's angst, they were whispering in French. Tavia Stewart wrote on a small notepad and showed it to Albert Dubois, whose face beamed back at her and he nodded.

"So, Monsieur Bernard, we are confident that ...", but Jaggs didn't get to finish his sentence, before Alex growled:

"Excuse me, but is there something funny you'd like to share?" He looked accusatorily at Dubois and Stewart, who looked back at him; shocked and a little mystified.

They looked across to Bernard, as if seeking to understand what they had done wrong.

"*Is there a problem, Monsieur Walker?*" enquired Bernard; his English heavily accented. Everyone glanced open-mouthed at Alex, who reached over and snatched the portfolio and the notepad from Tavia Stewart, who cowered a little, feeling threatened by the physical size of Walker and his explosive outburst. Alex glanced at the photos and then at the notepad. The writing was in French, so he dropped the open portfolio on the desk and showed the notepad to Jaggs. Alex then looked over to Bernard and said;

"*I don't know, is there? These two were laughing at my photos and scribbling notes to each other like school-kids. Not what I'd call professional or respectful!*" he yelled, pointing at a confused Dubois and a still-wary Stewart. Jaggs reached out and put his hand on Alex's arm to gently push it lower. Alex yanked it away from Jaggs and stood resolute; waiting for a response from the meeting's hosts.

"*I'm sorry, Alex, I don't speak French*", Jaggs stated quietly, looking to Bernard for help. Bernard reached over to take the notepad from Jaggs, but before Bernard could talk, Dubois shrugged his shoulders and held his arms out to indicate confusion, muttering in French to whoever would listen.

"*SPEAK ENGLISH!*" raged Alex, assuming Dubois thought it appropriate to continue to be rude. People outside the glazed office were starting to look over, alarmed and keen to see what the commotion was. It was Tavia Stewart who realised what was happening, and responded in defence of her colleague:

"*He doesn't speak English*". She then pointed over to the portfolio, adding, "*We were so happy to see your photos and were smiling because we agreed that you made our previous choice of brand ambassador seem very unwise*". She was beyond defending her actions now and her tone was becoming acerbic; she was going on the offensive. "*And the note on the pad says, 'I will translate everything for you later but, for now, be happy we seem to have the perfect candidate'*". She paused to calm herself before she made her final statement; "*But I think, on reflection, Mr Jagger, that I withdraw my approval*". She turned her attention to Alex and, leaning over to close his portfolio case, looked at him straight in the eye and said, "*Non, Bernard, une autre ambassadeur s'il vous plait*".

Alain Bernard slowly nodded his head and handed the notepad back to Tavia Stewart. He looked over at Alex Walker with disappointment. He then looked towards Jaggs. No words needed to be spoken, so Jaggs held out his hand and shook each of the hosts' hands as a respectful goodbye. He turned and looked at Alex and indicated for him to follow. Alex knew better than to attempt to say goodbye, so he meekly followed Jaggs out of the room and into the lift.

No words were said on the way down and, at the exit, Jaggs looked up at Alex and his eyes said all that needed to be said, so Alex just nodded and walked in the opposite direction.

Now, as Jaggs sat at the bar in Angelica, he sipped a Perrier and recalled the resulting four or five times he'd had to tell Alex that previous sponsorship deals were not going to be renewed.

The bar at Angelica was a favourite for Andrew Jagger. A city centre rooftop location with a wraparound glass terrace. It was classy and sophisticated, like the man himself. A perfect venue, from afternoon to evening, for hosting wealthy new sponsors who would be accustomed to such tasteful, vibrant surroundings. Jaggs used to regularly invite Alex here, too, but word quickly spread across the fashion industry about Alex's outburst at Le Echelons, and the mud certainly stuck. Jaggs had made a lot of money as Alex's agent in the past, but the safest decision for Andrew Jagger now was to distance himself as much as possible from his client.

Through a mixture of skill, charm and a few small lies, Jaggs had managed to rescue his own reputation from the Le Echelons magazine shambles without throwing Alex to the wolves. Jaggs still wasn't sure what had gone wrong, but whenever he tried to raise the subject, Alex either stormed out or told him now wasn't the time but he would explain everything later. Later never came.

Alex entered the bar, smiling at the hosts who he knew so well, and nodding to the barman who he knew even better. As he approached Jaggs, he beamed and held out a hand, giving his friend and agent a firm, enthusiastic handshake.

"Hey, Jaggs. Wow, feels like long-time no-see!" he said, warmly. Jaggs nodded and indicated that Alex should grab a seat next to him.

"How are you, Alex?" Jaggs enquired, not particularly interested in the response. Despite any inference in the note he had just left for his wife, this meeting was all Alex's idea and not a request from Jaggs in any sense. Despite Jaggs not having any sponsorship work for Alex, however, he did have something in mind for him to do. The men discussed football, old friends, even the weather for a while, before Jaggs raised the issue:

"Look, Alex, I don't have anything promotional brewing at the moment, but if you want to earn a few quid, I've got a favour to ask", he ventured.

"Sure, Jaggs, whatever I can do, mate", Walker eagerly replied.

"Well, it's not glamorous. In fact, it's a bit sensitive; sort of personal. That's why I'm offering £500 cash for your help". Jaggs looked round the room, slightly embarrassed at his imminent request.

"Oh that's... great. Yeah. I mean who doesn't want £500, right?" responded Walker, a little disappointed and unsure of what was coming next.

"A friend of mine has mistakenly delivered a package to the wrong address. It should have been collected and

re-delivered to the right address yesterday, but it wasn't. The contents are urgently needed to complete a secret photo shoot - they fly out next week", explained Jaggs. "I need someone I trust to go collect it and bring it to me, in the next day or so at the latest. I'd go myself, but I've got a couple of meetings this week that I really don't want to cancel. Maybe one of them might lead to something for you". Jaggs raised his eyebrows, as if indicating a promising future.

Eager to please and believing there could be an opportunity for real work at the end of it, Alex agreed to the request. Jaggs handed him a slip of paper and an envelope containing £500 in cash.

"Sorry to spring this on you, Alex, but I'm in a bit of a jam and, well, I knew I could trust you", said Jaggs. Alex smiled, encouraged by the words that temporarily boosted his crumbling self-esteem, and he promised to deliver the package to Jaggs as soon as he had it. With that, Alex Walker left the bar.

A couple of minutes later, Andrew Jagger's mobile rang. The voice on the other end was cool and collected. "Well done. I assume he agreed to collect the package. Now, you know what to do with it when it arrives, don't you?"

Andrew Jagger nodded and said, "Yes".

"Good", said the voice on the phone. "And once I've got it, I promise to send you the only remaining version

of the tape. What happened in Ilkley stays in Ilkley".
And with that, the phone line went dead.

Andrew Jagger felt very tense about his indiscretion
from several years ago now resurfacing. He'd told the
Police he didn't know the girl was only 14 at the time.
Fortunately for him, the Police dropped their enquiries
when they found her body and some fake ID a few
weeks later. The ID freed Andrew Jagger of any
accusations of knowingly having sex with a minor, and
he had a solid alibi for the date and time of the murder,
so his involvement with the girl never needed to become
public. The problem, then, was that a similarly drunk
friend had taken a short video of the pair having sex
some months earlier. In that tape, Jaggs and the girl
could clearly be heard talking about her true age. Jaggs
assumed the tape had been destroyed and was grateful
for this, as he knew it would have ruined him if it had
gone public. He was too ambitious to let a mistake like
that destroy his future. That's why, when a copy of the
video unexpectedly arrived in his inbox, he had no
hesitation complying with the written request that
accompanied the footage. Andrew Jagger remained
ambitious and, having seen the fall from grace Alex
Walker had suffered after his outburst (which was
minor in comparison to a case involving under-age sex
and murder), he didn't want to even think about how he
would fare if this old story resurfaced.

"Mud sticks", he reminded himself. He finished his
Perrier and left the bar at Angelica to wait for Alex to
deliver the mysterious package to his house. Andrew
Jagger truly had no idea what was inside.

Sat in a coffee shop, just across from Angelica, the caller watched as Jaggs left the premises. He put the secure satellite phone back into its Faraday pouch and finished his orange juice. That part of his plan was now underway, and now he had to get home because there was a trip to the beautiful city of York to finalise.

Chapter 16

The phone only rang twice before Ricardo Goas picked it up. His aged voice spoke softly and a little tentatively. He didn't usually get calls at home.

"*Hello?*" he enquired upon lifting the receiver to his ear. There was no immediate reply, but somewhere in his apartment, he could hear the faint bleeping sound of a pager.

The caller sneered. He knew this sound would initially confuse and then frighten the old man. He was right. Goas looked over his shoulder, startled. Without saying anything, he gently placed the receiver on the small table in his apartment lounge. The sound of shuffling was faintly audible to the caller, as Goas walked - unsteadily but with some urgency - across the wooden floor. At least, it seemed logical that the floor would be wooden, as the caller had disguised himself and recently taken a sales tour of an apartment that was for sale in the same block. Not that a disguise was necessary, but, as always, he had planned the visit meticulously and was fully prepared for any possibility. There was an extended pause before the caller heard the shuffling of Goas heading back to the phone. It was a markedly slower walk, as Goas undoubtedly now knew what the call was about. The scrolling text on the pager had announced a very clear message:

'Abercrombie is closed and Mercantile has recently gone into receivership.

Markets predict that Casa could be at risk of turbulent times.'

Goas picked up the handset once again but said nothing. He just held the phone to his ear, waiting for the inevitable confirmation that the call and the page were connected. The confirmation didn't come. The caller had all the time in the world to wait, and he knew that the longer the silence went on, the more Goas would suffer. Perhaps he'd have a fatal cardiac arrest from the stress? As much as that scenario temporarily amused the caller, though, he didn't want Goas to die that way. No, he wanted Goas to stare into his eyes, fully aware of his own impending and very painful death. Indeed, the caller had something very specific in mind for Ricardo Goas, just as he'd had for Yedlin down at the O2.

Goas waited for as long as his lungs, heart and willpower would allow him to, but eventually he could wait no longer. The silence was as painful as any knife wound Goas had received in his past. And he'd received a few.

"*When?*" was the first question Goas asked, but before an answer arrived, Goas followed it with, "*And which one are you?*"

"*Why?*" the caller replied, coldly. "*Were there really that many?*"

"It was my job", Goas said, standing as straight as he could and summoning up all the pride and justification he could muster. *"We were given orders and we were trained not to question. To kill someone was like being a soldier in a hidden, never-ending battle. We didn't wear uniforms or get medals, but we were just as proud serving our country. Maybe you never experienced that"*.

Despite the impassioned speech, Ricardo Goas's resolute tone was already starting to falter. After all, even legitimised killers feared their own mortality, and both he and the caller knew Goas didn't earn his immense fortune by being anything like a soldier or serving his country. In fact, it was probably the very opposite.

"Oh, I experienced it, but soldiers don't kill for personal gain, and I doubt you will remember which one I was, but – briefly - I'll make sure you know who I am. That is, until your heart stops beating", the caller responded to Goas. *"And as for when? Soon – but not too soon. Waiting builds the expectation, don't you think?"*

He took a slow, deep and deliberately elongated inhalation, as if breathing in to appreciate a rich aroma. Oh, the deep sense of thrill and desire was almost too much for him to bear. The caller clenched his jaws and then exhaled loudly. It was like an exclamation mark; such was its intensity and finality.

Goas knew that sound meant the call had reached its conclusion. There really wasn't anything else to say, so he slowly replaced the handset and ended the call. He turned the ringer off. He didn't want to hear that sound again today. He sank back into a chair, motionless and emotionless. He always knew that his past could eventually catch-up with him. Mercantile had spoken to him late last year to let him know that Abercrombie was dead through unnatural causes. It had been a short call, but it felt like a breaking wave had smashed its way through an imaginary protective wall around him; a wall he thought might just remain intact for the rest of his life. Clearly, that was not to be.

Goas picked up the rosary beads from the small table where the phone was and began to unconsciously play with them between his fingers as his mind wandered. Looking at his watch, he saw it was 3pm, so his only remaining contact, who happened to be over on the east coast of North America, would probably be out enjoying her grits and coffee at a nearby diner right now. He would call her later. Goas then looked out of the window and across the river. It was going to be dark in an hour, so he decided he would go for a walk and try to enjoy some fresh air. He knew there was no point in trying to run away. He had no desire to prolong the agony, as he knew the caller would find him quickly once again, and he was simply too old to fight back, even if it was an attempt to extend his life by just a few more days. He smiled at the thought of a walk along the banks of the river towards the Castle Tea Rooms. After that, he might even pop to a local pub and have a glass of sherry; watching people on their journeys home. How strange that his last few hours or days would be spent in jealousy of the monotony and regularity of other people's lives.

Goas walked into the hall and reached for his coat and scarf hanging on the wall hooks, and then shuffled into his makeshift library. Resting down on a chair so he could put his shoes on more easily, he noticed that the neon light on his answering machine extension was flashing. He had no appetite for more phone messages today. Besides, it might just be the previous caller taunting him again. Giving it no more thought, he walked out of his little library, glancing back at all the books he had read and all those he had yet to start. His lip quivered momentarily, as he realised, he may never again get another chance to open a book and lose himself in the contents for hours at a time.

Leaving the apartment, Goas slowly made his way down the single flight of stairs to the communal hallway and stepped out through the secure entrance door. He waited for the door to close behind him, before turning left and strolling along the path by the side of the river. He'd walked this route many times in the past, but rarely had the lapping of the water sounded so calming, or the sound of the seagulls been so hauntingly beautiful. Goas reflected on how sharpened his senses were this afternoon and took in a deep breath. His life was suddenly, if momentarily, wonderfully simple. He actually felt at peace, as he made his way towards the historic Clifford's Tower. From there, it would only take two minutes to walk to the Castle Tea Rooms.

"*Afternoon, Mr Goas*", said Jane, brightly, as Goas walked in. The lady owner of the tearoom always recognised and warmly welcomed this fine, quiet and well-mannered gentleman into her establishment. "*Will you be having the usual?*" she asked, excitedly.

Goas smiled broadly. "*Oh yes, please, but with straw-berry jam, if you have any?*"

Jane beamed back and nodded to confirm that they did, whilst Goas took a comfortable seat. The tearoom was compact, with only seven small tables, but Goas loved the location and took residence at his usual seat by the window. It was a friendly, warm atmosphere; not like the sterile repeatable format of those multi-national coffee chains. No matter how much they tried to match their outside decor with the strict Council rules on maintaining the heritage of the historic city, those places still showed no soul.

Goas took off his coat and scarf, laying them carefully over the back of the chair next to his. He sat, hands clasped in his lap, excitedly waiting for his tea and scone to arrive. He felt quite giddy and, in that moment, was free of all life's concerns and the fearful expectations of what the very near future might hold for him.

Within a matter of minutes, Jane returned and placed a plated-up scone and a blue and white floral teapot on the table, along with a matching cup, milk jug and sugar bowl. "*Last of the jar, Mr Goas, so best use it up, eh*", she said, whilst giving a conspiratorial wink, as Goas saw the extra-large lump of strawberry jam that sat beside the scone on his plate.

"*Oh, the little things*", he thought, and he beamed back up at Jane.

The tearoom owner left Goas to enjoy his late afternoon tea. He sliced open the scone, applying a copious amount of butter and jam to the two halves. It was delicious, and the sharpness of the hot tea complemented the sweetness of the food to perfection. As he took his time to savour the food, he looked out of the window and watched as people skittered here and there. Most were either walking to bus stops or their parked cars; trying to make an early escape before the peak-hour traffic snarled up the city centre and surrounding roads. A little boy, being gently pulled along by his mother, looked up at the window and smiled at Goas. Goas was happy to smile back, and he even gave a little fingertip-wave to the child, who thought for a moment and then waved back.

As Goas continued to scan the street, watching couples carrying armfuls of bags from the never-ending retail sales, his eyes suddenly fixed on a figure stood in the shadows of a shop doorway. The windows and entrance to the shop were boarded up, limiting the amount of light into the vestibule, so it was too dark to be certain, but Goas was convinced the shadowy figure was looking directly at him. The longer Goas stared, the more he was sure that the figure was calmly staring back. Could it be the caller? He was so fixated on the figure, that he started to shake and accidentally dropped his cup of tea. It clattered to the floor, smashing as it hit the dark wood, sending liquid and china fragments skidding across the tearoom floor.

Jane hurried out from behind the counter, dish towel in hand. Goas looked down at the floor, up at the proprietor, and then back out of the window. The shadowy figure had now walked out into the streetlight glare. He was warmly embracing a young woman, whom he had presented with a bunch of flowers. With his arms around her shoulder and her arms around his waist, the couple walked away, animated in conversation and without any trace of interest in Goas. Just an innocent, loving couple, heading home after a busy day.

"Not a problem, Mr Goas. I've been thinking those cup handles are probably a little small to grip... and the new dishwasher capsules seem to leave a film on them", Jane said, calmly, as she cleared the mess. Goas suddenly felt old, frail and very vulnerable.

"I ... I ... I'm so sorry", he mumbled, still a little distracted. *"I'll pay for the damage and the cleaning"*. He felt confused and embarrassed, as he once again glanced at the innocent couple in the street who were now disappearing out of sight.

"Nonsense, Mr Goas. Accidents happen", said Jane, breathlessly, looking up from the floor as she picked up what she hoped were the last shards of china. *"See, all sorted in a jiffy"*.

Goas smiled; feeble and humbled. He excused himself and gathered his scarf and coat. *"Err, I must be going, I'm afraid. Things to do before ..."*, but the words trailed off. He placed his shaking hand in his pocket and pulled out a £20 note. Jane was just about to tell him it really wasn't necessary, but Goas insisted. *"Please, you have always been a wonderful friend and, sadly, I think this might be my last time here. I'm ... going away, you see"*. He placed the £20 note in Jane's palm and held it in place, in a gesture intended to ensure his companion that he really wanted her to take it.

"Well, thank you, Mr Goas. It's been a pleasure to know you, and if you're ever back in the city, please pop in and we'll share a pot of tea", Jane said, warmly. Goas smiled back and shook her hand in fondness, whilst fighting back tears. He turned and made his way out of the tearoom, heading back to his apartment. He wasn't in the mood for more people, or even a sherry. In fact, he yearned to go to his room and sleep; hoping to wake up and realise it had all just been a bad dream. With his head bowed, the journey back home felt relatively quick, although he had drifted in a daze all the way. He deserved to die; he knew that, but the reality of this sudden feeling of mortality was one of such immensity that, no matter how much he thought he would be prepared for it, he now knew that he wasn't.

He arrived back at the communal entrance to his apartment block and rummaged in his coat pocket for the key to the lock. He paused. His sense of sadness and melancholy were suddenly replaced by a hollowness in the pit of his stomach. There was no sound but, instinctively, Goas knew 'he' was there, lurking in the shadows. This deadly game was suddenly close to its conclusion.

Goas didn't look round, but said to his visitor, *"You'd better come in"*.

Although there was no response, Goas stepped into the hallway and left the security door ajar. Taking the stairs to his first-floor apartment, he unlocked the door and left that one wide open, too. It was then he heard the quiet 'click' as the door downstairs was pushed closed. He walked on, into his home, and sat down in his beloved armchair that looked out onto the river. He sat in silence, his back to the door, and waited.

When he heard his apartment door click closed, all Ricardo Goas could do was close his eyes and wait for his imminent death. Sadly, for him, his death was going to take several hours.

Chapter 17

DC Hulme looked up and did a double-take, as he realised it was DS Walker striding into the office. Still slumped in his chair, looking over paperwork, he checked his watch and then gave Walker an inquisitive look.

Walker placed the palm of her hands on her desk, leant over and said to her colleague, *"Remember the journalist, Ferranti? The guy who stank of stale alcohol?"*

Hulme nodded, wondering what Ferranti had to do with his colleague coming back into the station just five hours after finishing an eleven-hour shift.

"Well, I've just had a call from DS Denton from the London Met. He was standing next to a crime scene at the Thames, near the O2. They had just found a body, screwed to a plastic chair, with a wine cork stuffed down its throat".

Hulme jerked back in his chair, puffing his cheeks and then blowing out the air, as he took in the shocking news. *"So, what do you want me to do, Guv? Bring Ferranti back in for questioning?"*

Walker paused for a moment and then nodded. *"Yes, let's see if there's anything he wants to tell us. We can hold him until The Met call back, in case they have anything else we need to ask him*". She then looked at her watch and smiled, adding, "*Who knows, maybe he's sobered up or at least had a shower by now*".

They both smirked at the idea and picked up their respective phones; Hulme to contact Ferranti, and Walker to talk to her most senior officer, DCI Colin Newsome.

Hulme rang the general office number at the Yorkshire Post. It was answered with a polished voice within a couple of rings. "*Yorkshire Post Newspaper Group. Emily speaking, how may I help you?*"

"*Hi, this is Detective Constable Hulme of West Yorkshire CID. I'd like to talk to…*", he paused, checking Ferranti's full name, "*…. Adam Ferranti, please*".

The line went quiet for a moment, before Emily responded, "*He's just away from his desk at the moment. He's only gone down to the post room to collect a package, so he shouldn't be long. Would you like to wait, or can I get him to call you back?*"

Hulme considered the options and, assuming the post room was probably a couple of floors down, thought he had better things to do than hold the line. "*Can you ask him to phone the CID at Millgarth please*", he said. "*He has the number*".

Whilst Hulme was busy calling the newspaper, Walker was busy in a phone conversation with her boss. "*Hello sir, it's DS Walker. In yesterday's update note, I mentioned an interview with a journalist ... Yes, that's the one ... Well this morning, a DS from The Met returned my call. They've found a body at the O2... They're checking with forensics as we speak. I just wondered if you thought we ought to call-in HMET now?... Yes, of course I can come up, sir. About 30 minutes? I'll see you then"*. She ended the call. It seemed a little strange that the DCI would take such an interest in a case so early on, but Walker assumed it was because he had already been considering handing the case over to the Homicide and Major Enquiry Team. Walker turned back to Hulme. *"Any news?"*

Hulme shook his head. *"Away from his desk, but they're passing a message on and I expect to get a call back shortly, Guv. If not, I'll call him again"*.

Walker nodded that she understood and then headed into the Scargill incident room. Maybe this case wasn't going to be shut down, just yet.

Meanwhile, at the Yorkshire Post offices, Adam Ferranti was making his way down to the ground-floor post room. He didn't know the temp on the post desk today, so he intended to keep the conversation to a minimum. She, however, clearly found him attractive and decided to flirt a little.

"Hmm, that's a nicely wrapped gift for you. I expect it's from one of your secret admirers?" she mused, as she pouted her lips and gave Ferranti a suggestive stare.

Ferranti smiled back and simply asked, "*Where do I sign?*", whilst looking for the iPad to put his signature on. He was slightly amused and bemused by the girl's response;

"*Either here, or you could buy me a drink later and I'll let you sign your name wherever you want to?*"

Ferranti suppressed his need to laugh out loud, and just sighed, "*The iPad is just fine, thank you*".

"*Suit yourself*", she said dejectedly, trying to sound as if she didn't care about his response to what was her wholly inappropriate behaviour. She chewed her gum loudly and dropped the iPad onto the desk, pointing to where he needed to sign. Ferranti scrawled his name and nodded a thank you, hearing the girl make the same offer to a young man who had just arrived as Ferranti was walking out. He smiled.

Back on his floor, Ferranti strolled across the office and gently put the package down on the desk. On the address label there was a return address; 'Staley's Clocks, 39 New Haven Road, Hampstead'. Ferranti racked his brain and wondered if he had been late-night browsing with his friend, Jack Daniels, and ordered something he couldn't now remember?

"*It wouldn't be the first time*", he muttered to himself. He looked in his drawer and took out a pair of scissors. Opening the blades carefully, he then slowly sliced through the tape that held the beautifully and symmetrically folded wrapping paper. Inside was a

box. He pulled the lid open and there, inside the box –
somewhat unsurprisingly – was a clock. As Ferranti
took it out of the box, he noticed it was set almost to
the right time. According to the leaflet that accompanied the clock, there was a small piece of red tape
underneath the clock; presumably to break the connection between the battery and the mechanism. As
Ferranti turned the clock around, to look at it from all
angles, his phone rang.

"*Ferranti, newsroom*", he answered.

"*I do hope you like your clock, Adam*", said a familiar
voice.

Ferranti stopped looking at the clock and concentrated
on the call. "*Sure*", he answered, slowly, "*So where do I
send the thank-you card?*"

The caller laughed a little and responded casually.
"*Cute, but the game's not over yet. Pull the red tape
from the base of the clock, Adam*". Ferranti froze. Was
this a bomb? The caller anticipated this reaction and
said, "*It's not an IED, Adam. Pull the tape and start the
clock ... please*".

Ferranti thought for a few seconds and then, slowly, he
pulled the red tape out from its resting place. It came
out and, despite Ferranti tensing himself, there was no
explosion. The clock started blinking and he set it down
on the desk.

"So, am I supposed to say thank you?" Ferranti asked, hoping for an answer that might help him understand what the hell was going on.

"You're not very good at deadlines anymore, are you, Adam? It made journalism so exciting when there was a printing deadline. None of this hourly upload deadline, day-in day-out…", the caller trailed off, seemingly waiting for an answer.

"What?" asked Ferranti, entirely confused.

"Well if you look at the clock for a few seconds…". The caller waited a moment, before continuing. *"You'll see what I mean"*.

Still confused, Ferranti watched as the clock ticked over, but now, after closer inspection, he was even more confused.

"Ah, I suppose you're wondering why the digits are going backwards?" asked the caller. Then, almost immediately, he gave Ferranti the answer in a harsher tone than before. *"It's because it's counting down, Adam."* Ferranti now understood what the clock was doing, but he still didn't understand why.

"To what?" he asked, nervously.

"To a fourth death", came the reply. *"The Police have found the body at the O2, and they're now expecting you to call them back"*, the caller added.

"I've not been asked to call anyone, so how do I know they've found a body; let alone if it's actually got anything to do with you?", said Ferranti, trying to sound scornful.

"Yes, you have", the caller replied calmly. *"There's a note on your desk ... do you see it?"*

Ferranti moved the clock packaging off the desk with his free hand and started to look around, shaking his head at the fruitless exercise, but then he suddenly stopped. He was now staring at a Post-it Note, stuck on his keyboard. On it was a hand-written message, asking him to call DC Hulme at Millgarth Police Station.

"You see, I told you, Adam. You really must start to take me seriously", said the caller, in a mocking tone.

Ferranti continued to stare at the note. He spun round quickly, looking across the office and out of the windows, but there was nobody in sight looking back. He then paused, in thought, as a revelation dawned on him:

"What do you mean, the fourth body? There are only tw .... ", but then he stopped. He could almost hear the caller's evil, self-satisfied smile, before the voice spoke and said:

"You missed the last deadline I set you, Adam. Tell the officer in charge of the Scargill case, she needs to talk to her colleagues in North Yorkshire CID. The smell from the apartment should really be strong enough by now to

offend the neighbours. It never fails to surprise me how flesh can rot so quickly in a hot room. Oh, and make sure the officers don't cut their hands on the wire. I'll be in touch again in a week, Adam. You need to do better with this deadline". And with that, the phone went dead.

Back at Millgarth, DS Walker made her way up to the 14th floor and knocked on the DCI's door. She was summoned inside, to find DCI Colin Newsome talking to what appeared to be a plain-clothed civilian.

"Come in and close the door", said Newsome. The plain-clothed man glanced over at Walker, but walked towards the back of the office and leaned against the filing cabinets.

"Sir, we appear to have confirmation that …", began Walker, but the phone on Newsome's desk rang. Agitated by the interruption, Newsome picked up the phone:

"What?" he barked down the phone. He listened intently and then furrowed his brow, glancing up at Walker. *"I understand, DC Hulme, thank you",* he said, and then replaced the receiver. He looked up at Walker and said, *"Before we continue this conversation, I think you might want to go back downstairs and talk to DC Hulme. It appears he's just had a very interesting call from your Mr Ferranti".*

Just as Walker was about to excuse herself, her superior added, *"Oh, and DS Walker, in view of our call earlier* today, I'll be moving DC Hulme off the case and replacing him with DC Mike Hobbs. Hulme is young and enthusiastic, but Hobbs has proven HMET experience, and I think we need a HMET set of eyes on this, don't you?".

This came as a surprise to Walker, but she accepted the order. "Yes sir. When will that be?"

"With immediate effect, Detective Sergeant. My assistant is briefing DC Hulme now and DC Hobbs will be with you first thing in the morning".

Chapter 18

Amelia Demetrious had left earlier than usual to get her grits and coffee at the Bang Bang Pie Shop on North California Avenue. The weather was always cold in Chicago in February, and the wind could bite through even the warmest clothing. Fortunately, she didn't have far to walk from her house and, having devoured the Fancy Grits and Candied Bacon, she was back home in good time.

She glanced at her watch. It would have been a little after 3pm in England.

The news she had heard yesterday, from her contact in London, wasn't good. They already knew that Abercrombie was dead and they suspected that Mercantile was, too. That could only mean that Casa was in imminent danger, so Amelia had to warn him. Only when Casa was safely on his way to her, would she rest.

She sat down in her window chair and drew a long, deep, calming breath before picking up the handset and dialling the number. The trans-Atlantic call connected almost immediately but, to her dismay, an answering machine cut in and she heard the soft deliberate voice of Ricardo Goas say;

"Thank you for calling. As I am either resting or busy with other matters, please feel free to leave a message and I will call you back when it is convenient".

The machine clicked and beeped. Amelia left the message they had all been trained to use, but had never needed to use it in all the years they had been operating:

"Casa, dirígirse al sureste a dodne se encuentra los tres mares".

She wanted to add a personal note to the message but, even as a lump formed in her throat and tears welled in her eyes, she knew she had to stay completely professional. She put the phone down, ending the call to Goas's machine, and then immediately dialled a different UK number. The call connected, but the recipient knew not to say a word. Instead, he listened as Amelia said;

"It might be lunch-hour. I cannot confirm if the house will re-open again later, or not". Having relayed the message, Amelia ended the call.

The man listening, known to her only as 'Republic', pressed a little harder on the accelerator and hoped that the 'house' was not already 'closed for good'. For several minutes, Amelia clutched the handset close to her chest, almost hugging it. Casa had been more than just a contact. Many years ago, he had approached her about the work of the syndicate, with his conscience weighing heavily on his mind. Their secret liaisons quickly turned into something far deeper, but before they could plan his escape, Scargill had found out and warned him; the only way out was death.

Casa and Demetrious had to bury their emotions; meeting rarely, and never able to live the life they truly wanted. It was a heavy price to pay, but she refused to be the reason for his execution. Now, as her 72nd birthday loomed, she gently wept for what could have been, knowing that she might never be able to look into the warm gentle eyes of Ricardo Goas ever again.

Meanwhile, over in England, as Republic sped north, he called his superior on the phone. *"She's been on"*, he said. *"Seems she's tried to contact him, but there's no answer. What do you want me to do?"* he asked, dutifully. He knew his superior wasn't bothered about Goas, who had no direct value anymore, but the man on the other end of the phone still needed to restrain the activities of Amelia Demetrious, until she was taken out of the picture, for good. It was therefore important that they at least seemed to care about Goas.

"We need her to think we are trying", came the reply. *"My bigger concern is who is killing off the old group and could it lead them to us? When you're there, let me know what's happening as soon as you can"*.

Simon McBride ended the call, hoping Republic wasn't going to be too late getting to York.

Chapter 19

Alice Hetherington happily kept herself to herself. A petite lady of 82, with white curly hair, she was not reclusive, but wasn't one to get involved with her neighbours, either. Today, she had put on a muted brown plaid skirt and her sensible shoes, in readiness for her morning coffee with friends in York's beautiful city centre. A long, warm overcoat covered her slim frail frame and a knitted cloche hat sat on her head. She applied just enough Chanel perfume to be appear stylish, but not wealthy.

As she opened the door from her apartment into the corridor on the first floor, a faint aroma caught her attention. At first, she dismissed it as if it were a passing bad smell carried in on a breeze. As she locked the door to her apartment, though, and was just about to turn toward the lift, the aroma caught her attention again. This time she shuddered slightly, as her senses reacted to the smell. A warm flow of air seemed to be coming from her left, so rather than walk toward the lift on her right, she turned her attention toward the curious smell.

The apartment next door belonged to an elderly gentleman; Mr Goas. As Alice reached his door, the aroma had developed into a slight stench. It was as if someone had the heating on and had also happened to leave some raw chicken out of the fridge. Alice's stomach turned and she pulled a lace hanky from her pocket to cover her nose. She knocked on the door, which opened ever so slightly, and a wave of nausea hit her as hot air rushed through the gap and carried with it the unbearable smell. With her hanky still over her nose and mouth, Alice gently pushed the door wider and called out, *"Hello?"*. That was when she saw Goas. She let out a horrified scream. The next thing Alice Hetherington knew, she was outside in a chair, being attended to by a paramedic. She didn't know where she was exactly, but she was aware that the back of her head was very painful.

"Hello, Mrs Hetherington? I'm Tom, and I work for the Yorkshire Ambulance Service", a young man said, glancing over at the police officers, so they knew the patient was conscious. Alice Hetherington looked around to try to work out where she was. Then the memory came flooding back and her eyes widened in horror, as she covered her mouth and stared up at Tom.

DS Bob Williams of North Yorkshire CID stood at the apartment doorway, surveying the scene. Nobody, especially an elderly lady like Alice Hetherington, should be exposed to this. He was an experienced copper and had seen more than his fair share of the dark underbelly of York's drug wars, but even this rendered him almost speechless. He wasn't allowed into the apartment, and the local Police had done well to protect the crime scene from the chance of any contamination. They had taped it off immediately and only touched the door handle; doing this simply to close off the ghastly view from anyone passing by in the corridor.

Stood by Williams's side was PC Sally Allsopp from York Police, who had responded to the 999 call. She was clearly shaken by the scene before her but tried to cover up her desire to vomit by flicking repeatedly through her notes.

"SOCO are going to complete their analysis, but I was the first responder, sir, after we had a call from another neighbour, Mr Chan, who had heard a lady scream and then heard a thud as something hit the floor", recounted Allsopp. *"I arrived on the scene and found Mr Chan knelt over Mrs Hetherington. The door was pulled slightly shut, which Mr Chan confirmed he had done. He didn't want Mrs Hetherington to wake up to that sight"*. She looked up at DS Williams, who nodded to confirm that he understood, and that PC Allsopp could continue. Allsopp flicked over the sheets in her notepad. *"After I had checked Mr Chan was okay, I put on two pairs of latex gloves and opened the door - by the handle - to look inside the apartment. I could see a body, probably male, with his neck in a noose attached to the ceiling, and his limbs lashed to the fridge on his left and the sofa on the right. Pools of blood were on the floor and the wire had cut into his neck, but not quite far enough to sever the head. The heating must have been put on high, which accelerated the decomposition of the body."*

PC Sally Allsopp paused, taking a moment to calm her queasy stomach, and then continued her recount. *"The victim has been identified as Ricardo Goas. It appears ...."*, she swallowed hard. This was her first sight of a murder scene, and she was finding it much more difficult to cope with than she could have ever imagined.

DS Williams put his hand on her shoulder and smiled, softly. *"Take your time, PC Allsopp, you're doing well. Your first murder scene, I assume? You certainly got thrown in at the deep end"*.

PC Allsopp smiled, grateful that this probably desensitised detective wasn't so insensitive as to not recognise her situation. She took a deep breath and pushed her drooping shoulders up and back, before resuming with her report. *"SOCO initial reports say that he had his wrists, ankles and neck tied with saw wire; perhaps whilst knelt on the floor. The saw wire was then pulled taught and tied to large, heavy items to provide resistance in case the victim tried to pull free. From the cuts, SOCO think his only choice of escape was to...."*, she paused, trying to remain calm, but swallowing hard again and squeezing her lips together to focus on not throwing-up, as she continued, *"... was to either stay perfectly still and wait for help, or try to free one hand in order to undo the other lengths of the wire"*. She closed her notebook. Her eyes glanced up at Williams for questions, but in truth, more hopefully for approval that she could stop.

"Guess he decided not to wait, then", DS Williams said, assessing the situation. *"SOCO said there's a severed hand on the floor and cuts to his throat and the remaining limbs. Looks like he struggled to free himself but..."*. His voice tailed-off as the rest of the account didn't really need to be said out loud. As Williams

ended the sentence, the lead SOCO came out of the apartment and stopped in front of him.

"*Bob*", she said, nodding her head in acknowledgement to DS Williams.

"*Grace*", replied Williams, acknowledging her in return, before looking at PC Allsopp and saying, "*Thank you, Constable. That was a good summary, but perhaps you might want to get some fresh air, now?*". It was not said so much as a question, but more of a suggestion to the pale-faced police officer.

PC Allsopp gratefully accepted the offer and walked away as quickly as she could, without it looking too much like she was trying to escape. As she reached the stairs, DS Williams turned his attention back to Grace Allen, the Senior Scene of the Crime Officer.

Allen removed some of her protective gear as she briefed Williams on her findings so far. "*I assume PC Allsopp briefed you on the background, so this is just my pre-liminary view, Bob. It looks like Mr Goas had been kneeling, perhaps in a stress position. The killer - or killers - had tied the wire so well that, perhaps as fatigue was overwhelming Mr Goas, he tried to free himself. The saw wire tore through his wrist, severing the hand. Then, with blood pouring from the wound, his frantic movements probably made the rest of the wire - around his ankles, remaining wrist and his neck - cut into him. The killer presumably calculated that this would happen. I'd say that this was designed to inflict maximum psychological damage, before a very painful physical death. I'll compile a full briefing after the team has gathered all the evidence bags and you've got the autopsy report".*

Williams listened, shaking his head and scratching his chin. *"Bloody hell. What sick bastard even thought of this, let alone did it?"* he asked, rhetorically.

Allen added her view. *"Someone very skilled, very patient and clearly very driven. I can't imagine this was an opportunistic killing".* Williams nodded his head in agreement and felt a pang of sadness for the frightening end to the life of Ricardo Goas.

Chapter 20

Adam Ferranti was waiting in the public reception area at Millgarth, when DS Walker reached the ground floor. He nodded a hello, with some urgency, to acknowledge her arrival. He walked towards the security door and she buzzed him through. To her surprise, he held out his hand to greet her.

"*Hi*", he said, with angst clearly evident in his tone and demeanour.

"*Mr Ferranti*", Walker said back, accepting his brief handshake. "*Let's go through here*", and they walked towards an interview room similar to that of their last encounter.

Ferranti was clearly anxious, and his previous machismo seemed to have now gone. Walker was initially unsure how to respond to this pretty dramatic change of character. They took their seats and then she looked at him. "*Your message said something about a clock. Do you have it with you?*"

Ferranti looked up; his hands nervously fidgeting with each other. "*Err, no. I called and spoke to a Detective Constable Mike Hobbs. He sent a car to collect it - along with me - so it didn't get damaged or disturbed*".

Whilst Ferranti had glanced at Walker, he seemed reluctant to make any kind of sustained eye contact at this point.

"*Look*", he started, nervously, "*Before we go on, I just want to say sorry for, well, being a bit … I might have come across as… as a little arrogant or … you know – a prick - when we first…*", but Walker was already nodding her head, accepting his apology.

"*Let's start again, shall we?*" she offered, still a little confused about the change in his manner, but allowing her frosty demeanour to ease a little, given the different attitude she was experiencing from Ferranti. She noticed that he seemed to then relax a little, too; perhaps relieved he didn't have to actually complete his apology. DC Hobbs entered the room without looking over at Ferranti. He glanced instead at Walker, who nodded and smiled, ever so slightly. Hobbs took his seat and nodded a quick hello to Ferranti. Walker turned the tape recorder on:

"*Friday 1st March 2013 at 11:27am. Second interview with Adam Ferranti. In the room are DS Stephanie Walker and DC Mike Hobbs*".

She looked up at Ferranti, ready to ask him her opening question, but Ferranti couldn't restrain himself any longer.

"*There's another body*", he blurted out immediately. "*You need to contact North Yorkshire CID, and I swear I didn't say anything, but he also knows that it's a woman in charge of the Scargill case*". Ferranti looked at both detectives, and whilst they were shocked at the news of a third murder, the statement that the killer knew some specifics about the lead on the case was an added – and unsettling - surprise.

"I've not even authorised a press briefing, yet", said Walker. *"How the hell does he know that information?"* After a few seconds, Walker composed herself sufficiently to turn to Hobbs and say;

"I want you to call upstairs and get someone to contact North Yorkshire CID. I want to know the moment they confirm if they're looking into the recent murder of an elderly man or not".

DC Hobbs stood, but then paused and looked at her, quizzically. Walker sensed the confusion and responded with, *"It makes sense, given that the other two bodies the killer contacted Mr Ferranti about were elderly gentlemen, doesn't it?"*. Hobbs paused again, and then nodded his head at the obvious conclusion, before heading out of the room.

Walker spoke into the tape recorder; *"11:29am, DC Hobbs has just left the room"*. She then turned to Ferranti, asking him to start at the beginning. Ferranti, having now shared the shocking news that felt like it had been burning a hole in his gut, had calmed down a little. He leant forwards, looked down at his shoes, and took a deep breath. He exhaled and sat back; his restless eyes looking around the room as he began to replay what happened.

"*The post room at work called me and said there was a package*", he stated.

"*What time was this?*" asked Walker.

"*Around 4:30pm, yesterday. I'd not been in the office that long*", replied Ferranti. "*I wasn't expecting anything, but I went down to collect it straight away. I think, on reflection, my mind was elsewhere; stuff about a friend I had lunch with yesterday*".

"*What friend?*" Walker asked, partially bemused that this man might have any friends at all.

"*A guy who drives me to work every day, but it's not as grand as it sounds ... he has a Leaf. I mean, he's not a chauffeur and we just talk, you know? About stuff. Anyway, he's got problems with his parents and...*", Ferranti gestured somewhat meaninglessly with his hands and Walker was surprised to find that this previously arrogant man now appeared to be lost and rambling. She nodded at Ferranti, which he was relieved at, as it meant he didn't need to continue talking about Khatri.

"*Anyway*", he continued, "*I went down to get the parcel. I came back to my desk and the phone rang, almost as soon as I sat down. I mean it was as if the guy was watching – waiting - for me to get back*". He paused, shrugged his shoulders and waited for a reaction from Walker. She asked whether he could see anyone watching him whilst all of this was happening, but he confirmed what she suspected; he couldn't.

"*Talk me through the phone call*", Walker said, prompting him to continue.

"*Phone rang; no ID showed, and I answered it - whilst looking at the package*".

At that point, Hobbs walked back into the room. Walker confirmed his return on the recording, and stopped the tape whilst Hobbs quickly got her up to date. "*The front desk is calling upstairs and will let us know*". Then he looked over at Ferranti and waited for Walker to continue with the interview.

Walker returned her focus to Ferranti and said, for the purposes of the tape, "*DC Hobbs has returned to the room. It is 11:31am. Mr Ferranti, you were telling us about the content of the phone call you received. Please continue*".

"*He asked me to look at the package that he knew I now had*", stated Ferranti. "*He told me to pull the red tape out from under the clock. I hesitated, but he told me it wasn't a bomb. I don't know why, but I believed him. He even used the word 'please', in a kind of comforting way, after he asked me to trust him*", relayed Ferranti.

"*Anything remarkable about the packaging?*", Walker asked, knowing that the forensics team would soon be looking at that and the mysterious clock inside it, for evidence of 'exchange'; such as fingerprints, fibres or DNA.

"*Nothing. The only thing that was odd was that the clock was set at the right time but was counting backwards*", added Ferranti.

Hobbs leant forward, scratched his head and looked confused. "*Backwards?*" he queried.

Ferranti nodded, rapidly. "*I know, right? I was confused, too. Then he asked if I still liked deadlines, because the clock was actually counting down.... to a fourth murder*". He paused for Walker and Hobbs to absorb the news, before finishing his recollection with, "*I started to say that there had only been two murders, and that's when I realised what he was going to tell me next. That's when he said about telling the woman in charge of the enquiry to contact North Yorkshire CID. He also said he hoped no-one cut themselves on the wire*".

"*And when is this deadline, Mr Ferranti?*" asked Walker.

Ferranti just stared, helpless, as he said, "*I don't know. He just said he'd be in touch again, in a week*".

There was a knock on the door, and a member of the front desk team popped his head into the room. "*Sorry to interrupt, DS Walker, but I was told it would be alright?*"

"*Sure*", said Walker. She looked over at Ferranti, who nodded that he understood. He knew this was a live police investigation and that everyone was a suspect until proven otherwise, so the police would need to talk in private. *"Interview suspended at 11:33am"*. She pressed pause on the tape recorder, before she and Hobbs left the interview room, and went to speak in the one next door.

"North Yorkshire CID are currently investigating the murder of a 78-year-old man. Apparently, it's a very theatrical and gruesome scene, so they don't suspect it was opportunistic, suicide or accidental", said the man from the front desk. He looked at Hobbs and Walker, who glanced at each other.

"Who's running the investigation?" asked Walker. Her colleague looked at his notes and confirmed that person as DS Bob Williams. He handed her a slip of paper with Williams's number on.

"Thank you", said Walker, and then turned to Hobbs. *"Mike, I'm going to close this interview down, for now. Get the Duty DI to sign-off a request to intercept and record calls to Ferranti's workplace, and find out who the sitting Judge is who'll be reviewing our request. After that, I'm going to set up a call with DCI Newsome"*. With three murders and a fourth predicted, Walker knew all three Detective Sergeants would be required to support the lead HMET officer. Best be ready - and united.

With that, Walker returned to the room where Ferranti was waiting. She turned the tape recorder on again:

"This is DS Walker returning to the room, alone, at 11:36am". She sat down and said, *"Mr Ferranti, thank*

you for the information you've given today. I'm going to close the interview now, but the same conditions still apply. As before ...", but before she could finish the sentence, Ferranti was nodding and finished her sentence for her;

"Stay local, discuss this with nobody, and remember to contact you if I hear – or receive – anything else. Absolutely no problem, Detective Walker. I'm more than happy to help".

Walker was, once again, momentarily thrown by the change in character and tone of Ferranti; from hounding member of the Press, to co-operative potential victim. She briefly pondered on her own change in character, recalling how, in her private life, she'd gone from attentive loving wife to actual domestic abuse victim. Walker held out her hand and smiled warmly at Ferranti. *"I hope we don't need to see each other again, Mr Ferranti, but thank you for your assistance".*

"I hope so too, Detective, but I'll gladly help wherever I can". Ferranti held her gaze for a couple of seconds. Why did he find this previously abrasive woman so interesting and, to his complete surprise, somewhat attractive all of a sudden?

Chapter 21

The SOCO team were finishing their analysis at Ricardo Goas's apartment. There were very few clues. There was a partial footprint, where presumably blood had spilt quicker onto the floor than expected, from Goas's wrists, but it wasn't large or distinctive enough to offer any insights. Senior SOCO Grace Allen had a final room to check, as her colleagues closely inspected a couple of the deeper pools of blood. The flooring in the kitchen was uneven, so there were three areas on the floor where blood had gathered to more than just a couple of millimetres in depth. There was also a smashed pager laying on the floor, which the team bagged and tagged.

Allen carefully walked out of the open-plan kitchen and lounge area through the tiny hallway and into a small study. An impressive array of books lined the longer wall, with a soft leather Chesterfield swivel chair next to a small desk over by the window. The desk had a banker's lamp, space for a notepad, and there was a small answering machine - with its red LED flashing. Following a recent case, where unplugging an electrical device led to a complete loss of data, it was now protocol to listen to or read anything on-screen that was immediately available, transcribing it, and then finally bagging and tagging the piece of kit as potential evidence. Allen completed a visual check of the machine and dusted it for prints, but if the killer had been stupid enough to leave a print on this – after such a meticulous murder – she would be amazed. Still, sillier things had happened in the past, so she took a series of prints from the machine and then called out to DS Williams.

When Williams came into the room, Allen explained; "*Bob, I've checked this for prints and now there's just the digital recording to transcribe*".

It took Williams several minutes to get some protective clothing on, so as not to run the risk of cross-contamination. He carefully fumbled inside his pockets and took out a pad, pen and a Dictaphone. He nodded to Allen, who pressed play on the answering machine.

"*Casa, dirígirse al sureste a dodne se encuentra los tres mares*", came the voice of what sounded like an elderly American woman. The phone message ended and the robotic voice from the machine announced, '*The caller withheld their number. You have no more messages*'.

Allen and Williams looked at each other. "*How's your Spanish?*" Williams asked. Grace Allen shook her head and asked Williams the same question.

"*Dos cervezas, por favor*", came the reply, which caused Allen to giggle.

"*So, not much better than mine, then*", she said. "*Okay, well Andreas down at the lab speaks Spanish. I'll get this translated and let you know what it ...*", but before she finished, a voice called for her, from the kitchen. "*Excuse me*", she said to Williams, and walked quickly but carefully towards the voice. It was one of her team and he was holding a piece of blood-sodden paper with some tweezers. Allen stared at it intently.

"*Can't read everything*", the SOCO said. "*It was in a pool, where the blood was deep enough not to have congealed. Most of the print is either currently obscured or obliterated, but we've allowed it to drip dry a little, and from what we can see, it looks like a VAT receipt… and it lists saw wire as a purchased item*".

Grace Allen gasped. "*Bob!*" she called out loudly, as she marched back towards the front door of the apartment in search of her colleague.

Chapter 22

He sat at the desk in his secure room, relieved that Goas was dead, but angry that he had been so careless as to step in some blood as he left the scene. He hoped he had not made any other mistakes. Looking at the stain on the bottom of his boot, it only covered a small section underneath his toes. He doubted there would be enough of a mark in the blood to trace him. He exhaled, with some relief, but with the doubts still creeping in.

"*Casa is closed*", he said, and crossed the name off a list he had recently written. He found it cathartic to write a list every time he killed. Once he had crossed the latest victim's name off, he would always burn the paper and flush the remnants down the toilet. "*Can't be too careful with lists*".

Once he had destroyed the paper, he reached into the desk unit drawer and pulled out an old iPod Shuffle. He chose his soothing playlist and, as 'The Wolves & The Ravens' by Rogue Valley began to play, he closed his eyes and sank into the words and melody:

"*Through the never-ending maze, where the way is seldom clear, is no map or compass near, drive a ship I cannot steer...*", he sang, quietly. A few minutes of solitude for his troubled mind.

As the song continued, he sighed, and he felt like himself again, or at least the person he used to be so many years ago. As the stillness washed over him, it reminded him of fading ripples in a pond, flattening out after a pebble has long since sunk out of sight. The peace felt so complete that even his darkest thoughts could not penetrate it. He remained calm until the end of the song when, involuntarily, the name "*Abi*" escaped his lips.

He opened his eyes, where tears had started to well. As he brought Abi's memory into focus, though, the sweet beaming smile on the pretty 23-year old's face changed. Her skin turned grey and her eyes became vacant. Blood started to seep from her mouth and the pretty dress she was originally wearing turned into Army fatigues; covered in bloodied mud. The flowery meadow he had imagined her sitting in turned into the earthen wall of a foxhole, with gunfire raging all around.

His mood darkened and the hatred began to rise again, like a seething storm. The image of an army officer appeared, shouting at him to leave her. As the officer screamed at him, he drew a long-bladed knife from its sheath and plunged it into the officer's gut. Once, twice, ten times he plunged the knife into him. As the frenzied attack peaked in his memory, he became aware that he was actually stabbing the desk with the ballpoint pen; two, three, four more vicious stabbing motions. His heart was thumping, his eyeballs were bulging, and his breathing was heavy from the exertion. He stopped and closed his eyes in an attempt to steady his breathing. Instead, those images of death were replaced by other bodies. A faceless woman lying on a kitchen floor, bleeding profusely from a head wound. A faceless man on the floor next to her, convulsing, with a kitchen carving knife buried deep in his chest.

He opened his eyes, wide; his fury had returned, and it felt more consuming than ever. "*How can you value life so much and yet disregard it so easily?*" he rasped.

He knew what he had to do next. It was what he always did when he relived this nightmare. He pulled back his shirt sleeve to reveal his existing scars. "*You reap what you sow*", he said, and scraped the ballpoint pen along his forearm, cutting into his skin and watching his blood seep to the surface. "*You need to remember what it's like to suffer pain*", he grunted, as he stopped tearing into his own skin, leaving a three-inch bloodied laceration. He had a sterile bandage ready, along with some antibiotic ointment. He knew the dangers of infection from his early days of self-harm. It wasn't the same as hurting someone else, but it sometimes still worked as a temporary measure to deal with the physical and emotional pain he carried with him every day.

His heartrate eased and his breathing returned to normal. It was now time to prepare for the next interaction with Adam Ferranti.

This time, he wanted witnesses.

Chapter 23

DCI Colin Newsome walked into what was being used as the Scargill incident room, with Detective Inspector Angela Clark following half a step behind. Newsome had been asked to head-up the Homicide and Major Enquiry Team and had personally requested DI Clark to run the day-to-day operation.

"*Afternoon all*", bellowed Newsome. The five HMET members, including DS Walker and her new assistant, DC Hobbs, all stood to acknowledge both their superior and DI Clark. The HMET incident room was on the 5th floor in Millgarth Police Station, and the walls were already covered with several wipe-boards and pinboards - all partially populated. A wipe-board on wheels stood in an open space and would be a focal point at every morning briefing. Today, it stood blank, but DI Clark picked up a marker and was ready to brief her team, once Newsome had finished his opening statement, of course. Newsome cleared his throat to attract attention:

"*This investigation is entitled 'Obelisk' and currently covers activities in three Police authorities: The Met, North Yorkshire and here in West Yorkshire. Shortly, DI Clark will brief you and you'll then take part in a conference call with the Detective Sergeants leading the investigations in London and York*", he started. "*Now,*

I don't need to tell you how important this is. Some of you will have been involved in HMETs in the past. Let's continue the proud tradition".

Newsome looked around the room and gently nodded his head, repeatedly, in acknowledgement and encouragement, before turning to DI Clark. *"Over to you, Detective Inspector"*, said Newsome, and then he left the room.

"Right", said Clark, stepping forward and taking the lid off the marker pen. *"Let me ensure we are all up to speed. I'll start by introducing DS Walker and DC Hobbs, who have both been seconded to the team. They have interviewed a member of the public – a journalist at the Yorkshire Post - who reported two separate contacts from someone who apparently knew of all three murders".* She looked over to Walker and Hobbs, who partially raised their hands to identify themselves, before exchanging a few quick hellos with some of the HMET they didn't already know.

Clark continued. *"Three victims"*. She pointed over to one of the pinboards, where the photos of the dead men's faces stared back at her. *"Currently, we do not know if their deaths are linked and have no clues as to the identity of their killer or killers; nor do we have any obvious motive. The only things that we do know are that all the deceased were over 75 years old, and that a single caller has alleged he knew about all of their deaths"*. She paused briefly for questions, but then quickly moved on. *"In a moment, DS Walker will brief us on what has happened in Leeds so far, but for now, let's all get into the comms room and dial into the conf call with The Met and North Yorkshire CID".*

The small comms room had 6 seats around a small circular meeting table. As the team walked over, a couple of the team shook hands with Walker and Hobbs, briefly introducing themselves. Once they were all seated, Clark dialled the number on the speakerphone and, when prompted, entered a PIN. Within seconds, the automated voice announced that there were two other people on the call, and then the voices of DS Williams and DS Denton were heard introducing themselves.

"Good afternoon, *gentlemen; this is DI Angela Clark. In the room, I have the Leeds-based HMET members, including DS Stephanie Walker and DC Mike Hobbs, who are seconded to the HMET for this investigation*", announced Clark.

"*Good afternoon*", replied Williams.

"*Afternoon Ma'am, and hello again, DS Walker*", said Denton.

"*Afternoon DS Denton*", acknowledged Walker.

"*I'd like to start the call confirming a few day-to-day operational rules*", said Clark. "*Firstly, I'll hold a daily call at 0930, six days a week. When I'm not here, DS Walker will be in temporary charge, as she has the background to the situation and, in my opinion, is best placed to ensure continuity*". She looked over at Walker, who wasn't expecting this, but was grateful for the opportunity. Everyone else in the room nodded in agreement that this seemed logical, for now.

Clark continued. *"Secondly, I want all information and evidence displayed on the boards in this incident room. DS Williams and DS Denton, if you can ensure your local teams provide us with copies of everything you have, that would be extremely helpful"*. This was more an instruction than a request, but DI Angela Clark didn't want to tread on any toes this early in the investigation, until she could presumably see all the toes first! Then, she'd do whatever she needed to do to enhance her already impressive reputation as an effective copper; even if that meant others had their noses put out of joint.

"I'm now going to hand over to DS Walker, who will brief us about Albert Scargill. We are referring to him as victim number 1". With that, Clark nodded to Walker.

"Thank you, Guv", said Walker, and then began to recount the case of Albert Scargill. *"On October 1st 2012, a local PC was approached by a member of the public who was concerned about an elderly neighbour; Albert Scargill. On entering a house on Gathorne Close, he found the dead body of an elderly gentleman. He'd suffered a major head trauma, which the coroner later confirmed was because his skull had been fractured by a golf club. The weapon, which appeared to belong to Mr Scargill, was next to his body. No signs of forced entry or exit, and no clues other than a note left on the victim's chest. It said, 'You reap what you sow'. After*

several fruitless lines of enquiry, we were about to close the incident room when, on Tuesday 26th February 2013, a walk-in here at Millgarth reported a call from someone who referred to the note on Mr Scargill's body. It's alleged that the caller also predicted The Met would find another body. The information was fairly specific, so I left a message with control at The Met". Walker paused to look over to DI Clark.

"Any questions so far?" asked Clark.

One of the team asked if the alleged call had been recorded, to which Walker shook her head and responded that it wasn't policy to record calls at the Yorkshire Post – where their source was based.

"Who was the walk-in?" asked another member of the team.

"A man called Adam Ferranti. He's a journalist at the newspaper", replied Hobbs. A few of the team looked at each other and nodded. They had heard of him. Clark looked at Walker and indicated she should continue.

"I'll now ask DS Denton to pick up the briefing from a Met perspective", said Walker.

"Thank you, DS Walker", replied Denton, as he began to brief the team on the body in the Thames.

"On Wednesday 27th February 2013, I attended a crime scene near the O2 Arena. A safety officer from

the Arena had found a dead body next to the River Thames. SOCO confirmed that the body appeared to have been fastened to a plastic chair with six corkscrews through his rib cage and spine. He also had two corkscrews in his eyeballs and a wine cork rammed down his throat. It is currently assumed that he had only been there a number of hours. As I was talking to…", he paused, knowing that Simon McBride had been quite explicit about what Denton should and shouldn't say. Denton pretended to need to cough, buying a little thinking time, and then continued. *"Apologies, I seem to have a frog in my throat. As I was saying, whilst I was talking to a colleague at the scene, I received a message that DS Walker had called Met Control and left a message. Her information appeared to be accurately matched to what we were unfolding"*. He paused again. No-one asked any immediate questions, so he handed back to Walker.

"Thanks, Steve", offered Walker. *"On Friday 1st March 2013, Adam Ferranti phoned Millgarth in response to a request from CID. We wanted to bring him back in, now that the claim from the alleged caller had been proven accurate. As it was, Ferranti had just received a package and a call from the same alleged informant who had originally contacted him about Mr Scargill. In the package was a digital clock. It was counting down. Not only did the caller report a third murder, but he also said the clock was counting down to a fourth. We'll come back to the package shortly, but Mr Ferranti alleged that the caller told him to tell us to contact North Yorkshire CID. DS Williams can pick up the briefing now, from a North Yorkshire perspective"*.

DS Bob Williams cleared his throat and said, *"Thank you, DS Walker. Also, on Friday 1ˢᵗ March 2013 here in York, a local PC responded to a 999 call, with reports of a body and, in addition, an unconscious elderly woman. At the incident, I talked to both the attending PC and SOCO, who had locked the scene down. The victim, 78-year-old Ricardo Goas, was found dead in his apartment. His neck, arms and legs were bound by saw wire. First SOCO assessment was that he had bled to death from injuries suffered as a result of a severed hand and deep lacerations to his other arm, both legs and neck. His head was also almost severed from his body. He appeared to have been lashed to several heavy objects in the apartment, whilst knelt in what's commonly known in the Army as a high stress position. Again, first assessment was that he had perhaps panicked and tried to free himself, leading to his left hand being severed at the wrist. As with the Scargill murder, there was no apparent forced entry or exit to Goas's home residence"*. Williams then asked if there were any questions thus far, indicating that there was more to the story.

"DS Williams, please talk us through the voice message", requested DI Clark.

"Yes Ma'am", replied Williams, dutifully. *"SOCO had walked the grid in all the rooms, with the exception of a small library. On entering said space, they noticed an answering machine with a live message flashing. After checking the room thoroughly, I was asked to go in and transcribe the message with the lead SOCO. The message seemed to be in Spanish and came from what*

sounded like an elderly American woman. We believe it was to someone called 'Casa'. We are currently assuming Goas was Casa, although that's yet to be confirmed. The SOCO interim report has arrived today, so rather than attempt to speak Spanish, I'll forward the English transcript. It doesn't mean a great deal to us at the moment, though".

"DS Williams, please can I ask you to share the translation now? I'm sure our interest is piqued!" said DI Clark, looking round the room. She was right, it seemed, based on the looks on the team's faces.

"Err, sure", said Williams, as he opened the SOCO file next to him. "One of the SOCO team in York speaks Spanish and although we're having it independently verified, we are pretty confident with the current translation. The message was, 'House, head south-east, to where the three seas meet'. We can't confirm that the message was definitely for Mr Goas, but we are currently assuming it was, as the machine's outgoing announcement is in his voice. BT has confirmed there were two calls to his line that day. Both calls are untraceable back to precise phone numbers, which BT says is highly unusual, although they can confirm that one was from within the York area and the other was trans-Atlantic". He paused, then added something of real interest to the investigation. "Odd thing to mention, but BT has said that whilst those two calls were within a couple of minutes of each other, the only previous call to his number – in early October 2012 – was also untraceable. Before that, Goas had rented the phone line for seven years, but never once received a single call".

"*And the receipt, DS Williams?*" enquired Clark.

"*Yes, of course. We recovered a receipt at the scene. It was for a number of hardware items, including saw wire, such as that used in the murder. The receipt was initially hidden from sight in a pool of blood. We don't know if it's for the precise saw wire used in the murder, but it seems an odd coincidence - or a pretty stupid mistake by the killer - for it to be there. He or she also left a partial boot print, but it's too small and too generic to be of real use, unfortunately. We're waiting for confirmation from Forensics on the receipt. That's everything we currently know*", said Williams, in closing.

Clark looked round the room. People were clearly processing a lot of information. She didn't want to overload them, but Walker had previously mentioned the presence of further intelligence. "*DS Walker, if you could conclude with the news about the clock and package you mentioned earlier, please?*"

"*Well, we too are waiting for a final report from Forensics, but the interim report confirms there's an address label underneath the label that was addressed to Mr Ferranti. As soon as we find out more about that and have checked the clock for trace, we'll share the info with the team*". Walker then closed her notebook and looked over to DC Mike Hobbs: "*Anything I've missed, Mike?*"

Hobbs flicked the pages of his notebook to go back to some prep notes he had made before the meeting. He started to shake his head as he ran down the list, but then looked up. "*Oh yes, couple of points. Firstly, Mr Ferranti said there was no ID on either of the calls he received, and that the caller knew his name. No obvious reason identified yet as to why the caller decided to contact him rather than anyone else, but the alleged calls did not come through the switchboard - they seem to have been direct dial. That's it, Sarge*".

"*I suppose it's not difficult to know his name*", stated DI Clark. "*It's splashed all over the weekend supplement along with his photo, but the alleged direct dial is interesting. Any way we can be sure he actually received the calls?*" asked DI Clark.

There was a hum around the room at this point, until Walker said, "*We are checking with BT, but the Yorkshire Post telephony software does indicate that Ferranti did indeed receive calls to his extension*".

"*So, no consistency in the method of killing...*", stated team member DC Sally Hobbs, rhetorically. She studied killing patterns as part of her PhD in Criminal Psychology and so this was of key interest to her.

"*No, but the untraceable calls could be part of some sort of pattern or link. It's interesting that the October 2012 call was Goas's only other call on that number - and so close to the Scargill murder, too*", mused DI Clark. "*Danny, please look into the tech behind untraceable calls, and find me some information of where 'three seas might meet' might be*", she requested from DC Danny Hardy. He jotted the notes down and said, "*Will do, Guv*".

In Leeds, DI Clark concluded the conference call by thanking everyone. They would all talk again on tomorrow morning's call. In London, DS Steve Denton ended the call and then immediately dialled a mobile number. The call was answered almost immediately.

"It's me. I've just been on the HMET call", Denton began. *"So far there have been three murders - all men over 75. Apparently, there's a fourth murder predicted, and a single informant is giving all this information to a journalist in Leeds. Now, what can you tell me about the three men?"*

Denton wasn't naive enough to reveal *everything* he'd heard today. He wanted to test whether the trust and information flow was two-way. The man on the other end of the call smiled. Denton had done as he had asked of him, but he still wasn't about to share everything he knew with Denton in return.

"Nothing yet, Steve", said Simon McBride, but quickly added, *"But I expect you'll be searching for an elderly American woman, soon"*.

McBride knew Denton would be surprised that he already knew this, given the HMET reference of the elderly American woman who had left a message on Goas's answering machine. McBride also knew though that Denton wasn't stupid, so he'd need to keep feeding him some snippets. He wanted Denton to feel this like this really was a two-way exchange. McBride ended the call and smirked.

"*What an idiot*". This would never actually be two-way. 'Company business' meant he could use and somewhat abuse his influence over Steve Denton - and he fully intended to do so.

Chapter 24

Aarav Khatri pulled up outside the Post Office in Barwick and walked briskly across the square to Ferranti's front door. He knocked loudly, expecting Ferranti to be asleep, as usual. Instead, though, the door opened almost immediately.

"*You're late*", jibed Ferranti, looking unshaven and unkempt, but rather more alert than Khatri had ever seen him.

As Khatri walked into the front room, he realised that the curtains were already open, and whilst a part bottle of whiskey and a glass sat on the small table, so did a copy of a technology magazine and a recent issue of The Times. There was also what looked like an almost empty bowl of porridge teetering on the edge on the table, although the familiar feint smell of stale alcohol still hung in the air. Khatri paused and consciously blinked, as if checking his eyes were not deceiving him.

Ferranti noticed this and, with a scowl on his face, said, "*What? Never seen a guy have breakfast before?*" He knew the scene was a little different than Khatri had grown accustomed to. In fact, it was different to what Ferranti had grown accustomed to, as well. Neither of them knew if it was a permanent improvement or a temporary aberration, but they both seemed to like it.

"No, it's just... well, I mean, erm". Khatri was struggling to hide his surprise, but Ferranti answered back with, *"Well don't get used to it"*, and he picked up the bowl and spoon, taking them into the kitchen. Khatri was almost speechless.

"I'll just put the paper and magazine away, shall I?" said Khatri, really not sure what to do next.

"No, leave them there. Jeez what are you, my cleaner?" shouted Ferranti from the kitchen, as Khatri heard the clatter of the bowl and spoon being tipped into a pile of other dirty pots and pans in the sink. Oddly, that sound made Khatri feel more relaxed; after all, a man can only handle so much revolutionary change in one day.

Ferranti shouted through from the kitchen, *"Want a coffee? I've got the kettle on and can sort out a travel mug for you soon enough"*. Khatri heard the clatter of the pots and pans again, and imagined Ferranti rinsing out a mug that probably needed thermo-nuclear cleansing to kill all the bacteria it had likely amassed since god knows when.

"No, I'm good thank you", he responded.

"Suit yourself", said Ferranti, with another clattering sound as, presumably, he dropped the mug back into the pile to be washed.

After a short silence, Khatri mumbled, *"Thank you, for the other day"*. He was unsure how Ferranti would feel about being reminded that he appeared to be a person with a heart. Several seconds passed and Khatri wondered if Ferranti had not heard him, so he started to say again, *"I said thank y...."*, but Ferranti gruffly cut him off.

"Yeah... heard you the first time", he barked, but didn't offer any other words, such as a friendly 'you are welcome', so Khatri let the subject drop. Ferranti walked out of the kitchen, travel mug in hand. *"Okay, let's go"*, he said, and the pair walked out into the crisp chill of the March mid-morning air and the deserted village street. Ferranti locked the door and shivered, pulling his jacket closer around his body before striding over to the Leaf. Khatri had never seen him walk so fast and actually failed to keep pace. Ferranti opened the car door and climbed in before Khatri could even get there. What was going on?

"So, shall we debate the North Korean threat of nuclear war with the US? The MP's girlfriend taking the speeding points for him? Or the Home Secretary's idea to pilot an entry fee scheme for immigrants?", asked Ferranti, as soon as Khatri had pulled away from the kerb and was starting to head up Main Street.

Khatri let the question settle in his mind, before turning around and looking at Ferranti in both wonder and concern. This sort of conversation usually started after about 10 minutes of driving, once Ferranti had woken up enough. It never happened straight away. Ferranti just smiled back, glibly, and lifted his travel mug to his lips in a mock 'cheers' gesture. He was just about to take a sip of the hot coffee when, suddenly, his expression changed to one of horror and he shouted to Khatri, *"LOOK OUT!"*

Khatri turned, just in time, as a blind man with a stick was crossing the street in front of them. Khatri slammed his brakes on, and the car screeched to a halt, inches from the startled pedestrian. Presumably, the blind man had not heard the quiet electric motor of the Leaf and so had stepped out into the road. When Khatri slammed his brakes on and the motion had thrown Ferranti forwards and then back into his seat, the scalding hot coffee had spilled out of his travel mug and splashed across his hands and clean white shirt. Ferranti began pulling at the front of his shirt to get it away from his chest, as the burning liquid threatened to scald his skin.

"Oh my god, are you alright?" howled a panicked Khatri. He didn't know where to look - at Ferranti or at the pedestrian. The pedestrian shook his fist and motioned in the direction of the car. In fact, it almost looked like he was peering into the car, before he put his white cane back down and then staggered to the safety of the kerb, muttering to himself all the way.

"I'm fine, I'm fine", said Ferranti hurriedly, trying to avoid spilling any more coffee in the car. He was also blowing down inside of his now sodden coffee-stained shirt, to ease the burning sensation. Khatri reached out and took the travel mug, handing Ferranti a clean rag to wipe his hands with.

"I'll take you back to get changed. Just let me....", and Khatri turned to see if the blind man was alright, but the pedestrian had already disappeared from sight. *"Wow, everyone is walking so quickly this morning",* he unconsciously said, out loud.

"What?" asked a confused and distracted Ferranti, still wiping his hands and wet shirt sleeve cuffs.

"Nothing, just me thinking out loud", said Khatri, and he slowly and carefully made a u-turn, to get Ferranti the 200 yards back to his house to get changed. As they pulled up, Ferranti told Khatri to wait in the car; he wouldn't be long. Nearly thirty minutes later, Ferranti appeared back at his front door. He now wore a blue shirt. He walked to the Leaf and climbed into the back seat.

"Hi. Sorry, but it took a little longer than I expected to change, and for some burn cream to dry on my skin. I had a scald mark, so thought I might as well deal with it", said an apologetic Ferranti.

"No problem, and sorry again", said Khatri as he turned to talk to look at Ferranti before focusing again on the road and easing away from the pavement.

"Eyes straight ahead please this time, driver, if you don't mind", said Ferranti, with a wry smile on his face. Thankfully, the rest of the journey into the city centre was uneventful.

When they arrived at the Yorkshire Post offices, Ferranti got out of the Leaf, with more apologetic words from

Khatri ringing in his ears. He climbed the stairs to the 2nd floor and walked to his desk. As he neared it, he was surprisingly apprehensive, but he found he had no reason to be. There was nothing untoward on his desk and, for the rest of the day, all his calls came from people he knew and who had their phone numbers displayed. He finished his draft 'doozer' in half the time it normally took, and he continued to feel surprisingly alert as the day went on. Barry Clements called him into his office to talk through his first draft of the article, and proudly beamed that it was almost print-perfect. Ferranti was buzzing, even when Charlie on reception rang to tell him a couple of plain clothes Police Officers had arrived and asked for him.

"Ok, thanks Charlie. Can you show them into the ground floor reception meeting room, please?" chirped Ferranti. Perhaps they had some news about the clock and caller. He made his way down to the ground floor reception room and walked in to see Walker sitting with a female detective he hadn't seen before.

"Mr Ferranti", said Walker, holding out her hand and noticing the smile on Ferranti's face. Could he really be pleased to see them? *"This is Detective Inspector Clark"*, she added, as Clark leant forwards to shake Ferranti's hand.

"Please, sit down", said Ferranti. *"Hope you have some good news about things?"* he enquired, expectantly. Then, as soon as he sat down, he stood back up and said, *"Oh, how rude. Sorry... would either of you like a tea or a coffee?"*. Both declined, so Ferranti sat back down.

DI Clark spoke first. *"Sadly, I'm afraid not, Mr Ferranti. We can confirm a third murder, the one you alleged the caller told you about".*

Ferranti sat upright, a little startled and more than a little taken aback by his visitor's use of the term 'alleged'.

"I'm sorry, but what do you mean 'alleged'?" he asked, now irritated.

"Well, up to now, Mr Ferranti, we have no proof of the calls or the content. I wasn't intending to suggest you are not telling the truth but, as this is an ongoing triple murder investigation, nothing can be taken for granted until proven otherwise", and Clark smiled weakly. She was fully aware of her use of the term 'alleged' - and was unsurprised by Ferranti's reaction.

"Look, Detective", started Ferranti, clearly riled by Clark's tone. He was just about to stand and explain exactly what he thought about her attitude, when Walker held up her hand to indicate he should calm down.

"Mr Ferranti. We have to avoid making assumptions, but I'm sure DI Clark didn't mean to upset you – it's simply a statement of fact, that's all. I'm sure we will get proof in the very near future", stated Walker, calmly. She looked over at her colleague, to indicate that perhaps Clark should support the tone of the conversation, which the DI duly did with a nod of her head and pursing of her lips in an apologetic gesture.

"So, have you got a wire-tap on my phone, yet?" asked Ferranti, knowing full-well that they would either have one already, or get one very soon. *"That will presumably give you the proof I'm not making things up"*. His voice was gently sarcastic and provocative.

Both Walker and Clark glanced at each other involuntarily but said nothing. *"So, that's a yes then I take it"*, said Ferranti, who had picked up on the body language. *"Good"*, he added, and then he relaxed back into his chair. Walker was just about to assure Ferranti that they couldn't confirm or deny his phone calls were being recorded, when the conference room phone rang. Ferranti looked at the ID. It was Chloe on the switchboard. He picked up the receiver.

"Hey Chloe", he said, but the voice that came back was not that of Chloe.

"Hello, Adam". Ferranti froze and he quickly looked up at Walker. She recognised the look in his eyes immediately and she indicated he should press the speaker phone button. He did so with speed.

"Didn't think I'd hear from you again for a while", said Ferranti. *"Are you manning reception now? Have Charlie and Chloe gone home early?"* The caller didn't respond to the jibe.

"I assume you know, or you soon will know, that they've found the third body, Adam. Just as I predicted", the caller said. *"How is the clock? Or have the Police got it? Oh, of course they will have, silly me"*, and he let out a faux chuckle.

"What do you want?" asked Ferranti. Walker and Clark were scribbling down notes, when Clark indicated to Walker that she would go out of the room and call Millgarth. Walker should stay and scribe.

"I just wanted to say hello", came the voice.

"Hello? Why would I want to hear 'hello' from a giant pain in my ass and the murderer of three innocent old men?" said Ferranti, disparagingly and with a slightly raised voice. Walker glared at him, but Ferranti nodded at her and indicated that his temper was under control.

The caller exhaled in exasperation. *"Oh, they are far from innocent, Adam, but I've clearly caught you on a bad day. Maybe it's because you had to change into that blue shirt you're wearing now? Hope the coffee you spilled didn't burn. You really should tell that driver to pay more attention to the road. I thought he was going to drive right over me! In fact, thinking about it, he was so busy looking after you, he didn't even take the time to check how I was! That really makes me quite angry, Adam".* His voice had taken on an ominous tone; so much so that it felt like a threat. *"You looked so much smarter in the white, this morning",* said the caller.

It took Ferranti a few seconds to assimilate what the caller had said, but then his jaw dropped and his eyes widened, but he said nothing. Walker looked at him, with concern. Almost in slow motion, Ferranti replaced the receiver, cutting off the speaker and the caller. He slowly sank back into his seat.

"What is it?" asked Walker.

Ferranti looked up with haunted eyes. *"He knows where I live".*

Chapter 25

Senior SOCO and Forensics Lead, Grace Allen, placed the blood-stained cotton wool bud carefully into the hazardous waste bin underneath her lab workspace. She had cleaned the dried blood from the receipt as much as she could without endangering the integrity of the paper and the ink on it. Fortunately, the eco-conscious retailer had used paper and ink, rather than the more prevalent thermal paper. The combination of that and the fact that the team had transported the wet receipt in a paper evidence bag, meant the print quality was more stable, and therefore cleaning had a higher chance of success of 'saving' the receipt. Allen put the receipt in a micro dryer, so the gentle warmth could ease the remaining moisture out of the slip of paper. After 30 seconds, she took the receipt out and placed it gently under a magnifying screen to help her see even the faintest of details.

"Right, let's see what you've got to tell us, shall we?" she said, talking to herself. She turned on the overhead microphone and started her review.

"Monday 4th March 2013. Analysis of artefacts from the Goas crime scene. The integrity of the print of the VAT receipt has been compromised, but the majority of the key details are visible", she began. *"Retailer check to be made on what looks like Fo_ K _nd_ _ s, in _*

ond___, with a partial postcode of W14 _ and what could be E or F and P or B. TID ends in 0198 and M-ID looks like it ends 87217".

*Allen paused briefly before continuing. "Precise date of purchase is unclear, but the final three letters of the month are BER, so that narrows it down to the latter part of the year. Last four digits of the card are either 4699 or 4698. The VISA algorithm will verify the optional prefix numbers and then NCA to cross-reference with the other detail on the receipt. The order was placed over the internet or the phone, as the payment was **not** verified by PIN. First five digits of the authorisation code are visible; 00872, but the sixth and final number has been obscured".*

Allen looked up and away from the lens. Even with this level of magnification, it was easy for a person's vision to blur slightly from focusing, especially after such a long day. After a minute, Allen returned to the magnifying screen and began to speak.

"Summary of findings:

One: Multitude of trace was found on the paper, but none of the DNA or fingerprint records matched anything on either the Police National Computer or the NCA's Echelon database.

Two: Paper receipt appears to have been stapled to a larger piece of paper – perhaps a delivery note – but had already been torn from the larger piece of paper when found at the Goas apartment.

Three: Specific details from the receipt will be recorded and passed to North Yorkshire CID, with a recommendation that The Met look into the address clues, given the postcode suffix.

Analysis and report completed by Grace Allen. Time is 7:43pm".

Allen turned the microphone off. She wanted to rub her tired eyes, but knew she needed to exit the lab and remove her barrier clothing first. She walked out of the lab and into the small changing area, flopping down onto a bench in front of her locker. It really had been a long day and she was already looking forward to her warm bed. After seven straight days in work, she had three days off at the ready, and had plans to visit a friend who had a cabin in the North Yorkshire Moors.

"No mobile signal, no WIFI", she said, with relief of what was to come. She sighed happily at the thought, only for the peaceful moment to be ironically broken by the ringing of her mobile phone.

In her tired state, Allen struggled to open the locker at first and hoped the caller wouldn't ring-off before she got to the phone. She also hoped that it wasn't her friend, postponing the two nights of solitude she was so looking forward to; with music, great food, wine and some good old-fashioned girlie talk. After a few seconds, she managed to open the locker door and snatched at her mobile. She was so pre-occupied with answering it before the caller rang off, that she didn't bother to check who was calling.

"Hello?" she gasped, as much with anxiety at potentially missing the call, as with her breathlessness from her frantic yet weary attempt to open the locker door.

"Hi... Grace?" queried the caller.

"Yes, this is Grace. Who's this?" she asked in return.

"Hi, it's DS Williams. Sorry to call so late, but I wondered if you'd completed the analysis of the Goas murder evidence? I wouldn't ask this late normally, it's just that I want to give the DI on HMET an update in the morning, if possible". He knew it was late and could tell from Grace's voice that she was tired. That's why he had rung at this hour, in the hope that Grace Allen would be happy to send over her findings without questioning if it could wait. She sighed and shook her head in disbelief, as well as in resignation that she knew her day had not quite finished after all. After a few seconds, she said, *"Sure. I'll send over the digital voice recording I've just finished and the report notes – I want this off my slate, so I can enjoy my days off".*

"Thanks, Grace. Let me know when you've sent it. I'm still in the office, so I can pick it up straight away", said a grateful Williams. The phone line disconnected, and Grace slumped back against the locker. She stared up at the ceiling, gathering her willpower and final reserves of energy, before she straightened her posture and then stood to head back into her office. She paused. Was that a door closing she had heard? Who else was working so late, she wondered? She didn't give it much of a second thought, though, as the whole team were currently

working double-shifts. Perhaps one of them had also just finished. Lucky things, going home rather than going to log back on.

Grace walked out of the locker area and into the corridor. She could see a couple of office lights still on and, as she walked past Annie Welbeck's office, she tapped on the window and waved. Annie waved back and, in an animated manner, looked at her watch and rolled her eyes. They both smiled at each other. Further down the corridor, the light was also still on in Pete Devonshire's office, but he wasn't sitting at his desk. *"Probably grabbing yet another cuppa and a cigarette"*, she thought out loud, and then looked round, giggling, in case anyone had heard her talking to herself. Thankfully, nobody had.

Grace reached her office and sat behind her desk. She turned the desk lamp on, rather than relying on the blinding white light from the overheads. She noticed Annie's light go off, so she waited a moment, as Annie would need to walk past her office to get to the secure exit. No point starting work only to then break off in a few seconds to wave goodnight to her friend. But Annie didn't appear. Allen waited a little longer, but still no Annie. *"Hmm, maybe she went to the ladies before heading home. Or maybe she's got a hot date and they're making out in her room"*, she chuckled. She turned her laptop on and heard the hum as the processor kicked in. Another light a little closer to her office went off. Presumably, Pete was finishing for the day. That just left Grace's desk lamp on and the corridor emergency beacons, with their dull, relentless glare.

Grace logged in to her computer and started to type the email to DS Williams, talking quietly to herself as she typed the words:

"DS Williams. Please find attached my report on the evidence gathered at the apartment of Ricardo Goas. I have yet to document the details of the receipt analysis but, to help you with your briefing tomorrow, I have attached a .WAV file of the review I have just completed. I do not have the email address for your DS colleague in The Met, but suggest you forward this to him, as he will need to investigate what looks like a London postcode. I'm going away now for a few days, on leave, but my inbox will be monitored by the duty officer, who I have cc'd into this email. Regards ..." and, with a flourish, she typed her name and said out loud, *"Who is now going home, to sleep, and then will be getting pissed over the weekend with her mate, so don't even think about fucking calling me"*.

She attached the .WAV file and the report and then pressed send. That's when she heard what sounded like someone kicking a waste-paper basket or bumping into a cupboard. There were no other lights on along the corridor and the motion sensors hadn't picked up any movement. Allen looked at her watch. It seemed a little late for the cleaners to be working in the kitchen, but *"Yes, that must be it"*, she thought, even though the hairs on the back of her neck had started to prickle.

"Oh, relax for fucks sake", she told herself, to try and ease the anxiety she felt tickling away in her stomach.

As hard as she tried, though, something was making her nervous. *"Stupid Spidey-sense"*, she joked, nervously, but she made sure she turned her ceiling light on before turning her desk light off. As she stepped into the corridor, the main lights came on with the sensors detecting her movement. She breathed a sigh of relief and berated herself for being so worried. She turned to flick the switch of her ceiling light to the off position, only to realise she was not alone. Someone was behind her. In a split-second, a pair of men's hands grasped her shoulders in a vice-like grip. Grace gasped as she was spun round to face her attacker! Then she exhaled in relief, her shoulders dropped as she relaxed, and then she grabbed his hands.

"You fucking idiot! You nearly gave me a heart attack!" she shouted, as the loving eyes of her latest boyfriend beamed back at her. He smiled and offered a softly-spoken *"Sorry"*, before leaning forward and kissing her gently on the lips. His hands slid from her neck to her shoulders, and then down to her waist. After a soft, slow, lingering kiss, she pushed him away and looked quizzically at him. *"I thought you weren't due back from the conference in Berlin for a few more days?"* she asked, creating air quotation marks as she said the word 'conference', to suggest it was perhaps just a drunken business trip.

"Oh, I finished it early and the boss told me to head up north and give my girlfriend a surprise", he said, raising his eyebrows suggestively. He gently squeezed her buttocks, whilst burying his head into her breasts.

"Oi, not here", said Allen, feigning shock and disapproval.

Just then Annie Welbeck and Pete Devonshire walked around the corner, laughing and joking. They had been washing their cups in the kitchen area and were now a little startled, catching the lovers in a raunchy embrace.

"Oops, sorry. Hope we weren't interrupting anything?" teased Welbeck. Grace blushed and her boyfriend hid his face in embarrassment. He let go of her, taking a step back.

"No, not at all", he said, clearing his throat, while glancing guiltily up at Grace.

"Well remember, Big Brother is watching you", said Devonshire, in reference to the various CCTV cameras around the lab.

When her colleagues said goodnight and had left, Grace Allen squeezed her boyfriend's buttocks and said, *"Come on, let's go get laid at my place."*

Grace had only met this latest boyfriend a few weeks earlier, but he was so in-tune with her, that it was almost as if he'd known her for years. They walked down the corridor, hand in hand. He was joking and tickling her, making his girlfriend laugh out loud. She was so happy to see him that it never even crossed her mind to ask who let him into the secure facility to surprise her. She was also so distracted that she didn't notice him glance up at every CCTV camera along the corridor.

He smiled. The camera LEDs were not flashing. Hardly surprising as, earlier that evening, he had accessed the secure facility without anyone's help, and disabled the lab's CCTV security system single-handedly.

There must be no record of him being there.

Chapter 26

Walker and Hobbs were in the HMET incident room. It was past midnight, but they both felt there was something staring them in the face that they just couldn't see yet. Fatigue was starting to set in. They were still staring at the collection of photos and notes on the incident room pinboard, when Walker asked;

"*So, how long have you been on the force, Mike?*" Such informality wasn't unusual when a DC and a DS were working late, alone together, but it was unusual when the pairing was so relatively new. Hobbs took the gesture as an attempt to create a rapport.

"*It seems like a lifetime*", he joked. Walker smiled warmly in response. She knew the feeling. "*What about you?*" he added.

"*Five years, so far*".

"*And I see you're married? Guess it can be tough on the relationship*", said Hobbs.

Walker snapped her head round, with a look of shock plastered on her face. How could he know about the situation between her and Alex? Did it show that much?

Hobbs continued, seemingly unaware of Walker's sudden sense of vulnerability. *"Don't look so surprised. I am a detective, you know ... plus the wedding ring kinda gave it away"*, he added, gently mocking his colleague.

Walker relaxed. Hobbs's observation was purely in relation to her being married.

"Oh, yes. I forgot about your investigative prowess and deductive powers, Holmes", she joked; trying to calm herself down. Happy to move away from the subject of her troubled marriage, she then asked, *"What made you join the force?"*

Hobbs quickly looked down at his hands, as Walker realised it was now her turn to unwittingly hit upon a sensitive point. *"Mike, I'm so sorry... It really is none of my business. Please don't feel you have to tell me anything"*.

Hobbs pursed his lips. Not so much in anger or disappointment, but as if in internal debate as to whether to say anything to his colleague or keep his private life just that; private. After several seconds, he nodded to himself and looked up. He was clearly struggling to keep his sadness in check, but he replied;

"It's okay, Sarge". He took a conscious breath and gathered his thoughts, before continuing with his answer. *"I joined a few years ago, because I wanted to help bring people to justice. You see, my sister was in an abusive relationship and none of us realised it, until it was too late"*. Walker was listening intently; absorbed.

"The guy got off on a technicality; two weeks after we buried her. It burned a hole inside me and, even though I knew the technicality was down to human error, I vowed I'd never knowingly let someone abusive – or a criminal of any other kind – slip through my fingers".

Silence hung over the room. Neither of them wanted to say anything or indeed knew what to say, and neither of them knew how to ease the atmosphere without it feeling awkward, either. Slowly, they both turned back towards the information on the wall in front of them and pretended to study it. Hobbs suddenly sprang out of his seat.

"I've got it! I know what we're looking for!" he exclaimed, excitedly, and in a way that lifted the mood of the room, considerably. Walker looked at the information on the wall, and then stared back up at Hobbs, expectantly. He looked back down at her, clearly excited. *"Pizza! We need pizza!"*, he said, loudly, and then smirked. Walker exhaled in relief, and suddenly realised she was actually very hungry.

"I'm buying", she said, as she laughed in both good humour and relief. She found herself feeling a lot of empathy with Hobbs, and now felt like she was starting to trust him. *"And thanks for your trust in telling me the things that you did, Mike. It can't have been easy"*.

"Well, in this line of work, Guv, I guess we need to trust each other … sometimes with our lives", and Hobbs

looked directly into Walker's eyes. She started to slowly nod; both in understanding and in appreciation that Hobbs had shared such an intimate part of his life. This was an important step in the growing trust between the investigative pair.

Chapter 27

Khatri pulled up outside the Yorkshire Post building at 9:56pm; waiting to take Ferranti home. He tried to relax by turning the radio on, singing quietly along with 'Skyfall' by Adele. He'd had a day from hell but, somewhat surprisingly, was looking forward to seeing Ferranti again.

The news came on the radio next, but Khatri's mind drifted as they announced the election of a new Pope in the main headlines. He looked in his notebook and reflected on a very eventful twelve hours of driving today:

"Right, let's see… twenty-seven customers. One who nearly vomited in the taxi. That would have been a £50 cleaning bill. Err, two drunks who ran off without paying, even though they had reserved using their credit card". He smirked as he shook his head at their stupidity. *"And that moron… I mean, what sort of idiot racially abuses their driver?"* Khatri wrote a note to let his cousin know that they must never pick up that client again.

As the news and sport bulletin continued, Khatri glanced at his watch. It was 10:03pm and Ferranti was late. He stared into the reception area, but other than a security guard, there was no sign of movement. Then, from the side of the building, he saw a shadow emerge and the security lights came on, flooding Adam Ferranti in blinding white light.

"What...?" mumbled a somewhat puzzled Khatri. He continued to watch a furtive Ferranti glance around as he made his way to the car. He then opened the door and sunk into the back seat.

"A little bit old for hide and seek, aren't we?" teased Khatri. Ferranti glared at him, before scanning the surrounding area through the window. *"Just drive"*, he snapped. Khatri was taken aback by the blunt nature of Ferranti's tone, but he turned to face forwards and put the car into gear, setting off towards Wellington Street and their usual route home via the A64. After a few minutes, Ferranti glanced up at Khatri, who had been checking on Ferranti in his rear-view mirror since he got in. Ferranti realised his behaviour was wildly different to this morning's demeanour. He sat up slightly in the seat.

"Do me a favour?" he asked. *"Take me home a different route. Don't go through Crossgates and Scholes. Take a right, up towards Temple Newsam, and head to Garforth"*.

Khatri nodded to confirm that he understood but kept looking at Ferranti in the rear-view mirror. He noticed that his passenger kept glancing out of the side window and over his shoulder. As the car eased right at the traffic lights and headed up Selby Road, a concerned Khatri finally asked;

"Are you okay? You seem agitated".

Ferranti shuffled awkwardly in the back seat and looked into the reflection of Khatri's eyes.

"I'm fine. Thanks. Just… well I can't talk about it in any detail". Ferranti began, as if debating what he could and couldn't tell Khatri. *"It's just… well, that blind guy this morning. He, erm, I… I had a visit from the Police about everything and I need to find somewhere safe to hang-out for a while. I'm just a little on edge, as a result"*.

Instinctively, Khatri looked round at Ferranti, and the car drifted towards the pavement. Ferranti shouted at Khatri, who realised what was happening and over-compensated, swerving back towards the centre of the road and the oncoming traffic. Car drivers beeped and headlights flashed at Khatri, with irate faces and abusive hand gestures all pointed in his direction. Ferranti gripped the car seat and door handle, as it seemed a certainty they would crash. Thankfully, Khatri gathered himself just as a brewery lorry seemed to be bearing down on them. He veered the car away from danger and re-gathered his composure. For several seconds, neither man said anything; nor did their state of panic subside. Then, they saw the flashing blue lights of a Police car coming up behind them. Khatri's shoulders slumped as he realised he might be in serious trouble. He pulled the car into a lay-by and waited for the Police car to pull in behind him. The passenger of the Police car got out and walked to the passenger window of Khatri's vehicle.

"*Good evening, officer. I'm so sorry about that*", said Khatri, "*But a cat ran across the road*", he lied.

The officer looked into the back of the car and saw Ferranti, who he nodded to, before saying; "*Evening, sir. DI Clark asked us to make sure you got home safely. We'll be around the area for tonight, in case you feel nervous*". The officer then looked at Khatri and added, "*But perhaps your driver here is trying to give you a heart attack before you get home?*"

Khatri gave a pathetically weak smile in response.

"*Thank you, officer, but I'm sure we'll be fine from now on*", said Ferranti, checking Khatri's guilty expression in the mirror. "*And I appreciate you staying local tonight, but I don't intend to be home for long. Just enough time to pack and grab a ride somewhere*".

The officer nodded, and then gestured goodbye to Ferranti. He gave Khatri one final look, before returning to the police car.

Khatri let out a long sigh and sat back, visibly relieved. Ferranti then startled him momentarily, as he gently put his assuring hand on Khatri's shoulder:

"*I know you didn't mean that, but do you think you could just get me home? Alive? I've had a really bad day and I'd appreciate it if you didn't shred my nerves any more than they already are*", said Ferranti, softly. Khatri gently nodded his head and then, in an unconscious response to their overwhelming relief, both men started to laugh. Khatri rested his hand on Ferranti's, which was now squeezing Khatri's shoulder in an assuring way.

"Thank you. I'll be more careful. We don't want to tempt fate a third time", said Khatri, and Ferranti sat back, still glancing out of the window, as the car eased back into the night-time traffic. He assumed that if anyone was following him, the sight of the Police car would make them think about giving up for the night.

Twenty minutes later, Ferranti was home. He raised his hand in thanks and farewell, as Khatri pulled away from the kerb and headed up Main Street on his own journey home. Ferranti opened the front door and immediately switched the lounge, kitchen and stairway lights on. He felt insecure tonight and only relaxed a little being back in the comfort of his own home. Still nervous, he strolled into the kitchen and opened a cupboard, pulling out a bottle of Jack Daniel's and a glass.

"Now is not the time to die", he said to himself, as he unscrewed the bottle top and poured a generous measure into his glass. He sighed, shook his head as if to dispel an image from his mind, and raised the glass towards his lips. He stopped. He lowered the glass and looked at the amber hue of the whiskey for a moment, before gritting his teeth and slamming the glass onto the worktop. The liquid splashed across the kitchen and his shirt, as the glass splintered into several pieces. Ferranti formed a fist around the remainder of the glass in his hand. He snarled and flung the broken glass across the room against the kitchen wall. Blood seeped from his fingers where the sharp edges of the broken glass had

cut the skin. He stared at them, as the blood oozed from several minor cuts and started to trickle down into his palm. His anger subsided and he began to take deep, calming breaths, before he whispered, "Not yet".

Khatri's subsequent journey back home was smooth, but the events of the day had taken their toll on him. As he opened the front door, he could hear his housemates talking in the kitchen.

"*Bloody hell, that's the end of old Wilkinson, then*", laughed Harry.

"*You're kidding. Wilko will outlast the whole Government and I doubt Hulme has the balls or the capability to drive this through. Besides, I reckon Hulme will be out before Easter*", scoffed Alix.

"*Well I think it's a great move*", announced Celia. "*About time we allowed people to reveal the lack of care in some hospitals*". It was then she noticed Khatri. "*Hey Avi*", she said, brightly. "*There's a letter for you in the basket, hun. Looks official!*" And with that, she gestured to a worn wicker tray on the kitchen worktop.

"*Thanks*", said Khatri. "*I'll grab it, but I'm heading to bed. I'm shattered. Keep the noise down you lot, yeah?*" he requested.

His housemates all mumbled in agreement but, by the time Khatri had reached the top of the stairs, he could already hear loud laughter and voices from the room below.

Chapter 28

DS Steve Denton dialled the number at 8:50am as requested. It was answered promptly.

"Did you get the information I emailed you?" Denton queried.

"And good morning to you too, Steve. Yes, thank you. Was that everything SOCO sent you?" asked Simon McBride. He didn't trust anyone. It was his way of life, so he felt no reason to trust Denton in particular.

"I didn't get it direct. It came via the DS running the North Yorkshire murder enquiry. It's everything he sent me", lied Denton. *"I'm just waiting for the final information - about the receipt".*

"Odd they sent through an incomplete report, isn't it?" McBride was no fool and his bullshit sensor was screaming right now. Denton expected his question, though, and responded without pausing:

"The DS in North Yorkshire wants to brown-nose the DI at this morning's briefing. Think he's angling for a transfer and wants to look like he's working at pace. Besides, Senior SOCO is now on a three-day weekend. I guess this is as far as she got before she left". The line

189

was silent for a few seconds as Denton waited for his story to land.

"Okay. Well let me know when you get the analysis of the receipt. Shoddy work by such a supposedly meticulous and careful killer to have left a possible clue behind", McBride mused, out loud.

"They all make a mistake at some point", said Denton before changing the subject. *"So, McBride, what's my quid pro quo?"* he asked. After all, their informal agreement was that they would share information in a two-way process.

"Ah yes. Well, even though this remains 'company business', Steve, I can tell you we have found a link between Goas and the American woman who left him the message. We're looking into a specific person of interest with our FBI colleagues. Maybe we'll uncover precisely what's at 'where the three seas meet' too. I'll keep you posted". With that, McBride ended the call abruptly. No courtesy, no professional respect. Denton muttered his disgust under his breath, but then started to prepare for the morning's 09:30 HMET call. Simon McBride, however, immediately dialled another number. It rang a couple of times before a hushed voice answered, *"Yes?"*

"Find out what she knows", said McBride. *"The boys in blue aren't telling me everything"*.

"And afterwards?" asked the man, known as Republic.

"Leave her be. There's no need to spill more blood.... just yet". McBride then ended the call as abruptly as he had done with Denton. Republic slipped his phone into his holdall, just in time.

"Who was that?" asked Grace Allen, entering the bedroom with a damp towel wrapped around her body.

"Oh, just work, honey", he replied, feigning a sigh. *"Looks like I now need to head out to Spain later this afternoon"*, he lied.

"Hmm", said Grace, grinning seductively. *"So, we have time to kill before we both have to go?"* she said, dropping the towel to the floor to reveal her naked body. He smiled and threw the duvet back, so she could climb back into bed with him. He was unsure what excited him the most; the thought of more sex with Grace Allen, or knowing his trusty switchblade was hidden only inches away from her throat. After all, she was just another assignment for him. Just another pawn in the game.

And an expendable one at that.

Chapter 29

DI Angela Clark sat patiently as the HMET team gathered in the conference room, waiting to dial-in DS Williams and DS Denton. Last into the room was DS Walker. *"Apologies Ma'am. I was finishing up with another enquiry"*, she said, glancing over at DC Hobbs, who knew the truth.

"Right, well let's not make it a habit, DS Walker", said Clark, in a cold matter-of-fact way. She wasn't used to people keeping her waiting.

"No Ma'am. It won't happen again", said Walker, opening her notebook and busying herself to avoid the looks she was getting from others. Clark dialled the conference call number and heard the automated voice tell her that two people were already on the call.

"Morning, DS Williams. Morning, DS Denton", she barked authoritatively.

"Morning, Ma'am", they both responded.

"First topic this morning; the forensics report. DS Williams, thank you for sending it through earlier but, for the benefit of the rest of the team, can you explain the key points, please?" Clark requested.

"*Morning all*", said Williams to the group. "*The report on the crime scene arrived late last night, along with a voice recording of findings re: the receipt we found at the scene. Having sent the information onto DS Denton... I believe you've made some further progress, Steve?*" continued Williams.

Denton picked up the story and said, "*Yes we have, Bob. Ma'am, we had some missing digits and characters from parts of the receipt but, with the information SOCO gave us, we've filled in some of the blanks*". Denton was pleased with the pace his team had solved some of the riddle already. "*We know the retailer in question is a hardware store on the North End Road in London, so we've sent a car down to question the owner*". He paused, in hope of hearing how impressed Clark was with the work they'd done already, but she just asked;

"*Is that it, DS Denton?*"

Slightly disappointed, DS Denton replied, "*Err, no Ma'am. Now we have confirmation of the retailer, we have requested the National Crime Agency review the relevant data and liaise with the card issuer to find a name and address. We expect some feedback later today, but I can't commit to it being complete or actionable at this stage*". Denton waited for a reply from Clark, but as nothing seemed to be forthcoming, he ended his update with, "*That's all for now, Ma'am*".

"*Very good*", said Clark, without actually sounding like she meant it in any way. She turned her attention back to Williams and asked, *"Any update on the translation of the voice message, DS Williams? Or anything further on motive? Who was Ricardo Goas?"*

"We have translated the message, Ma'am, as you know. For the benefit of the rest of the team, it is an American woman telling Goas to head east to where the three seas meet. We're researching that at the moment, but a Google search brings back a general location in India: Kanyakumari. No further insights yet, but we're hopeful we'll have more information on that for tomorrow's call, Ma'am".

Having heard the lack of response to the excellent progress Denton's team had made, Williams didn't expect anything of gratitude from Clark - and he wasn't disappointed. He didn't wait for an extended uncomfortable silence and moved on to Goas.

"Nothing so far on Goas. Residents told us that, although he was pleasant and courteous whenever they did meet him, he was very private. Local boys on the beat are also canvassing the area. They're following up with a local tearoom where he was a regular. NCA has responded, though. They've told me Goas's background search has security restrictions, thus limiting their access. It's unclear at the moment why and who has authority to bypass the restriction. They're looking into it".

That piece of information piqued Clark's interest. She shifted in her chair and furrowed her brow. To those that didn't know her, it was unclear why. To those that knew her, though, it was a tell-tale sign of her providing an opportunity; the opportunity to shine with something further that would get DI Angela Clark really intrigued. Such was her enthusiasm on this, that she suggested they close the call early so the team could spend time on their already allocated tasks. That would free her so she could talk privately with a contact at the NCA. The team dispersed, with Walker and Hobbs heading back to their desks.

"Good job Her Majesty doesn't know why you were late", said Hobbs, as he jogged to catch up with Walker. *"Any news on Alex?"*

"Isn't it just", replied Walker. *"And no, no reply on his mobile or at home"*, she added. She'd found herself in the unusual situation of worrying where her husband was. She had not seen or heard from him since she found the note about him going to meet Jaggs. She'd called Jaggs that evening and he said he hadn't seen him since lunch but was due to catch up with him again soon. Walker was late to the daily call this morning because she was trying to reach Alex and Jaggs via any means possible.

The day progressed, with enquiries ongoing. At 3pm, the phone rang on Walker's desk. She snatched it off the cradle and spoke in eager anticipation that it was Alex. It was actually DS Bob Williams, who had just finished on the phone with the NCA.

"Oh, hi Bob", said Walker, a little disappointed it wasn't her husband finally getting in touch.

"And I'm thrilled to be talking to you, too", he replied. "You okay? Is Clark the Shark getting to you?" Williams asked.

Clark the Shark. Seems fitting, thought Walker. "Err no, it's just a family matter, but thanks for asking, Bob. What can I do for you?" she said, brightening up her tone.

"I've had a chat with Steve Denton, and the Met boys have come up with some info. I was going to tell DI Clark. Seems she's not at her desk, though – brown-nosing the top brass I expect – so I thought I'd talk to you - you know, as you're her deputy".

"Okay. Well tell Deputy Walker what you've got, Bob?" laughed Walker. Her mood was improving and any concerns about Alex were momentarily gone as she immersed herself in her work.

"The owner of the hardware store tracked the transaction. He said it was easy to remember because, whilst they often get orders for saw wire, knives and corkscrews, it's unusual to get repeat orders of all three together for the same name. He's got an address for the first transaction and NCA confirm it matches the VISA number recorded... it's in Leeds. He's looking for the other addresses, but their records are all manual, so it could take a while".

Walker was scribbling furiously whilst listening to Williams. Hobbs sat opposite her. He hadn't seen her this frantic for quite a while and wondered if the call was someone contacting her with news about her husband.

"Give me the address, Bob", squealed Walker, excitedly. Williams provided the detail and Walker promised him she'd get right back to him and Steve Denton as soon as she had an update. She put the phone down and stared up at Hobbs.

"What is it?" asked Hobbs, relieved that the bright eyes and smug smile on Walker's face meant at least she didn't have bad news about her husband. Walker held her smug smile for a moment and said, *"We have an address for the first saw wire parcel. It's here in Leeds"*.

Hobbs opened his mouth, dumbfounded. He waited for Walker to pick up the phone to call DI Clark, but she didn't. Instead, she took her jacket off the back of her chair and started to stride out of the office. She stopped, mid-stride, and looked back at Hobbs.

"You coming?", she asked, teasing him.

Hobbs rose and grabbed his jacket. He jogged after Walker and, as he caught up with her, said, *"Aren't you going to report it to the DI?"*

Walker kept striding to the lift, smiling. *"Nope. DS Williams tried her phone, but there was no answer and, as I'm her deputy, I'll take this lead on this, Mike"*.

Hobbs was a little unsure. Protocol in a HMET-led incident would be to report the news to the lead officer, letting them direct activities from that point. He slowed down a little before stopping, but Walker just called back over her shoulder;

"The killer might be there right now, Mike", and then she stopped and turned to look at him. *"Are we going to let due process get in the way of a possible arrest?"* She stared at him, impatiently, awaiting an answer. He hesitated, looked behind him towards his desk phone, and then decided to follow his colleague.

As they climbed into the car, Mike asked, *"Where to, Sarge?"*

"8 Park Avenue, Roundhay", said Walker, as she fastened her seatbelt.

The journey to Roundhay only took ten minutes. They had not used lights or a siren, but the late afternoon traffic had only just started to build, going out of the city centre. As they entered Park Avenue, they slowed; not wishing to attract any attention. They pulled to a stop outside number eight and looked at each other, mystified.

"It's... a retirement home", said Hobbs first. *"Our killer is an OAP?"* he quizzed, half-joking.

"Maybe it's just a cover, Mike. Might be a janitor or even a member of staff. Someone using the address to help cover their tracks", pointed out Walker. Hobbs nodded, still looking quizzically at the property. Walker looked at Hobbs and said, *"Only one way to find out"*. She opened the car door, and Hobbs followed promptly.

Together they entered the reception. It was a small but welcoming area. A young woman was working behind the counter. She looked up and smiled at Walker and Hobbs.

"Hello. Welcome to Park Avenue Nursing Home. How can I help you?"

"Hello", said Walker, flashing her Police credentials. *"I'm Detective Sergeant Walker and this is my colleague, Detective Constable Hobbs"*. Hobbs flashed his credentials as well and returned the warm smile of the receptionist. *"We are making some enquiries about a parcel that was delivered here a couple of weeks ago. It came from a company called For Kandles in London's Leadenhall Market. I believe it was addressed to a Mr Paul Reynolds. Is he a member of your staff?"*

The receptionist smiled. *"Oh no... Mr Reynolds is 89 and has been bed-ridden for a number of months, I'm afraid"*. She smiled again and then shook her head, adding, *"He certainly seems to be popular at the moment ... or at least that parcel he had delivered does"*.

Walker and Hobbs glanced at each other before Hobbs said to the receptionist, *"What do you mean, 'popular'?"*

"Well, it was delivered a week or so ago, but when we opened it for Mr. Reynolds, he assured us he hadn't ordered it. We didn't know what to do. It would have been expensive to return it, but when we spoke to the sender, they said they couldn't accept it back if the

parcel had already been opened. Then, yesterday, a guy came in – gorgeous he was – and said he'd come to pick it up. Well, we didn't want it and so I said he could take it. Couldn't say no to that smile", and her face melted into a memory that she was obviously very fond of.

"Yesterday?" checked Hobbs

"Yes, I think, or the day before... it's been a long week... He said he needed the stuff before he went away on a photo shoot or something. It all sounded very exotic". A mischievous smile appeared on her face as she added, "I said I'd happily carry his bags on his trip, but he just winked at me and showed me his wedding ring. Shame. Oh, he was ...", and the distant look of reflective pleasure reappeared on the receptionist's face again. She soon realised that her visitors were both looking at her, though, and so she cleared her throat, her cheeks going pink with embarrassment. "Sorry", she said. "It's just, when you're staring at people over 70 all day every day, talking to concerned family members, or watching trolleys full of bedpans being wheeled back and forth... well... let's just say he was a welcome distraction", and she shrugged her shoulders, as if to indicate 'I'm only human'.

"So, you'd remember his face if you saw it again?" asked Hobbs. As soon as he asked, he realised it was a stupid question, and Walker and the receptionist just stared at him. Walker then looked up above the reception desk and into the corner of the ceiling.

"CCTV camera?" she asked, hopefully.

The receptionist looked up and said, *"Yes. You'd be amazed how much we need that, to provide us with a sense of security"*.

"How long do you keep the recordings for?" asked Hobbs.

"A week, usually", answered the receptionist.

"Show me the CCTV records for whenever the parcel was collected, please", requested Walker.

The receptionist paused. *"Don't you need a warrant or something to be able to view those?"* she challenged.

"No", answered Walker. *"You can give us access voluntarily, unless you're hiding something, of course? Well, then we'd just have to arrest you and close access to the building once we had the warrant"*. She smiled at the receptionist, just enough to make sure the girl knew she was serious. The receptionist didn't hesitate. She popped a 'Be back soon' sign on the reception counter and led the two detectives into a small room behind reception. In the room were three CCTV monitors mounted on a wall, with a control panel sat on a desk in front of a small chair. The receptionist mulled over her dates whilst looking at the library of CDs. She finally nodded to herself and took one out of the racking. She popped it into the player and the larger monitor turned into a replay screen.

As the receptionist scrolled through the recording on fast forward, she suddenly said:

"That's him". A blurry image of the back of a man's head, face hidden by a baseball cap, filled the screen. *"Hmm, that's no use, is it"*, she said, as she pressed fast-forward again, but this time at double speed. A minute later, the same man emerged from down a corridor with a large parcel in his arms. His face still wasn't visible, but then the receptionist said, *"Oh hold on, this is the bit I was thinking about"*. On screen, the man held up his left hand to show the receptionist his wedding ring. The receptionist was mainly out of shot, with the camera being above and behind her, but you could just see her shoulders shrugging. Then she pointed up above her, at where the camera was. Just as Walker was about to thank the receptionist for her time, the man on the screen took off his baseball cap and ruffled his hair. Then he stared straight up at the camera and smiled.

"I asked him to do that so I could have a picture. Told you he was gorgeous".

Walker froze, open mouthed. Staring up at her, on freeze frame, was her husband - Alex.

Chapter 30

It was a mild spring day in Washington DC. Senator Nikki Swati sat on a bench overlooking the Constitution Gardens lake. She found being outside and surrounded by nature to be a pleasant break from the melodrama of Capitol Hill, but she wasn't here to admire the view; she was here to meet her contact, Amelia Demetrious.

Demetrious and Swati had first met back in 1996, before Swati was married. Swati had approached the FBI with some disturbing information she had been privy to. Demetrious had been the officer on duty at the time and had handled the query. Demetrious was impressed by the then young, ambitious woman's analytical capabilities and, whilst they had not communicated for many years after that, Demetrious had followed the would-be politician's career. She saw elements of herself in the young woman, and harboured the hope that the FBI would be able to persuade her to join them. As it was, the young analyst decided to enter politics, and it wasn't until after the September 11th attacks – when Demetrious was officially retired – that she reconnected with the newly elected Senator Swati. The reconnection took place at a security conference that Swati was attending - and where Demetrious had arranged to be hired as a hostess.

"*Excuse me*", said Demetrious, who suddenly appeared just behind Swati, "*But would the Senator like a cup of Wagh Bakri tea? I think perhaps it would help sustain your interest*". Swati smiled to herself and, only partially turning her head in the direction of the voice, quietly thanked the attentive hostess, whilst still trying to focus on the presentation. Two minutes later the hostess returned and, placing the tea on the small table at the side of Swati, said, "*Your invigorating tea, Ma'am. One that, I believe, is the preferred blend of those who love Kanyakumari*".

Swati smiled, broadly, realising that the hostess had apparently done some research and knew of the Senator's Indian husband. Again, a partial head-turn from Swati, and a softly-spoken and gracious, "*Why, thank you*", in the direction of the hostess.

A few seconds later, as Swati lifted the cup to take a sip of the hot tea, she noticed a carefully folded slip of paper sat on the saucer underneath where the cup had been. Swati quickly turned her head to seek out the hostess, but she was gone. The Senator's sudden movement was noticed by the Secret Service agent nearest her, and he took a step forward. Swati gave a weak smile and signalled with her hand that there was no problem. Once the agent had resumed his post, Swati opened the carefully folded piece of paper and was troubled to see the shocking statement it held. It informed her that US intelligence secrets and the identities of its intelligence officers overseas were once again being sold for personal gain.

It took another two years to get to a point where the two women felt they had enough trust in each other to make their connection work. Both had proven they were acting honourably, and Demetrious had seen how adept the Senator was at using the information that had been provided to place subtle pressure on various Security sub-committees; pressure that allowed them to enforce governance on some questionable activities. Similarly, Swati had come to trust that whatever Demetrious knew, she always managed to guide the Senator away from any possible direct link to her - and from any immediate and obvious personal risk or danger.

Demetrious strolled along the pathway on the east side of the lake, and took her seat near Swati; close enough to hear, but far enough away that any casual observer might think it merely a coincidence that the two women were sitting on the same bench. Both women stared into the distance rather than at each other. They shared not even a glance.

Demetrious was feeding some birds with wild seed from a paper bag she carried, when she heard Swati say, "*I'm sorry about Casa*".

Demetrious paused. The birds looked eagerly at the handful of seed that was suspended in mid-throw. "*Thank you*", she said, pulling her hand back and then launching the seed into the air. "*A hazard of the life we …. led*", she continued, with a faint and sad tone in her voice.

"*I believe the Metropolitan Police in London will have news on Mercantile later today, too*", added Swati.

Then, after a few more minutes, she enquired, *"Is anyone still trading on Main Street?"*

Still struggling to keep her emotions in-check, Demetrious didn't answer straight away. The terrible news about Goas had been confirmed by Republic in a short text a couple of days ago - and it still lingered heavy in her heart. It had read:

'Lion Insurance regrets to inform you that premiums are no longer necessary for your house'.

Demetrious had been sitting at home when the text came through. Although she feared it might be the case when she had first tried calling Casa last week, reading that the worst had actually happened - that the man she loved had been executed – simply crushed her. She had heaved with tears and held herself tightly, whilst rocking gently back and forth in her chair, for what seemed like an eternity. The last strand of hope that she and Goas might ever be together again was gone. As she sat on the bench at the lake, she subtly wiped a tear from her cheek and stabilised her breathing, before responding to Swati:

"One. It's a new business which appears to be slowly blossoming. A heritage bank is funding it, but channels are open and language is positive. I'm thinking of investing my life savings". Demetrious then emptied the remaining wild bird seed out of the bag onto the grass at her side of the bench.

Swati's shift in body language was subtle and unconscious but visible. The last sentence drew her attention.

"*ALL your savings?*" she asked, checking what she thought she had heard.

"*Everything I own*", replied a bitter and vengeful Demetrious. She then stood and paused to look over the lake, before slowly walking away.

The meeting was over. Amelia Demetrious had decided to place her faith in the man she only knew as Republic. With his help, she would destroy the illegal operation, even if it took her dying breath. Then, she and Ricardo Goas could be reunited in death and never have to leave each other ever again.

Swati glanced sideways towards the departing Demetrious. It was then she noticed the two dying long-stemmed roses Demetrious had left on the bench; tied together with a black ribbon. A heart-wrenching symbol of her unbearable grief.

Chapter 31

DI Clark called the HMET morning meeting to order. Already on the conference call were DS Denton and DS Williams. DS Walker was in the room, looking as if she hadn't slept a wink during the night.

"Morning all", Clark announced, loudly, to ensure the chatter around the room was silenced. Various clearing of throats, coughs and scraping of chairs signalled that people were now paying attention.

"First up, DS Denton. I believe you have the Coroner's report on victim number 2?" Clark asked, firmly.

"Morning Ma'am. Morning all", replied Denton. *"Victim number 2 has been confirmed as David Yedlin. Fingertips were seemingly sandpapered off, though"*. The team in the room all glanced at each other. Sandpaper seemed a bizarre tool to use in a murder, although they were yet to find out about the hardware store link.

Denton continued. *"Dental records and a bank statement - the latter found in an inside jacket pocket - confirm the name and an address. Upon searching the NCA Echelon database..."*, he paused for effect, *"... it's been confirmed that, like Mr Goas, Yedlin's background search has restrictions, limiting even their access"*. The buzz in the room was palpable as another fact that seemed to link the two victims had emerged.

"Please continue", said Clark, both as a request for more information and a ploy to quieten the room.

"Yes Ma'am. Autopsy report confirms cause of death was partial drowning and eye trauma. It seems that a killer - or killers - did something consistent with waterboarding, but with red wine instead of water. When Yedlin couldn't swallow any more, he began to take wine into his lungs. At that point, the coroner believes a cork was rammed into his throat to stop the wine from escaping". Several team members pulled faces in shock, but Denton was far from finished. *"As the victim began to struggle, whilst apparently held down – as evidenced by lesions consistent with restraints around his wrists, ankles and across his torso - the killer or killers pushed corkscrews into his eyeballs and twisted them into the sockets. The coroner says it's impossible to tell whether he drowned, or from convulsions when his brain was punctured. The corkscrew shafts were entirely buried in his skull, with just the wooden handles protruding from the sockets"*. Denton stopped, to allow the information and image to be absorbed. He then cleared his throat and said, *"And, I'm afraid, there's more detail"*.

"Please continue, DS Denton", said DI Clark, seemingly unfazed by the descriptions or by the reactions of the HMET attendees; many of whom were hardened coppers, but who were clearly shaken by the brutality of the scene that had just been described.

"We believe the victim was transported from the murder location, wherever that was, as there was a minimal amount of blood at the scene. His body was screwed into a plastic chair with six more corkscrews into his back. He and the chair were placed at the water's edge of the Thames, out of plain sight, but found by an O2 Arena Safety Officer, Julie Pritchard, on her morning safety routine. She said it was 8:30am and she just assumed someone had remained drunk through the night and decided to sit near the river to help sober up". Denton closed the file on his desk and concluded with, *"We're looking into the evidence and CCTV in the area to see if we can trace the body back to where he was murdered and how he was transported".*

DI Clark pondered the information and didn't respond to Denton's closing remarks. She sat, silent, reflecting. As the silence started to become uncomfortable, DS Williams spoke up.

"Ma'am, it's DS Williams. To add to the information that you've just been given, yesterday we got the SOCO report on the Goas scene. You may recall that we found a receipt there? Well, SOCO found sufficient information from the receipt to allow DS Denton to identify where the purchase had been made. It was a hardware company down in London. The company had taken three such orders; all for saw wire, knives and corkscrews ... same name on the order, but deliverable to three different addresses."

Williams waited for Denton or Walker to pick up the story, but neither of them did, so he continued. *"We talked to DS Denton, and his team confirmed that the first order was delivered to an address in Leeds. You were unavailable yesterday, so I passed the information onto DS Walker*". Williams stopped and everyone in the incident room looked over to Walker, but she was distracted and had clearly not heard Williams introduce her into the sequence of events.

"DS Walker?" asked Clark, prompting her to pick up the story, but Walker appeared to be elsewhere in her thoughts, as she kept looking at her pad and doodling; her mind wandering, as she kept recalling seeing Alex's face on the CCTV at the retirement home.

"DS Walker?" said Clark again, in a raised voice, having become clearly irritated. Still, Walker didn't appear to hear anything. She just kept looking down, hunched over her pad and wallowing in deep thought.

Hobbs could see that DI Clark was just about to yell at Walker, so he nudged his colleague instead. *"Err, Sarge? Over to you"*.

Walker looked up, startled and a little confused. *"Yes Ma'am?"*, she said, not knowing what else was expected and hoping Clark would re-state whatever the question was. Clark just glared at her expectantly, before adding, *"Keeping you awake are we, Detective Sergeant?"*

Walker glanced around the room and realised everyone was either staring or smirking at her. Luckily, DC Hobbs stepped in and said, *"Long night for you, Sarge. Don't worry, I'll update the team"*, and he looked into

Walker's eyes to give her a sense of confidence. She looked back, suddenly realising Hobbs might have to tell them everything, and that would give her no time to figure out what the hell was going on with Alex.

"It's okay, Mike. Yes...", Walker said, looking around the room, *"... hardly any sleep last night... neighbours from hell... but I can confirm that DC Hobbs and I visited the Leeds address yesterday. It turned out to be a retirement home. The recipient of the parcel - an infirm 89-year old resident - states he had definitely not ordered the items. We took a statement from the receptionist and we're continuing enquiries today"*.

Walker smiled apologetically at Clark and flipped her notebook shut. Hobbs sat perfectly still next to her. He had no idea why Walker hadn't mentioned the CCTV footage of the man collecting the parcel. Maybe she had yet to check an assumption, before confirming a key fact with the team.

"Thank you, all", said Clark, after checking there was no more information to share. Everyone shook their head and the meeting was over.

Walker strode out of the room. Her concentration was back on whatever was going through her mind earlier in the meeting. Hobbs followed her and wanted to ask her about the CCTV footage, but another officer called over to her with a handset pressed against his shoulder; muffling anything the caller might hear:

"Sarge? Phone call for you", he said.

Walker looked over, quizzically, screwing her face up as if to ask who it was. The officer shrugged his shoulders. *"He just said it's a private matter"*. Walker paused, and then asked for the call to be put through to the conference room phone. She headed in and closed the door.

"Hello. This is DS Walker", she stated, after thanking the officer for patching through the call.

"Steph? It's Alex", came the voice of her husband on the other end of the phone. He sounded stressed and upset.

"Where the fuck have you been? I've been trying to call y...", Walker exclaimed, about to vent both her frustration and her relief that Alex was finally in touch, but he interrupted her.

"Jaggs is dead. He's fucking dead", shouted Alex. He sounded as if he was going to burst into tears.

"What?" said Walker, in disbelief and shock.

"He's dead. He was dead when I got there", Alex replied, replaying the scene in his head. *"I never touched him. He was just ... hanging. I wanted to cut him down to see if he was still breathing, but when I got to the wire he was hanging from, I couldn't do anything. It just cut through the skin on my hands"*.

Stephanie Walker temporarily stepped out of Police mode and softened her tone.

"*Where are you, Alex?*" she asked, calmly.

"*I don't know*", her husband replied, dazed and distracted. "*I just ran out of there and drove. I slept in the van last night. I kept waking up and driving some more. Anywhere. I don't know where I am, Steph*". His trembling voice made him sound like a lost, helpless child. "*I don't know what to do. I've got blood all over my hands and on the steering wheel. There's blood on my boots…*". The phone went quiet for a few seconds and then Steph Walker could hear her husband sobbing softly; "*So much blood*".

Stephanie Walker felt a pang of sorrow for her husband. This giant of a man, seemingly reduced to a little boy, faced with the sort of incidents she had to deal with every week as part of her job. Death, blood and Alex not knowing how to process it. Indeed, she had some insight into what her husband must be going through. She changed tack in the conversation, in an attempt to snap Alex away from the terrible pictures in his mind.

"*Alex… Did you collect a parcel from a retirement home in Leeds earlier in the week?*"

There was no reply at first, but then Walker heard her husband gently sniff back tears, before he replied, weakly; "*Yeah, it was for Jaggs. He gave me £500 to go collect it for him*".

"*And where is the parcel now, baby?*" Walker continued. "*What did you do with it?*"

Alex Walker thought, concentrating a little better on the conversation than he had been. Still weepy and still sounding a little woozy, he said, *"I dropped it on the floor at Jaggs' place. I just wanted to get up the stairs to help my friend, Steph"*, and he slipped back into sobs of sadness and confusion.

"Alex, I need you to listen to me. Can you do that?" Walker asked.

Silence followed, as Alex Walker calmed his nerves, before answering with a timid, *"Yes"*.

"Alex, I need you to turn on your mobile data and then Google Maps. Then come home. Let me know how long it says it will take you to get there - and where you're setting off from - and I'll meet you at the apartment, okay?" Her voice was gently encouraging and soft as silk. Her husband complied and relayed the information regarding his location before the phone clicked off and he was gone.

DS Walker leaned forwards in her seat, burying her head in her hands before sliding them to the back of her bowed head. *"Fuck"*, she muttered and exhaled with puffed cheeks as she sat back up. She closed her eyes and allowed her head to flop backwards, so she was looking straight at the ceiling. After giving her brain time to stop screaming, she knew what she had to do. She took in another deep breath, sighed, and clambered to her feet. DS Walker, the no-nonsense cop, had returned. She flung the conference room door open and strode over to Hobbs. She ripped a sheet from his notepad and started to explain what she needed as she wrote:

"Mike, get a squad car over to this address with a SOCO team. Dead body."

Hobbs looked up and stared at her; more than a little startled. Walker looked back at him and calmly but assertively demanded, *"Now!"*. As Hobbs nodded his head and started to dial, Walker strode over to where DI Clark was sitting. Clark looked up. She was intrigued about the approaching and suddenly assertive-looking Walker.

"Ma'am, we need to talk. We have a bit of a problem. Well, I have a bit of a problem", emphasised Walker.

Chapter 32

Aarav Khatri woke with a terrible headache. He didn't remember what time he had finally fallen asleep the previous night, but he had gone to bed very dehydrated. This morning, he was suffering as a consequence.

"So, this is how alcohol makes you feel every morning, Mr Ferranti!" he thought to himself, adding a casual, *"Why the hell would you do it?"* to the end of his thought process.

As his eyes adjusted to the opaque morning light, he rolled onto his back and wished he could close his eyes and go back to sleep. Sadly, he knew he couldn't.

"Things to do; money to earn", he moaned, in exasperation. He sighed again, and then slowly rolled over onto his side, in readiness to get up. That was then he saw the envelope that had arrived by post for him the day before, still laying unopened on the floor. He reached for it and pulled it close to his face, to see if he could see who it was from. Even with tired eyes and a slightly woozy head, it didn't take him long to realise what it was. He sat bolt upright, stared at the envelope for a few seconds, and then closed his eyes. Running his fingers through his hair and puffing his cheeks out, he whispered;

"Please don't be... please. One more written warning, please. Just a bit more time". He hoped his god might be listening, but he doubted it. He gathered his inner strength, opened his eyes, paused again, and then opened the envelope, quickly. He pulled the crisp white paper out and unfolded the letter to read it. His heart sank immediately:

'Dear Mr Khatri,

As you know, the medical school at St James's Teaching Hospital takes great pride in the attendance and endeavour of its students. We are also grateful to our overseas student sponsors, who provide their sons or daughters with the opportunity to literally save lives. It has come to my attention, however, that you have not attended a single class in the last 3 months. We are also aware that you have had two previous written notifications about unexplained absence. Our records show that the last classes you attended were Anatomy and Anaesthesiology, in mid-December 2012.

This letter is to notify you that we intend to cancel your association, and study, with this hospital.

St James's prides itself in being both grateful to, and open with, our sponsors. We do not, and never will, accept a sponsor's generosity, if it is not being spent as intended. It is therefore with great regret that I must inform you that unless you return to class immediately, we will assume you have decided to abandon your study.

If there are extenuating circumstances, please contact the Registrar's Office within 5 days and we will be pleased to consider your appeal. If you do not contact us or re-start your course within those 5 days, we will allocate your place to another prospect and write to your sponsor; confirming our decision.'

The letter was signed, but Khatri didn't bother to look at the name. He was too busy re-reading *'and write to your sponsor; confirming our decision'*. He had known this day would come, and no matter how brave he promised he would be, he felt a wave of over-powering guilt and self-loathing bury itself in his gut.

"Five days before they decide to write the letter to my parents. Two days to type it and mail it. Three days for it to arrive... One minute for my family to feel devastated because of my lies", Khatri muttered to himself. *"I was supposed to be on my way to my first million pounds by now, but where am I? Nowhere"*. He shook his head, reflecting on what he had done with his life since he left home.

He shared a rented five-bedroomed Victorian terraced house in the Headingley area of Leeds. His room was on the first floor and was easily the best of the five, with its high ceiling and tiny en-suite. On one side of his bed was a free-standing mirror and a large wardrobe, with a small desk and chair at the other side next to the window, which overlooked Carnegie Stadium. The walls were plain and painted magnolia, with the only personalisation in the room being a set of family photos and a banner for the cricket team he followed; the

Kolkata Knight Riders. Apart from that, a part-share in the Leaf and £1200 in his savings account, Aarav Khatri had nothing and no-one. Tears welled in his eyes as he fell back onto his pillow, surrounded by all his worldly possessions. His only thought now was how he could earn enough money to avoid creating shame and embarrassment for his parents, and a lifetime of spite from his sister. In less than two weeks.

He hauled himself out of bed, drank half-a-litre of water in an attempt to ease his throbbing temples, and then changed for work. He had to pick Ferranti up in less than an hour and, no matter how he felt, he had to keep that lucrative contract. He raced downstairs, grabbed a pain au chocolate from the cupboard, and ran out to the street. As he drove the nine miles to Barwick to collect Ferranti, his mood swung into deeper despair. His body language was that of a despondent man when he finally knocked on Ferranti's front door. He waited for several seconds but could see the curtains were closed and no internal lights shone through the frosted glass of the front door. He was just about to look through the letterbox, when he heard the door being unlocked from the inside. A scruffy but reasonably cheerful Ferranti opened the door, with the usual accompanying aroma of stale alcohol escaping into the fresh outside air.

"Wow, you look how I feel", said Ferranti, squinting through the mid-morning light and seeing Khatri's despondent expression.

"Got any headache pills?" asked Khatri, as he stepped up and into the house. Ferranti was already walking to

the kitchen but stopped and looked back over his shoulder at Khatri. A gentle smile broke out on Ferranti's face, as he replied sarcastically;

"I might have one or two in a cupboard, somewhere. Give me a minute to look", and he walked into the kitchen to get them both some tablets and a glass of water. Khatri glanced around the lounge. An almost empty bottle of whiskey sat on the table, along with an empty tumbler. Next to them were some first aid items and a bloodied hand towel. Khatri recalled seeing the bandage around Ferranti's right hand as he greeted Khatri, but given the problems Khatri had right now, he really didn't have the patience or interest to ask – let alone listen to – what had happened. Ferranti came back out of the kitchen and passed two tablets and a glass of water to Khatri, who gave a weak nod of thanks and swallowed the tablets along with two gulps of water. Ferranti looked on, still smiling, and took his tablets as well.

"So, what were you drinking last night?" asked the amused Ferranti, as he took the now empty glass of water from a grateful Khatri.

"Nothing. I'm just tired and have a lot to think about", Khatri replied, quietly.

"Parent trouble again?" asked Ferranti. Khatri looked up, puzzled at how Ferranti could have guessed. Ferranti could see the question in Khatri's eyes, as if he'd said it out loud. *"It's the only thing I've ever seen you get worried about"*.

Khatri briefly pondered his reply, before realising Ferranti was both right and perhaps far more observant than he had realised. *"Wanna talk about it on the way down?"* offered Ferranti, as he headed upstairs. Khatri didn't respond at first, but he liked the idea. He just wasn't sure how much to tell Ferranti about the letter, but they had discussed his life and aspirations once before, of course, in a lunchtime chat at Pizza Express.

"Ok, if you don't mind hearing about my problems?" enquired Khatri.

"Hey, what are friends for, right?" Ferranti called back from the top of the stairs. Khatri smiled involuntarily. Did Ferranti really just refer to him as his friend? A warm feeling flooded through Khatri's body as, suddenly and surprisingly, he didn't feel quite so alone in facing his challenge. He knew it couldn't be the tablets working that quickly, but his headache felt a little less over-bearing and his mood had definitely lifted. When Ferranti came back downstairs, he looked remarkably fresh-faced and alert. He looked at Khatri.

"Let's go. The counsellor's surgery is open for business", he said, whilst smiling, warmly.

The journey into Leeds city centre was a blur, with Ferranti and Khatri discussing his situation that had been thrown up by the letter. Actually, Khatri did most of the talking and Ferranti mainly listened, whilst providing a few good ideas and helping his friend feel that perhaps there was a way forward after all. As they pulled up outside the Yorkshire Post offices, Khatri turned to Ferranti and said;

"Thank you, Mr Ferranti. You have ...", and a wave of emotion started to well up inside of him. *"You have been a wonderful listener today. Please accept this journey for free, as a gesture of my humble gratitude"*.

Ferranti smiled and opened the rear door. As he got out of the car, he stopped, turned, leant back in.

"Kid, never give your services for free. Besides, you need the money more than I do", he said, as he winked at Khatri. Khatri sniggered in response at the humorous way Ferranti had made the rather critical point. Ferranti started to close the rear door, and then pulled it open again. Leaning back in, he said; *"And it's Adam, not Mr Ferranti"*. And with that, he closed the car door shut and turned to enter his workplace. Khatri had a beaming smile, as he watched Ferranti walk through the reception doors and into the building.

"You are an enigma, Adam Ferranti. Just when I thought I knew you inside out, you present a different hidden side". Khatri was still smiling and shaking his head at how lucky he felt this morning, as the Leaf gently eased away from the pavement.

Chapter 33

PC John Turner was just about to end his shift, which had been remarkably dull to say the least, when his radio crackled into life:

"Come in, 4-7-1-3", the Control Room dispatcher said.

"4-7-1-3", Turner replied into his radio.

"Can you attend an address in the Adel area, please. Report of a possible dead body".

Turner confirmed he could attend and noted the address. He turned on the car's flashing blue lights and sped towards the leafy and very affluent neighbourhood of Adel; carefully weaving in and out of the late afternoon traffic as he drove. Within minutes, he was pulling into the sweeping gravel driveway of a remarkably beautiful house.

"4-7-1-3 to Control", radioed in Turner, as he waited for a response.

"Go ahead, 4-7-1-3", crackled the radio confirmation.

"I'm at the address and am about to enter the property. No sign of SOCO yet, so I'll just secure the scene", said Turner.

"Understood, 4-7-1-3. SOCO say they are close - just working their way through some traffic", came the reply from Control.

"Roger that", said Turner, and he ended the call.

Getting out of the car, Turner walked towards the double-doors of Andrew Jagger's home and suddenly found himself feeling apprehensive. The house was modern, yet it had a kind of dark, gothic grandeur. All the windows had thick, heavy curtains drawn in full, and the front doors were huge and imposing; almost eight feet tall and crafted out of the darkest wood he'd seen. Turner could see that one of the doors was already slightly ajar, so he rapped on it and called out; *"Hello? Police"*. There was no response, so he decided to open the door further.

As he entered the property, in front of him was a grand entrance hall. At the rear of the hall was a huge window that looked out onto a football-field sized and perfectly manicured lawn. Two stairways swept in opposing semi circles up to a spectacular balcony, with another huge window behind it, reaching all the way up to a vaulted ceiling. Turner would have been breathless at its magnificence, had it not been for Andrew Jagger's body, perfectly centred against this magnificent backdrop, suspended by his neck in front of the balustrade of the expansive landing. His arms and legs were held taut by ropes, to create a deeply disturbing star-shaped pose on the balustrade. His trousers were missing, and there was the largest pool of blood Turner had ever seen, gathering on the floor twelve feet below Andrew Jagger's lifeless body.

Turner assumed the body had been there several hours, as blood was no longer dripping from the open wounds, yet Andrew Jagger's eyes seemed to be staring right at him; imploring him to help. There was nothing Turner could do, just as there had been nothing Jagger could do in the moments before his death.

"4-7-1-3 to Control", Turner stammered, with his eyes fixed on Jagger. *"Reported dead body, confirmed"*.

"Understood, 4-7-1-3. SOCO should be with you in less than one minute".

PC John Turner clicked off the radio. He looked up at Jagger's face one more time and then turned away from the morbidly hypnotic scene. He vomited.

Less than an hour later, SOCO had completed their initial sweep of the grid at the house. Once all suspicious items had been tagged and bagged, carefully erected scaffolding was brought in to examine the body in situ, whilst it still hung from the grand balcony. DI Clark attended the scene, along with DC Hobbs. The Lead SOCO, Brian Glazier, provided them both with an update:

"Cause of death appears to be asphyxiation resulting from hanging. We found a bottle and syringe near the body, and what could be a rather clumsy injection point at the back of the neck. You'll need the post-mortem to

confirm if that's what it is, though. If you're looking for a time of death, I'd guess anywhere between 7pm yesterday evening and 4am this morning, but it's only a rough estimate, given the condition of the body. After we checked for prints, we swabbed the bottle – in case the contents were hazardous. Again, I can't say for sure, but indications are that it's an NMB. The Coroner will find out, as there's still some blood in the legs; below where there are cuts to the inner thighs", offered Glazier, in summation.

Neither Clark nor Hobbs knew what 'NMB' meant, so Glazier explained. *"They use NMB's – Neuro Muscular Blockers - in surgery. They help control the muscles, so there's no involuntary spasms. Spasms are never a good thing when a surgeon is about to slice your chest open"*. He winked and smirked at the two detectives, but from their stony-faced expressions, realised SOCO humour didn't necessarily work that well outside of the department.

"Erm, you'll have the full autopsy report within 48 hours", he said; somewhat embarrassed, before shuffling is paperwork, nodding his head at the detectives, and striding back to where his team had gathered.

Hobbs puffed out his cheeks and exhaled. *"Pffff, someone is going to a lot of effort to kill people so the-atrically. I assume we're linking this murder with those of Scargill, Yedlin and Goas, Ma'am?"*

"For now, yes. But let's not forget this could be pure coincidence - or a copycat", said Clark, although she

knew the chances of it being either were incredibly low. *"Any sign of the parcel from the hardware store?"*.

"Yes, Ma'am", Hobbs responded. *"SOCO found it – unopened and laying on its side near the door. They can't say for sure, but damage to the corner of the box is consistent with it being dropped and having rolled; as if someone discarded it in a hurry"*.

"Either that or it was already damaged", Clark replied, as she reflected on the scene that was playing out for them. DS Walker had briefed her on the call she'd had with Alex, so they knew he'd been in the house, specifically so to deliver the box. The question in Clark's mind was, did Alex Walker drop the box because he was rushing to help his friend, or because he was rushing to catch him before murdering him? *"What do we know about Mr Walker's background?"* she asked DC Hobbs, looking to keep a train of thought going.

Hobbs pulled a smartphone from his pocket. *"Got a summary sent to me earlier, Ma'am... one moment, please"*. He scanned the phone for a text and read it aloud to Clark. *"Male model. Very successful until recently, but NCA says he currently has credit card debts of over £350k. Prior to that, a period in professional sports until his rib injury and, before that..."*, Hobbs paused as he re-read the final line of the text. He looked up at Clark and said, *"He was a trainee paramedic"*.

Clark raised her eyebrows in surprise. *"Was he know? I think I want to talk to Mr Walker"*.

Chapter 34

As soon as she'd seen Alex on the CCTV, DS Walker knew the likely outcome of any discussion with DI Clark. Once it was then confirmed that Andrew Jagger was dead, and that the parcel at the crime scene appeared to be the one that Alex had collected from the retirement home linked to the evidence of the prior murders, she knew she would have to be removed from the HMET investigation immediately.

In the surprisingly supportive meeting, however, Clark showed a lot of compassion for the situation Stephanie Walker found herself in. She even agreed to allow Walker to go with the team that would bring Alex in for questioning; thus, hopefully managing any volatility in such a tense situation. This was an extraordinary gesture by Clark. Walker knew her superior was putting herself in a vulnerable position by approving this, and so vowed she would take a few days off work as soon as her husband was in custody. She was just about to thank DI Clark when Hobbs knocked on the door. Clark sighed and waved him in.

"What is it, Detective Constable Hobbs?" asked Clark, seemingly a little annoyed at the interruption.

"Apologies, Ma'am, but I thought you should both see this immediately". He dropped a copy of a tabloid

newspaper on the desk in front of them. Clark and Walker looked down at the headline blazed across the front page:

'*Dead Businessman Was Under-Age Predator*'.

Underneath the headline was a slightly fuzzy image – a still from a video. It showed the back of a naked man, whose head was turned towards the camera. He had a broad smile on his face. It was apparent that there was a naked female underneath the man, but only a leg, an arm and some long blonde hair were visible. The beaming face belonged to Andrew Jagger. Walker and Clark looked up at each other, and then across to Hobbs.

"The article states that the Editor received a video from an anonymous source, yesterday", explained Hobbs. *"They claim that, in the video, Jagger admits he's having sex with a 14-year old girl. They also go on to report that, sadly, he will never be brought to justice, as Police found his dead body this morning. According to a 'Police source', he died in a bizarre and intricate sex-related suicide"*.

Hobbs looked at Walker and Clark, waiting for an explosive reaction. Instead he was surprised when Clark looked at Walker, with a somewhat sympathetic expression, and just said;

"You'd best go now. Take two uniformed officers with you".

Walker looked at Clark and pursed her lips, then nodded slowly, before turning and walking out of the office. As she passed Hobbs, she only gave him a quick glance, but he could see tears welling in her eyes. Hobbs looked over to Clark, in a silent plea for her to explain what was happening. Clark just stared back and, in a softer tone than he had ever heard from her, she said, *"Get me that video tape"*. Hobbs nodded to her, and then turned to catch up with Walker. She was scribbling something on a piece of paper at a desk.

"Hobbs, get two uniformed officers to meet me at this address", she barked, throwing the scrap of paper in his direction, whilst trying to hide her real emotions behind an assertive façade. As determined as she tried to be, Stephanie Walker was struggling with the situation. It wasn't that she felt guilty bringing Alex in for question-ing; just surprised that she felt some compassion towards her usually abusive husband.

The drive to the apartment complex took Walker 15 minutes. When she arrived, two uniformed officers were already parked outside, waiting. She briefed the officers and explained that she would take the lead as they entered the apartment, but that they must remain visible and within earshot at all times. Walker did not want any possible accusation of her perverting the course of justice as this played out.

As they entered the lift in the residential complex, the uniformed officers glanced at each other, quizzically, as Walker slid a security card into the reader that allowed them to travel to the luxury penthouse apartment. Their expressions were that of incredulity once they entered the expansive home of Stephanie Walker. Neither of them said it, but they were both wondering how a newly-promoted Detective Sergeant could afford such luxury. Their questions were answered when they saw Alex Walker. Both of them recognised him immediately from previous billboard campaigns they had seen dotted around the city, although neither was expecting to see him in such a dishevelled state right now.

"Alex", said Stephanie, softly but firmly. He turned to look at his wife and saw that she was not alone. He was expecting her, but quickly realised they must be there to take him in for questioning. He suddenly felt betrayed.

"Why are they here?" he asked. *"I thought you wanted me to come home so we could talk, and then you could help explain what had happened? Instead, you've got these two with you?"* His voice switched from sounding hurt to sounding angry. His speech was also slightly slurred; partly from the physical and emotional fatigue of the last 24 hours, but Alex Walker also held a large dram of whiskey in his hand... and probably held several others already in his stomach.

"Alex, I can't talk to you alone. That would mean your defence and my involvement would be deemed compromised and inadmissible as evidence", explained Stephanie. She spoke to him with the gentle, supportive tone of a wife. He, however, just heard the phrase 'your defence' and immediately became aggressive.

"Defence? Why do I need a defence?" he asked, angrily. He stared at the two officers and then glared at his wife.

"You think I killed Jaggs, don't you? You think I'm a fucking murderer?!" The animosity in his voice was increasing with every word.

"No, no of course I don't, Alex. But I have to be impartial, so no-one can suggest I'm covering anything up". She moved towards him and held out an assuring hand.

"What is there to cover up? You fucking bitch! All you're interested in is your career. Fuck me, I'm just an innocent victim of circumstance, but you're already judge, jury and fucking executioner, aren't you?" He slapped his wife's hand away, scowling at the uniformed officers as they both took a step forward.

"What do you two think you're doing?" he snarled. Stephanie Walker looked behind her and held up her hand to indicate that the officers should stop. They both did, but one of them spoke up;

"Come on, Mr Walker, we all want to avoid a scene. We just want to ask you some questions down at the station", the officer said. Whilst this was intended to calm the situation, it inadvertently added to the tension.

"You're going to stick me in the back of a Police car, like a common criminal, you mean?" replied Alex, who was clearly furious at the thought. He turned his attention back on his wife. He stood tall and glared down at her. Stephanie Walker had seen this look before and reacted just in time as Alex Walker made a lunge for her. The uniformed officers didn't need an

instruction. They instinctively raced forwards and caught Alex off-balance. They slammed him onto the floor and put him in an arm-lock. Alex struggled and, at first, started to swear and thrash. *"Get off me, you bastards! I wasn't going to do anything. Fuck!"*

Alex Walker squirmed and flexed, as the officers tried to apply the plastic constraints around his thick wrists. Stephanie Walker could see her husband's face was red with rage. He twisted his neck to look directly at her.

"What the hell are you doing? Why are you doing this?" he yelled, and his expression turned from anger to one of submissive confusion. His tone softened measurably, as his eyes caught those of Stephanie's. *"Steph? Please, I'll come quietly. Just stop them and I'll answer any questions you have"*. But Stephanie Walker wasn't falling for the fake charm. She had believed him far too often in the past, only to then see him become angry and return to his abusive ways. She turned away from him.

"Steph?" he pleaded, but when there was no reply, the burning rage returned.

"STEPH!" he roared, as his mood darkened. He began to struggle again, with his muscular frame pushing back against the arm-lock. One officer had her knee pressed into his back, but he pushed her aside as he managed to stand up. He then pulled the other officer towards him and, with his free arm, knocked the officer backwards onto the sofa. The power of the blow from Alex meant the officer fell awkwardly. His taser, handcuffs and baton came free from their supposedly secure holders

and went skidding across the floor. Alex Walker gathered himself and towered over the scene, menacingly.

Suddenly, the air fizzed and four darts slammed into Alex Walker's back. An electric current raced through the copper wires and sent his muscles into spasm. Stephanie Walker held the taser that had just discharged. As her husband fell to the floor, the look of determination on her face dissolved, as she dropped to her knees. She was drained of all her temporary resilience. She knew what he was physically capable of, and, as the compassion waned and the contempt for her abusive husband rose, a little part of her felt satisfied that she'd had the opportunity to bring him down.

"Feel the pain, you bastard", she muttered to herself, quietly.

As the officers took control of the situation again, Stephanie Walker called DI Clark, and then DC Hobbs, to say that she was taking a few days off. She told them where she would be if they needed to contact her. She couldn't stay in the apartment, but she knew the perfect place she could go and be completely anonymous for a long weekend.

Chapter 35

Adam Ferranti had taken the advice of DI Clark to lay low, but rather than take refuge in a Police secure house, he decided he needed some time away from Yorkshire. He hired a car and toured the North West, before finally spending a few nights at a hotel in the Lake District. He didn't drive often, but he was adept at what he liked to call driving on the wrong side of the road.

He booked into a hotel in Grasmere and spent most evenings sitting in the beautifully named 'Poet's Bar', reading a book called The New Few. On his fourth and final night in the hotel, a familiar face appeared. Ferranti was sitting in his usual cosy corner, with his book in his hand, and a small glass of red wine sat, untouched, on the small table next to him. His peripheral vision registered that someone had flopped down in the chair opposite. He didn't bother to look up, as he assumed a fellow resident was taking a seat. There was no need for him to expect a visitor.

"Well, well. Look who it is", said a woman's voice, sarcastically. Ferranti glanced up from his book, to see who the person was talking to. He did a double-take, as he realised a tipsy Stephanie Walker had sat at his table and was now talking directly to him. He paused, stunned at the coincidence.

"*Detective Walker*", he said, with more than a hint of surprise, but acknowledging her presence. "*It's a... surprise but a pleasure to see you again*". He carefully folded the corner of the page he was reading and placed the book down on the table. He smiled at Walker, who was staring back at him with no obvious expression. "*Enjoying a tipple, I see*", he added, in an attempt to enter into some sort of conversation. She blinked a couple of times, as her brain slowly processed what he was saying. Then she smiled and said, sarcastically;

"*Well, my husband seems to think being drunk is an acceptable way to live, but look at who I'm talking to. Preaching to the converted, aren't I?*". She raised her glass into the air and said "*Cheers*", before chuckling at her own joke, and then taking a swig of her drink.

Ferranti ignored the obvious taunt and sat back in the armchair; interlocking his fingers and resting his hands in his lap. He waited for Walker's glazed eyes to re-focus on him, and then mockingly asked, "*So, do you come here often?*"

Walker guffawed at the joke and decided to play along. "*You'll be asking me 'What's a girl like you doing in a place like this?' next, Mr Ferranti*", and she laughed at her own joke, again.

Ferranti smiled. "*You're far too intelligent to fall for that kind of line*".

Walker stopped laughing and looked at him. She seemed to be considering how to respond, and a warmth appeared in her expression. *"Thank you, Mr Ferranti. It's been a while since a man in my life said that to me - even if it was meant as a joke"*. They both now felt a little uncomfortable at where the sentiment in the conversation seemed to be heading.

"I was just about to get another drink", lied Ferranti, in an attempt to break the tension. His glass of red wine still sat untouched in the middle of the table. Walker looked at her own rather more empty glass and nodded her head.

"I think another one would be good", she said, and her gaze caught Ferranti's.

To further relax the situation, Ferranti added, *"And it's Adam, please. Mr Ferranti sounds like I'm being interviewed"*.

Walker smiled a little wider at the joke and, like a shy schoolgirl, responded in the same manner. *"It's Stephanie"*. She then looked at her glass and added, *"And mine's a vodka and orange juice. Just go easy on the orange juice"*. Neither wanted to admit it, but their pupils started to dilate.

Ferranti rose and walked over to the bar. As he ordered Walker another drink and got himself a Diet Coke, he looked over at his guest. She had picked up the book he had been reading and seemed pleasantly surprised in his choice. Ferranti added the drinks to his tab and eased himself back into his seat opposite Stephanie Walker.

"You like politics?" he asked, indicating that he had seen Walker pick up the book.

"Not really, but the book offers an interesting insight into who might hold the real power and influence over society. And it's not the politicians, thank goodness", Walker replied.

Now it was Ferranti's turn to be impressed. He put Walker's drink down on the table and took a sip of his Diet Coke before resting back in the armchair. Walker looked inquisitively at Ferranti's drink. He looked at the glass, and then back at Walker. *"Rum and Coke - easy on the rum"*, he lied.

They sat in silence for a moment, savouring their drinks. Ferranti broached the elephant in the room first by asking, *"Are we allowed to be talking to one another?"*

Walker's face saddened a little as she replied, *"Sure. I'm no longer on the case and we're not talking about anything to do with it, anyway, are we?"*

"I'm pleased that we can keep on talking, then", said Ferranti. Now it was his turn to raise a glass and say, *"Cheers"*.

For the next 90 minutes, Adam Ferranti and Stephanie Walker spoke about many things; from the weather, to the book, and even their favourite places to go on holiday. Both agreed that the Lake District was beautiful, even when it was pouring with rain. Stephanie

Walker remained tipsy, even after downing a strong coffee at the end of the evening. Adam Ferranti remained completely sober. He had not touched alcohol all evening, or any evening that week, despite the constant presence of a glass of red wine at his table.

As the barman called time and the residents finished their drinks, Walker and Ferranti sighed a happy sigh. They'd had the most relaxing evening either of them had experienced in months, and they'd both thoroughly enjoyed it. They left the bar area and stood at the bottom of the stairs, with Stephanie looking to head up to her 1st floor room, and Ferranti facing in the direction of his own room on the ground floor.

"Thank you for an entertaining evening, Stephanie", said Ferranti. *"It was a very pleasant way to end my final night here"*.

Walker smiled and responded in agreement. *"And it was nice to talk to you too, Adam. It's nice to be respected as an intelligent woman. Thank you"*. Her words were genuine, as was her smile. They stood for a moment, before Ferranti broke the silence.

"Right, well I'm along here, so goodnight, Stephanie".

Walker nodded, and was about to turn to head up the stairs when impulse took over. She leaned forward and kissed Ferranti on the cheek. He blushed and she became quite shy in response, but she looked into his eyes and said, *"Sleep tight"*.

Ferranti watched her go upstairs and disappear out of sight, before turning down the corridor and entering his bedroom.

As he shut the door and went to turn on the light, an arm wrapped round his neck and a blade pressed firmly against the side of his throat. Ferranti slowly and carefully put his arms up, as if to signal that he surrendered, but then he swiftly dropped his left arm and swung his elbow low into his attacker's gut. The man with the knife bent over double, releasing his grip and dropping the blade, such was the speed and power of the blow. Ferranti, however, did not stoop to pick up the knife. Instead, he straightened his shirt and stared at the intruder.

The attacker slowly rose to his feet and looked at Ferranti. Both men started to smile.

"*That was poor*", said Ferranti.

"*I was being gentle - unlike you!*" said the man, removing his mask and ruffling his hair. Ferranti picked up the blade, closed it and handed it back. His visitor nodded, in gratitude.

"*We need to talk*", he said, sounding serious. "*McBride is close to finding the truth, and faster than we thought. I think he's getting inside information from that Met guy - DS Denton*".

Chapter 36

Simon McBride sat in his office, staring blankly out of a window that overlooked the Thames and Lambeth Bridge. His mind was elsewhere. On his desk was a slip of paper, with the handwritten English translation of the voice message left on Ricardo Goas's answering machine. He had been in an open discussion earlier today with a group of the smartest thinkers in MI5. They didn't know why they were in the room – protocol dictated that McBride didn't have to give them context – but they were asked to create theories about what the message could mean.

"What if 'three seas' is in reference to a trio of people, who each represent one of three seas in question?" proffered one attendee. *"A Bengali, an Indian, and an Arab? A terrorist meeting, perhaps?"*

"Chances of finding any match is a trillion to one, unless there's a piece of intelligence that ties them all together", countered McBride, despondently.

"Kanyakumari is also known as 'Thriveni Sangamam'. Could that be an anagram of a place or a person they need to meet there?" suggested another attendee. McBride seemed a little more interested in that offering, but not much. As more random theories were generated,

he began to grow weary, so he excused himself from the session. He knew the process they would go through; generating more theories, before spending much of the afternoon on their databases, disproving each and every one of them.

McBride looked out at the throng of people who swarmed over Lambeth Bridge, heading home at the end of the day. He noticed a cyclist pulling an advert trailer across the bridge. As he watched the cyclist reach the end of the bridge and turned right, the poster on the trailer came into sight. McBride was mesmerised:

'Supporting people with learning difficulties and/or mental health challenges, through supported living and social inclusion. A joint initiative across Southwark, Lewisham, Greenwich, Newham and Redbridge. Control and Choice in the Community'

In the bottom right of the poster was a logo. It depicted the same three letters, overlapping. Underneath it, it read, *'Three Cs'*. McBride slowly sat upright as he recalled a recent - if fuzzy - memory from this morning. His brain worked frantically as he turned to his desk. He rifled through a pile of papers in his tray and some on his desk. He then pushed them all aside and reached under his desk for his confidential waste bin. He held it up, in both hands, and stared at the lock. If he broke it, questions would be asked, so he picked up his phone.

"Hello, Facilities? This is Simon McBride in office third-west-seven. I need someone to unlock my confidential waste bin.... yes please... well it seems I've

dropped something in that I now want to review... yes, it was careless of me". That last sentence was said through gritted teeth, as he hated to admit a fault. *"Thank you"*, he said to the voice on the other end of the phone, before placing the receiver down.

Ten minutes later, a facilities manager arrived and unlocked the bin. McBride tipped the receptacle upside down and the paperwork from inside cascaded out onto his desk. He sifted through the pile and there it was. A satisfied smile spread across his face. He felt he now knew what the message meant. All he had to do was confirm his suspicions and the net would start to close.

Chapter 37

Ferranti and the night-time visitor talked for nearly an hour in the small ground floor room of the hotel in Grasmere. It was clear that McBride was a lot closer to the HMET case than they had originally thought. They felt sure their assumption that someone senior in the investigation was leaking information to him, was correct.

"So, you're saying Denton has a history with McBride?" asked Ferranti. *"What about DS Walker? Anything there?"* The visitor shook his head. *"I only ask because she's off the case, now. I wondered if that might slow McBride down"*, explained Ferranti.

"I think I need to create a distraction", said the visitor. *"Something to confuse or delay the work of the HMET. Something that will either slow McBride down or perhaps mislead him entirely"*.

"Or something to make them focus on McBride instead, perhaps?" added Ferranti. *"We need to plug the leak - and fast. I have to get the proposed expose in front of my editor. I can't face the failure of 1996 all over again"*.

* * *

What happened in 1996 had actually all started in 1995. Adam Ferranti was already making a name for himself within the Washington Post, when he approached the editor, Seth Athenberg, to talk about collusion between senior British Intelligence operatives and their counterparts in the States. Ferranti felt he had evidence that they were trading state secrets for personal gain. Athenberg encouraged Ferranti to run with his proposed expose, giving him access to some highly connected and influential people in his own business network.

For months, Ferranti painstakingly gathered enough pieces of the jigsaw to create what seemed to be the perfect storm. He had evidence to hand to the Justice Department, just before going to press with the article and re-establishing The Washington Post as the premier newspaper in the country. After he felt he had enough information of both historical and possibly current illegal activity, he presented it all to Seth Athenberg in late 1995. Upon seeing the proposed article and supporting evidence, Athenberg engaged a private risk analysis firm – Politico-Risk Inc - in an attempt to establish the impact of the findings. Going straight in at the top, both he and Ferranti met with the CEO – Callum Dennison.

A Senior Risk Analyst - a young woman called Nikki Griffiths – was also present at the meeting. It wasn't hard to see that she was talented, astute and ambitious, with aspirations of her own of entering mainstream politics. It was her energy and her commitment to working extraordinarily long hours that meant the analysis on the impact of the expose, on the United States and Great Britain, was ready within three weeks.

When presenting their report back to Athenberg and Ferranti, Callum Dennison announced the expose as the story of the decade; bigger than Watergate, in terms of the tremors it could send through the American political system and beyond. Athenberg and Ferranti planned the next steps and, with the newspaper owner's direct blessing, were on the verge of publishing the article. It never went to press, though.

Athenberg had been sitting in his office late one night, finalising the front page for the first paper of the new year. Two senior officials from the FBI – together with the newspaper owner - walked into his office. It was a short and succinct meeting with a clear ultimatum.

"Print the article and go to jail, or pull the article in the interests of national security and hand over all your evidence to the FBI right now", said one of the feds.

Athenberg never knew whether the newspaper owner or Callum Dennison was responsible for leaking the news to the authorities, but it didn't really matter. He knew Ferranti would be devastated at the news.

At the same time, Ferranti was waking up from an alcohol-infused snooze. He had been out celebrating as it felt like an almost unbearable weight had been lifted from his shoulders. He awoke in a hotel room; surrounded by empty champagne bottles and wrapped around a naked woman he plainly didn't recognise. The phone was ringing. It was his friend and fellow journalist, Josh Lucas.

"Man, everyone is trying to get hold of you", panted Lucas, before Ferranti could hear him shouting back across the Washington Post offices, *"I've found him!"* Lucas turned his attention back to Ferranti. *"Adam, Athenberg needs you down here - now!"* Lucas was sounding more than slightly exasperated, but Ferranti just rubbed his head and closed his eyes, trying to understand what he had missed.

Ferranti understood the principle of what was being said to him, but he'd never spoken to any witnesses in any court case. *"I don't understand...?"* he mumbled.

Lucas lowered his voice and whispered down the phone. *"Athenberg is in his office right now, screaming at a couple of Feds who were asking for you and him. You'd better get down here"*.

Ferranti had heard enough. He slammed the receiver down and sat, contemplating.

His hungover mind was still trying to process what he'd been told, as he marched into Athenberg's office, just after midnight. His editor was sitting at his desk, head bowed, and hands resting on the back of his neck. He looked exhausted and defeated. As Ferranti closed the office door behind him, Athenberg looked up and slowly said, *"I'm so sorry, Adam. I tried"*.

Ferranti could see tears in his boss's eyes, as Athenberg regaled the events of the previous two hours.

"That article was a Pulitzer Prize offering", concluded Athenberg. *"And you'll produce another one, soon.*

You're that damn good, Adam". Athenberg had nothing else to offer in way of explanation, as Ferranti raged and wept, and then raged again. Eventually, Ferranti felt his shoulders slump in exhaustion and defeat. He looked down at the floor for a few seconds, before he turned and walked quietly out of the office, out of the building, and into the nearest late-night bar.

"So, what will it be?" asked the bartender.

"Open a bottle of Jack, and don't put it away", said Ferranti, slamming down a fistful of cash. The bartender did as he was asked.

When Ferranti requested his sixth double, the bartender said *"You look like you've had a long day my man?"*. Ferranti fumbled to get more cash out of his pocket, but the bartender shook his head. *"This one's on me. You look like you need a lucky break, so enjoy this one and then maybe you need to sleep it off. I'm sure tomorrow will bring a new perspective"*.

Ferranti knew this was true. He drank the final whiskey in a single swig, put the glass down on the bar, and thanked the bartender. *"Time to disappear for a while"*, he thought to himself.

* * *

"You okay?" asked his night-time visitor, aware that Ferranti's attention had clearly drifted.

"Hmm? What? Oh, yeah. Sorry. I was just thinking about ... stuff. Where were we?" questioned Ferranti, apologetically.

"A diversion or something, to buy a little more time", replied the man.

"I have an idea", said Ferranti, and he took out a digital Dictaphone.

Five minutes later, when the idea was in motion, Ferranti smiled and said, *"Ok, that will be useful. Now, you find out what you can from the investigation and McBride, and I'll look a little closer to home"*. With that, Ferranti focused back on the task at hand.

The men shook hands, then hugged, before the visitor left via the ground floor window in Ferranti's room. Ferranti sat in silence on the bed, contemplating what to do next. He suddenly found the room a little suffocating and felt the urge to go for a midnight walk. He needed to clear his brain and assess his options.

Having dressed appropriately for the cool, damp night air, he left the room and exited the hotel via the front door. He shivered as the chill nipped around his face, and he decided to zip the jacket completely closed. As he was doing so, a quiet voice said, *"Sobering up, or just restless?"*

Ferranti looked to his right and saw Stephanie Walker, huddled in a thick padded full-length coat on a bench, outside the hotel entrance.

"Restless", he replied. *"You?"*

Stephanie Walker laughed nervously and said, *"Both"*.

"I'm thinking of going for a short walk. Care to join me?" asked Ferranti.

Walker thought for a moment and then looked up at Ferranti, smiled softly, and said, *"Sure"*. She rose from the bench and they set-off down the wide gravel driveway and into the sleepy village of Grasmere.

Chapter 38

The pair didn't say a great deal for the first few minutes of their walk, until Ferranti asked, *"Mind me asking what's making you restless? After all, I don't need to ask you why you need to sober up"*. They both smirked as they glanced at each other.

"Are you always this charming, Mr Ferranti - sorry ... Adam?" enquired Walker.

"Oh, I think you know I can be an asshole. I mean you were in the interview room the first time we met, right?" joked Ferranti. Walker smiled weakly, but it wasn't natural. Ferranti spotted the change in her expression and said, *"Sorry. Wasn't wanting to talk about the case... Just letting you know I can be self-aware... Stephanie"*.

Walker looked up and smiled gratefully, saying, *"Not a problem"*.

They continued to walk in silence towards the lights of the village half a mile away. Without looking at Ferranti, Walker said, *"Ever think you know someone, only to find out they're not what you thought they were... Not what you hoped they were?"*

Ferranti looked perplexed. He didn't look at Walker, but said, *"We still talking about me?"*

Walker gave a short laugh and looked at her companion. *"No, not you. Someone close; someone you felt you could trust with anything and everything"*. Her tone of voice became melancholy.

Ferranti didn't say anything immediately, but then offered, *"Yes. Sounds very familiar to discover that about someone"*. His voice had lost its playful tone. He sounded a little downcast now, too.

They continued their stroll in momentary silence, before Walker probed a little deeper. *"Your wife? Girlfriend?"* then held up her hand in apology, hastily adding, *"You don't have to say. Sorry, that was wrong of me to pry. I ..."*, but Ferranti took her hand and gently lowered it with an assuring, almost affectionate, squeeze.

"It's okay. My father. Well, stepfather, to be exact. My real dad died when I was really young, and my Mum tried to cope with the grief and with me on her own. I wasn't the easiest kid to bring-up, surprisingly". He smiled, reflectively. *"But, after a few years, she started to date this guy who seemed great at first. He adored my Mum and paid enough attention to me. He didn't buy my affection, nor did he starve me of respect"*. Ferranti's expression grew darker. *"It's a long and complicated story, but my mum suffered from some injuries she'd received at his hands. She'd made it through a series of operations, but never really recovered, in many ways. She passed away several years afterwards, having never quite got back to her normal self"*.

Walker stopped. She had a look of empathetic sadness on her face, and she rested her hand on Ferranti's shoulder; returning the soft affectionate squeeze of assurance that he'd given her. Ferranti took a deep breath and sighed, before starting to stroll again. Walker matched his steps.

Ferranti glanced over at Walker and said, *"And your story? Again, no need to share if you don't want to"*.

Oddly, Walker found herself torn between not wanting to bare her soul, and somehow feeling that she and Ferranti had more in common than she ever expected. *"Err, just … well let's just say your story struck a few chords"*, she proffered. Ferranti didn't probe, but he instinctively knew Walker was talking about domestic violence.

"Isn't violence an everyday risk in your line of work?" he asked.

"Not as much as the TV cop shows would have you believe", she replied, smiling.

Not wanting to probe into her private life, but not wishing her feel that he didn't care, Ferranti pushed on. *"It's tough when it's someone you love or loved. I'm so sorry"*.

They walked a few more paces and Stephanie Walker stopped, turned to Ferranti and said, *"I feel like a drink. I have some vodka in my room – but no ice. But there's two glasses, so… "*, and she screwed her nose up, as if in an apology about the ice. She found herself really hoping Ferranti would say yes. He pretended to be disappointed at the faux pas of no ice, but the corners of his mouth turned into a smile, and he accepted Walker's invitation. They returned to the hotel and Walker led the way up to her room. It was smaller than Ferranti's, so they had to sit on the edge of the bed. Walker poured two large vodkas and handed one to her guest.

They talked for over an hour and, without sharing any of the specific details, Walker felt that Ferranti seemed to 'get' her story. His responses were empathetic and it felt as if she was talking to a close friend, as he listened intently. He didn't seem to have the time to touch his vodka.

As the clock showed 3am, Walker was becoming sleepy and Ferranti announced that he had an early start. As they stood, Walker was a little unsteady on her feet and Ferranti held out an arm, to steady her. She held onto his hand and said, *"Thank you. Oopsie"*, but then, she didn't let go.

Ferranti didn't pull away either. It wasn't awkward in the slightest and Ferranti gently placed his other hand on her waist, as if to steady her further, saying, *"You can let go ... if you want to"*.

Walker stared into Ferranti's eyes and whispered, *"I don't want to."*. She took a half-step back, towards the bed, still holding his hand. She pulled Ferranti closer and, after a momentary hesitation, she kissed him gently once, and then again. He didn't resist. They fell into a long, soft, emotionally-fuelled kiss and, slowly, she sat down on the bed, pulling him down with her. Ferranti began to undo the buttons on her blouse. She didn't stop him.

As they continued to undress each other, Ferranti winced. Walker checked, in case he was having second thoughts, but he assured her that he wasn't. *"You just caught my forearm"*, he said, showing her the bandage he was wearing. *"Burnt my arm on a kettle at home. Guess I don't heal as well as I used to"*.

"Then I'll kiss it better", said Walker, and began to kiss the bandage gently. She slowly worked her way up his arm, to his neck and chest.

The rest of night was spent in the sort of warm, soft, all-consuming sex Stephanie Walker wished she could still have with the man she married; except the Alex Walker of today couldn't have been further from her mind. In fact, at this moment, she didn't care whether she ever saw him again.

Chapter 39

Less than 24 hours ago, Alex Walker was lying on the floor of his luxury apartment, having been tasered by his own wife, DS Stephanie Walker. When he had been given the all-clear from possible after-effects and complications, he suffered the humiliation of being led from their palatial home, in handcuffs, and put into the back of a fully-emblazoned police car. He saw at least three people get their mobile phones out and take photos or videos of the scene unfolding.

Once they arrived at Millgarth Police station, Alex had had to sit in the charge room next to a drug addict and a drunk. Both stank of urine and both were aggressive. He spent the night in a holding cell, cold and dishevelled, until he was taken to an interview room the next morning.

Alex Walker sat down, and two officers took their positions at either side of the door. Two minutes later, DI Clark and DC Hobbs entered the room. Clark nodded to the two officers, who then left.

"Mr Walker", said Clark; *"I'm Detective Inspector Angela Clark and this is Detective Constable Mike Hobbs. I'm going to record this interview... do you understand?"*

Alex nodded, and Hobbs turned on the recorder.

"Monday 11th March, 2013, at 07:40. Interview with Alex Walker. This is DI Clark. In the room with me is DC Hobbs. Mr Walker has been informed of his rights but, at this moment, has declined the right to a solicitor being present", stated DI Clark.

"Mr Walker, can you tell me anything of your whereabouts since last Thursday?" asked DC Hobbs.

"Sure. Last week, I spent most days making calls to agents and dealing with some private matters; before I...". Walker's voice faltered. He knew what he was going to say next. *"Before I met with Jaggs, collected a parcel for him, and took it to his house".* His lip trembled and he looked down at his hands, which were resting in his lap. He was struggling to compose himself for what was to come.

"And, for the record, can you confirm this gentleman's full name?" Hobbs asked, in a flat matter-of-fact tone.

"Andrew Jagger", mumbled Walker.

"For the record", stated Hobbs, *"Mr Walker confirms the name as Andrew Jagger. Mr Walker, why were you delivering a parcel to Mr Jagger?"* Hobbs continued.

"He asked me to", responded Walker.

"When did he ask you?" enquired Hobbs.

"A day or so before. I can't think, I'm exhausted. We met at Angelica's for coffee. He asked me to collect the parcel as a favour. He said it was needed urgently, but he didn't have the time to collect it himself".

"Who's Angelica?" enquired Clark.

Walker looked up at her, confused. "It's a bar, not a person", he responded, almost scornfully, thinking 'How does she not know that – everyone in Leeds knows that'.

"Did Mr Jagger tell you what was in the parcel?" asked Hobbs.

"He said it was some stuff for a photo shoot, and they – whoever they are - were due to fly out in the next few days with it". Walker was starting to sound weary of their questions. Surely, they couldn't really think he had killed Jaggs?

"Were you not curious? Didn't you ask?" quizzed Clark. "What if it had been drugs?"

Walker tilted his head to one side and stared at Clark. He couldn't believe she had asked such a bold question. He snorted in derision. He started to shake his head and just said, "No. Never. Jaggs is the most above-board bloke I know".

"When did you take the parcel to Mr Jagger's house?" interjected Hobbs, aware of the rising tension between DI Clark and Alex Walker.

"Saturday night", said Alex, still looking at Clark and becoming even more irked. Why were they questioning him, rather than looking for the real killer?

"Please tell me, in your own time, what happened when you got to Mr Jagger's house on Saturday night".

Walker's weariness suddenly disappeared. The images of that night started to flood back into his memory. His eyes began to well with tears, as he prepared to re-live the evening. He paused, as if returning to the scene in his mind.

"I arrived around 7pm. All the lights were on, as usual - he liked it bright, did Jaggs", said Walker, smiling gently at the thought of his friend. *"I got out of the van, knocked on the door, and then went back to get the parcel out of the back of the van"*.

"Go on", said Hobbs.

"Jaggs opened the door. I went in and we walked through to the kitchen and had a bit of a chat. He said he had guests coming, so he didn't want to be rude, but could I put the package back in the hall and leave". He glanced at Hobbs, who he felt was the more amiable of the two detectives, and added, *"He has a bad back – he had a bad back, rather"*. Walker paused, as he came to terms with having to use the past tense about his friend, Andrew Jagger.

"How did that make you feel? Being asked to leave so quickly by a supposed friend?" asked Hobbs.

"A bit weird, to be honest. I used to be the person who got invited to Jaggs' house for his events". Alex looked down in reflection and then back up at Hobbs, with a slightly guilty expression: *"I told him as much and... well, he was dismissive. That's not like Jaggs at all, but he just said, 'Yeah, well that was how it used to be before', and then he apologised. He said he'd talk to me properly later"*.

"And then you left?" Hobbs checked. Walker nodded. Hobbs confirmed that was the case, for the recording.

"Would you say Mr Jagger seemed on edge when you were there, Mr Walker?" Clark enquired.

Walker thought for a moment and then said, *"Yes. Yes, I would. Jaggs rarely got nervous - even when the big deals were being negotiated"*. Walker hadn't really thought about Jaggs's behaviour at the time. His mind had been focused mainly on his own feelings of disappointment and awkwardness.

"So, Mr Jagger was alive when you left. Was that the last time you saw him?" challenged Clark.

Alex snapped out of his reflective moment and looked up at Clark. With the sadness on his face reflected in his voice, he answered, *"No. That wasn't the last time I saw Jaggs"*.

Clark and Hobbs waited, in silence, for Walker to continue.

"A couple of hours later, around 10:30 that night, he called me. He sounded upset and frightened. He was almost pleading for me to come back, but it just didn't sound like the Jaggs I knew. He sounded like a little boy, afraid, but trying to sound calm and cool". Walker was looking at both Clark and Hobbs, as if needing them to say they understood how difficult this was for him; for signs that they believed him.

"What did he say, exactly?", asked Hobbs.

"He said 'Alex, please come back. I need you here, urgently. Please', but sort of like someone who is desperately trying to sound calm, but actually wanting to cry. I'll never forget that call". Alex's eyes had a haunted look. That call was going to be a recurring nightmare for the rest of his days.

"And what happened then, Alex?" asked Hobbs, his voice soft and encouraging, as if it was Walker who was now the frightened little boy. Alex sniffed and wiped a tear from his eye. He swallowed hard and then began to talk, staring only at the table throughout the recollection.

"I got there around 11pm. All the curtains were closed and the only lights I could see were from the hallway. I could tell they were on, because the front door was slightly open. I just knew something wasn't right, so I went up to the door and shouted to Jaggs. There was no answer. I pushed the door open, wider, and looked inside. That's when...". Alex Walker buried his head in his hands. He stayed in that position for nearly a

minute; his body gently rocking as he sobbed quietly into the palms of his hands.

Hobbs passed a small pack of tissues across the table, leaving them just in front of Walker. Walker glanced up and pulled the packet under the table, with a tearful but heartfelt, *"Thank you"*. Alex Walker cleaned his face and blew his nose. He finally composed himself and then looked up, embarrassed.

"Are you alright to continue, Alex?" asked Hobbs, sounding genuine and concerned. Walker nodded. He took a few more seconds for deep breaths, and then, tissue in hand, he re-started the recollection.

"Jaggs was hanging from the balcony; strung out in a star-shape. I ran towards the stairs, bumping into the box I'd delivered earlier; kicking it over. I didn't know what to do, really, but I ran up the stairs and reached to try to free one of his arms, in case he was still alive and could undo the ropes. But as soon as I grasped the rope that held his left arm, there was some sharp wire that slashed my fingertips and palms. I then tried the same with rope holding his neck, but the same thing happened. That's when I saw the note". He stopped, ashamed of what he would have to admit next.

Clark and Hobbs quickly turned to look at each other, before Clark asked, firmly, *"What note?"*

Walker drew a deep breath and said, *"There was a note on the balcony, addressed to Whom It May Concern. I opened it, thinking it was a note from*

Jaggs, but it wasn't. Someone had written a note, with my name at the bottom, saying I had killed Jaggs because he had destroyed my life". He gulped, audibly, and then confessed. *"I ran. I ran out on my friend, because I didn't want to be thought of as a murderer. I thought about asking Steph what to do, but all I could imagine was her calling me a murderer and throwing me in jail. So, I took the note and drove all night, just anywhere. I wasn't even looking at the road signs; just following the biggest main road I could find, until I was too tired to drive any more. That's when I called Steph".*

"Why would you imagine your wife would throw you in jail, Mr Walker?" Clark's cold, demanding tone had returned. Whilst Hobbs was acting the 'good cop' role well, Clark had no intention of being anything other than an inquisitor. Walker looked up, realising he had talked himself into a delicate corner. He couldn't tell them about the physical abuse he'd already shown his wife he was capable of and how he knew he could be jailed for that, but he also couldn't stay quiet, either.

"I don't know. Maybe it's just a thing I was thinking", he said, shrugging his shoulders, hoping they could return to the murder conversation and he could once again be acknowledged as also being a victim in the piece. But that wasn't where Clark was going.

"Let me go back to a phrase you used earlier, Mr Walker. You described Mr Jagger as the 'most above-board bloke' you knew. That's what you said, isn't it?" Alex didn't know where the conversation was heading,

but the accusatory nature of Clark was making him feel uncomfortable.

"Yes, because he was", Walker declared, putting on a poor attempt at being self-assured. He even sat upright and stared Clark full in the face as he said it.

"Mr Walker, let me tell you what I think happened", began Clark, putting the palms of her hands down on the desk, assertively. *"Andrew Jagger asked you to pick up a parcel for him, from the Park Avenue Nursing Home. You collected the parcel because you wanted the opportunity to challenge Andrew Jagger, face to face but in private, over why he hadn't given you work for nearly three months. After all, last year you were fulfilling a series of contracts that had been worth hundreds of thousands of pounds, through him. Isn't that correct? He threw you out of his house the first time, but yes, he did call you back later. Not because he wanted your help, though. No, it was because on your first visit, you had threatened to release a video of him and Alicia Robertshaw; the 14 year-old girl he had sex with a few years ago".*

Walker looked startled. How did they know about the video?

"You blackmailed Mr Jagger into paying you £100 000, promising to give him the only copy of the video that YOU made, Mr Walker".

Alex was shaking his head vehemently; both at the accusation, but also in disbelief that the Police knew of the video and the fact that he had filmed it.

Clark continued, becoming slightly more animated as she fed on the reaction from Walker. *"But you got greedy, didn't you, Alex? Not only did you take the money, but you also sent the video tape to the newspapers. You needed Andrew Jagger to suffer, and he did. You used your basic paramedic training to paralyse him, before - with your clear athletic strength - hoisting him up. The blood on your hands isn't from trying to release him; it was from tying the ropes nice and tight in the first place, wasn't it, Alex?"*

DI Clark paused, but Alex Walker just kept shaking his head slowly, open-mouthed. Hobbs could see his confusion, so he took up the narrative. *"The newspaper gave us the video; a video they say you told them you sent to them, to clear your conscience"*.

"And you didn't call your wife straight away, did you, Alex? Because you are guilty. Guilty of blackmail, guilty of murder, guilty of aiding and abetting sex with a minor....", Clark said. She paused before adding, *"And guilty of physically abusing your wife. Yes, Mr Walker, she confided in me when she said we needed to bring you in"*. Clark slammed shut the file she had laid out on the desk in front of her.

Alex Walker sat, momentarily unable to speak and trying to process everything he had just been accused of. He looked at Clark and said, *"I never blackmailed Jaggs. Why are you accusing me of asking for 100 grand?"*

Clark smiled, satisfied she was about to nail Alex Walker to the wall. *"If you didn't blackmail him, then why else did Andrew Jagger transfer £100,000 into your bank account on that Saturday night? And whose private account did you transfer £25 000 to on Sunday afternoon, just before placing a call to your wife?"*

Chapter 40

The dashcam on the bus confirmed the driver had no chance of reacting, as the man stumbled from the pavement and out into its path. His head and shoulders were crushed under the front wheels of the 10-ton vehicle. There was no identification on the body, and the coroner had no recognisable facial features or dental impressions he could use, to compare. His hands were crushed, so fingerprints were impossible, too. The main defining physical feature left was a series of unique tattoos on his left leg. The only other clue was a mobile phone found in his pocket, which had a single, unlisted, London number stored on it.

Did the man simply stumble? Was he drunk? Or did he perhaps have a medical condition that rendered him unable to maintain his balance? All questions that needed answers, so a coroner could record the reason, before closing the file on an accidental death. Unbeknownst to the coroner and the Police though, this man had been carefully selected; all based on his height, build and specific appearance.

He was targeted to die today.

Annie Welbeck, of the North Yorkshire Forensics team, had been assigned to the case, and she read the provisional post-mortem report, which had been submitted three days after the accident took place. She also had in her possession some photocopies of all personal effects. The male, around 40 years old, had had no obvious medical episode which could have caused him to lose his balance. Nor did he have a spasm that threw him into the road. He also had no alcohol or substances in his bloodstream that would indicate impairment or negative influence. Welbeck was completing her final notes in the case file, when Grace Allen walked into her office; refreshed and relaxed after what appeared to have been a period of truly excellent annual leave.

"*Hey Annie*", said Allen, brightly. She had her coat on, as she had been on the early shift and was now finishing for the day.

"*Well, don't you look like the cat who got the cream?*" teased Welbeck. "*Good time away? Do anything you really shouldn't have done - perhaps with that gorgeous guy we saw you with the other night?*"

Allen smiled, knowingly, and then turned her face into a picture of innocence. "*Why, Annie Welbeck, whatever do you mean?*" she said, as she threw her head back in laughter. "*Oh, it was just wonderful!*" Her whole face beamed with satisfaction.

"*Hmm, well while you were away doing 'things', some of us had to work, you know, so a little less happiness in your voice and attitude, if you don't mind?*" said Welbeck, mockingly.

"*Actually, he had to leave early again. He had an emergency sales conference to get to, so I haven't seen or heard from him for three days. It was lovely whilst it lasted, though*". Allen's mind wandered back to the happy memory.

"*So I see*", said Welbeck, genuinely pleased Grace Allen had enjoyed a relaxing break. She worked such long hours, after all. "*Well, I'm just finishing this file and then I'm due an early finish, too*", she added, "*So if you're alright to wait a few minutes, I'll walk out with you?*"

Grace Allen nodded and then looked over Welbeck's shoulder and asked, "*What's the case file on?*"

Welbeck glanced up, as she started turning the pages of the file. "*Some poor guy stumbled in front of the 2A bus. Got his head and shoulders crushed. Not pretty, and the local patrols tell me there were over twenty witnesses, who now all need some sort of trauma support*".

As Welbeck flicked over the pages, Allen had a fleeting view of what appeared to be a handwritten note. Something registered in her mind as her eyes flicked across it.

"*Wait up, Annie. Can you just go back to that last page?*"

Welbeck paused and looked up at Allen, whose expression had suddenly changed into one of deep concentration. Welbeck turned back a page and Allen scanned the words, before reaching over and tapping a word on the list. The note was a photocopy of a list of names; some crossed out and some still clear to see. It said:

Scargill

Yedlin

Goas

Jagger

Rodriguez

McBride

Ferranti

"*I know that name. Just before I went on leave, I worked on a crime scene and some evidence for a murder victim called Goas. It's not exactly a common Yorkshire name, is it?*" quizzed Allen. She leaned around Welbeck and started to log herself into the computer her colleague had been using.

"*Hey!*" exclaimed Welbeck, in surprise. "*I hadn't saved those notes!*"

"*Hang on, Annie, I want to check something*". Allen started to flick through her online files to review what she had noted about Ricardo Goas. After looking at a few documents, she covered her mouth with her hands.

"*Grace, what's wrong? What is it?*" asked Annie Welbeck, with a strong hint of anxiety in her voice.

"That name on the bottom of the list... I think it's the name of a witness in the Goas case, or something. Bob Williams mentioned it and I must have doodled it on my notepad for some significance. Annie, I think this guy might be in imminent danger", stated Allen, boldly.

At around the same time, in the North Yorkshire CID offices, DC Ahmed Akbar was showing DS Bob Williams some CCTV footage from two sites that overlooked the scene of the bus incident.

"Sarge, I was looking at the recording from one of the nearby CCTV cameras. I wanted to see if there was evidence of our victim having a fit or something, when I noticed this", he stated, as he played five seconds of a recording to his colleague, that showed the incident playing out from the view of a camera above and to the right of the scene. Williams watched the recording, but then looked up at Akbar with a quizzical expression. Akbar was smiling at the screen, assuming Williams had spotted what he himself had seen, but then he looked down at Williams to meet his gaze.

"You didn't see it, Sarge?" Akbar asked, surprised. Then he remembered that it had taken him several viewings himself to see what he was trying to show Williams right now. *"Look"*, he said, replaying the clip and freeze-framing a particular image. *"There!"*

In the somewhat grainy image, Williams could make out an outstretched arm, seemingly pushing into the victim's back a split-second before he stumbled into the road and was crushed by the bus.

"And there's more", smiled Akbar. He closed the current .WMV file and opened up a second one. This one showed the incident from a different and much wider angle - behind and to the left of the incident. Immediately before the victim fell in front of the bus, a man in a beanie hat and overcoat standing at the rear of a group of pedestrians seemed to lean forwards. As soon as the bus hit, the same man turned and strode away, which didn't register as normal bystander behaviour given the incident. Akbar then switched to a final film clip, some fifty metres further on down the road. The man in the beanie hat was walking towards a crossing and, after glancing behind him – presumably to ensure no-one was pointing towards him – he took off the hat and looked up. His dyed white hair and distinctive birthmark on his neck were as clear as his face.

"Well, well; Bryan Rodriguez", said Williams. He then looked up at a smiling DC Akbar and said, *"Great job, son. Now go find him and bring him in"*.

"With pleasure, Sarge", replied Akbar.

Chapter 41

Ferranti was drinking coffee. His suitcase was packed and he was ready to return home from his stay at the hotel in Grasmere, when his mobile rang.

"Hello?" he said, as he flopped into a chair by the window.

"Mr Ferranti? This is DC Hobbs from West Yorkshire CID". Ferranti recognised the name and the voice from his involvement with the case.

"Morning", Ferranti said, trying to sound casual and friendly. *"What can I do for you, DC Hobbs?"*

"Mr Ferranti, we'd like to temporarily increase the security on you", explained Hobbs.

Ferranti furrowed his brow and leant forwards in the chair. *"Why?"* he asked.

"I'm afraid I can't divulge any information, sir, other than tell you that we feel it would be safer, at this time, for you not to return home".

Ferranti didn't respond immediately, as he was processing the information and deciding what to say in response. After what felt like an incredibly long silence, Hobbs re-started the dialogue. *"You can stay in a hotel, although we don't like to pay for the Marriott and such"*, he admitted, before adding, *"But then the safe houses we have are functional but not luxurious, Mr Ferranti"*.

Ferranti hesitated, before suggesting, *"And do I need to tell you where I'm staying if I'm prepared to pay for it myself?"* He had no intention of staying in a city centre B&B or budget hotel.

"Provided we can contact you, that's fine. We'll need to set up a security word or phrase, so you know it's us calling you", explained Hobbs.

Ferranti stood, looked around the room and opened the curtains wider to see the magnificent Lake District laid out before him. He smiled. *"I think I'll stay where I am, thanks. And how about 'Is that darn laptop fixed yet?' as the phrase?"*

"I'll make a note of that, Mr Ferranti", replied Hobbs, smiling at the phrase. *"If you're going to be staying where you are, we're happy to go into your house and pick up anything you think you'll need, from any of your rooms?"* offered Hobbs.

"No!" snapped Ferranti. Hobbs was taken aback by the apparent ferocity of the reply, but Ferranti quickly recovered his tone. *"I mean, let's not give anyone a clue that I need anything or don't plan to return home. They might follow you over here. I'm sorry – I guess your call*

has just made me a little jumpy. It's okay, I can buy stuff while I'm away", he added, now sounding far more composed.

"I totally understand", said Hobbs, *"These sorts of calls are always a shock to people, but I'm sure there's nothing for you to worry about. Would you like me to inform the local police that you're... wherever you are?"* asked Hobbs, realising he had no idea where Ferranti currently was.

"No, I'm fine", said Ferranti. *"I'm sure they've got enough on their hands without bothering about where I am and if I'm in or out for a walk. Oh, and I'm pretty sure I need to tell someone that I've secured a piece of tech that means I'm going to record all calls I make or receive; you know, just in case"*.

"Sounds a wise idea Mr Ferranti. I'll make a note of the tech in the case file. Just remember your responsibilities to the caller though, even in this sort of pressure situation, we still need to be mindful of personal privacy", reminded Hobbs.

"Preaching to the converted, DC Hobbs", replied Ferranti, as he looked out at the beautiful view from his Hotel. He really would like to collect a couple of things from his home, but he didn't want the Police opening up every room and trying to find the very specific items he might want or need.

"I appreciate the call, DC Hobbs. Have a good day. Now, go get that darn laptop fixed", he joked, to

Hobbs's amusement. Hobbs ended the call after assuring Ferranti that if he ever felt in any danger, he should call 999 and tell the operator it was a secure location emergency. The assurance from Hobbs didn't make the situation any less stressful for Ferranti, but at least he was now aware of the procedure.

Ferranti flopped back down in the chair and reviewed how his plans for the days ahead would need to change. He knew he'd have to call Barry Clements to tell him he'd be working away from the office for a week or two. He would need to tread a fine line between letting him know enough, without panicking him. After all, Ferranti needed the work and didn't want Clements deciding he was a liability. He also found himself wondering if DS Walker was still here at the hotel. It felt strange to feel a sense of warmth with such an authority figure and, on reflection, a woman he seemingly detested just a couple of weeks ago. He also knew that feeling was mutual; both then and now.

As he sat at the window, smiling gently to himself, his phone rang. It was Aarav Khatri.

"Hello. How are you?" asked Khatri.

"What's new, my friend? Missing me?" teased Ferranti in response.

"I just wondered when you might be back? There's something I would like your opinion on, please", said Khatri.

"How about we talk in a couple of days?" said Ferranti.

"Okay. Thank you. But any chance of some time now? It's just that…", but Ferranti had already ended the call and Khatri was abruptly cut off.

"Enough", muttered Ferranti. He threw the mobile on the bed behind him and sank back into his thoughts. The phone rang again. Ferranti sighed. He understood. Khatri was excited and Ferranti had just cut him off mid-conversation. He answered the call.

"I get it, you're excited about something, but enough, already", said Ferranti, wearily.

"Enough already?" came a calm and familiar voice. *"But Adam, I've not finished yet. In fact, I think you might like to know I have new plans. Big plans"*.

Ferranti recognised the voice, and the walls of the hotel room felt like they were closing in on him.

"How the hell did you get this number?" has asked, instinctively scanning the grounds of the hotel from his window for any sight of the caller.

"Adam, I know everything. I have for years and years. You recognise my voice, don't you?"

Ferranti checked the phone. The tech he'd told DC Hobbs about just minutes earlier indicated that it was doing its job in recording the call, which provided him with some sense of relief.

The caller remained silent, waiting patiently for Ferranti's next question.

"Who the hell are you, and why are you doing this to me?" Ferranti asked, with a touch of frustration and fear creeping into his voice.

"You know who I am, Adam", came the reply. It threw Ferranti, but he wasn't kept in suspense for very long, as the caller continued. *"Some people would be pleased to hear from their long-lost stepfather"*.

Ferranti's jaw dropped and his eyes bulged. Barely able to believe his ears and with his blood beginning to boil, Ferranti uttered the name through gritted teeth: *"Reynolds"*.

"Sorry about your mother. So sad she died from her injuries, but she really was... weak". The last word was said in utter disdain. Ferranti stood, holding the phone to his ear, shaking with fury. He was stunned and utterly speechless. He felt every emotion right now.

"But don't worry, daddy's home, now. After all, you and I have unfinished business, don't we?"

Ferranti cut the call off and immediately dialled 999. Anger was coursing through his veins and panic was causing his hands to shake. The man who'd caused his beloved mother's death was apparently alive and well – and looking for a family reunion. But before the emergency operator could answer his call, Ferranti ended it. He thought it might be a better idea to talk to Stephanie Walker first. He raced out of the room, along the corridor, and up the stairs to rap on the door of her room, hoping she hadn't left yet.

Chapter 42

DS Steve Denton picked up the ringing phone.

"*Denton*", he said, with his mouth still partially full of a limp salad sandwich he had brought with him from home.

"*DS Denton? Malcom Peters from For Kandles*", came the reply.

Denton took a couple of seconds to realise that the call was coming from the hardware store in London that had been of particular interest in the investigations so far. "*Ah yes, thanks for calling back, Mr Peters. Any luck finding the information we asked for?*"

"*Yes. Sorry about the delay… we keep comprehensive paper records, so sometimes it takes longer to find a copy of an order*", offered Peters, apologetically, though the apology was wasted on Denton. Malcolm noted the silence and cleared his throat, slightly embarrassed at his misplaced enthusiasm for his desire to maintain a paper filing system; loose as the term was.

"*Can I have the addresses of the deliveries please, Mr Peters?*" asked Denton.

"Well, that's the thing", replied Peters. *"It appears that the other two boxes were collected in person, by a delivery driver who paid cash"*.

Denton sighed, put his pencil down and scrunched his tired face with the palm of his hand. He had hoped for and expected progress; something to move the investigation forwards. He picked up the remains of his limp sandwich, stared at it for a couple of seconds, and then dropped it in the bin to the side of his desk.

"That's a shame", Denton said, forcing politeness, whilst staring up at the ceiling. He was feeling as stale and limp as his lunch at this moment in time.

"Yes, sorry. I mean, we know the name on the boxes but the delivery driver didn't seem to have any addresses on his collection paperwork. We've searched the CCTV image but can't read the rest of the handwriting, sadly", replied a somewhat despondent Peters; apologetic, once again, though this time for his failure to provide the information that the Police clearly wanted.

Denton sat up, abruptly. *"CCTV image?"*

"Yes", replied Peters; the smile on his face coming through loud and clear over the phone. *"I installed it a couple of years ago, just after we..."*, but he was cut-off by a revitalised DS Denton.

"Can I send down a member of CID, to view the tape?", Denton asked, eagerly.

Three hours later, DC Olwyn Jones sat down next to DS Denton. He held a copy of the CCTV clip, saved onto a memory stick, in his left hand, and had the names of the two recipients of the parcels scribbled into his notebook. Denton snatched up the memory stick and plugged it into his desktop USB slot. As the file opened, he looked up at Jones, who anticipated the look and said, *"Name on both of the deliveries was Paul Reynolds, Sarge"*.

Denton was intrigued, as that was the same name as the man at the retirement home, but that was nothing compared to his reaction when he saw the delivery driver's face on the CCTV. *"Got you!"* he exclaimed. He smiled at Jones and then picked up the phone to call DI Clark.

Chapter 43

Ferranti raced upstairs and sprinted to the door of room 8, where he and Stephanie Walker had spent most of the night together. He rapped on the door and found himself tapping his foot, impatiently, as he waited for someone to open it. After a few seconds, he rapped on the door again but, this time, he heard footsteps and a voice mumble, *"Okay, okay, I'm coming"*. The door opened and, to Ferranti's relief, Stephanie Walker was still there.

"Oh. Morning", said Walker, clearly embarrassed to see Ferranti and secretly wishing she had left the hotel earlier. Ferranti saw the embarrassment on Walker's face but, right now, he really didn't care.

"I'm sorry to bother you, but I really need to talk to you", said Ferranti, apologetically, but clasping his hands together as if praying.

"I'm actually just about to leave", replied Walker, trying her hardest to avoid eye contact. *"I'll be back in Leeds later today, so maybe ..."*, she continued, but Ferranti cut across her.

"Look, I realise this is a little embarrassing, but I need to talk to you", and he reached out and grabbed Walker's hands, clasping them gently but firmly within his own.

"Err, I don't know. Last night was... well, it was prob-ably a mistake. I'm married and it... it was great...", Walker started to say, glancing up and smiling, nervously, *"But I'm not...".* Before she could continue, though, Ferranti interjected again.

"He just called me". Walker looked up in confusion at Ferranti, as he continued. *"It's my stepfather. He's the killer! He says we've got unfinished business".*

Walker was struggling to catch up with Ferranti's story, which he realised from her puzzled expression and the slight shaking of her head, so he was said, *"I recorded the call",* before holding up his phone, as if in evidence.

Before Walker could say anything else, Ferranti slid past her and into her room. It was clear from the open suitcase, and untidy piles of clothes around it, that Walker was a long way from 'just about to leave'. Ferranti sat at the table by the window and set the phone down. Walker was still staring out of her door and into the corridor, in shock at Ferranti's presumption that he could just walk in.

"Come in", she said, sarcastically, and then closed the door. She walked slowly over to the table to face the clearly agitated Ferranti. She felt like she had a lovesick teenager pursuing her, who just didn't know the difference between a one-night stand and a first date. Truth be told, though, Walker was unsure how she felt. Seeing this previously confident man who, last night, was gentle yet assertive during an amazing night of sex, now fidgeting in his seat, brought out a surprising and

almost maternal instinct in Walker; not something she had ever imagined possible.

"Listen to this", said Ferranti, and he pressed play on an app that Walker had never seen or even heard of before. She listened to the replay of the call and was visibly shocked; mainly at the effect the call was having on Ferranti, rather than at the content of the call itself. The recording ended and Ferranti looked up at Walker, eagerly awaiting her response and hopeful of instructions for what to do next. Walker noted his anticipation and her expression turned to one of helplessness.

"Adam, I'm sorry but I'm not sure what you want me to do? I'm off the case, and you and I simply cannot be seen to be discussing it. We actually shouldn't even be seen together...", she paused, before looking into his pleading eyes, and ending her sentence with, *"... at all"*.

Ferranti swallowed hard and looked down at the floor. He knew, of course, that what Walker was saying was technically correct, but he needed her to give him some advice. He drew a deep breath and then exhaled, before looking up at her. *"I get that, Stephanie. Last night was... well, it was last night. I need you, but to give me some advice about whether what I'm planning to do is the best way forward"*, he explained.

Walker relaxed and took a deep breath, before slowly nodding her head in understanding and saying, *"Talk to me"*.

"I'm done hiding. I'm going to head back to Millgarth and give them a copy of the recording, and a statement.

Then, I'm going home. He knows where I work, I believe he's already found out where I live, and now he knows my private mobile number. There's no such thing as protective custody. For all we know he could be here, right now".

Walker pondered on the statements and then nodded in agreement. *"I see your logic. I don't think it's safe to go back to Leeds but, as you say, maybe nowhere is safe. I can't see us being allowed to allocate a protection team to you, but you can't just live your life normally, either. That will open you up to danger"*.

Ferranti paused, in thought, and then said, *"What's normal, anymore?"*

Walker knew he was right.

"Why do you think he's killing people?" asked Walker, instinctively reverting to her Police training.

"Same reason he killed my mum, perhaps. Because he can?" offered Ferranti.

"No", Walker replied, firmly, shaking her head. *"There's so much more to this spree of killings than that. We just don't know what, yet"*. Walker then looked down at the phone. *"What's the tech you used to record the call? I've never seen that on a mobile device before"*.

Ferranti smiled. *"Something my buddy gave me a while ago. He's got all sorts of tech gadgets that the general public - and most of the authorities - just don't know exist. I took a few with me when I left the company".*

Walker tilted her head inquisitively and, with his mind momentarily off the call, Ferranti was happy to expand on the statement. *"Justin runs his own corporate communications company down in London. He gave me a job after my mum died and, well, it's scary what tech is out there that you'd think only existed in science fiction movies".* As he had done the night before, Ferranti felt himself so easily being able to open up to Walker. He continued. *"Justin and I go way back. He went into Black Ops before he left the military. With his contacts in there, he gets first dibs on any tech that's being released by the military into the Police forces around the world. You know, people were so excited when targeted listening devices came out in the nineties. Chances are, though, that the military Black Ops teams were using that tech six or seven years earlier, until they got something better. Their Research and Development facilities make Disney's Epcot look like a garden shed with sock puppets".* He chuckled at the comparison.

"Your stepfather; he's English?" asked Walker, abruptly changing the subject. Ferranti looked up, surprised by the question. *"His accent, on the message. It is English, isn't it?"* checked Walker.

Ferranti's mood darkened. *"Yes, he was"*, he replied.

"Was?" asked Walker, wondering why Ferranti had used the past tense.

"Is!" Ferranti responded, sharply. *"I just prefer to think he's in the past; gone from our lives, I guess"*.

Walker nodded, showing she understood and that she realised she was back on very sensitive ground. She wanted to ask what Ferranti meant by 'our lives', but decided to save that until a later meeting, or perhaps an interview. He was clearly upset, and she didn't want to hurt him.

Ferranti sighed, and then stood. He was smiling again, although it was a weak and almost apologetic smile. *"Thank you, for listening"* he said.

Walker smiled and nodded back. *"You're welcome"*. They held their gaze far longer than two people would, if having just a polite farewell. Ferranti slowly walked out of the door; glancing back and smiling, as Walker gently closed the door.

Stephanie Walker giggled. How wonderful it was to feel so playful with a man. It was an emotion she had long since forgotten. Then she realised that she felt happy and sad, both at the same time. *"Like characters in a 'forbidden love' movie"*, she said to herself.

The situation she faced was delicate and, whilst her choice would be both unwise domestically, and potential career suicide to boot, all she wanted to do right now was to pull Adam Ferranti close to her and feel the warmth of his body against hers, and hear his breathless whispers again.

Chapter 44

Alex Walker slumped back into the now familiar chair in the police interview room. DI Clark and Acting DS Hobbs sat across from him. Clark clicked on the recording machine and said, *"Friday 29th April, 2013, at 10:03am. In the room are DI Clark and Acting DS Hobbs, interviewing Mr Alex Walker"*. She looked up at Walker with a stony expression and asked, *"How do you know Bryan Rodriguez; the man you paid £25k to shortly after the death of Andrew Jagger?"*

Walker exhaled, in exasperation. *"Look at my bank account. I'll even show you it myself, if you give me my phone back. I've not got £25k to give to anyone, and I've never heard of Bryan fucking Rodriguez"*.

"It's a lot of disposable money, Mr Walker", said Clark, *"Even for a man with such a high celebrity profile as you. Presumably you invest your money, rather than keep it in a common current account?"*

Walker looked at Clark with a degree of unease. He was sure she knew he had no savings and probably knew about his debt, but he tried his best to avoid the indignity of admitting it. *"Yeah, well I mean it's all secure, isn't it, in... you know... offshore accounts and stuff"*, he bluffed.

Clark smiled, and Walker was now certain she knew all about his debts. He shuffled in his chair, crossed his arms, and tried to look defiant.

"So, why don't you now tell me the truth about the money", said Clark, leaning forward with a determined glint in her eye. *"And about why you paid Bryan Rodriguez to murder someone?"*

The suspense was broken unexpectedly, when a colleague from the front desk knocked and entered the room. He leant over to whisper that he needed five minutes with DI Clark. Clark looked irritated at the intrusion but recognised the expression on the Desk Sergeant's face. The information must be urgent and material to the interview. She paused the interview and the tape and excused herself from the room.

As soon as the door was closed, the Desk Sergeant passed his superior a piece of paper with a scribbled message he'd hurriedly written down after a phone conversation with DS Denton from The Met. Clark looked at the note. A grim smile of satisfaction spread across her face.

"We're sure about this?" Clark asked.

"Apparently he's got CCTV footage that confirms it", replied her colleague.

Clark didn't say anything else. She turned and walked back into the interview room. She started up the tape, announced the continuation of the interview, and slowly began; *"Mr Walker, I'm led to believe you've recently been in London, collecting some more hardware-related parcels, no less?"*

Alex Walker was speechless. He looked like he wanted to say something, but he couldn't get the words out of his mouth. He glanced from Clark to Hobbs, and back again, looking confused and at a complete loss. Suddenly he stopped still; sat back in his chair and said, *"I think I need to call my solicitor now, if you don't mind"*.

Chapter 45

DI Clark called the morning HMET meeting to order. "*We have a lot to get through this morning, so let's keep questions limited to must-asks*", she said, glancing around the room to ensure she could see that everyone understood. "*First up, as some of you know, we currently have DS Walker's husband in custody. She is therefore no longer assigned to the case. So, I've asked DC Hobbs to step-up to Acting DS as the West Yorkshire lead*".

If the mention of DS Walker's removal from the case was news to any of the team, they did their professional best not to let any emotion register on their faces. Hobbs looked around the room and nodded casually in acknowledgement of his new assignment. Everyone in the room knew Hobbs would have been the logical choice, and he was happy to be given the opportunity.

"*Everyone will find a photo of Alex Walker in the HMET SharePoint file*", continued Clark. "*DS Hobbs, please update the team on the Jagger post-mortem and forensics*".

"*Morning all*", said Hobbs. "*Post-mortem report from the coroner's office states cause of death was asphyxiation resulting from hanging, but there was also a recent needle puncture in the back of his neck, consistent with a syringe needle. Forensic analysis confirmed low level traces of neuromuscular-blockers – NMBs - with a very small trace of anaesthetic. After analysis of a small blood sample that was still in the body, and from looking at some contusions on the arms and legs, their conclusion is that the victim was deliberately paralysed – unable to resist being bound and hanged. There were no obvious marks from the victim trying to resist or fight back"*. Hobbs took a breath and surveyed the room. *"Arms and legs were bound with rope, with saw wire threaded around the rope in question; presumably to make untying the binds hazardous to anyone who tried to help. Cuts to the inner thighs... gravity drained most of the remaining blood once the victim's heart had stopped pumping it out. Jagger would have been unconscious, if not dead, by then, though"*.

"You mentioned a trace of anaesthetic?" quizzed Clark.

"Yes. The coroner commented to say he couldn't be sure there was enough anaesthetic injected to relieve any pain for the victim, so Jagger would have most definitely suffered". Hobbs closed the file containing the coroner's report, and opened his case notes file, in readiness.

Clark picked up the story, ready to hand back to Hobbs. He was her golden boy, and anything she could do to shine a light on his work would only enhance her reputation. She was tired of being a DI and had already decided that this case would be her springboard for consideration in an upcoming DCI vacancy. *"As I mentioned earlier, we have Alex Walker in custody. DS Hobbs?"* she said, referring back to her colleague.

"Thank you, Ma'am. Whilst looking into Mr Walker's financial position, NCA discovered he has – or had - debts of over £300k. This debt was building until fairly recently, when a single deposit of £100k was made into his account - the day after Andrew Jagger's murder, in fact. There was also a payment out of the account later that same day for £25k. Last night, the bank confirmed who it was paid to: Mr Bryan Rodriguez - a local thug known to North and West Yorkshire Police, and currently out on parole".

On the other end of the conference call, DS Bob Williams had been casually listening, until the name of Rodriguez was mentioned. He sat bolt upright and, almost unconsciously, exclaimed, "What?"

"DS Williams? Is there a problem?" enquired Clark.

"Sorry Ma'am. Did DS Hobbs just say 'Bryan Rodriguez'? Would that Bryan Rodriguez be a Latino man with bleached blonde hair and a distinctive birthmark on the side of his neck?"

Clark and Hobbs looked at each other, astonished that DS Williams had described the man they had identified as the recipient of the payment. "You know of Bryan Rodriguez?" asked Hobbs.

"Know of him? One of my DCs is currently trying to establish his whereabouts. We want to question him. He's a known thug in the criminal fraternity here, and we have reason to suspect he was involved in a recent death - possibly a murder", exclaimed Williams.

The room fell silent for a moment. Everyone was absorbing the information and starting to theorise about possible lines of enquiry, when Williams spoke again. *"Ma'am, I'm sending you a couple of video files from local CCTV to look at"*.

"I'll put them up on the screen here in the room, DS Williams - thank you", said Clark, with sincere gratitude.

"I'll forward them to you too, DS Denton", added Williams.

"Thanks", said Denton, brightly.

After a few seconds, the clips were sent. Both Clark and Denton confirmed the arrivals.

"Ma'am, please open the clip 'file reference CCTV724' first, please", requested Williams. Clark opened the file and played it as Williams narrated. *"At 3.42 seconds into the clip, please freeze frame – you should notice an arm pressing into the back of another man. That arm appears to belong to our Mr Rodriguez. Now press play again, and you'll see the man at the front-middle of the frame fall forwards"*.

"We see it, DS Williams", said Hobbs, *"But it's too hard to identify the person doing the pushing"*. As they watched the clip, everyone was focusing on the aggressor. No-one noticed the uncanny resemblance of the victim to Hobbs, other than Hobbs himself. He gave an involuntary shiver, but wanted to ensure no-one was

distracted. He then asked Williams to take the HMET team - including DS Denton - through the remaining video clip, with it being paused at the point that Bryan Rodriguez looked up and inadvertently gave the CCTV cameras a good long look at his face.

"That's him", said Hobbs. *"That's the Bryan Rodriguez who received the £25k"*.

"Ma'am", said Williams, *"The victim in this incident had a list of names in his lower jacket pocket. It was unspoilt by the blood from the scene as it was in a clear plastic wallet. Forensics flagged it as a possible link to this case, but I was going to check it out, first. I've just emailed you and DS Denton a copy"*. He paused and waited for his colleagues to receive and react to the emailed list. Five seconds later, as the email was opened and the photocopied list was pulled up on-screen, Williams heard the confused gasps and mutters he was expecting.

"This is very interesting, DS Williams", said Clark; leaning forward and eagerly staring at the screen. *"So, we know about Scargill, Yedlin, Goas, and now Jagger... Rodriguez speaks for itself... I think we need to put our Mr Ferranti into protective custody as soon as possible – it's not exactly a common name... Anyone recognise the other name on the list?"* she asked the team, thus signalling the end of her stream of consciousness.

Everyone was still in shock but muttered in agreement that they didn't recognise the one remaining name on the list.

"*DS Denton, what about you? You recognise the name 'McBride'?*" DI Clark enquired.

There was a short pause, before DS Steve Denton replied with a clear and assertive, "*No Ma'am. I don't recognise that name at all*".

Chapter 46

Simon McBride pressed 'end' on his secure mobile phone. He needed to check something with the man he knew as Republic but, for the fifth time in the last 24 hours, Republic had not answered the call. McBride put his phone back in his jacket pocket and returned to the sheet of crumpled briefing paper he'd recently recovered from the secure confidential waste bin. It was a general briefing document about a visit by the British Prime Minister to Washington DC. Nothing untoward in the document itself; just the usual detail about the itinerary and specific locations, either for PR opportunities or areas of concern to the security forces. This morning, McBride had glanced at it and discarded it within minutes, but after watching the cyclist on the bridge, he recalled a specific lunch appointment listed in the itinerary.

"So, whilst everyone is looking to the three seas in India, little do they know the truth. Not so much 'south-east to where the three seas meet', but...". McBride trailed off, smiling to himself. Oh, how everyone had been misled by what they thought they'd heard. He'd even struggled with it himself, until he'd seen that cyclist on the bridge. The poster he pulled behind him sparked the memory of the security briefing note, and the details related to one of the stop-offs in the itinerary. It read:

Red status – 11:30am arrival at Democrats Triple C: 430 South Capitol Street, south-east entrance.

"So, who would be calling Goas and telling him to go to the south-east entrance of the DCCC?" pondered McBride, aloud but to himself. He assessed the options he had. He knew it would be unwise for him to call his contact in the FBI directly, given that their conversation would probably be recorded and maybe even monitored live. He reflected on what seemed to be the most obvious option open to him in that instance. *"Can I use Denton to verify the identity of the American voice, and how do I tie that back to the Democratic Congressional Campaign Committee; the Triple – or rather 'the three' - Cs?"*

Denton certainly wasn't stupid though, so he'd have to tread carefully. The time was 09:35am, and McBride assumed that Denton would be out of the daily HMET meeting by now. He pulled his phone out of his pocket and dialled. After a couple of rings, Denton picked up.

"DS Denton", came the response from the end of the line.

"Steve, it's Simon. It occurred to me that we hadn't spoken for a while and... I might have something for you".

"And I might have something for you, too", replied Denton. That took McBride by surprise, and the silence made Denton smile. *"You first though, Simon"*, he offered.

McBride was momentarily thrown by Denton's confident tone, but he gathered his composure and began.
*"My contact at the FBI believes he's found the truth
about the Spanish translation. You're looking in entirely
the wrong place. In fact, you're looking in the wrong
direction and on the wrong continent"*. There was
silence at the other end of the line. Now it was McBride's
turn to smile. He waited for a few seconds for Denton
to begrudgingly acknowledge the news, before proceed-
ing to brief Denton on what he needed him to do.

*"Do I mention the source is you - or the intelligence
services at all?"* asked Denton.

"No", answered McBride, firmly. *"Don't mention my
name. I don't currently want this getting back to me, as
the instigator, as there are certain protocols we need to
manage through our overly-sensitive American colleagues. Let's keep me as a hidden asset, for now, OK?
Anyway, that's my news – what do you have for me?"* he
asked with the usual smug tone back in his voice.

*"Your surname appeared on a list that North Yorkshire
CID found on a body in a suspected murder case. It
features alongside the names of the four murder victims
the HMET are currently investigating"*, replied Denton.
There was a quiet but audible gasp from McBride; then
silence. The silence continued for so long that Denton
looked at his mobile phone to check the call had not
dropped. *"You there, McBride?"* he asked.

"Yes, I'm here", replied a slightly shaken McBride,
slowly. Whilst he'd worked for British Intelligence for a

long time and his life could be a little 'James Bond' at times, he had never truly felt he was ever in any danger - until now. *"So how did you find that out?"* he asked, trying to disguise his angst.

"There was an incident in York last week. Someone got crushed by a bus. The SOCO team recovered a piece of paper from the victim's jacket pocket, and the Forensic Lead recognised one of the names on it from having done prior work on our case", replied Denton.

"So, do you think the victim was the killer - and now he's dead?" quizzed McBride, a little too hopefully.

"We don't know if he's the killer, Simon. Local CCTV seems to have identified a person of interest in the case, though – the person who appears to have pushed him under the bus. We're looking into both men's pasts, but, if they're like any of the other bodies in this HMET case, they'll likely have some kind of security clearance that we don't have access to. Don't suppose you can help on that front, Simon, old chap?" asked Denton, enjoying having the upper-hand.

McBride hesitated. Just how far would he need to bend to get what he wanted out of Denton? *"Let me take a look"*, he offered. *"Send me the details. It might take a few days, but I'll see what I can find, and what, if anything, I'm at liberty to share"*. He was about to end the call, but then quickly added, *"And send me those CCTV clips, would you? I'm intrigued"*.

Ten minutes later, McBride received the email from Denton. As he stared at the familiar names on the list photocopied and filed as evidence from the recent bus incident, he clicked on the first video file. McBride glanced at it and started to write some notes. Like everyone else had done, he freeze-framed the clip as per the instruction, but his eyes weren't focused on the out-stretched arm. Instead, Simon McBride stared at the grainy image of the victim. His jaw slowly dropped. He sat staring at the screen, mouth wide open. He regained some of his composure and opened the secure browser on his device, to book a first-class seat on the next available flight to Washington DC. He needed to talk face-to-face with the American lead in the illegal transatlantic operation – sooner rather than later.

Chapter 47

DI Clark called a special HMET meeting to order. Although she wasn't expecting any significant progress in this morning's session, DS Steve Denton had announced a couple of key developments he wanted to discuss.

"Acting DS Hobbs and I have interviewed Alex Walker, and he has finally requested a solicitor, following confirmation that we now have CCTV footage of him collecting two more packages from the hardware store in London. Packages with contents much like the one found at Andrew Jagger's home. I think DS Denton deserves some credit here for the excellent work carried out by The Met", Clark said, as she looked around the room to gather some momentum from her audience.

There was a general mumbling and the faintest sound of congratulations from the HMET meeting room in Millgarth, as Denton listened in from his desk in London. He was pleasantly surprised at the congratulations bestowed by Clark, as it was certainly not her usual behaviour.

"Thank you, Ma'am", Denton replied, almost hurriedly, as if to capture the praise and build on it. *"If I might add, we should be close to a couple of other breakthroughs in the next 48 hours, too"*.

"*Sounds like positive news, DS Denton. Would you like to share any insights into your lines of enquiry, or is it a little too early?*" enquired Clark, rather warmly.

"*Happy to share what we are looking at, Ma'am, but obviously we're working hard to validate our current assumptions*", replied Denton. "*Firstly, I think we might be about to disprove the assumption that Alex Walker knew anything about the £100,000 or £25,000 transfers. This would therefore cast doubt on any link between Walker and Rodriguez*".

"*What?*" asked Clark, audibly unsettled that Alex Walker might not actually have been involved.

"*Yes, Ma'am. I think we can also expect to find out a little more about the three Cs; that's the letter C, and NOT s-e-a-s, as in water, which we'd previously assumed from the transcription on the Goas message. I have some provisional information that it's not a reference to India, as we first thought it might be*".

"*Steve, it's DS Williams here*", cut in Bob Williams, who was now keen to wade in on the conversation. "*Our SOCO team said we had a native speaker translate the message, which spoke of three 'seas' – very much as in water.*"

"*A tactic or code, Bob*", replied Denton. "*We actually think it refers to an address in North America*". There were some startled gasps in the room, and whispered conversations started to build.

"*Enough, please*", barked Clark to the meeting attendees, in a slightly raised voice. As the room fell silent again, she returned to Denton. "*DS Denton, I take it that's everything?*"

"*One more thing, Ma'am*", came the reply. Clark glanced around the room and noticed a few open-mouths. She suddenly felt as if the meeting was getting out of control; or rather, out of *her* control.

"*DS Denton, please stay on the line*", requested DI Clark, in a thinly-veiled order. "*Everyone else, please return to your current lines of enquiry. I'll instruct you on any new investigations shortly*".

Everyone was surprised at the sudden and unexpected curtailment of the meeting, but they stood and left the room, quickly and quietly as instructed. DS Bob Williams also left the call. Those who had worked with Clark previously knew silent obedience and no eye-contact were essential when she was in this mood.

As soon as the door was closed, Clark returned to the call with Denton, in a far more formal tone than she had used before. "*DS Denton, before you share your final piece of news, I need you to answer me this: How did you find out about the query over the £100,000? That news has only been released to me. Do we have a problem with chains of command at the National Crime Agency?*"

Denton realised he had slipped-up. He had been told the information about the transfers in confidence by Simon

McBride. *"No, Ma'am. I have some inter-departmental contacts who appear to have a similar interest in our investigation"*, he replied, whilst waiting for the fury of DI Clark to erupt. Instead, she exhaled, and said, *"Yes, MI5. I know about it. DCI Newsome said he had a visit a couple of months ago from one of their agents. Apparently, one even turned up at the O2 murder scene?"*

"Yes, someone did show up unexpectedly at the Yedlin murder, Ma'am. He told me he was there on company business and was unwilling to share any information".

"And did you share any information with him; either then, or subsequently, DS Denton?"

Denton paused. He was thinking about how to respond, but the silence was in itself an admission. This clearly didn't come as a surprise to Clark. She knew how MI5 worked and that they were very adept at offering snippets of information to gain favours and disproportionate amounts of intelligence in return. The fact that Denton may have been in collusion with them, as evidenced by his knowledge of the money, angered her greatly though.

"So, what do they know, Steve" she asked, softening her tone, markedly. On the other end of the line, Denton closed his eyes, leant back in his chair and slowly exhaled. He assumed that Clark calling him by his forename was a gesture of openness, but even if it was actually a trap, there was little he could do to hide the information any longer. He also had to admit he really

didn't have any clue as to how much Clark already knew.

"He told me about the probability of the address being in North America", admitted Denton. *"He also told me about the NCA report on the £100,000"*.

"And what did you tell him?" asked Clark.

"I told him about his name being on the list found on the bus victim's body and he's seen the CCTV footage of the accident. I did recognise his name and I thought he should know, I'm sorry, Ma'am. I can promise you I've not heard from McBride since".

"Interesting", muttered Clark to herself, not sure if she was surprised by any of what she'd heard or not. *"Do me a favour, Steve; keep this conversation between us for now, okay? It seems an agent – presumably this McBride - has recently flown out to Washington DC. We also now know that there is a building in the capitol, known as the Triple C"*.

Denton was stunned and impressed at how ahead of the game Clark really was. He cleared his throat, sheepishly. *"Yes Ma'am. What do you need me to do now, DI Clark?"*

"Absolutely nothing, DS Denton. I'll take it from here. Just let me know if you hear from Mr McBride again – that's an order". Clark punched the 'end' button to cut the call dead. She would deal with Denton's conduct

later, and he would realise what a dreadful mistake he had made.

She walked out of the HMET meeting room, to find a number of the team were huddled by the large pinboard that was mounted on the longest wall in the corridor. Hobbs was pinning a piece of paper to it and appeared animated whilst answering questions from his colleagues. He turned and saw Clark approaching.

"Ma'am. New development", he said, as the others cleared a way for Clark to get to the pinboard. She looked up at the new piece of paper.

"Paul Reynolds? That's the name on the three hardware orders, isn't it?" she asked. *"How is that a new development?"*

"Adam Ferranti came in earlier, Ma'am. He dropped off a voice recording and we've taken a statement. If you have ten minutes, I'll be happy to brief you", said Hobbs, breathlessly.

Chapter 48

Aarav Khatri was sat in Mrs Atha's Tea Shop, deep in a heated discussion with another man, when Adam Ferranti strode in.

"Hi", said Khatri. He was pleased to see Ferranti, but was clearly in the middle of an argument with his guest. Ferranti walked over to them and glared at the man.

"Excuse us for a moment", he said, more as an order than a request. The man was about to object, but Ferranti gave him a ferocious frown, so he sat back down.

"What's his problem?" asked Ferranti, as he and Khatri moved into a different corner of the room. He was clearly in a no-nonsense mood, so Khatri didn't even try to embellish the truth.

"He's done some work for me, and I don't have the cash to pay him until the weekend. He's now threatening to destroy the work, but I really need it for tomorrow", said Khatri, dejectedly.

Ferranti looked over at the man and then back to Khatri. *"How much?"* he asked.

"Oh, I need it a lot", replied Khatri.

"No, no", said Ferranti, shaking his head in mild frustration. *"How much do you owe him?"*

Khatri paused, glanced over at the angry man and then back at Ferranti. *"Two hundred and fifty pounds, but I just don't have it"*, he said. He slumped further into his seat, looking embarrassed.

Ferranti stood swiftly, looked at Khatri as if assessing him, and then said, *"Wait here"*. He walked over to the angry man and spoke quietly to him. The man nodded, showed Ferranti something that was in his backpack, just as Ferranti then pulled out a fistful of twenty-pound notes. He counted them into the man's hand and then held out his empty hand; gesturing that he wanted something in return. The man looked over at a bemused Khatri and then back at Ferranti, before reaching into his backpack and handing over a USB stick and a laminated folder. The man then stood and walked out, without looking at or saying a word to Khatri.

Ferranti returned to the table where Khatri was sitting and passed over the folder and the USB stick.

"Better be worth it", said Ferranti. *"That just cost me two hundred and eighty pounds, given the 'inconvenience and shame' you apparently created for your friend"*.

Khatri was dumbstruck. Tears welled in his eyes at the kind and unprompted gesture by Ferranti. He was just about to thank him and started to reach over to hug him, but Ferranti, who had been looking around the tea shop, glanced back over to Khatri and saw the tears.

"Oh, for fucks sake, not that emotional shit again", he said, and he held up a hand to signal that Khatri should stay exactly where he was. *"What is it, anyway?"* Ferranti asked, as a tearful Khatri regained his composure.

"Well, you know I said I wanted to ask your opinion about something?" said Khatri, whilst opening the file and spreading it across the table. *"It's this".*

On the table was a glossy promotional sheet, featuring a photo of Khatri proudly posing in a suit. He was stood in front of five sparkling new BMW E1 electric cars. The headline above the image announced, 'For environmentally-friendly trips and multi-lingual drivers, book your journey with Khatri Executive: the greener way to get to your business meeting'.

Khatri was beaming with pride at the brochure, but Ferranti looked concerned.

"You've bought, or leased, five new cars? What the hell? How much is that costing you?" he quizzed, perturbed at the scenario. Khatri, however, was still smiling.

"No, I have only leased one, but the man promised to photoshop me in front of a fleet of five. Now I can send this to my parents, tell them I own a fleet, and announce my intention to quit my medical training. With this, my

father will be proud and I will have time to make enough money to perhaps invest in a second car".

Ferranti was lost for words. He couldn't decide if he applauded the tactic by Khatri, or whether he thought it would only make the situation with his family far worse. As he reflected on the situation, his phone buzzed and a text appeared:

'Meet me tonight at midnight - Westgate Warehouses in Otley. Let's bring this to a conclusion.

Love, Dad x'

Ferranti stared at the screen, both shaken and frightened. The text had no caller ID showing, a tactic consistent with all the other communications he had received over the phone. He recalled all the conversations with Justin, back in London, about how easy this was to do.

Meanwhile, Khatri was still talking to him, but it was all a muffled background sound, as Ferranti's world seemed to implode. He was busy thinking about what he might do, when Khatri touched his hand, in an attempt to catch his attention. Ferranti jumped.

"Oh, sorry", apologised Khatri. *"I thought you were listening, but hadn't decided how to answer my question"*.

Ferranti hurriedly stuffed his mobile into his pocket. He couldn't think rationally about his options and listen to Khatri at the same time. *"What? Sorry, what was the question?"* he asked, struggling to return his focus to the conversation.

Khatri looked hopefully at Ferranti, but witnessed the blank expression on his friend's face. *"The marketing poster - what do you think?"*

"Err sure, great, Or, maybe not, I don't know. Sorry, but I have to go", mumbled a confused Ferranti.

"Need a ride? I can take you?" asked Khatri, both help-fully and hopefully. Ferranti stared at Khatri, with what felt like a million thoughts racing through his head. His expression then changed, as a look of determination took over. Ferranti knew he had to find a way to end his torture, and so he looked Khatri square in the face and said, *"I'll need a lift later. Are you available tonight?"*

Chapter 49

McBride had agreed to meet her outside the Ariel Rios Federal Building in Washington DC. She was attending a briefing by the Head of the Bureau of Alcohol, Tobacco, Firearms and Explosives as part of her role on Capitol Hill. It was lunchtime, and they each bought a hotdog from a street vendor, as they attempted to maintain the façade of a casual conversation between friends or colleagues.

"I got your message, but I'm still not sure what you're doing here? It feels as if you're panicking a little... and we have no need to panic", she said, casually monitoring their immediate area, which was busy with scores of anonymous central government employees.

"Well, I have some news. News that makes me worry - and should worry you, too", hissed McBride, a little irritated at his companion's condescending tone. Her body language and tone remained non-plussed at the statement and they walked-on a few paces. She smiled as they passed a group of federal office workers racing from one building to another. A few steps later, McBride broke the enforced silence and said, *"I think Republic is dead"*.

Those five words had the desired effect. She stopped walking and, whilst her expression remained calm, the information had clearly taken her by surprise. After processing the statement, she re-started their walk and asked, *"When - and how?"*

McBride explained; *"Crushed to death, a week ago. I've seen the CCTV footage, and I'm pretty sure it was him. It clearly shows him being pushed. The police recognised the man who pushed him and are searching for him, but he seems to have disappeared".*

She took time to process this information, reflecting on its significance. McBride remained silent, until he saw her body language change, from a slightly tentative gait to her more composed and assertive one. He then continued with his briefing. *"The man they recognised had received £25,000 in his account the day before Republic was pushed. It apparently came from the husband of one of the detectives associated with the case - Alex Walker, who's married to DS Stephanie Walker. She was removed from the case, just before Alex was arrested on suspicion of blackmail, fraud and murder".*

"Who did he allegedly murder?" she asked.

"His agent. Mr Walker was a commercially-successful male model. All legit and, up to last year, very lucrative; but then the work - and the money – appear to have suddenly stopped. The police have accused him of murdering his agent after extorting £100,000 from him; apparently something to do with an incriminating video of his agent knowingly having sex with a minor".

"Is there any kind of doubt about any of this?" she asked.

McBride realised he had been non-committal in his report with his repeated reference to the 'apparent' situations that had unfolded. He smiled, fleetingly, in admiration at her analytical mind. "Yes", he announced. "The HMET team are about to receive a report from the UK's National Crime Agency, but I've already seen it. Amongst their conclusions is that Andrew Jagger's and Alex Walker's accounts were hacked, and that the same device was used to access both accounts". He paused for a few seconds for the information to sink in, before continuing. "The NCA tried to trace the device used, but it has no digital footprint. I doubt Walker had any kind of access to such specialised equipment... we're talking military-grade tech. Black Ops".

"So, you think Walker has been framed?" she quizzed.

"Yes, I do", said McBride, without hesitation. "And no, we don't know why... yet".

She began thinking out loud, asking a series of rhetorical questions: "Who, outside of the intelligence services, would have access to that sort of equipment?" She paused, as she stared into McBride's eyes. "What are the chances that Alex Walker really is involved but is clever enough to make it look like he was being framed - killing the one person who might know all about him?" She took time to pause and reflect on her own questions. "You were right to come here. I apologise for questioning your motive".

McBride smiled graciously at the admission.

"We've spent too long and have too much invested to let this slip now", she continued. *"I'd hoped we'd killed off and buried any suspicion twenty years ago, but it seems we haven't"*. The look on her face had turned to one of seeking assurance, and McBride replied to her silent plea;

"I'll keep digging - until we strike gold", he promised.

*"And I need to fix the leak that we seem to continually suffer with - and fix it **permanently**"*, she said. *"It's time to take all of someone's savings. I'll call my plumber"*.

McBride put a broad smile on his face and extended his hand. He raised his voice to the normal level, appearing to end an innocent meeting with a cheerful, *"Thank you so much for your valuable time, Senator"*. The pair shook hands, and Senator Nikki Swati turned and headed back to her security briefing.

McBride watched her walk away, before turning and hailing a cab. He missed her glance back at him. She was no fool, and she knew Simon McBride was a greedy, ambitious and ruthless man. An extra share of the $100m their illegal scheme was about to pay-out was possibly worth killing one more operative and framing an unsuspecting Alex Walker.

"Who knows", she thought. *"Perhaps you're the one actually responsible for killing Abercrombie, Mercantile and Casa too, Mr McBride"*.

From a vantage point, just a few hundred feet away, Amelia Demetrious frowned. She had found out that

McBride had flown to Washington following a phone call from Republic. He wasn't dead, but the man who died underneath the bus was partially selected because they looked vaguely similar. The fact McBride was here to brief Senator Swati on the apparent murder, led Demetrious to the only obvious conclusion there was.

She now knew what she needed to do.

Chapter 50

Acting DS Hobbs and DI Clark sat in the meeting room and listened to the recording Ferranti had left for them; the recording of the call he had received from Paul Reynolds – his stepfather. Hobbs pressed 'stop' and looked up at Clark.

"Where is Ferranti now?" Clark asked.

"He went home, Ma'am. Said he had some business to deal with, and that he plans to head to a new location. He says he doesn't feel safe staying in one place, and doesn't want a Police presence for fear of attracting attention", replied Hobbs.

"Understandable, yet foolhardy at the same time", sighed Clark. *"Still, we can't force him, so let's not waste our energy worrying about him. Let's spend it finding out more about Paul Reynolds"*.

"We've already started enquiries, Ma'am, with the usual research. NCA are searching for links, as Mr Ferranti gave us some useful insights and background, so we're hoping we can get something sooner than usual". Hobbs spoke in a confident tone as he relayed the detail.

"What do we know about him?" asked Clark.

Hobbs flicked open his notebook and began to run through the key points. "He's English, according to Ferranti. He recalls seeing Reynolds' passport some years back, when he was looking in a set of drawers for money to borrow", he said, whilst placing emphasis on the word 'borrow' that made them both smirk. "Reynolds was the long-term boyfriend of Ferranti's mother, but disappeared after he had beaten her near to death. Ferranti says the local and State Police couldn't find any trace of Reynolds after he fled the scene. We've sent a request over to Washington PD to ask for a copy of their files".

"Good", said Clark, whilst thinking of further instructions to give. "Once you get a firm ID, let's check credit cards, travel, any bank details etc, and see what the NCA can find". She stood to leave the room, but hesitated. "And let's see if the Washington PD can get an up-to-date statement from Mrs Ferranti. Maybe Reynolds has been in touch with her recently, but she just hasn't told her son".

"I'm afraid that won't be possible", said a resigned Hobbs. "We're checking, but Ferranti says his mother never truly recovered from the beating, and subsequently died from her injuries three years ago".

Clark appeared initially saddened by the news, before enquiring, "What were the injuries to Mrs Ferranti, do we know? If not, can we ensure we ask the Washington PD for any information they have?" Hobbs looked a little puzzled at the question, but Clark answered his query before he had time to ask it himself. *"It's probably nothing, but it would be good to know if there were any similarities to any of the injuries suffered by the victims we're looking into"*.

Hobbs nodded his head; both impressed at, and agreeing with, the logic of the thought process. Maybe this new avenue was even more promising than he had originally thought. He checked Clark had gone back to her desk and then closed the door. He pulled out his mobile and dialled a number well-known to him. It rang and rang, before eventually going through to an answering facility.

"It's Hobbs, just returning your call. I'll call you back in a couple of hours with an update. Please don't call me back". He ended the call and looked up through the internal glazing. Thankfully, nobody was looking over, because he was convinced that he had 'guilt' written all over his face right now.

Chapter 51

It was dark, with rain in the air and a thick fog threatening to mask the area like a blanket. Khatri pulled up outside Ferranti's house, and the front door opened immediately. Ferranti had been looking out of the window, as he'd expected Khatri ten minutes earlier. As he exited the house, pulled the front door closed and locked it, he glanced across the village square, and then up towards the church, and back. He felt he couldn't be too careful. He strode across the pavement and opened the rear door of the Leaf, putting a holdall in the back seat, before climbing into the back himself.

"Where the hell have you been?" demanded an extremely nervous Ferranti. *"You were supposed to be here at 10:30pm – it's 10:40 already"*.

Khatri was a little taken aback by Ferranti's mood, but he reminded himself just how on-edge Ferranti had been earlier in the day at Mrs Atha's Tea Shop. *"Sorry... accident on the A64 at Seacroft, so I had to come via Crossgates instead"*, Khatri explained.

The explanation helped Ferranti relax a little and Khatri could see him nodding in his rear-view mirror. With that, Khatri also relaxed, and the tension in the air subsided, slightly.

"So where are we going?" asked Khatri.

"Otley. Take me to Westgate and I'll walk from there", said Ferranti, but Khatri noticed him looking out at the weather.

"I can take you wherever you need to go, and I can wait for you, if you like?" Khatri offered.

"Too dangerous", mumbled Ferranti, absent-mindedly. Khatri looked up at him in the rear-view mirror, inquisitively. Ferranti noticed and responded accordingly. *"I mean the place I'm going probably isn't safe for your car - pot holes and jagged brickwork on the track"*, he lied, still staring out of the window into the gloom.

"Oh, I didn't realise you'd been there before?" Khatri said, somewhat surprised.

"I went to check the place. Important to know the location, especially if…", but his voice faded, as he realised he was about to say too much. He didn't want Khatri to know why he was going there and no doubt offer unwanted support that would complicate the situation. Khatri decided not to ask about the rest of the sentence, as he'd grown to know that when Ferranti didn't say something, it only annoyed him if you queried it.

They drove in virtual silence for the rest of the journey, passing through Seacroft, Weetwood, Adel, Bramhope and onwards into Otley. The rain had started to fall and the fog had thickened, so visibility had fallen to less than two hundred metres. As they turned right into

Westgate, Ferranti piped up. *"Slow down. I need to see which way I'm going"*. Then, in less than a minute, he exclaimed, *"There!"*

Khatri glanced to his right and saw a series of derelict warehouses. *"What, the old Jeffries Haulage place?"* he asked, with some surprise. He checked behind him and, with nothing coming, he stopped the car and then started to reverse back up Westgate.

"What are you doing?" asked Ferranti, with a degree of both nerves and anger in his voice.

"I'm taking you in there, parking, and waiting for you. I don't know why you're here and I don't want to know, but you're a friend and it's a scary place this late at night. There were drug junkies living in there last month. They might have come back for all we know".

Ferranti started to protest, but he had to admit, the warehouse site did look daunting. He sat back, feeling a little defeated, but quietly grateful.

The Leaf trundled over the old concrete and tarmac, coming to a stop behind a single derelict office block that sat perpendicular to the extensive warehouses. Nobody from the street could see the car, and Ferranti was pleased, as he didn't want an inquisitive local police officer spotting the Leaf and calling it in.

"Wait here and lock your doors", said Ferranti, as he pulled the hood up on his dark jacket and opened the car door. As he climbed out of the car, Khatri hissed,

loudly, *"Don't forget your torch"*, but Ferranti had already gone and was disappearing into the gloom, to the front and right of the single storey office block. Khatri locked the doors and put his headphones on, pressing play on his new Sony Walkman CD player. He sank low into his seat, and whilst pretending to listen to the music, was actually starting to feel quite exposed. He moved the wing mirrors and rear-view mirror on the car, so he had a wide peripheral view around the vehicle.

After a few minutes, he saw a figure emerging from the fog. It was heading to the car from the rear and left of the small office building. Khatri smiled to himself, muttering, *"Knew you should have taken the torch"*. He unlocked the doors in time for the rear door to fly open. Khatri, still smiling, looked into the rear-view mirror and started to say, *"I did try to tell you to take…"*, but he froze when he saw a pair of unfamiliar blue eyes staring back at him. Before Khatri could say anything else, in one rapid movement the passenger hooked a piece of saw wire over the headrest and around Khatri's neck, pulling his head backwards and cutting into Khatri's throat with dreadful ease. Khatri's eyes widened in terror as he tried to halt the progress of the wire, but it was futile. After a brief struggle, Khatri's bulging eyes dimmed and his body slumped down into the car seat. His hands, with his now blood-soaked fingers, dropped from his throat and flopped onto his thighs. Aarav Khatri was dead.

The killer released his grip on the wire and opened the rear door, removing his jacket and throwing it onto the back seat. He then turned and ran to a large bush nearby, pulling out a petrol canister he had hidden there the previous night. He smiled at his preparedness and returned to the car. He opened the driver's door and emptied the contents of the canister over Khatri and then into the rear of the car. The holdall Ferranti had placed in the back seat was also doused with petrol. The killer stood back and took out a hand-held flare. He pulled the cap off and struck the tip of the exposed flare; igniting it. He then tossed it into the car and ran back behind the office block, heading in the direction of Westgate and the anonymity of the town centre. He removed the rest of his subtle disguise, as he went.

The flames caught quickly and soon engulfed the interior of the car. A sudden whoosh echoed through the night, as a large pool of petrol in the back seat ignited something in Ferranti's bag – something that sounded like a small rocket launching. The sound and the flash from the sudden wall of flames caught the attention of several passers-by heading home from the local pubs. It was also heard by Ferranti, who raced out the office block and saw the burning wreckage. The inside was ablaze, but Ferranti could just see the profile of Khatri's body. He sprinted to the burning car and, pulling his jacket sleeve over his hands, tried to pull Khatri from the flames. The seat belt was still holding Khatri in place, so Ferranti pulled a knife from his pocket – something he'd brought for his own security and peace of mind – and started to hack through the seat belt. The fire was starting to burn the skin on his hands, but he continued, like a man hell-bent on saving his friend.

Locals were now running into the warehouse parking area but were fearful of the car exploding, so all but one of them stayed back. One man, however, ran forward and grabbed hold of one of Khatri's arms, as Ferranti finally cut through the seat belt and freed his friend. The two of them pulled Khatri from the car, but his badly burnt body was clearly lifeless.

Ferranti sank to his knees. *"No!"*, he cried-out into the darkness of the sky. "NOOOOOOOOOOOO!"

The man who had helped him pull Khatri from the car put a hand onto Ferranti's shoulder in sympathy. He felt Ferranti's body quiver, as the tears flowed. For the first time in nearly four years, Adam Ferranti broke down and sobbed, openly and uncontrollably. His friend lay dead in his arms, as the sound of sirens drew ever closer.

Chapter 52

The news of Aarav Khatri's death reached DI Clark in the early hours of the morning. The local Police had secured the inner and outer perimeters of the scene, and SOCO had arrived a little after 1am.

The fire crews had put the fire out, but in doing so had unavoidably contaminated any evidence that might have held trace material from the killer. The ambulance crew had tended to Ferranti's burns and those of the man who had helped at the scene. The man was local and known to Police, but not because he had a criminal record. He ran the local youth football team, where the sons of some of the officers regularly played. He had offered Ferranti his condolences, which were gratefully accepted but of little help. Adam Ferranti was sat, very much alone, feeling hollow, when DI Clark arrived at the scene just after 6am.

She first spoke to the Lead SOCO before taking a seat next to Ferranti on a broken brick wall, not far from the warehouses. He glanced up, momentarily. *"I've already told them everything I know"*, he said, solemnly.

"I know, Mr Ferranti. I'm not here to interview you; just to see how you are? You've suffered a terrible shock and, despite what you or others might think, we're

human, too. We still feel people's pain", said a surprisingly softly spoken Clark.

Ferranti looked up; his eyes red from crying and dark from a lack of sleep. He looked at Clark for a few seconds and then said, *"Thank you"*, before looking back down at the ground.

"Is there anyone we can call for you?" asked Clark.

Ferranti shook his head, then changed his mind. *"Perhaps you could tell my boss I'm not going to be in for a few days. I don't really feel like talking to anyone right now"*. He looked at Clark in hope and she nodded.

"Of course. Is there anyone else?" she asked, still speaking softly.

Ferranti stared up at the skyline, as the faintest rays of sunlight pierced the dark shroud of the night. *"I suppose you'll be talking to Aarav's parents?"* he asked, already knowing the answer, but still wanting to talk about his friend.

"Yes, that's already being handled through our contacts in the Kolkata Police Department", replied Clark. *"No one else? A wife, girlfriend, partner... boyfriend even?"*

Ferranti wanted to talk to Stephanie Walker, but he knew he couldn't let Clark know they were on personal terms. He shook his head, adding, *"I'm sure everyone who needs to know will know. Apart from Aarav, my most frequent contacts these days are with the Police.*

You, DC Hobbs and DS Walker", he said, sounding lonely. He wondered whether or not Clark would reveal that Walker was off the case.

"Well, if you think of anyone, I'll be here for about an hour and then I'll be heading back to the station", she said, rising from the makeshift seat. *"I believe your mobile phone was destroyed in the fire, so please let me know when you manage to get a replacement. We'll want to talk to you again soon, I'm sure. Acting Detective Sergeant Hobbs will be taking over the scene shortly"*. Ferranti nodded, but didn't break his gaze from the watery sunrise.

Fifteen minutes later, a genuinely subdued Hobbs wandered over to Ferranti and offered him a lift home. Ferranti smiled weakly and said he was grateful for the offer, but he thought a taxi would be the best choice once the paramedics had agreed he was able to leave. *"Oh, and congrats on the promotion, Acting Detective Sergeant Hobbs"*, he offered. Hobbs smiled and nodded, whilst retaining a polite solemnity in Ferranti's presence.

The taxi duly arrived and Ferranti walked into his messy lounge almost nine hours after he had last left it, with the cold cup of tea still sat on the table and a half-eaten pack of biscuits resting next to it. He dropped onto the sofa and rested his head on the back. He closed his eyes; drained in every way. He was about to fall asleep, when he suddenly felt the need to speak to Stephanie Walker. He wanted to hear her voice.

In the drawer in the kitchen, he had a spare mobile phone - a pay-as-you-go model which still had some credit. He gently teased Walker's business card out of his wallet, careful not to hurt his burnt and blistered fingertips, and dialled Walker's number. The call went to her answer phone, so he left a short message, trying to ensure his voice didn't crack with the raw emotion.

"Hi, it's me. Look, I know this is inappropriate, but I really need to hear your voice. Aarav Khatri – my friend - was murdered last night and…". His voice quivered with emotion. He held the phone to his chest as he composed himself, and ended the message with, *"Please, just give me a call"*.

Stephanie Walker was at home when Ferranti was calling. With her husband in custody, she knew he wouldn't be walking through door and creating a scene any time soon, so she had completed her domestic chores in peace. She noticed her phone ringing but was busy loading the washing machine at the time. She was really quite enjoying not talking to anyone. An hour later, however, she looked at the phone and saw she two missed calls and two voicemails. She didn't recognise one caller ID, but when she heard Ferranti's message, and the emotion in his voice, she was relieved not to have answered the call. She had things to do before she spoke to Adam Ferranti again.

Stephanie walked back into the bathroom, with her mind on the immediate problem. She picked up a small pen-like device and momentarily closed her eyes. She said a little prayer and then opened them again; staring down at the device.

"Fuck", she whispered to herself. This was the last thing Stephanie Walker needed right now. She was only a couple of days late with her period, but the device confirmed that she was pregnant.

Chapter 53

John Zander had been a 'cleaner' for a number of government agencies for over 20 years. He had resolved several issues for them, leaving a trail of seventy-nine bodies in his bloody career. He was just moments away from making that eighty.

He knew the house on Mozart Avenue had standard locks on the rear door, as he had been in the house earlier in the week to check for creaking floorboards and squeaky door hinges, and to plan his subsequent escape from his upcoming kill. Tonight, the front room was in virtual darkness, with only shafts of moonlight from the cloudy night sky sporadically spilling into the room and illuminating the area around the window. The streetlights outside the house had been switched off two days earlier, as part of the preparation for tonight.

Amelia Demetrious was sitting in her favourite window-side chair as usual at this time of night. She was apparently fast asleep. Zander entered the room, altering his night-sight goggles to accommodate for the moonlight. He could see the back of the chair and the top few inches of Demetrious's head, showing just above the backrest. His Maxim 9 was already in hand; a gun not yet known – let alone available - to the American public. With its integrated silencer, it looked like something from the movie 'Blade Runner', but Black Ops and the CIA had been using it for several years.

Moving deftly to his left, to avoid a creaky floorboard he had noticed on his previous visit, Zander stepped onto a rug, muffling his near-silent movement even more. He slowly raised the Maxim and pulled the trigger, with the semi-automatic sending three bullets into the back of Amelia Demetrious's skull. Her head lolled forward and the outline of her body slumped to the right. Zander moved forwards, so as to be able to confirm the kill. As he lifted his foot from the rug however, a series of tiny sensors were activated and shouts of *"Freeze"* and *"Don't move"* rang out, as five heavily armed law enforcement agents appeared from the hall and darkened corners within the room. Red dots appeared all over Zander's head and chest. He froze, momentarily assessing his chances of escape, before realising he would die trying. He smiled, smugly; not at being caught, but because he fully expected his superiors would get him released, without charge, within the hour.

As he was being searched, hands firmly bound with plastic flexicuffs, Amelia Demetrious looked towards the window of her house, from the security of an undercover Police car parked out in the street. She could just make out the makeshift mannequin in the chair, with its wig still in place, but its head now featuring holes where the bullets had shattered the moulded plastic. She was actually impressed by the skill Zander had shown and, maybe in a previous life, she would have liked to hire him herself. For now, though, she was just happy to be alive. She also had to make a call; a call she was very much looking forward to.

Senator Nikki Swati was awoken by a distinctive ring tone on her mobile. She roused quickly, checked the display, and smiled. She clicked 'answer' and put the phone to her ear. *"Is the job complete?"* she asked, confidently.

"Not yet", came the reply from a voice that Swati was not expecting to hear. *"But it will be very soon"*, said Demetrious, who then ended the call and handed Zander's phone back to the officer in charge of the operation. Demetrious smiled, as she retrieved her own mobile from her cardigan pocket, and dialled a different number. When the phone was answered, she uttered just one word: *"Now"*.

The window of Senator Swati's bedroom was suddenly ablaze from floodlights, and someone began hammering on her front door. Startled, Swati raced to the window and peeked out through the blinds. To her horror, the street immediately outside her house was filled with two news crews and three Police cars, all with their lights on and camera crews at the ready. The hammering at the door continued, but one of the TV crews had spotted the movement at the window and instantly turned their camera in its direction.

CNN and Sky carried the broadcast live as Breaking News. The cameras followed the scene from the bedroom window, all the way through to a startled Senator Swati being led from her home in handcuffs, wearing a large overcoat which covered her pyjamas. Most of Europe and the entire United States were watching the drama unfold. No-one knew where the information had come from, but the ticker-tape banner headline read, *'LIVE: US Senator, Nikki Swati, arrested over intelligence leak and abuse of office'*.

It was the early hours of the morning in England, but in his townhouse in Kensington, Simon McBride was wide awake as he watched in horror. At the same time, in his cottage in Barwick, Adam Ferranti turned away from the coverage and picked up his mobile, reading the text message that had just arrived. It said *'An exclusive information file is in your inbox. Now you have your doozer. Regards, Amelia'*.

Chapter 54

Mike Hobbs was at home. It was his day off, and he was just about to get ready for bed, when his phone rang. He saw the caller ID and gathered himself before answering it.

"Hey, Mike. Sorry I didn't call back earlier and thanks for doing this. I know you're sticking your neck out for me", said Stephanie Walker.

"No problem", replied Hobbs, clearly sounding nervous. They both knew that if he was caught talking to her about the case, when she had been officially removed from it, he would certainly face disciplinary action. It was only because of a deep loyalty to Walker that, somewhat reluctantly, he said he would help wherever he could.

"So, did you get to hear the tape from Ferranti's stepfather?", asked Walker.

"I did", replied Hobbs. *"How weird was that; his own stepfather?"*

"I know", Walker responded. She then paused and, with a genuinely concerned tone in her voice, tentatively asked, *"What can you tell me about Alex? How is he*

holding up?" She knew this was a risky topic for her and Hobbs to be talking about. Hobbs hesitated, unsure how much or how little to say. "*It's okay, Mike, don't feel you have to tell me anything*", said Walker, breaking the uncomfortable silence. "*I appreciate it's not a fair question, given the circumstances*".

Hobbs thought a little longer and then braced himself. "*He's asked for a solicitor*".

Stephanie Walker felt that this was an odd statement to make. "*Of course he's asked for a solicitor - doesn't everyone?*" she challenged, in somewhat of a mocking tone.

"*He didn't at first*", said Hobbs. "*I can't tell you what or why, but at his first interview, he declined the offer, saying he didn't need one*". The line went silent again, and Walker sensed that Hobbs was debating whether he could or should share any more information with her. She didn't have to wait too long, before Hobbs spoke again. It was as if he couldn't hold it in any longer and seemed to think that if he said it quickly, it would be fine. "*What do you know about £100k going from Andrew Jagger's account into your husband's, or £25k sent from Alex to a man called Bryan Rodriguez, who later deliberately pushed a member of the public under a bus?*" Hobbs was almost breathless by the time he had finished the final hastily shared sentence.

Walker was speechless. Her brain couldn't comprehend what Hobbs was asking her, so her only reply was a bemused, "*What?*"

Hobbs didn't respond. He waited for Walker to process the questions and deduce that Alex must have been challenged with some new evidence - damning evidence.

"*No*", said Walker. "*This doesn't feel right*". She was over the emotion and confusion, and her analytical brain was now at work. "*Mike, my husband is physically abusive to me, but he's not a murderer and he's not got or done anything to earn £100k. There has to be another way to look at this. Maybe the question has to be who's trying to frame him?*"

Hobbs, meanwhile, was breathing a sigh of relief. His loyalty to Walker was in no doubt, but he had suspected she was hiding something for weeks, and so was pleased she had now confirmed that Alex Walker was a wife-beater. Had she not revealed that hugely private fact, Hobbs wouldn't have felt that she trusted him; but she clearly did.

"*You're right*", he said, calmly. "*Denton from The Met seems to think the same*".

Stephanie Walker gripped the phone a little tighter and smiled, softly.

Hobbs continued, "*Denton seemed to have information that DI Clark didn't*".

"*What is it?*" gasped Walker, eagerly.

"*Dunno*", he replied. Hobbs knew Walker would be disappointed to hear that, so he quickly added, "*But

I do know that Clark immediately dismissed everyone from the morning meeting, but asked Denton to stay on the line. Boy, she was pissed off. Oh, and Denton seemed to think he had a clue about the Spanish message on the answering machine at the Goas scene, too".

"Anyone looking into a possible link between Reynolds and Jagger?" asked Walker.

"The DI seems to be keeping her cards close to her chest at the moment, Sarge".

Walker smiled at the reference to her as 'Sarge' by Hobbs. *"Thank you, Mike... or should I say, Detective Constable Hobbs"*, and they both laughed, lightly, as the tension broke and things felt a little more normal. At least temporarily.

"It's actually Acting Detective Sergeant, if you don't mind", Hobbs replied. Walker laughed a little more, but he could hear the sadness coming through; not that he had been temporarily promoted, but at how quickly Stephanie Walker was becoming seemingly irrelevant within the team.

"Well, congratulations ADS Hobbs", Walker added. She had been thinking about what to say next, and knew she had to protect Hobbs from any involvement, should things go awry. *"Mike, you should know that I'm going to talk to someone - someone close to Ferranti. I'm not going to say who or when or why, because the less you know the better, but I HAVE to*

find out more. This waiting is killing me and I hate feeling helpless", she said.

Hobbs was nodding his head and had a look of gratitude and acceptance on his face when he said, *"Understood, Sarge. Be careful"*. He was just about to say "good luck", when a thought popped into his head. *"Sarge?"*

"Yes, Mike?" Walker replied.

"I'm not sure this is relevant, or why I'm telling you this, but I think Denton has an insider in British Intelligence feeding him information. I've seen a note on DI Clark's notepad. It's a man called Simon McBride from MI5. I don't know why, but her notes suggested this guy has something to do with America and someone called Senator Swati. Well, that's the woman who just got arrested in Washington… for abuse of office. It feels like more than just a coincidence if Clark had it on her radar". He stopped talking for a moment, before concluding with, *"That's all I can tell you"*, and then he ended the call.

Walker sat for a moment and reflected on what Hobbs had told her, but in particular the final comment he made: 'That's all I can tell you' rather than 'That's all I know'. It struck her as a peculiar phrase for a normally reserved Hobbs to use. She was tired, but her brain was buzzing. Tonight was not going to be a peaceful or restful night for her.

Chapter 55

DI Clark called the HMET meeting to order. The murmurs around the room quietened and then stopped, as all eyes fixed on her in anticipation. For the first time in several years, Clark now felt the pressure from a team's expectation of her next move.

"*Morning all*", she said in a commanding voice that hid her sudden and unexpected nerves. "*We have just received a report from the National Crime Agency, and will be subsequently dropping some of the charges against Alex Walker*".

Mumbling rippled round the room like a Mexican wave, before Clark cleared her throat to announce continuation of the rest of her report. "*The NCA confirm that the transfer of funds, to and from Alex Walker's account, were carried out on the same device. This device has no IP address and the NCA confirm it was probably completed from a piece of specialist tech that Alex Walker is very unlikely to possess*". Clark glanced around and realised that this didn't seem to be a surprise to anyone in the room. It certainly wasn't a surprise to DS Denton logging in from London, and this troubled DI Clark. "*Forensics have also returned their analysis on Andrew Jagger's body and have cast doubt that Alex Walker had any involvement in the murder.*

Local CCTV corroborates Walker's story that he was at the house twice that evening".

Postures around the table became slumped and a couple of the attendees flipped their case files closed, in disappointment. *"Let's not forget, though"*, Clark said, with some enthusiasm, *"We still need to nail this bastard for aiding and abetting the under-age sex crime"*. Her enthusiasm fell on relative silence, though. It was an interesting and serious development, but the investigating force at the time would resurrect that case; not HMET.

"Ma'am", began DS Denton. *"Any news on the other two boxes from the hardware shop that Walker collected?"*

"Not yet", replied Clark. *"We'll be following that up with Mr Walker, but my expectation is that he's being used as a diversion or a fall-guy by someone else"*.

"Yes Ma'am", came a dejected response from Denton, nodding along to himself that this was likely the truth.

"DS Williams", began Clark. *"Any news on your search for Bryan Rodriguez, the man who pushed the man we now believe to be Harold Fry into the path of the bus?"*

"Not yet, Ma'am", Williams replied. *"He seems to have gone into hiding. Knowing Rodriguez, though, if he really has got £25,000 in his pocket, he'll do something very stupid, very quickly, and be nicked before the week is over"*.

Clark was about to thank Williams for the update, when he spoke again. *"We do have some news on Harold Fry though, Ma'am. He has a security background, but we know he had no ties whatsoever to any of the previous victims or names on the list. We can also confirm he has no known associates called Paul Reynolds"*.

Clark was stumped. She was never stumped and, for the first time in her meteoric career, she had no idea which way to turn. Either she was too late in drawing conclusions, or someone was staying a few steps ahead of her, leading her into a maze of confusion and chaos. Her mind immediately turned to DS Steve Denton, along with his intelligence connection, Simon McBride.

"So, what will your next move be, Detective Sergeant Denton?" she mused.

Chapter 56

A local police officer climbed the stairs of the stoop leading up to a house in Plainfield, Wisconsin. He knocked on the door and took half a step back. It was early in the morning, but he had no choice other than to wake the person or people living inside. He heard noises from within the house, as someone shuffled across the front room and a woman, who looked to be in her 40's, peered out through a gap in the curtains. She waved at the officer in acknowledgement and made her way to the door.

"Morning, Ma'am", said the officer, touching the tip of his hat in a gesture of courtesy, once the door was opened.

"Officer", the woman replied, acknowledging him in return. Though she was relatively young, she had a cane in her right hand, which she was leaning on, heavily. *"How can I help you?"*

"Is this the residence of Abi Ferranti?", the officer enquired, looking at his notebook to check the name and address.

"I'm Abi Ferranti", the woman replied, a little concerned. *"Is there a problem, officer?"* Her expression

then turned to one of exasperation, as she exhaled loudly and said, *"If it's Mrs Getz complaining about the mess again…"*, and with that she raised her voice and bent forward, as she looked across to the property next door, *"I swear I've told her a thousand times not to leave trash outside. It attracts animals and I'm not the only neighbour with a cat, you know!"* She turned back to the officer and shook her head in frustration, whilst she shuffled with her walking cane; re-positioning herself to reduce the discomfort she was in.

The officer looked sombre and shook his head. *"No, Ma'am, it's nothing like that. I'm afraid we might have some news about your father"*, he said. Abi suddenly went pale, and momentarily lost her balance. The officer quickly leant forwards and held her elbow, to help steady her in the doorway. She instinctively grabbed the officer's arm, and slowly re-found her balance and her composure. *"Are you alright, Miss Reynolds?"* he asked, in a concerned voice.

Abi was breathing heavily, but nodded her head. *"Yes, thank you. It's just… I'd managed to forget all about him"*. She looked into the officer's eyes with a haunted expression, before asking, *"Is he back?"*

"No, Ma'am. He's definitely not back, but the Chief sure would appreciate you coming down to the station, just to help with some enquiries".

She looked at the officer, trying to second-guess why the Police would need her help again. She had always feared her father's return, after his brutal attack on her and her mother many years ago. Reluctantly, she went inside the house, gathered her things, and prepared to accompany the officer to the station.

Four hours later, Abi was back home. She collapsed into the swing seat that sat on the decking at the front of the house. Tears suddenly flowed from her eyes. Mrs Getz, the old lady from next door, was walking back from the local store. As she passed the house, she saw Abi crying. She stopped and paused to consider what to do with her angry, irrational neighbour. After a few seconds, Beatrice Getz nodded to herself, as she came to a decision. She opened the garden gate to her neighbour's house and made her way up the path and onto the stoop. She plopped her aged frame onto the swing seat next to Abi Ferranti, and wrapped her arms around her. Abi stopped crying, and her red, puffy eyes looked up at the caring face gazing back at her. She smiled and Mrs Getz smiled back, pulling her close again as the tears restarted. Abi Ferranti had found comfort in the arms of another human being for the first time in over twenty years.

She had one phone call to make and it felt like her nightmares would soon all be over.

Chapter 57

The second floor was empty in the Yorkshire Post offices, and most of the lights were already switched off. The day team had long finished and gone home, and Barry Clements was just about to close his laptop down for the day, too, when an email notification pinged onto his screen. It was from Adam Ferranti and the subject line simply said, '*Doozer - of international proportions!*' The body of the email was empty, but there was an attachment.

Such displays of enthusiasm were rare from Adam Ferranti, so Clements paused to ponder. Should he wait until morning, or open the email now and stay a little later in the office than usual? His wife was out with friends tonight on a rare social event that didn't require him to reluctantly attend, and she had already suggested he get fish and chips for himself for dinner. Simply put, he could leave work whenever he wanted to.

"*No reason to rush, I guess*", he said to himself as he looked to open the email, but then his stomach rumbled and he remembered just how hungry he was getting. Just as he decided to go home after all, a second email arrived. The subject line said, '*I know you want to go home, but you **really** need to read this first*'. Ferranti had clearly second-guessed what Clements was thinking.

"*How the hell...?*" thought Clements, smiling. He realised everyone knew he operated like clockwork – the polar opposite to Ferranti. Clements chuckled at the thought and decided to see why Ferranti thought he should be so excited by the emails. He picked out a bar of chocolate from his desk draw to fend off the hunger a little while longer.

Over an hour later, Barry Clements eased himself back in his chair and stared at the screen. "*Fuck*", he said quietly to himself; drained and in awe of the amazing article Ferranti had sent him. It was, without doubt, the biggest doozer Adam Ferranti had ever produced for the Yorkshire Post and, in all honesty, was probably more the type of explosive feature The Times or one of the big Sunday broadsheet papers would release. Apart from saying "*Fuck*" one more time for emphasis, Barry Clements was speechless. Could the content of the article be correct? And yet, why was he even asking that question, given the article contained names, dates, leaked documentation and sources who were willing to be identified. It deserved an edition all to itself. As an experienced editor and journalist, Clements could find no fault – no flaw – in the revelations. His priority was to now call the owners and their legal team, because if this went wrong, it would be the end of the paper.

Fifteen minutes later, Clements pressed 'Send' on the meeting invite he had just arranged with the lawyers. He tagged it as 'Private', so even the secretarial team wouldn't be able to see who the meeting was with or what it was about. He then typed an email back to Ferranti. The subject line simply read, 'F*ck!' When the email arrived in his inbox, Ferranti couldn't contain his joy. He punched the air and genuinely felt happy for the first time in years.

Back at the Yorkshire Post, Clements closed-down his laptop, flipped the lid shut and placed it into his desk drawer. Just as the draw slid closed, there was a knock on his office door. One of the security team from reception had escorted DS Stephanie Walker up to the second floor.

"I'm sorry, Mr Clements, were you about to leave for the evening?" Walker asked, flashing her badge.

Clements knew that her question and gesture probably meant that he wouldn't be going anywhere soon. He put a file and his sandwich box into his holdall, and said, *"No, not quite. Just tidying up. Please, come in"*.

Walker smiled graciously and sat on the chair opposite Clements. She placed her bag on the floor and pulled out her notebook. *"I'd just like to ask a few questions about Adam Ferranti. You may not know, but there's an ongoing investigation he's helping us with right now"*.

"Err, no... I wasn't aware, but of course, we're more than happy to help the Police with any investigation", said Clements, momentarily wondering whether the Police were also on the track of the subjects in the draft revelations he had just read in Ferranti's article.

From his reaction and his body language, Walker could tell that Clements truly didn't know what she was talking about. That helped her, as she wasn't supposed to be there questioning him, but she could leverage the need for utter confidentiality in keeping her involvement a secret.

"*Well, we're trying to keep it low key and not cause any alarm. I'd appreciate it that, unless I authorise otherwise, you do not discuss this conversation - even with Mr Ferranti*", said Walker, firmly.

"*Of course, of course*", replied Clements.

"*Mr Clements, I don't want to alarm you, but it appears that someone is using Mr Ferranti as a messenger. That person is someone we suspect to be a multiple murderer. Mr Ferranti has been extremely co-operative, but we fear for his safety. That's why, on our advice, he took time off, recently*", regaled Walker, in an attempt to put Clements in the picture.

"*I just thought that was because he wanted to sober-up and rest? I knew he'd been under a lot of pressure recently, but I had no idea that...*", and then Clements just shook his head in shock. "*How can I help?*"

"*Ordinarily, we wouldn't involve an employer and, as I mentioned earlier, I urge you to keep this whole conversation to yourself, Mr Clements*", said Walker, making sure that Clements truly understood their position. "*Now, my first question is this. If someone wanted to find out about Mr Ferranti's habits and routine, how easy do you think that would be to do, in terms of his work?*"

Clements chuckled. "*Routine? Adam Ferranti? Those words don't belong in the same sentence, Detective. He has what he likes to call 'flexible working', but we call it 'turns up when he's sober enough to function'. Although, to be truthful and fair, I've actually never seen him drunk, and he has made some effort over his appearance lately*". He guffawed, before concluding, "*I suspect there may be a woman on the scene!*"

Walker looked down at her notebook and made some scribbles. She couldn't help but smile and blush a little at the thought of Adam Ferranti making an effort just for her. "*Does he have a routine at work? Does he always sit at the same desk, for example, or does he move around?*" she asked, after composing herself.

"*Same desk. He's not the tidiest person in the world, so everyone in the office agreed they didn't want to hot-desk with him. He sits over there, by the window*", said Clements, standing up and pointing to the far corner of the office.

"*May I take a look?*" Walker enquired.

"*Of course*", replied Clements, and he stood so he could lead her across the room to Ferranti's desk.

As they arrived at the window, Walker noticed the desk was extremely untidy. A half-empty mug of milky coffee looked like it might be growing bacteria, and the desk was strewn with post-it notes and scraps of paper. Walker looked around the desk and out of the windows that were behind and to the left of the desk chair. She noted that there were no buildings or vantage points that overlooked where Ferranti would have sat, which puzzled her, as she recalled him saying that the first time the caller rang, he knew what exactly Ferranti was doing.

As she was about to thank Clements and return with him to his office to ask a couple more questions, Walker's peripheral vision caught sight of a flashing red light up in the corner of the ceiling. She looked up and saw a CCTV camera. Clements followed her gaze.

"Ah yes, we have CCTV. Adam hates it; says it's a vulnerability. He said that at his previous job, in London, he was shown how easily people could hack into those systems and see what was on the screens in the offices. I don't really think any of our competitors believe we have any news worth stealing, to be honest, but Adam insisted on having a security screen on his monitor, because we certainly had no intention of turning off the CCTV. The potential for theft, by employees, is a serious matter, Detective", Clements said, raising his eyebrows to accentuate the point.

Walker had a hunch. After a couple more questions for Clements, she asked to see the visitors' conference room, where she and DI Clark had interviewed Adam Ferranti some weeks earlier. Clements agreed to show her the room, but preferably on their way out. *"Mrs Clements will be waiting with my evening meal"*, he lied.

As they made their way down the stairs, Walker noted a number of CCTV cameras; all able to monitor the movement of people throughout the building. When she and Clements entered the visitors' conference room, Walker immediately looked up to see if there was a CCTV camera in that room as well. There was, and Clements noticed that this was where her apparent interest lay.

"*Are you seriously thinking we might have a problem with our CCTV security?*" asked Clements, increasingly concerned at the implications.

Walker smiled a placating smile and said, "*I doubt it, Mr Clements, but it's an interesting common feature when there's contact from our suspect*". She broadened her smile and put away her notebook, in a further attempt to distract Clements from her train of thought, but yes, she was indeed intrigued by the presence of the CCTV cameras. What she didn't know was how easy, or difficult, it was to get access to the coverage they provided.

"*Thank you for your time, Mr Clements. I hope I haven't made you too late to get home?*", Walker said, apologetically. "*I'll walk out to your car with you, if that's okay?*" she asked, as they walked out of the conference room and through the reception area together. She was hoping to spend a couple more minutes casually extracting more information from Barry Clements.

"*I'm heading for the train, actually. It's a nice ten-minute stroll to the station from here*", Clements responded, in response to her offer.

"*Oh great, I'm heading that way, too*", Walker lied. "*Mind if I join you?*"

"*Not at all*", Clements also lied. He really wanted to use the short walk to reflect on the article Ferranti had sent, but to say he had a problem with a detective walking with him for a few minutes would be awkward.

They walked, making small talk for a few hundred yards, before Walker casually asked, "*When are you expecting Mr Ferranti back to work?*".

"*I'm not sure when he'll be in the office again, but he's already working*", said Clements, puffing out his chest as he remembered how amazing the work was that Ferranti had just completed.

"*Oh... really?*" said Walker, surprised.

"*Yes. In fact, part of the reason I'm late leaving tonight is because he's just submitted an article for my consideration*", said Clements, proudly.

"*Must be some article to keep you behind when everyone else has left*", stated Walker, keen to understand a little more.

"*Oh, it is!*" said Clements, emphatically. He then turned to Walker and said, "*And hopefully, we can get it published in the next few days – be sure to look out for it, Detective Walker*".

"*I know it's a silly question, Mr Clements, but it's not got anything to do with our immediate investigation as discussed tonight, has it?*" asked Walker, cagily.

Clements smiled back at Walker, dipping his head and looking at her over the top of his glasses. "*Of course, it isn't*", he replied, with a light laugh.

"*Apologies. I wasn't thinking*", said Walker, sheepishly, "*But it must be pretty exciting, though. I mean, your enthusiasm is obviously hard to hide, Mr Clements*".

Barry Clements stopped walking and smiled conspiratorially to Walker. "*Oh, it's what Adam calls a doozer*", he said.

Walker looked confused by the statement, and that made Clements smile. "*A doozer is what you and I might call a belter, a stormer, or a cracker... but this is so much more than that. I can't say much more than I have, I'm afraid, Detective*", smiled Clements apologetically. Walker could see that he was barely able to contain himself. "*But it will make Watergate look like a journalistic titbit!*" he added, excitedly.

Walker still looked confused, and so Clements assumed that those words were, perhaps, from a different era than the young detective. "*It's fantastic*", he summarised. "*Truly fantastic*". He couldn't help himself from clenching his fists and quaking in excitement, and Walker noticed it.

From a vantage point in a late-night coffee shop, a weary Adam Ferranti watched the pair shake hands and head in their separate directions. He had been waiting for Clements to leave the office, but, when he saw Stephanie Walker with him, he sat back down in his seat.

"Now, what are you two talking about?" he wondered.

Chapter 58

Stephanie Walker had a crushing headache. The last three weeks had turned her life upside down and something was tugging at her sub-conscious, which was probably why she lay awake for most of the night with her brain buzzing. The thoughts of her pregnancy didn't help simplify things, either.

Her brain felt like it was going through the same frustrating sensation as when a word is on the tip of your tongue, but you just can't quite recall it. She knew she was onto something, though. Her instinct told her that the article Barry Clements had mentioned, and the last conversation she'd had with Mike Hobbs, had some significance. It was almost as if Clements's tone had suggested the publication of the 'doozer' would be more than just a professional article by Ferranti. She checked a list of notes she'd been compiling in order to help clear her head:

1. Find out what I can about the stepfather, Paul Reynolds – do I ask Adam?
2. Check Khatri's background. What links could there be to his murder and that of the others?
3. See doctor about pregnancy – false positive?
4. ~~Establish the latest on Alex.~~ Question remains over sex-tape, and do I prosecute for abuse?

5. Justin Grant: seems an important friend to Ferranti. Find out more.

As she studied the list, she said to herself, "*Well, let's start at the bottom of the list for a change, shall we*", and with that, she searched the internet for Justin Grant's company - Meretseger Communications. She carefully dialled the number on the screen.

The call was answered within two rings. "*Meretseger. This is Justin*".

"*Mr Grant? My name is Detective Sergeant Walker, of West Yorkshire CID. I believe we have a mutual acquaintance in Adam Ferranti?*"

"*Err, yes, of course*", pondered Grant, whilst running the call through a piece of tech to establish who – and under what authority – the number calling him was assigned to. "*How is Adam? I hope you're not calling me because he's in any trouble?*" he asked, seemingly concerned.

"*I'm afraid I'm limited in what I can say, as we have an ongoing investigation, Mr Grant, but Mr Ferranti is certainly helping us resolve something, rather than presenting as the problem himself*", Walker responded, before hearing an audible sigh of relief from Grant.

"*So, how can I help you?*" quizzed Grant.

"*I have a few questions, which unfortunately I'm not at liberty to give you any context for. Suffice to say, though, Mr Ferranti tells me you're an expert in your field?"*

Walker's plan to flatter Grant worked, as his voice took on a more confident – perhaps over-confident – tone. *"Ah, that's very kind of him. Yes, I do have some expertise and I'll be more than happy to help the British Police. I am, after all, a law-abiding businessman operating in your country. God save the Queen, and all that"*, he chuckled, proud of his joke.

"Law-abiding, in the work you do? What a load of fucking bullshit", thought Walker, but she swallowed her desire to ridicule the man, and instead proceeded with her questions. *"First of all, Mr Ferranti has been receiving calls regarding our case, but there's no Caller ID. My colleagues at the National Crime Agency tell me this is due to specialist tech, because even the telephone companies can't identify what line has been used to make the calls. Mr Ferranti tells me you know all about this tech, so I wondered if you could share some insights?"*

"Of course, although Adam knows about all of this. He even asked me about it a few weeks ago", replied Grant.

"Well, I've not spoken to him myself for a while, so if you could give me the same insights you gave to him, that would be most helpful", explained Walker.

"Adam reviewed that kind of tech when he worked for me, so I reminded him of all the tests he did to check it out", began Grant. *"How were the calls delivered, anyway? Live, or triggered delay?"*

"I'm sorry", said Walker, "I'm afraid I don't understand the question".

Grant apologised and explained. "Was the call live, or was it a voice message that was played minutes or hours - or days - after it was originally recorded?"

Walker hesitated. "Well, live. I was there when one of the calls came through and it was a conversation, not a message".

Grant smiled and, with a touch of condescension, said, "Just because you were there, still doesn't make it live, Detective Walker. You can still trigger an announcement you've made, either by setting a time and date for the call to be made, or by starting it whenever you feel it most appropriate, with a small trigger device. The responses can be planned too, which is how many radio hosts sound live when interviewing, but the interviewee has been pre-recorded".

"I see", said Walker. "Thank you, Mr Grant. My second question relates to CCTV hacking".

"Pfft", came the somewhat condescending reply. "Do you know how easy it is to do that, Detective? There is no such thing as a secure commercial CCTV offering. Hell, even you could get the components you'd need to do that from Maplins! Download some software, too, if you know where to shop. The whole thing would cost you about fifty pounds. With a day's prep for a beginner, such as yourself, you can then be sitting outside a building, in a coffee shop, or even your car, and hack *into pretty much ninety percent of the world's CCTV signals, just by accessing their WIFI".*

Walker was shocked. She knew that in the right – or wrong – hands, hacking was easy, but she didn't know it was almost *too* simple for anyone to do. *"So, if you wanted to know exactly what someone was doing, just before you made a call to them - and during it, perhaps - and a CCTV camera was focused on or near them…"*

Grant interrupted her. *"Yep, it's that easy".*

Walker paused. Her brain was racing through a number of scenarios. Grant listened for a few seconds, and then asked, *"And is there a third question?"*

That 'tip of her tongue' sensation was back, and the question came out instinctively. *"Tell me about Mr Ferranti's drinking?"*, Walker asked, rather boldly.

Grant was slightly taken aback at the question, as it seemed to have no immediate relevance to the discussion, but he assumed there was a reason for it, and he certainly didn't want to give the police reason to question his transparency. Meretseger had enough skeletons in the cupboard, so he was more than keen to avoid any inquisition by the authorities.

"Sure, what do you want to know?"

"How bad was it, and has he always had a drink problem - I mean, ever since you've known him?"

Grant sighed. He felt he was about to share some intimate information about his friend that, now he thought about it, really made him feel uncomfortable. *"Well, he kinda liked a drink when we were over in Afghanistan, but didn't we all, in that hell-hole".* He gave a forced chuckle, before continuing. *"But, after his mum and sister were hospitalised – you know, after the attack – he seemed to go downhill".*

"Attack?" queried Walker. *"I didn't know anything about an attack? All Mr Ferranti told us was that his mother died from some injuries she sustained?"*

"Well, that's true. It was a savage beating they took, though. They both recovered, in a manner of speaking, but never fully. They were never the same again, that's for sure. It hit Adam hard. By the time his mom eventually died, Adam was swimming in Jack Daniel's every night, and most days too, to be honest. When he came over to London, to work for me, he tried to kick the habit, but... well it just interfered with a couple of really high-profile clients. It could have wiped millions off my revenue, and so, in the end, we had a meaningful chat and, he left. He was pretty determined to kick the drinking into touch, though".

"Very interesting, Mr Grant, thank you. You mentioned that Mr Ferranti has a sister?" probed Walker.

"Yeah, Abi. Stepsister, to be factually correct. Great girl, but wow, has she been through hell and back", regaled Grant, adding a new element of detail that intrigued Walker.

"He's never mentioned a stepsister", Walker said, almost as if to herself.

"Really? That surprises me. They were close, until he came across to London. I think she felt kind of abandoned, like he was more focused on his issues than hers. Mind you, he had more than enough of his own demons to deal with", relayed Grant.

"You mentioned Abi was in hospital, too, so I'm guessing it must have been a severe assault?" continued Walker. It increasingly felt as if her instincts were egging her on and on with this line of enquiry.

*"A really **bad** assault, and more"*, said Grant, vigorously emphasising word 'bad'. *"Beaten into a coma, after she'd been raped by the bastard. Seriously, Adam didn't tell you any of this?"*

"No", said Walker. She actually felt a little hurt that Adam hadn't shared this important part of his life with her. *"Is Abi still alive?"*

"She is, or rather she was the last time we spoke... probably a couple of months ago. I know she struggles with the cane and still has nightmares. Fuck, I'd have nightmares too, right? She doesn't really hear from Adam, so I ring her or email her every couple of months; you know, to make sure she's ok". His voice noticeably softened, and Walker smiled a soft, caring smile after hearing what Justin Grant had just told her. Perhaps he wasn't quite the arsehole that she first thought he was.

"Thank you, and sorry to keep you, Mr Grant, but just one more thing, if I may?" she ventured.

"Shoot. No meetings today, so happy to help", he replied in eagerness.

"Mr Ferranti told us he met you in Afghanistan after he asked to be moved there on an assignment?" she quizzed.

"Yes, that's right. So?" replied Grant, a little puzzled that this was actually her question.

"What do you know about an article he'd written, some time before he asked for a transfer? I believe it got quashed by the authorities? It seems to have had quite an effect on his career. I wondered whether it ever came up in conversation?" probed Walker, clearly digging even deeper with Grant than she first thought she'd be able to.

"Don't know much about it", said Grant. "The most he ever said was – and these are his words, not mine, so apologies for the cussing – 'the bastards got to Seth before we could print it. It was my chance to put things straight, for my dad, as well as my mum'. I guess 'Seth' would know more?" he suggested, in an attempt to answer Walker's question.

"Yes, I'll try to contact him via Adam's current editor. I'm sure he'll have a way of getting in touch with Mr Athenberg", said Walker. "Mr Grant, you've been most helpful. Thank you. As I said earlier, please do not *discuss this conversation with anyone else; we are at a delicate stage in our enquiries".*

"Understood, Detective Walker", responded Grant. *"If there's anything else you need help with, please let me know".*

"Actually", Walker interjected hurriedly, *"It might be useful if I could talk to Abi, if you could ask her if she'd be willing to speak with me?"*

"Sure. Got an email address I can send her details to?" asked Grant.

Walker hesitated. She didn't want Grant to suspect something was wrong if she didn't give him her official West Yorkshire CID email address, but if Abi Ferranti emailed her at work, she'd need to be careful who saw her screen. After all, she had officially been removed from the case.

"Phone is best", she replied.

The pair swapped details, and Walker was just about to thank Grant again when something came into her mind. For no obvious reason other than the fact he was American and possibly was more au fait with current affairs over there, she asked one final question. Grant was bemused by it, but yes, he knew more than she did.

*"Senator Swati? Sure, every American is transfixed by **that** story. It's yet to really break, but my sources tell me she's been involved in an abuse of power, related to*

either the security of data or data about security. I'm still digging. I tell you what though, she ain't climbing out of that hole!" came Grant's emphatic review.

Walker noted the obvious enthusiasm in Grant's voice. Clearly, his apparently legal anti-espionage activities bled over into a private interest, in what seemed to be an illegal espionage activity.

Justin Grant had certainly been a useful investment of Walker's time, and later that night she pondered on the nature of the article Clements had referred to. That then made her think again about the mysterious article Ferranti had tried to publish all those years ago. She returned to her notebook to review the list she had made earlier. She referenced it quickly, and made a new list:

1. Adam has a sister - Abi! Talk to her, if possible.
2. An original article was quashed. Talk to Ferranti's ex-editor, Seth Athenberg – contact through Clements.
3. Senator Swati – find the news feature online. If this is to do with data, is there some link to Clements's comments on the upcoming 'doozer'? Probably not, but let's not assume.
4. Check into Khatri's background. What links could there be to his murder?
5. Approach DI Clark with any suspicions... could risk suspension owing to involvement.
6. Look into Simon McBride as per Hobbs's tip-off.
7. Alex – do I prosecute for abuse?
8. Doctor.

The next stop might be another discussion with Barry Clements, and then she possibly needed to ask Mike Hobbs for one more favour. Hopefully, by then, Abi Ferranti might have contacted her.

Chapter 59

Constable Steven Griffiths was responding to a call. A local restaurant had needed to close because of a pungent smell emanating from their waste bins. Later, the owner had been found unconscious.

A local Public Health Officer, Ben Rothwell, who had been dining at the restaurant on his day off, had first noticed the aroma. He was a regular visitor and knew the owner, John Sumner, very well. *"Hey, Johnno, what's that smell?"* he'd asked him.

The owner paused and took in the scent. He pulled his nose up and said, *"Not sure, Ben, I've been in the kitchen all morning, so hadn't noticed it over the meal prep. There are so many smells in the kitchen, I think my nose is punch-drunk"*, he joked, whilst well aware that Ben Rothwell was a regular second, and a Public Health Officer first. *"Let me take a look out back"*.

There were five large steel waste cannisters in the back yard of the restaurant; all almost six feet high. Sumner took a small stepladder from the exit porch at the rear of the kitchen and examined each one in turn. As he reached the fourth bin, the smell seemed the strongest. He set the ladder next to the side of the bin, and climbed up the four small steps, allowing him to just peek over the edge and into the cylinder.

"Ooof, yep, that's the one. I bet bloody Georgiou has been chucking unbagged rotten meat in again!" he fumed. He reached over and carefully started to pick card and plastic wrapping from the top of the container, to see if he could spot precisely what was responsible for the smell. As he moved yet another piece of cardboard out of the way, he saw the source and reeled backwards; falling off the ladder. His head hit the edge of a brake pedal on one of the other bins, and he was knocked out cold; blood seeping from a small laceration on the back of his skull.

Constable Griffiths arrived to find a paramedic tending to Sumner's minor injury and checking him for concussion. Ben Rothwell stood nearby. The smell was nauseating, and Griffiths had to put on a scented health mask that Rothwell had provided him with.

"Tools of the trade are always in the car", said Rothwell, smiling proudly. *"You never know when you might need them, right?"*

"Boy Scout, were you?", asked Griffiths, referring to the Scouts' code to always be prepared. Rothwell looked baffled, clearly unfamiliar with the saying. *"Obviously not"*, muttered Griffiths to himself, as he stood the stepladder next to the bin and climbed up. *"More like a ruddy Girl Guide"*, he added, and chuckled to himself at his own joke.

He peered over the top of the bin and immediately saw what had caused Sumner to fall backwards. A shock of peroxide blond hair stood out amongst the kitchen waste, along with a lifeless eye, staring up and beyond Griffiths. The slashed, bloodied throat of the victim was also just visible, with what looked like a prominent birth mark underneath. Griffiths climbed down and asked everyone to move back, slowly and very carefully, as this was now a crime scene.

"6-1-9-7 to base", said Griffiths into his radio.

"Go ahead, 6-1-9-7", came the reply.

"I need SOCO down to an address in the city centre, and please pass a message onto DS Bob Williams for me. Tell him, I think I might have found Bryan Rodriguez".

Chapter 60

Stephanie Walker had returned home to the apartment. Alex was still in custody, even though the more serious charge of murder had since been dropped against him. She wandered round their home and felt like a total stranger in it. Whatever emotion she had previously felt for the property was now gone. Her mobile rang. *"Walker"*, she said, without looking at the ID.

*"Is that **Detective** Walker?"* came a woman's voice, with an American accent.

"It is. Who is this, please?" enquired Walker.

"My name is Abi Ferranti. Justin Grant gave me your number. He said it was alright to call you?" the voice asked, tentatively.

"Oh, it is. Thank you for calling, Miss Reynolds".

"Call me Abi", she said. She now sounded more relaxed than she had done at first.

"Abi it is", said Walker. *"And please, feel free to call me Stephanie, if you want to?"* offered Walker, in an attempt to retain the sense of trust she felt had started to build.

"How may I help you, Stephanie?" asked Abi, taking the lead in the conversation. "Is Adam alright?"

"He's fine, but I'm afraid I need to talk to you about a very sensitive and personal subject. Mr Grant explained about your past, so, I'm sorry to have to say this, but it's about your father".

Abi Ferranti didn't respond at first. Walker knew the subject was going to be a tricky one, and only hoped Grant had at least prepared Abi somewhat before the call. After a moment, Abi was heard to sigh, before saying, "What do you want to know?" Her tone was unexpectedly non-plussed.

"Well, first of all, let me tell you we believe your father might be in England, and we need his help with an ongoing investigation. I'm sorry to ask this, Abi, but has he been in touch recently?"

Again, there was a moment of silence before Abi responded. This time, it wasn't so casual. This time it was with incredulity. "Is this some sort of sick joke?" Abi cried. Walker was unsure how to respond, but Abi filled the silence. "Let me get this straight. The British Police are calling me, to ask if my bastard of a father has been in touch recently?" Her voice sounded less outraged; more like confused.

Walker was hesitant; "Err, yes. Look, I know this is a very sensitive subject for you, and if I didn't need to....", she continued, but Abi cut her off.

"Detective Walker. You are a detective, right?"

"Yes", replied Walker, slowly, and unsure where this question was leading.

"Then answer me this. How could my father be in England, or have been in touch with me recently, when I've just identified his rotted carcass down at the morgue in Plainfield? May he be burning be hell right now!" she hissed, as she choked back the tears.

"Yeah, erm, err... what?", stuttered Walker, reeling from what she'd just heard.

"Yesterday, I was asked to go down to the local Police station and identify some possessions they had found in a shallow grave, just out of town. The bones have all the markings you'd expect from someone who had been stabbed to death, and I recognised a few of the personal items", relayed Abi Ferranti. *"The reason I'm surprised by your question, Detective Walker, is the coroner here reckons that bastard's been dead for over fifteen years"*.

PART 3 – THE RIPPLES IN THE POND

Sunday 12th December, 1971

Chapter 61

Scargill walked into the large, oak-panelled meeting room and calmly closed the door; too calmly for their liking. They knew this meant he was furious.

"*So*", he said, as he slowly sat at the head of the table, "*Tell me what the hell happened*". With his teeth lightly gritted, the words came out as a hiss.

"*The teams followed Cleaver from the office in York. The only stop he made after leaving the office was to put an envelope in a post box*", said the first man. Scargill looked quizzical, but before he asked his next question, the first man added, "*It was a birthday card. My Blue Team waited for the collection van and then followed the postman back to the sorting office, whilst David's Omega Team stuck with Cleaver. The Delivery Office Manager was more than happy to comply with our request and he personally searched the mailbags himself. Cleaver was sending the card to his little boy. We checked the card for micro-dots and inserts, as well as the written message itself for trace of a code. There was nothing*".

"*After the crash, before we removed Cleaver from the equation, we asked the local Police to search the wreckage of his car*", said the second man. "*There was nothing*".

Scargill pondered this for a moment, then rose from his seat and started to walk around the room, as he asked a series of actual and rhetorical questions.

"How did you know which was Cleaver's envelope?" he asked, first off.

"He had coloured the envelope with bright crayons", replied the first man.

"Maybe he wanted it to be a fun envelope for the boy's birthday, given that he knew he might not make it to any celebration in person", said the second man, smiling.

"Or, if he thought he might be followed, he'd want to make it distinctive, to be sure we saw it. That would make finding it a better possibility amongst the hundreds of other envelopes, don't you think?" responded Scargill, sardonically. *"Clever boy, Anthony; giving us a lead you knew we'd then want to follow".* He stopped walking and smiled, almost admiringly, at the sheer cunning of the man.

"So, if Cleaver didn't have the file, does that mean he destroyed it, or passed it to someone else?" Scargill then mused, before turning to the others. *"I assume he didn't put it back in the filing system?"*

He was about to re-commence his walk, when he glanced at the two men from one to the other but saw that both had awkward expressions on their faces. *"You have checked to make sure the file isn't there, haven't you? TELL ME YOU'VE AT LEAST CHECKED THAT?"* Scargill thundered.

The two men looked at each other, before the first man said, *"I doubt it's there, sir, but I'll get someone to check as soon as we've finished this meet..."*, but he quickly noticed Scargill's expression darken even further, and so hastily added, *"I'll go check it, personally - now"*, and he left the room, relieved, and not the slightest bit concerned for his colleague, who he'd left to face Scargill's wrath in his absence. Scargill watched him leave and then began walking around the room again.

"I assume, sir, you're thinking he might have put it back and then hoped to go on to deny ever having seen it in the first place?", said the second man, trying to sound as if he too had drawn the same conclusion as his superior. Scargill stopped walking again and gave the man a contemptuous glare. No words were necessary.

"We are on the verge of the largest illicit breach of security protocols and yet, a clerical officer who decided to sabotage our little operation has now been executed without the ticking timebomb he held ever being recovered. How can you all be so bloody incompetent?" he screamed.

The second man started to raise a hand, as if he wanted to answer the question in defence, but he quickly withdrew the gesture, as Scargill began to raise his voice again. *"Three years of covert activity. Just days away from all becoming very rich, and now this"*. He pinched the bridge of his nose, screwing his eyes tightly closed.

After several seconds, calmness returned to the temporarily tortured mind of Albert Scargill. He had spent years planning, and then carefully building, an illicit operation, where he could sell state secrets for personal gain. He was now only moments away from either untold wealth - or a charge of treason. He turned to the second man. *"Where's Cleaver's wife and son now?"*

"Customs have confirmed they boarded a BOAC 747 to New York last night, sir. Do you want me to contact the FBI and ask for them to be detained?" the second man asked.

"On what charge?" asked an incredulous Scargill. *"We cannot afford to draw any attention; either to ourselves or to our American contacts".* He again had to take time to let his anger subside before he exhaled, loudly, and then stared at the second man. *"Get me a number for The Migale. We'll send him across. The cover story will be that he's attached to the British Embassy and is on a fact-finding mission".*

The second man rose and left the room with a nod, to assure Scargill that he would indeed return with a contact number for the mercenary known as The Migale; The Shrew. Scargill nodded in satisfaction at his choice of solution. *"If he can't find anything, nobody can".*

Twenty minutes later, Scargill dialled a number and waited for the call to be picked up. Within three rings, the phone call was answered and Scargill announced,

"This is Abercrombie. Await contact from Mercantile. Travel is being arranged. Contact Quantum, but only if absolutely necessary. Instructions to follow".

The voice on the other end of the phone simply answered, *"Understood"*, and then hung up. The Migale then went straight to his bedroom and pulled a suitcase down from on top of the wardrobe. He unzipped the lid and reached inside for a leather pouch. Inside it were seven passports, each with a different identity. He picked one up and opened it, checking the details inside.

"That one will do", he said to himself, as he prepared to adopt his new persona for however long this under-cover operation was going to take. The name – Mr Paul Reynolds.

Chapter 62

Jean Cleaver and her son, Peter, had arrived safely at New York's JFK. They hailed a cab that took them to a hotel where there was already a reservation in her name. They were to stay there for a week, before a friend of Anthony's would be in touch. The trip was supposedly a birthday treat for Peter as he approached his 7th birthday. His father had always said that Peter meant the world to him, so it was time for him to start seeing the world and all it had to offer.

Jean didn't know how her husband had found the money to fund such a trip, nor why he said he possibly wouldn't be joining them, but all of that was about to become much clearer. As she unpacked their case, a large bulky envelope, addressed to her, flopped out onto the bed. On the front it said, 'To my darling Jean - for safe-keeping'. She didn't know why, but as her son wandered into the bedroom, she instinctively hid the package under her pillow. They had never been abroad before and rarely travelled anywhere without Anthony, but he'd said it was important that his wife and son fly to New York and that he would follow; if and when possible.

"Work is simply murder at the moment, my darling, and I just don't know if I'm going to be able to escape

to join you right away", he had told his wife. At the time, Jean had accepted her husband's explanation and gleefully started planning what she and Peter would do on the trip for the first few days. Now, feeling very alone in the largest city she had even seen, she felt anything but gleeful. A sense of foreboding ran through her body and she involuntarily shivered.

"Are you cold, Mummy?" asked Peter, as he wrapped his arms round her waist.

"I was – just a little, sweetheart - but your lovely hugs are making me all toasty now", she replied, trying to hide tears that had unexpectedly welled in her eyes.

They continued to unpack, until the weariness of the travel hit the boy and he fell asleep on a sofa in the small lounge area of their mini-suite. Jean gently lifted his head and placed it on a cushion, before pulling a small blanket over the top of her sleeping son. She waited to ensure he didn't wake up, and then headed into the bedroom.

After quietly closing the door, Jean went over to the bed, lifting the pillow and removing the envelope she had stashed away earlier. She sat on the side of the bed and stared at the package for a minute or two; inexplicably apprehensive about opening it and what she might find. Finally, she ripped open one end. Inside was another brown bulky envelope, with the name and address of an attorney in New York. There was also a hand-written note. It said:

"To my darling Jean,

I am truly sorry, but if you are reading this, it means I won't be able to join you on our trip. Please give all of my love to Peter; hold him tight and make sure you look after each other.

You and our son are my world. I would - and will - do anything to protect you. The world is full of good people, but for reasons I can't tell you, there are a few who would think nothing of harming our family. I have to stay here and protect you from those few. You have given me such joy and happiness in life, that the most I can ever give you in return is peace and happiness; whatever the cost to me.

As a matter of urgency, and to help me ensure your safety, please post this via the hotel receptionist as soon as you can. Tell nobody, my darling Jean.

I love you both. Anthony".

As she read the words on the paper, Jean's heart-breaking sadness turned to tears; then her tears turned into sobs.

The door to the bedroom opened slowly, and Peter walked in, rubbing the sleepiness from his eyes.

"Mummy, are you crying?" he asked, quietly.

Jean Cleaver looked over and smiled at her son's innocent, caring face and said, *"Peter Adam Cleaver,*

*you are my absolute world and, on this holiday, I might
need you to be the man of the family".*

She held out her arms and her son ran into them. He
gave her a warm and tight hug that she so desperately
needed. She knew Anthony would not be coming to
New York at all. In fact, she had an inexplicable feeling
that she would never see her husband again.

PART 4 – UNMASKED

May 2013

Chapter 63

Amelia Demetrious sat in the window seat in her house on Mozart Avenue, and turned her digital voice-recorder on.

"I am Amelia Demetrious, former head of the FBI's Counter-Intelligence Unit; 1989 to 1998. This is my sworn testimony. On 17th December 1996, I was the Duty Officer on the FBI's confidential helpline. Calls only came through to me once junior analysts had triaged the initial call, and senior analysts had identified the hoaxes, or the attention seekers. Once the information was qualified, they would decide if the caller should be forwarded to the Duty Officer. It was rare for calls to get through, but on that day, it was different. I have attached to this testimony a recording of the call I received that day".

She paused the recorder and turned to her laptop; clicking on the .wav file and replaying the call for her own reference. As it played, she closed her eyes and listened in silence; reliving every word.

"This is Officer Demetrious. Please tell me what it is you're calling about, from the very beginning".

"Hello. Do I need to give you my name?" asked the female caller.

"Not yet, but you and I will decide together if that status needs to change later on. Please, go ahead", said the dispassionate Demetrious.

"Okay. Well, I work for a company in DC. We assess proposals from clients and advise them on the scale of risk they are facing if they do, or don't, proceed with certain actions".

Demetrious was familiar with risk assessment and knew there were always risks with things whether you changed something or just maintained the status quo. Both approaches could be just as dangerous as each other. *"I understand the principle"*, she said. *"So, specifically, what is it you want to talk to the FBI about today, Ma'am?"*

Demetrious recalled hearing the caller take a deep breath, as the woman must have realised that she was now into a serious and potentially dangerous situation. Demetrious waited and listened.

"Neither my boss nor his client know I'm making this call and, if they found out, it would be the end of my career. I don't want to put that at risk. I want to remain working in DC politics", the caller said. Again, there was a moment of hesitation, before she continued. *"I have highly credible information that US and British Intelligence operatives are collaborating to sell state secrets to the highest bidder"*.

Demetrious remembered being dumbstruck and, as she sat there in her window seat this evening, her finger twitched, as if she was again hitting the alert button, which meant the call was flagged as 'sensitive' on the recording facility that the FBI had on all phone lines. Nobody would be able to listen to the call without Demetrious, or the Director of the FBI, authorising it. That way, anyone potentially involved couldn't delete the call or warn the targets of any FBI investigation.

"Ma'am, I'm going to need you to talk me through every little detail, and then I'm going to need you to sign a statement", stated Demetrious.

The caller complied. *"Alright, well it started about four weeks ago when…"*.

The call continued for over an hour. The caller spoked, and Demetrious probed and double-checked the information she was being given. The caller sounded increasingly convincing and was growing in confidence as the two women spoke. With her substantial experience, it was clear to Demetrious that the caller was reporting a ticking timebomb, metaphorically speaking.

As the call recording neared its end, the voice of Demetrious announced, *"Ma'am, this conversation is between you and I. You mustn't mention it to anyone, no matter how close or trustworthy you think they are. I'll make some calls and, as I mentioned to you earlier, you'll need to sign a statement, as well as handing over whatever documentation you may have to support your claims. Please act carefully, as we do not want to alert anyone to this"*.

The caller said she understood and agreed, so Demetrious asked for her contact information. *"My name is Nikki Griffiths, and I work for Politico-Risk Inc, in DC. I'll give you my personal cell number, if that's okay?"*

The .wav file recording ended, and Demetrious opened her eyes. They were moist and sparkling, as the recalled emotions almost overpowered her. She restarted her recording device, and continued with the revelations that she intended to share with the world; including all she knew about Albert Scargill and his murderous profiteering colleagues.

Chapter 64

Seth Athenberg was sitting in a wheelchair. An oxygen tank that was secured underneath fed a mask he wore to support his failing breathing. In his prime, he stood at over six feet four inches tall, but now, he was a frail skeleton of a man; slightly slumped in his wheelchair. His body was devastated by the effects of emphysema, and Stephanie Walker now understood why he wanted to talk to her before the launch party for Adam Ferranti's 'doozer'. She hadn't been able to read the article yet, but Athenberg had certainly done so, and, by all accounts, it clearly made a terminally-ill man very happy.

"Good afternoon, Mr Athenberg. I'm Detective Sergeant Walker and this is my colleague, Detective Sergeant Hobbs. It's so good of you to agree to meet us", Walker said, as she offered her hand.

"Well, I couldn't stand the idea of trying to talk at the event itself. As you can see, I might not have the strength to talk for too long anyway. I need my rest", replied Athenberg, as he tapped his oxygen mask. *"Call me Seth, please"*.

"Thank you, Seth", replied Walker, graciously. *"Barry Clements said that perhaps you could help us fill in some gaps in an investigation we're running"*.

Athenberg nodded, taking some deep breaths to assist his concentration. *"Yes, Barry told me it concerned Adam Ferranti. Happy to help"*. He took some more deep draws on his oxygen. Walker and Hobbs glanced at each other. They would either need to take a lot of time in asking their questions, or make the interview very brief.

"Have you read the article?" Athenberg asked his guests. They both shook their heads, and Athenberg raised a weary arm and tapped the air with his finger, in the direction of a brown envelope that sat on the table. *"Why don't you read that first, and then we can talk. Might save you asking me too many questions, or me dying before I can answer them"*. With that, he gave Walker and Hobbs a weak smile. Gallows humour. Hobbs stood and retrieved the envelope. He opened it and handed it to Walker, who gestured that he should sit next to her on a sofa in the suite, so that they could read it together.

Twenty minutes later, Walker and Hobbs sat and stared. Her complexion had gone pale. The content of the article was explosive, to say the least, but they were more stunned at how the revelations were linked to their current investigation. Walker slowly slid the article back into the envelope and allowed the thoughts to filter through her mind.

"Looks like you might be more in need of some of this than I am", said Athenberg, chuckling as he tapped his oxygen line.

"I think you might be right", replied Walker, still processing the information she and Hobbs had just read, and still with a stunned expression on her face. Hobbs fiddled with his hands, nervously, as if he was washing them, over and over. He didn't have a thing to say, which was most unusual. Walker looked up at Athenberg and asked, *"Is this essentially the same topic that was quashed back in the nineties?"*

Athenberg's eyes were moist. He felt joy that this article was finally going to be published, but disappointed that it would be almost two decades later than it should have been. *"Well, it's been updated; a lot of new information and a couple of new names are featured now, but from Adam's perspective, yes; it's the story he wanted to tell back in '96. Wouldn't be surprised if he wants to print it under his real name, actually"*.

Walker assumed using a pseudonym might offer Ferranti some protection as a journalist; shielding him from those he named in this article. After all, if the new names identified in the piece wanted to reap some revenge, at least they might be temporarily fooled into looking for someone different.

"Seth, did Adam know the names Scargill, Yedlin and Goas back in 1996?", asked Walker.

Athenberg nodded, whilst holding his hand up to indicate he needed a moment. He closed his eyes and focused on his breathing for several seconds, before re-opening them and saying. *"He did. It was as if a dark cloud had been lifted, and Adam wanted his revenge"*.

Walker and Hobbs looked at each other, as if communicating telepathically, before Hobbs spoke. *"Revenge? As in killing them?"*

Athenberg gave a gentle chuckle and shook his head. *"No. I mean, don't get me wrong, Adam had a temper like no other, and if someone wronged him, he would explode, but this was different. Adam was convinced the best way to get his revenge AND the best way for him to protect his family, was to call out these people in public. That way, any hint of trouble, and the police would be onto it".*

"But it never got published, did it?" quizzed Hobbs.

Athenberg once again became emotional and had to pull his mask away from his face, so as to dab the tears trickling down his cheeks.

"No, it didn't. We had the article risk-assessed by one of the top politico-analyst companies in DC before we decided whether to publish, or not. They provided our lawyers and the owner with their assessment, and we finally got the okay to go to print. It was risky, for sure, but the owner saw it as a worthwhile gamble. We just had to time it, so we could share the information with the Feds just before it went public. Believe me, you don't want to piss them off". He started to chuckle, but then began to cough and heave. Walker stood to go help him, but Athenberg held up a hand to indicate he was alright. After a minute of wheezing and gradually getting his breathing back under control, Athenberg continued with the story. *"We were setting the front*

page, ready for printing, when I had a couple of surprise visitors".

"The Feds?" queried Walker. Athenberg was a little surprised she knew this, but he assumed - correctly - that Ferranti had shared that information with her himself. He nodded.

"Someone had leaked the article to them. I was mad as hell, and when they told me it had to be quashed in the interests of national security, I laid into them like a man possessed. I was so pissed off. I even accused Bob Grogan, the owner, of chickening out", recalled Athenberg.

"And had he?" asked Hobbs.

"No, I genuinely believe he hadn't. Bob wasn't the kind of man who would go down without a fight, and I had to apologise to him and grovel a bit, once the Feds had gone. I think he wanted to string me up, and it wasn't by the neck!" A saucy smile appeared on his face, just before he looked over at Walker, and added, *"Apologies. I shouldn't talk like that in front of a lady".*

Walker blushed a little. *"It's alright, Seth. So, with your balls still intact, what happened next?"*

That made Athenberg roar with laughter, before his whole chest was consumed by a heaving gasp, and his lips began to turn blue. He put his hand on his chest, as if suggesting he was having cardiac issues, but once again, as Walker stepped forward to help, he raised his hand.

"*I'm so sorry*", said Walker. "*I shouldn't have joked like that*". She felt guilty at accidentally causing this man so much pain and suffering, but as he regained control of his breathing, he shook his head and his hand at her.

"No *need to apologise. If I'm going to die soon, I'd rather it be because of laughter. I have so many well-meaning people around me, who avoid any sort of joy in life for fear they'll kill me. It was good to laugh for a change... even if I did probably pee my pants*". He winked, conspiratorially. Walker held her hand to her mouth, smothering the smirk trying to escape. She couldn't help but like this man and his sense of humour.

Athenberg drew a deep breath and then continued. "*Next thing was, I had to tell Adam. That had to be the hardest thing I've ever done in my life. He cried. He raged. He even accused me of chickening out; of making the gagging order up, just to protect myself*". Another set of tears welled in his eyes at the memory.

"*Presumably though, he was at least happy he wasn't putting his family in danger anymore?*" proposed Hobbs, but Athenberg's expression darkened in response.

"*Oh no.., they were in danger alright*", he said.

"*Reynolds?*" quizzed Walker. Athenberg narrowed his eyes and gazed at Walker. A gentle smile of hope spread across his face, as he realised she was piecing everything together.

"Go on", he requested of her.

"Reynolds returned. He must have worked for the same people Adam was trying to expose". Walker looked to Athenberg for confirmation. He nodded gently and, in doing so, encouraged her to continue with her theory. *"Back in the 70's, Reynolds must have been trying to find out if Adam or is mother knew anything about the file. Maybe Scargill sent him?"*. Athenberg was smiling even more now. He loved the intelligence and logical reasoning from Walker.

"Seems likely, doesn't it", said Athenberg, leaning forwards in his chair.

"So, when Reynolds couldn't find anything, he eventually left", said Walker reflectively. *"Then, when Adam's draft article was discovered in the mid 90's, Scargill realised the evidence was still out there and sent Reynolds back?"*, Walker asked rhetorically. Her brain continued to appraise the scenario. *"Okay, so Adam said his father died when he was young, and that Reynolds turned up quite soon after. Thinking back, that would have been around 1972..."* Walker suddenly stopped. She had remembered something but couldn't pinpoint its significance. She flashed a look at Athenberg, asking him, *"What did you mean when you said Adam might publish the article under his real name?"*

Seth Athenberg slowly eased back in his chair. A peaceful smile spread across his face. *"I meant he might actually print it in his birth name; Peter Adam Cleaver"*.

Hobbs sat upright again and calmly recalled the information from within the article and started piecing it together. *"The man Goas and Yedlin were ordered to kill back in 1971... the mystery man Adam talks about in his article... the one who was going to expose the illegal operation within MI5... Anthony Cleaver. That's Adam's real father, isn't it?"*

Everything about Athenberg visibly relaxed, as he sank back into the wheelchair. His face softened and the tears gently flowed, as he too was finally released from a secret that he had had to contain for nearly twenty years. He too had been subject to the restrictions of the suppression order back in '96, under the American Espionage Act of 1917, and had been told to never speak of the incident again.

Walker looked at Athenberg and then at Hobbs. *"So, Adam is actually Cleaver's son and..."*, she paused in realisation, adding, *"... and now he's had his revenge"*.

"Had?" questioned Athenberg, surprised. *"Don't you mean WILL have, now the article is going to be finally published?"*

Walker no longer felt confused. It was all becoming crystal clear. *"No"*, she said, in an ominous tone. *"I mean he's had his revenge already"*.

With Athenberg staring at her in confusion, Walker stood up; confident and assertive, but saddened. *"Thank you, Seth. I hope tonight goes well, but I have a feeling Adam isn't going to be there to celebrate with you"*. She gently took his hand and squeezed it softly, but the mood didn't last long. She knew what she needed to do, and as she and Hobbs left the room and returned to the car, she got out her mobile and dialled a number.

"Who are you calling?" asked Hobbs, but before she could answer, the call connected.

"Hello Adam", she said, coldly, *"Or should I call you Peter?"*

On the other end of the line, Adam Ferranti smiled to himself. *"I wondered when you'd call. Justin said you two had chatted. He said you seemed lovely, and that it was nice to hear someone in authority finally helping me. He also told me Abi had agreed to talk to you, so I guessed it would only be a matter of time before you'd pick up the phone. Especially now you've spoken to Seth as well"*.

"We're coming to arrest you, Adam. I'll make it easy for you, if you tell me where you are right now", said Walker, as Hobbs stared wide-eyed and open-mouthed at his colleague.

"I always liked the seaside", said Ferranti, and he gave Detective Stephanie Walker a location where they could meet. *"See you there"*, he added, before he ended the call with a smile.

CHAPTER 65

An hour later, Walker parked the car. She and Hobbs walked up the steep pathway to Scarborough Castle. As they reached the top, the moonlight illuminated the grassy banks that stood on either side of the locked ironworks, blocking their way through the imposing gatehouse. Large warning signs had been erected, presumably by the local Council, stating:

'DANGER: RESTORATION WORK UNDERWAY – DEEP HOLES AND RISK OF FALLING MASONRY'

'CASTLE CLOSED: DO NOT ENTER. DANGER TO LIFE'

Orange and black hazard tape was strung from tree to tree, blocking their way forward, but Ferranti had insisted that this was where they had to meet. Walker and Hobbs stepped over the hazard tape, clambered up and over one of the banks, and eased their way down into the inner bailey area. The security flood-lights came on and there, over in the farthest corner, stood Adam Ferranti. His back was towards them as he gazed out over the darkness towards the sea. Whilst the whole area was ringed by more hazard tape, they saw no deep holes or evidence of safety nets or scaffolding.

The crunching of gravel underfoot announced their arrival, and Ferranti's head tilted to one side, as he checked that he had heard two sets of footsteps. He didn't turn around. He knew it was Walker and Hobbs. He started to gently nod his head, as if confirming his hearing was indeed correct, and contemplating what he already knew Walker had to say. The footsteps stopped, several feet short of Ferranti, and Walker pulled her coat closer to her to protect herself from the brisk night-time breeze. She could see Ferranti look down at his shoes as he gathered himself. Against the shrillness of the wind, she called out;

"Hello, Adam. Or is it Peter?"

Ferranti, with his back still turned to them, sighed in such an exaggerated manner that both detectives could see his shoulders visibly rise and then sag. He now knew for certain that DS Stephanie Walker understood that Adam Ferranti and the killer they'd spent so long tracking were one and the same person. He raised his head, looked out toward the darkness of the sea once more, and said, *"Sounds like you brought re-enforcements"*. He turned to face them, before asking, *"When did you make the connection?"* The wind rose sharply. *"Was it something I did, or something I said?"*

Walker had to raise her voice to be heard over the howling of the wind as it whistled off the sea; up and over the cliff top. *"It wasn't any one thing. It only came together after I spoke to Seth, Justin and your half-sister, Abi. Suddenly, apparently unconnected pieces of a jigsaw started to fall into place, Adam"*.

Ferranti smiled. Ah yes, his half-sister. *"How is Abi? Relieved to hear her father figure is dead, I assume?"*

"She was, once she was sure it actually was his body they found near Plainfield. She was confused when I suggested Paul Reynolds was actually alive and well, though, and 'working' in England", stated Walker.

"Did you know that wasn't his real name? I never found out what his real name was", said Ferranti, letting out an ironic chuckle, before adding, *"He seemed to enjoy dying knowing that he still held a secret over me"*.

"I'm still unclear on a few things myself", asked Walker. *"Care to enlighten me, Adam, or will you enjoy sitting in jail; still holding secrets over me, like your stepfather did with you?"*

"Oh, I'm not going to jail", replied Ferranti, matter-of-factly.

"I have armed officers down at the gate and the helicopter is on stand-by. Believe me, you are definitely going to jail. There's no escaping it, Adam", Walker said, with a tone of confidence and determination in her voice.

"You've not brought anyone, Steph", smirked Ferranti. *"You're off the case, and if you'd told your superiors that you were meeting me here, I'd not be talking to you right now. You'd be sat at home, waiting for your disciplinary hearing date. Me, though? I'd probably be*

talking to your DI, who I hear likes to grab the spotlight in these matters. Ego – it's a terrible thing". He paused, knowing he was right. Nobody else knew they were here. Walker's posture and expression softened. A clear indication that Ferranti was right.

There was a slightly uncomfortable pause, before Ferranti continued. *"I'm happy to tell you everything you want to know though, Steph. That will make it even more enjoyable for me; to show you just how hopelessly lost you really were"*. He took a step forward, with Walker and Hobbs instinctively retreating a step. Ferranti smiled, but there was a sadness behind his expression. *"You have no reason to fear me, Steph. I'm just tired of shouting in this wind"*. With that, he took another couple of steps forward; watching for Walker's reaction. This time, she didn't move, and Ferranti smiled again. Hobbs looked across at Walker and moved to be by her side. *"Where would you like me to begin?"* smirked Adam Ferranti.

"It's your story. Start wherever you want to", replied Walker.

Ferranti glanced over his shoulder and gave a brief nod in the southerly direction. *"See that over there? That's Valley Bridge"*, he said, looking back at Walker. *"My father was murdered there in 1971"*. He shivered a little as the wind bit, and he moved over to a slightly more protected corner of the castle ruins. He found a large rock and sat down. Walker hesitantly followed suit in finding a rock to perch on, maintaining what she felt was a safe distance between them both, but keen to mimic Ferranti's movements as if to establish some kind of rapport – a rapport that prior to today, she already thought they had.

"My father was a good man; momentarily tempted by greed", began Ferranti, clearly keen to share his story, though his motives for doing so were unclear. *"He'd uncovered an illicit operation within MI5 whilst serving as a clerk for them. One of their top agents, Albert Scargill, had established a network of intelligence officers who were willing to help him sell state secrets for personal gain. My father was offered the chance to join and, at first, he did, but the killings started to frighten him. He didn't think murder was ever going to be part of their operation, so he decided to do the right thing. He secretly compiled a dossier with names, dates and incriminating evidence, but when he initially contacted the FBI, Scargill was on to him"*. Ferranti looked melancholy and appeared to be struggling with his emotions. He looked down at the ground as he re-gathered his composure, and then back up at Walker before continuing. *"He knew we were all in danger, so he sent my mum and I away, on what we thought was a holiday to New York. But it wasn't. It was intended to be a new start - a safe start - with US Intelligence offering us a safe haven. Mum knew nothing about any of it until we got there. The FBI knew why we were there, and they helped us as much as they could. They tried to make us feel safe in a place where supposedly nobody knew us, but it didn't last long, because Scargill had ways of tracking us. He sent one of his mercenaries, Reynolds, over to befriend us very early in 1972. Christmas had hardly been a celebration, so his arrival*

was a comfort to my mother. He claimed he was a friend of my father's, and that he'd received a letter just after his death, asking him to check we were okay". He paused again, reflecting on the moment Reynolds arrived on their doorstep all those years ago.

"My mum fell for the story, and eventually for him. He was kind to her and generous to me, too, although, at the time, I never understood why he was so interested in everything my father had ever given to me". Ferranti rose slowly from the rock, so as not to startle Walker, and began to stroll along the side of the wall. Walker rose too, and walked in a parallel line to her target. Hobbs stayed where he was.

"And then Abi was born?" asked Walker, gently.

Ferranti nodded. *"Yes, mum gave birth to her in 1973 but, a year later, Reynolds said he had to leave us. He told my mother he had instructions to work with the Americans and the Chinese as a secret liaison for the British Government. Both countries were involved in the growing Angolan War and the British wanted to help but wanted to avoid being directly linked to the FNLA and UNITA. We accepted his reasons and carried on with our lives. It was a good few years later, in 1979, that we were informed he was missing-in-action. My mother was devastated that another man in her life and father to her kids was presumed dead, and she struggled from that point onwards. She never really recovered, emotionally. You can imagine the impact then, when he turned up again in 1996. He said he'd been held captive, unable to contact us, until UNITA forces had found the* camp and released him. We wouldn't have known any different, and even though she probably had a lot of questions, mum was just over the moon to have him back".

"And then what?" pushed Walker. "He got nasty one night, battered your mother and half-sister to near to death?"

Ferranti stopped walking, as a cold, hateful glare formed in his eyes. "I should have realised earlier. I could have saved them", he growled in self-loathing. He was breathing heavily now and his eyes became skittish as he re-lived the experience. "He was a different man when he came back and I didn't see it at the time. There was no reason for me to link his sudden and somewhat surprising return with the impending release of my proposed article that would expose corrupt forces on both sides of the Atlantic. Reynolds, or whoever he was, was instructed to come back purely to find and destroy any evidence of the corruption. And, with me being prominent as the journalist set to add petrol to the fire, I'm guessing the order was given to destroy my family along with it all".

Ferranti's nostrils flared and his eyes were ablaze with hatred. Walker started to feel apprehensive about what he would do next, so she slowly put her hand in her pocket to grasp the police baton she was carrying. Ferranti saw the movement and suspected she had some means of defence with her, but did nothing to indicate to Walker that he had noticed. He forced himself to calm down in response, and his face returned to one of guilt and sadness. "*I was too consumed with my work*", he said, as if confessing this publicly for the first time. The remorse in his voice was palpable.

"*Your article... You mean the one about the Scargill operation? The one that Seth told me got quashed 'in the interests of national security'?*" Walker asked. Ferranti nodded in response. He looked up at Walker and his tear-filled eyes showed a broken man. Walker momentarily found herself somewhat sympathetic, but she now knew that Ferranti had many personas, and this one could be as temporary - and as dangerous - as any of the others.

"*As soon as we arrived in New York back in 1971, my mother posted a package to a lawyer in the city. She was told to trust nobody*", continued Ferranti. "*She didn't know what it was, but it contained the original dossier from my father. He suspected he was being followed, so he couldn't have posted it himself. He planned it so carefully so that my mum would find it in her suitcase*". Ferranti smiled in admiration at his father's attention to detail. "*He'd already written a 30th birthday card to me and left it with a solicitor's firm in London. The solicitor had specific instructions to contact the New York lawyer's office when that date came, to ascertain where the card should be sent*". Ferranti began to stroll slowly alongside the wall again. "*The birthday card gave me instructions to collect a package which would explain everything. He said he hoped it would mean I would finally understand everything and forgive him for sending us away. Initially I hadn't forgiven him for apparently abandoning us, but now I had the information*

I needed to punish the men who had taken him away from us in the first place. That's where I found the names of Scargill, Yedlin and Goas". He looked across to Walker and then looked back across towards Valley Bridge. *"The latter two were the team in the car that followed my father to that bridge and subsequently murdered him. Scargill would have given them the order"*.

"Why do you think your father wanted to wait so long for that information to get to you?" asked Walker, somewhat puzzled.

Ferranti's smile was a mix of sadness at the memory, but admiration at his father's forethought. *"He knew the people he was dealing with had long arms and even longer memories. I guess he hoped we'd be out of danger after 20 years, and perhaps I'd be happy to finally get closure"*.

Walker paused, hoping this moment of melancholy would reduce the tension in the air. When she felt that things had calmed, she continued to probe. *"So, you then had the names of the implicated men. Why didn't you just turn the information over to the authorities back in the 90s when you received it?"*

Ferranti smiled, but shook his head. *"That wasn't enough for me. There was every chance they'd avoid prosecution – corruption is everywhere. I wanted to expose them and hurt them hard. You know; the pen is mightier than the sword? I wanted to use my connections at the paper and my reputation as a journalist to bring as much of it all down as I could".* He paused, before quickly adding, *"I didn't ever plan on killing anyone, and I didn't have the guts to do it even if I wanted to. Not until... ",* but his voice trailed away, as he reflected on his memories of a past filled with hurt.

"Until you killed Reynolds?" asked Walker.

Ferranti's head snapped round to look at her; angry at the use of the man's name. Walker remained calm externally but realised she had made a mistake with her probe. Her hand tightened round the baton in her pocket, as she scrambled for a different line of enquiry. *"He'd come back, to finish the assignment he'd been given in 1971, find out what you all knew, and silence you if necessary?"* she suggested, tentatively.

"Yes", replied Ferranti, a little less agitated by this summary, it seemed. *"I didn't know the link, of course, but it was Scargill's final throw of the dice, according to US Intelligence. They knew the dossier was still out there, even if the article wasn't".*

So, what happened? Why didn't Reynolds just go for you instead of your family?" Walker asked.

"Reynolds had become an alcoholic after the supposed stresses of the Angolan War work. It gave him such a short temper. We reported him four or five times for the physical abuse, but the local police just didn't seem that interested. It's weird, but my mum was so glad to have him back. Every time he was taken down to the station, he'd be back within hours; apologetic, but smug".

411

Ferranti was exasperated at the recollection. He looked up at Walker. *"You know how victims of abusers are, Steph; so many seem ready to accept it's actually their fault"*, he said, rhetorically. Walker was taken aback at the statement by Ferranti, and felt annoyed at how much of her married life she had drunkenly revealed to him that night in the Lake District.

"Whoever was pulling the strings back in London kept getting Reynolds released and letting him loose, so he could find out, covertly of course, what else we knew and who we'd shared it with", regaled Ferranti. *"One day, back in early '97, I got to mum's house. I'd been helping her redecorate the kitchen and to turn the basement into something usable. Reynolds didn't care about helping her, but I wanted to. I thought the project would give her focus and make her happy. I'd put thick polythene all over the floor. I found Reynolds relentlessly punching and kicking her. Abi was already laid on the ground with blood seeping from her mouth. She was unconscious but breathing and, according to the surgeon who saved her, she'd been raped in the attack, as well. When I saw her lying there, and saw that monster punching my mother almost unconscious, I felt a seething rage burst inside me. I threw myself at him. I was blind with anger and just started pulling at his throat, hair and arms; anything to get him away from my mother. At first, he just threw me off, as if I was an irritating bug biting a bear, and that made me even more angry. I saw the kitchen knives and I grabbed one. I stabbed him in the back, and as he twisted to grab me, I started stabbing him in the gut; over and over and over, until he fell to the floor. I stood over him, as if I'd slain some kind of monster in an epic battle... I*

remember his shirt soaked in blood, but he was still moving. I couldn't stand that he was still breathing, so I sank the knife into his chest".

Walker could tell from his face that Ferranti was now back in the moment when he'd murdered Reynolds, as he continued. *"There was this hissing sound that came from his mouth. That's when I knew he was dead and that I was capable of murder. It actually felt good".* A sneer appeared on Ferranti's face, with the thrill of killing Paul Reynolds burning brightly inside him.

Walker realised that this was a dangerous moment in their meeting and chose to change the focus of the discussion to one which would hopefully calm Ferranti down, bring him back to the present moment and make him realise he was capable of doing the right thing. *"And then you called the emergency services and subsequently saved your mum's and Abi's lives?",* she asked. Her tactic worked, and Ferranti's face softened again, as he recalled what happened next.

"Yes, although I knew I also had to hide Reynolds's body. I managed to wrap him in some of the thick polythene that we had covered the floor with, for the decorating, and dragged him down the stairs to the basement, laying him behind a false wall. I couldn't take the risk of being put in jail. I'd done too much to him for it to be viewed as self-defence". He looked up at Walker, as if pleading for her to understand and accept his actions.

"I cut myself a few times, on the arms, to suggest we'd had a struggle. With no body, and given the statements

my mother gave to the homicide detective and the information Abi eventually gave, the Police and DA agreed there were no charges against me for attacking Reynolds before he 'ran off'". Ferranti smiled at the untruth. *"After I'd hidden the body, I sat down next to my mum. She was bleeding, shocked and in pain, but she told me she needed a hug, so I lay next to her and she held my hand in hers; telling me,* 'It's okay sweetheart, I'm here. I'll make sure everything will be alright'. *For a moment, I believed her".*

Walker and Ferranti both turned and started to slowly walk back to where the large stones were that they had previously sat on. Hobbs continued to watch closely, as the tensions both rose and abated.

"So, the body the Plainfield Police found in a shallow grave, recently... that's definitely Reynolds?" Walker asked, still a little confused.

"Yes, it's him. After the attack, the FBI stepped in and agreed to relocate us and change our name - to Ferranti. They were concerned in case Reynolds - or someone else - came looking for us to finish the job on Scargill's behalf. Little did they know the mercenary was already dead. I moved the body once I knew they were moving us to Wisconsin. I also decided to drop 'Peter' and assumed my middle name - Adam".

Walker paused, in thought. *"How did Scargill know about the article before it was published? Seth Athenberg told me the FBI just turned up, out of the blue?".*

"There were only two other people who knew about it", said Ferranti. *"Both worked for a private risk analysis firm in DC: Callum Dennison was the CEO, and the other person was a very ambitious young risk analyst, called Nikki Griffiths. As it turns out, Miss Griffiths was so ambitious, that she called the FBI to share the information. It turns out that she'd spoken to Amelia Demetrious, who was also the link for us, throughout our time in the States. When Demetrious got the call from Nikki, she then spoke to her trusted contact over in British Intelligence to ask if he could recommend someone trustworthy to dig for more information and find out if Scargill knew about the article"*. He paused, for effect. Walker shrugged her shoulders in frustration and held her arms out:

"And... ?" she quizzed, with a hint of irritation in her voice.

Ferranti raised an ironic smile, and said, *"She was put in touch with an up-and-coming intelligence officer, called Simon McBride"*. He continued on a line that then further confused Walker. *"You heard about that US Senator getting arrested recently, right?"*

Walker recognised McBride's name and recalled the information about the US Senator, but still didn't know the relevance. *"Something to do with abuse of position?"* she asked, furtively.

"Well, Senator Nikki Swati – nee Miss Nikki Griffiths – was contacted directly by McBride, back in '96. Demetrious had trusted McBride with some information

as she sought to get Ricardo Goas some immunity from prosecution if he offered up evidence on Scargill. McBride, however, contacted Griffiths and offered her untold wealth - or death, it would seem – to collude on something that could work very well for both of their careers. So, they hatched a plan to take over the scheme Scargill had developed. McBride and Griffiths decided to build a new network and had access to so much more information for sale than was available under the original operation. Then, when Griffiths married, she decided to make a career move onto Capitol Hill. You won't find a better powerbase than that to develop an illegal operation, and by then, of course, she had a real taste for it".

Walker acted as if she knew nothing and pretended to be trying to make sense of all the information. She needed to make Ferranti think he was one step ahead of her while she planned her next move. She glanced up at Ferranti. *"How do you know all this, Adam?"*

"It took her a while but Demetrious eventually found out she was being double-crossed by McBride, and decided to expose Swati in the way that would hit her the hardest. On the night Swati was arrested, Demetrious sent me her own dossier. It explained what had happened after the original article had been supressed, and confirmation that, many years ago, she had tried to get Goas out of the illicit operation, too. They'd fallen in love during the plan for Goas to turn state evidence, but Scargill got to him first and threatened him. He couldn't have just gone ahead and killed him outright; the inner circle would have panicked.

Whatever he threatened him with must have been more than enough to ensure his silence".

"So, the woman who loved Goas sent you a dossier to help you expose McBride... does she know you killed Goas?"

Ferranti's nostrils flared as he pursed his lips and hissed. *"Goas had murdered so many people and yet, there he was, that afternoon, smiling at kids and watching the world go by, while he waited for fucking tea and scones",* he said, in an attempt to further justify his actions.

Walker decided to switch to a different topic, in an attempt to reduce the tension. *"Why did you leave the country, Adam?"*

Ferranti didn't even look up at Walker as he re-started his story. *"After I killed Reynolds, I was starting to feel the pressure and had started to drink, heavily. Everyone knew it, and my credibility plummeted. Seth was really great, but a whispering campaign across the industry and the city made it untenable for me to stay at The Post - or in a local role. The only thing he had to offer was an overseas war correspondent vacancy".* He shrugged his shoulders. *"Clinton had just launched holy hell on the Afghans. Seth asked me if I wanted to go out there, and I was desperate to leave. After that, it was just one hell-hole after another for me: Kosovo, Ethiopia, Liberia, Kurdistan, and then back to Afghanistan. One pile of bloodied bodies and senseless death after another, and the ways in which some of the bodies appeared to have been tortured... Jesus. The shrinks told me my 'fear response' was on fire by then and I used drink as a way to drown out the screams I heard in my nightmares every night. Hell, I was fucking PTSD before anyone could spell it! At least I met Justin on my last tour of Afghanistan, though. He led a Special Forces team and we became close. There were a couple of times, out on assignment, we thought we were going to die, so we shared some really dark secrets back then. What happens in Helmand stays in Helmand, right?"* he grinned at his own joke.

Walker had seen what she thought was her fair share of blood and bodies, but the recount by Ferranti left her open-mouthed. She stared at him, in sympathy, for several seconds, before reminding herself why she was there. *"When did you return home?"* she asked, softly.

"October 23rd, 2010. I remember I was in the Philippines, covering 'Operation Enduring Freedom', when I was told that my mum's health was declining rapidly. She'd never fully recovered since the attack, but she always hid her pain from me. I was at the hospital when she died. She held my hand and told me it was all going to be alright again, and then her hand let go of mine as she slipped away". Walker could see Ferranti biting his lip as he fought the emotion. She straightened her posture, which had softened as she succumbed to the memories of Ferranti's living nightmare. It was time to get the conversation back on track.

"I cannot condone it, Adam, but I do understand why you felt you had to kill Scargill, Yedlin and Goas, but what about all the others?" she asked.

"They were a distraction. We felt we needed to throw the Police off the trail, as you seemed to be getting close to a breakthrough whenever I spoke to you. Jagger was the first distraction and he deserved to die. When I saw the video of him and that girl, all I could think of was Reynolds and Abi. The guy under the bus – whoever he was – and the other criminal? They created a break in the pattern of elderly men being murdered. Clever, don't you think?" he smirked.

Walker found herself once again repelled by the monster in front of her, and any sympathy for the position Adam Ferranti had been in as a child or younger adult, was gone. Walker was about to question Ferranti further over the murders of Jagger, the man under the bus, and the involvement and subsequent death of Brian Rodriguez, but she suddenly hesitated. A word Ferranti had used had thrown her:

"Who is 'we'?" she asked.

CHAPTER 66

Ferranti smirked, and glanced towards Walker's right-hand side. She turned to look over her shoulder, in case someone was about to attack them from behind, but there was nobody there. She was confused, but her confusion turned into astonishment almost as soon as she turned back towards Ferranti. A double take at her partner revealed that DS Mike Hobbs seemed to be smiling too; almost apologetically. He then took a deep breath and walked over to stand at Ferranti's side. Walker opened her mouth to speak but couldn't find the words. She felt many emotions right now, and all of them confusing her brain's ability to process what had just happened.

"Let me introduce you to Mike Hargreaves from MI5 Internal Security, although you know him as DS Mike Hobbs. Sorry, 'Acting' DS Mike Hobbs", said Ferranti, clearly amused at the whole introduction. *"Others simply know him as Republic – it's a codename thing"*, whispered Ferranti, doing absolutely nothing to hide his smugness.

"We've been working together for a few months", said Hobbs, with at least a hint of willing to put his partner in the picture with the facts. *"For Adam, it was revenge, but for me? Just doing my job"*, he added, almost

indifferently. Walker's mouth remained open, but she stayed silent as she struggled to come to terms with everything she was processing right now.

Ferranti threw a theatrical arm around Hobbs's shoulder and began to fill the silence. *"Mike was originally leading the case to find out if there was a link between Scargill's death and my original article for the Washington Post back in the 90s. I was originally his target, but it seems what happened to Abi as an indirect result of that bastard Scargill was very similar to what happened to Mike's own sister. You may recall him telling you about it, Steph?"*

Walker flashed back to when she'd been taken off the case, and she'd spoken with Hobbs about everything with Alex. She involuntarily dropped her head in anger and shame at having opened up about something so private.

Ferranti took Walker's continuing silence as an opportunity to give her more information about the partnership he had with Hargreaves. *"Mike needed to get close to me and needed an 'in'. He was working for Demetrious to spy on McBride, so he convinced McBride to get him onto your HMET. You probably remember the transfer when DC Hulme was removed?"*

Walker remembered it clearly. At first, she'd wondered who was giving those orders for the transfer, but having come to trust Hobbs, she hadn't given it too much thought.

"*McBride thought Mike was working for him when, all along, Mike was feeding him mis-information. He was actually updating Amelia Demetrious throughout, though; so that she could ultimately destroy McBride's illegal operation. It was always part of the plan for McBride to have the bright idea of transferring Hobbs to join your little HMET*", Ferranti regaled, as if belittling the entire operation.

Hobbs smiled at Ferranti before turning to Walker. "*Adam had suffered enough and I knew how corrupt the justice system was – and still is. We knew that even if everyone was caught, Scargill and the others wouldn't suffer. They'd see out what was left of their lives in the equivalent of a high-security five-star hotel. They murdered - or ordered the murders of - over fifty people; just to protect their get-rich scheme. These weren't sweet old men, Steph; easing their way through their golden years. They were cold-blooded killers, who put the security of an entire country at risk. They met the end they deserved*". In summation of his point, Hobbs's smile turned into a sneer.

Walker processed everything she was being told, and everything she felt and believed now forced her to view Hobbs as no different to the monster she now knew Adam Ferranti was. She glared at both of the men in front of her and allowed the words to come confidently and vehemently. "*And why the hell did you get my husband involved in it all?*"

Ferranti nodded a little, as if acknowledging that DS Steph Walker had posed a fair question. "*Justin – who you of course know, Steph - had stayed in contact with me after the war. We were friends. As part of his line of work in his new company, he'd come across dark web video footage of Andrew Jagger's under-age sex tape. You know, the one I eventually leaked to the newspapers?"* He spoke in an almost light-hearted self-congratulatory manner that sickened Walker to her stomach.

There was a pause as Ferranti seemed to play to an invisible crowd. Then, he began to speak again. *"When Justin told me about the tape he'd found, all I could see was Reynolds raping my little sister, and all Mike could see was the abuse that his sister had suffered, too. Jagger needed to be punished, and so did your loving husband in playing the part of the cameraman, Steph".*

Walker bowed her head in shame. Shame for the actions of her husband, shame for ever having shared a bed with him, and shame that, as a Detective, she'd known nothing about any of it.

"He never knew who we were, of course, but Mike and I started to put pressure on Alex, which is when his contracts started dropping and – I'll bet you noticed this - his demeanour changed somewhat 'inexplicably'", continued Ferranti, almost mocking Alex Walker's wife in doing so. *"We continued to put the pressure on and drove him into a position where he'd seek to earn money any way he could to fund his lifestyle, keep up the pretence, and feel like a man again. We even paid for him to go to London and pick up those packages from the hardware shop. I'm sure it was a lovely day out for him".*

Walker was filled with a wash of emotions. Regret at being so unsupportive of her husband, but also sick at the thought of his involvement in the sex tape, and how during all of his downfall he treated her so abhorrently. She tried to take some solace in the fact that Alex's turning point was nothing to do with her. None of this was her fault.

"And what about Khatri?" Walker asked, suddenly feeling deflated. Ferranti pursed his lips. Walker could tell he was considering what to say about the death of his loyal friend, Aarav Khatri, and for a moment he looked genuinely remorseful.

"He was a good kid, just in the wrong place at the wrong time. I hoped the death of Jagger, the guy under the bus, and the list we planted in said guy's pocket with my name on it, might have distracted suspicion from me. I wasn't sure it had, though, so what better way to throw the Police off than to kill someone I actually liked? I'll regret it for the rest of my life, of course, but sometimes the ultimate sacrifice is needed". Ferranti looked almost amused as he relayed this part of his story, and Walker began to retch at the thought not only of what Ferranti had done, but the thought of having slept with this monster several weeks earlier.

She looked at Ferranti and, through gritted teeth, asked, *"And what about me?"* Ferranti's expression seemed to change in response, and he looked down at the ground but he didn't say a word. Walker's anger rose. *"I said, and what about ME. What about US?"*

Ferranti smiled, almost genuinely, as he lifted his head and looked directly into Walker's eyes. *"You? Us? That was all real, Steph"*, Ferranti said, and bowed his head.

"I'm sorry, Steph", said Ferranti, his voice now trembling a little. *"I never intended to fall for you, and now it's all just gone… wrong. I'd hoped that, when all this was over, I could put the past behind me and make a fresh start - with you"*. He started to slowly walk towards her, as if he might want to embrace her or to apologise. Instead, he stopped five feet away from her and said, *"Steph, if you clench that baton any tighter, you're going to get hand cramp. Mike, take it off her, please"*.

Hobbs strode towards Walker and held out his hand. Walker assessed her options. She slowly started to pull the baton out of her pocket whilst hunching her shoulders in an apparent gesture of defeat. Hobbs then made an amateur error for a man of his experience; he momentarily stopped watching her. As he took another step forward, Walker screwed her face up in anger and determination, and in one swift movement, she flicked the baton out of her pocket, extending it with ease, and swung it at the right temple of Hobbs. As the baton struck his skull, Hobbs crumpled like a scarecrow without a stake. Walker glared up at Ferranti and re-raised the baton.

"Give it up, Adam", she yelled. Ferranti glanced at the unconscious body of Mike Hobbs and then, in an animated manner, exhaled and pulled both his hands out of his pockets; raising his arms in surrender. He looked at

Walker, who was suddenly hesitant. In his right hand, Ferranti held a revolver. As hard as she tried to hide her fear, Walker couldn't help but take an initial half a step backwards. Whilst she quickly recovered her composure, Ferranti had noticed the shift and held the gun at his side; not wishing to make Walker feel she had to run.

"They destroyed my life, Steph. First, they killed my father and covered it up, and then, when I could have exposed them at The Post, the truth was buried under bullshit reasons of national security", cried Adam Ferranti, with a tone of helpless resignation and a defeated shrug of his shoulders. *"I tried to move on; tried to forget it and lose myself in another investigative piece. I thought something new would be a distraction, and I could push the anger to the back of my mind, but it didn't save me. All it did was delay the explosion inside of me, until I ....."*, he pinched the end of his nose in an attempt to suppress the tears that were beginning to well in his eyes ... *"until I found you"*. He looked into Walker's eyes. He had tears streaming down his cheeks.

Ferranti paused for a few moments, with both disgust and innocence inter-mingling as he spoke. *"I thought I'd never be able to find anyone like you, and now it's come to this"*. Suddenly, though, the anger subsided and he visibly crumpled, almost dropping to his knees, as he burst into tears.

Walker had no intention of feeling anything other than disgust at the calculating murderer kneeling before her. More than ever, DS Stephanie Walker wanted to see this man rotting in jail for everything he had done, but she knew she needed to be seen as supportive and understanding in order to have any chance of making that happen. "*Adam, let me help you*", she said, as she leaned towards him with her hand outstretched.

Ferranti saw her move, though, and quickly raised his arm to signal she should stop. Sniffling, and trying to stop the flow of tears, he wanted to re-take control again. "*Wait. Just ... stop. Please. Don't come any closer, Steph*", he pleaded. The gun was pointing down at the ground, but his arm was locked firmly in place, as if to indicate he was ready to shoot, if necessary. He looked into Walker's eyes and fought hard to stem the tears. Then, he raised the gun to his own head.

Walker moved as if about to walk towards him, and Ferranti quickly pointed the gun back at her, until he was sure she was staying where she was. He then returned the gun to his temple.

Walker tried a softer approach. She knew exactly what to do and say next. She took a small step backwards, but kept eye contact with Ferranti throughout. "*I know you don't want to hurt me, Adam. We've been through so much together, and I know, underneath all this, we feel strongly about each other. We're so alike. Please don't hurt me... or our baby*", she said, letting the final words hang in the air, as she touched her stomach with a soft caring stroke.

Adam Ferranti froze. His face showed a mixture of confusion and disbelief, and the colour drained from his complexion. He fought with feelings of surprise, joy and confusion, whilst the other part of his persona – the part that sat in his secret room in the cottage in Barwick, the part that tore into his own skin when the desire to understand how others felt when they were killed - found it disgusting and un-nerving to the point of suspecting it all as a ploy. Adam Ferranti looked behind him at the cliff edge on the far side of the castle grounds, and stepped back towards it.

"*Yes, I'm pregnant, Adam; from our night together in the Lake District. Don't do this. I don't want our child to grow up not knowing its father*", she said, softly, whilst all the time re-assessing whether she was reducing the danger or merely adding to the instability of the situation. Ferranti's eyes started to blink rapidly; his mind was increasingly fighting itself to decide what to do. He looked at her with ever-changing expressions of rage and hatred, and then those of love and hope. Was Steph really pregnant with his child? Could she be lying in an attempt to fool him? He looked at her, disbelief in his eyes, but almost begging her to tell him if it was true. She nodded back at him and smiled, softly.

"*Yes, it's true*", she said, as she slowly and deliberately motioned to Ferranti that she was opening her coat and reaching into an inside pocket. Ferranti tensed and re-tensed his arm, pointing the gun back towards her, but it was more of a gesture than a threat. He watched her with anticipation and hesitancy, unsure of what she was going pull out of her pocket. It was a letter from the hospital, and an early precautionary scan of her unborn baby. Walker gently extended her hand so that her baby's father could snatch the items from her grip. He unfolded the letter and glanced at the scan, all the time keeping the gun trained towards her, whilst his eyes scanned the content. His mouth opened slightly, as if he wanted to say something, but he couldn't find the words. He looked up as he put the scan photo and the letter in his pocket.

"*You can keep them if you like?*" Walker said, warmly, as if giving Ferranti permission to do what he actually had already done. Ferranti, however, had begun to steel himself. He'd made a decision. He quickly raised the gun back to his own temple. Walker was surprised and frightened by the response and blurted out, "*Adam, no!*" as she involuntarily moved forwards.

Ferranti looked the mother of his child straight in the eyes; tears beginning to well up again. The pair were so close he could whisper. "*It's no use, Steph. We both know this can't go on. I don't want to be a father who's locked away from his partner and kid; unable to hold them or protect them. A man with no chance of building a relationship with his kid and unable to hug the woman he loves every night*".

He looked to the sky, with a finality behind his next move. He cocked the hammer on the gun, pressing the barrel firmly against the side of his head. "*Goodbye, Steph*", said Adam Ferranti.

A single shot rang out.

CHAPTER 67

For a couple of seconds, both pairs of eyes met.

Ferranti's cold stare was absent of emotion, but Walker's eyes danced erratically.

She couldn't bring herself to speak.

The pain she suddenly felt, grew as warm blood began to seep from the bullet hole in her stomach. Her expression was one of utter disbelief and confusion. She sank to her knees, gasping for breath in shock; totally unable to comprehend what had just happened. Adam Ferranti had not shot himself but had, instead, turned the gun directly on *her*; on their child.

Ferranti stooped and looked down at Stephanie Walker with utter contempt. His hateful eyes scanned her face for some semblance of a pitiful plea for help, but she was lost in her own terrified thoughts. Not only was her life possibly ending, but the child she carried inside would surely die before she did. She eventually managed to look up into Ferranti's eyes and, even without words, clearly begged to know, 'why?'

"I told you I couldn't live with that scenario, so... I thought I'd kill you. It saves me the problem of being a

man locked away in a cell, watching my bastard kid grow up despising me", came Ferranti's cold response to the silent plea.

Stephanie Walker slowly, painfully, but instinctively rolled over onto her side; trying to hold and protect her unborn child whilst she still had the strength to do so. Adam Ferranti took the scan photo from his pocket and placed it in Walker's hand, gently closing her fingers around it. Walker glanced towards Ferranti, helpless and more frightened than she had ever felt in her life.

"Oh, and just so you can die knowing the truth - I haven't touched a drop of alcohol in over a year, Steph. I just wanted to present myself to you all as some stereotypical, alcohol-dependent failure; y'know, to gain your spite and then your sympathy. A quick spray of some diluted alcohol every morning really fooled everyone – Eau de Jack Daniels, if you will". Ferranti sneered at Walker, and then aimed the gun at her one more time. Just as he was about to squeeze the trigger, though, he heard a groaning sound behind him. Hobbs was stirring. Ferranti looked at him, and then at Walker. He smiled. It was a smile of pure evil.

"What a shame", he said aloud, as if addressing an invisible audience. *"Two police officers – partners, in fact - inexplicably killing each other"*.

Ferranti stepped over Walker and squatted down. He ripped the scan from her hand and, whilst cleaning the gun on the scarf she was wearing, he placed the weapon in her hand. He took her hand and raised it; pointing the weapon at Hobbs, who was by now pulling himself up into a sitting position. Hobbs's vision remained slightly blurred from the baton blow to his head, but when he was able to focus, he realised what was happening. His eyes opened wide and he raised his arm; holding an unsteady hand out in a gesture to stop Ferranti.

"No", grunted Walker, but she was physically unable to stop Ferranti from squeezing the trigger of the gun that now only had her fingerprints on it. The bullet thudded into Hobbs's skull and – given the security floodlighting in the inner bailey of the castle - blood, fibres and cerebrospinal fluid could be seen exploding out of the back of his head. It was a joy for Ferranti to watch. Walker was horrified and tried to scream, but she had no energy. Ferranti's macabre smile showed his pleasure at the grim scene. He stood, took the gun from Walker's hand, and tossed it onto the grass, out of her reach. He then walked back towards the low castle wall, glancing at Hobbs's corpse as he passed.

Walker watched as Ferranti vaulted the wall and disappeared into the darkness. She could hear sirens slowly drawing closer, meaning perhaps help was nearly there. She managed to pick-up the crumpled scan from her side, and slowly raised it to her chest. She held it tight in her fist and closed her eyes, to pray.

CHAPTER 68

People were talking in hushed tones; uncertain of the correct protocol for such a gathering. Photos of Stephanie Walker and Andrew Jagger stood in IKEA frames on the low mahogany sideboard in the small house that Alex Walker now rented. The photos were tastefully offset by small bouquets of lilies, with a scattering of unscented candles and several cards of sympathy.

Alex had been released on a technicality – for now - but had needed to sell almost everything he owned to clear his debts. This terraced rental was all he could afford, but he appreciated it was a lot more enticing than a 10 x 8-foot prison cell. A large mirror stood atop a mantle-piece, to help make the room appear larger than it was, and the lace curtains allowed the soft sunshine to glow through the window.

Stephanie Walker had died in the cold, damp Scarborough moonlight. The sirens she had heard were not for her. Her body, and that of her partner, Mike Hobbs, were found the next morning, after a council worker had been sent to inspect the castle. Sightseers had complained that the site was closed without any prior notification. The council worker found the fake warning signs and hazard tape that Ferranti had so meticulously placed there, before he pushed open the iron gate and went to check inside the walls.

Next to the photo of Steph on the mahogany sideboard was a small frame that held a crumpled ultrasound scan that had been found in the young detective's hand when her body was discovered.

The front room was too small for the 30 people who had gathered, even with the cheap concertina doors between the lounge and the dining room pushed open. As the two rooms quickly became full, small groups spread into the kitchen and the hallway. The background music was quiet enough as to be unobtrusive but, for those who had run out of small talk and idle chit-chat, it was loud enough to fill the gaps, and allowed those fortunate enough to find a seat some respite, as they pretended to be lost in their thoughts. Those who had moved into the kitchen were primarily friends of Jaggs, and the chatter in there was a little louder than the other room; not least because they had found that easy-access to cheap wine helped lift their mood a little.

Although there were more people than expected at the gathering, the phone also occasionally rang with calls from people who couldn't make it in person, but wanted to express their condolences. Alex had already taken half a dozen calls when the phone in the hallway rang again. He eased his way through a couple of groups who seemed to have moved on from talking about Steph or Jaggs, and were now onto the subjects of the weather or how difficult it was to find parking nowadays in the city centre. He reached the phone on the 7th ring and picked up the receiver, whilst pointing and mouthing some directions to the upstairs bathroom for a guest.

"*This is Alex*", he said, turning his attention back to the phone.

"*Hello, Alex*".

There was a long silence, as Walker struggled to place the voice, but after a few more seconds, the caller spoke again.

"*Sorry about the death of your wife. And my baby*", said the caller.

Alex was confused. The room suddenly seemed to close in on him. With his accelerated pulse and suddenly dry mouth, he struggled to get any words out as anything more than a whisper.

"*What?*" he stammered, in confusion.

Adam Ferranti's voice replied, with a twisted and taunting tone. "*Yeah, it was my baby, not yours, Alex. Don't believe me? Maybe we could dig her up and do an autopsy on what's left of the foetus? You know, just so you can be sure?*"

Alex Walker struggled with his emotions; a rising hatred clashed with an all-consuming sadness, as his confused and grieving mind tried to make sense of what he was hearing. "*You bastard. If I ever see you...*", he started to snarl, but Ferranti casually cut across Alex's fury.

"Oh, don't worry, we'll meet again", said Ferranti. *"After all, Andrew Jagger got what he deserved as a paedophile. Next, it's the turn of his cameraman!"*

Before Walker could respond again, he heard the receiver click to end the call. As Alex Walker sank to the floor in the bricks and mortar shell of what was left of his life, 200 miles away, Simon McBride was in his Kensington townhouse; packing a suitcase.

The last few weeks had been traumatic, to say the least. His boss, Sir Trevor, who still to his knowledge knew nothing of McBride's illicit link with the recently arrested Senator Swati, had encouraged him to take a break. Sir Trevor knew he had been working extra hard on something, and was keen to show how his efforts were appreciated by those who knew him - and by the millions of UK citizens he had probably helped keep safe in his upstanding role.

"Simon, you remain one of our stars, but even stars need some respite. I don't want you to wear all that sparkle out now, do I?" Sir Trevor had said to him one day, after finding McBride seemingly having a mild form of a panic attack.

Though McBride had indeed been struggling, he smiled at the words of his superior. *"Oh, if only you knew, old man"*, he mumbled to himself.

He needed time to lay low and to decide what to do about the operation. There were still plenty of organisations out there that would be willing to pay him millions for some of the secret data he had access to, but now of course, without the Senator, he was alone.

As he flipped the suitcase closed, there was a loud knock at the door of his Kensington townhouse. McBride walked through into the hallway and could see the postman through the slightly frosted glass in the doorway. McBride opened the door and, in the postman's hand, was a small and beautifully wrapped box. A card was attached.

"Morning, Mr McBride", the postman said, cheerfully.

"Morning, Sandy", replied McBride. *"For me?"*

"Yes. Just need you to sign here, if you don't mind?" said Sandy, pointing at the screen on a small digital device. McBride signed using his fingertip and handed the device back to Sandy. He said goodbye, closed the door and quickly glanced at the parcel, before detaching and opening the envelope.

'*Sorry we missed you. See you soon*', it said inside. It was unsigned, but this wasn't unusual. Nobody in the Intelligence Service ever signed cards. McBride assumed the package was a small token of his team's gratitude. *"A bit cheesy, but still a nice touch"*, he said, with a small degree of begrudging respect.

McBride ventured into the living room and sat down on the sofa. He turned his attention back to the box and read the return label on the packaging. *"Hmm, Staley's Clocks, Hampstead"*, he said aloud.

As he began to unwrap the package, his mind wandered, trying to place where he'd heard the company name before. Hoping for a modern but tasteful clock to be inside, he was disappointed that the beautifully-wrapped box instead contained a cheap digital alarm clock.

"Very funny, gents", he said, as he shook his head and gave a wry smile. Surely this was a cheap joke, but McBride did at least have a sense of humour. He looked underneath the clock and saw a red tab, sticking out from under the battery housing. He pulled it, to start the clock. He turned the clock the right way up again and placed it on the coffee table to his left.

Within seconds, his expression changed from a smile to a look of confusion.

"Why the hell is it going backwards?"

AUTHOR'S NOTE

This story first popped into my mind as I walked my children to their primary school, nearly 20 years ago. At the time, it was a broad idea, but specific elements were well-formed and I have stayed true to them in this final version of the book - elements such as:

- The book would open with a car chase across Valley Bridge in Scarborough, and a small child would survive being an innocent victim of the crash.
- The key character would be a journalist, who would appear to be the killer's messenger.
- A blind man would be featured, who wasn't blind at all (and the sentence "... *you looked so much better in that white shirt* ..." was created all those years ago, too).
- I knew that Khatri would be killed exactly the way he was.

What I didn't know at the time, was why it all happened. I thought I knew when, in November 2018, I sat down at a pool-side table whilst on holiday, and scribbled out the high-level story... but the plot   twisted and turned over the subsequent 18 months. So, after several notepads, hundreds of post-it notes, and almost 39 days of typing and editing, I've finally arrived at my first edition.

It's at this point I want to acknowledge a number of people who, without their support, I would never had reached this point. For their endless hours, reading and critiquing the book in its various stages, and for their undying words of encouragement, I want to say thank you to Gary Hibberd, Jon Taylor and especially to Jenni Shields. For all that, and more (including making great cups of tea), I want to thank my long-time friend Iain Clark. He was my subject matter expert on Police procedures.

My thanks also to Tracy Sheldon, Rob Evans and Sheila Hardwicke, for their role in the informal Reader Review Panel I wanted - and needed. There's nothing quite like constructive feedback, and yours will help me get to a point where I made a decision on whether to go to print.

Above all of those though, I want to thank my wife – Lucia – who not only accepted that I needed to 'scratch the 20-year itch', but actively encouraged me to do it. My loving wife; you supported my decision to take time away from work to try this. I was self-employed at the time, and that meant we took a BIG drop in income, yet you did nothing but praise me for following my dream.

At the time of writing this, I also want to acknowledge a real-life event which resonated with me and added to the feeling that we rarely see how the deeper, darker elements of global intelligence, corruption and power-mongering really work:

In February 2019, The Observer newspaper printed an article about the former Lib-Dem peer and ex-MI6 chief; Sir John Scarlett. The report stated that Sir John was accused of using retired intelligence officers to gather "sensitive" information from secret sources in the Romanian Government. This information was intended to help a wealthy businessman avoid extradition from the UK, on allegations of bribery and money laundering.

As I came towards the end of drafting this book, the quote from Lord Acton came to mind: *'Power corrupts; but absolute power corrupts absolutely'*. As a counter to that, I prefer the quote from the first Spiderman film, which states, *'With great power comes great responsibility'*. I can only hope there are more of the latter on this earth than there are of the former.